MW00447963

John Coltrane
and Black America's
Quest for Freedom

John Coltrane and Black America's Quest for Freedom

Spirituality and the Music

EDITED BY LEONARD L. BROWN

OXFORD
UNIVERSITY PRESS
2010

OXFORD
UNIVERSITY PRESS

Oxford University Press, Inc., publishes works that further
Oxford University's objective of excellence
in research, scholarship, and education.

Oxford   New York
Auckland   Cape Town   Dar es Salaam   Hong Kong   Karachi
Kuala Lumpur   Madrid   Melbourne   Mexico City   Nairobi
New Delhi   Shanghai   Taipei   Toronto

With offices in
Argentina   Austria   Brazil   Chile   Czech Republic   France   Greece
Guatemala   Hungary   Italy   Japan   Poland   Portugal   Singapore
South Korea   Switzerland   Thailand   Turkey   Ukraine   Vietnam

Copyright © 2010 by Oxford University Press, Inc.

Published by Oxford University Press, Inc.
198 Madison Avenue, New York, New York 10016

www.oup.com

Oxford is a registered trademark of Oxford University Press

All rights reserved. No part of this publication may be reproduced,
stored in a retrieval system, or transmitted, in any form or by any means,
electronic, mechanical, photocopying, recording, or otherwise,
without the prior permission of Oxford University Press.

Library of Congress Cataloging-in-Publication Data
John Coltrane and black America's
quest for freedom : spirituality and the music / edited by Leonard Brown.
        p.   cm.
Includes bibliographical references and index.
ISBN 978-0-19-532853-0; 978-0-19-532892-9 (pbk.)
1. Coltrane, John, 1926–1967—Criticism and interpretation.
2. Jazz—History and criticism.
3. Jazz—Religious aspects.
4. African Americans—Music—Religious aspects.
5. Jazz musicians—Interviews.
I. Brown, Leonard, 1946–
ML419.C645J63 2010
788.7'165092—dc22   2009053086

3 5 7 9 8 6 4

Printed in the United States of America
on acid-free paper

Foreword

T. J. ANDERSON

"You plod up into the electric city—
Your song now crystal and
the blues. You pick up the horn
with some will and blow
into the freezing night:
a love supreme, a love supreme—"

—Michael S. Harper, "Dear John, Dear Coltrane"[1]

A long-awaited testimonial to the influence of John Coltrane, this book includes contributions from several knowledgeable voices, each one articulating a particular aspect of our musical culture.

Why now? What is the importance of these works? At this time, we are experiencing a crisis—the lack of intellectual respect for a culture that has been subjected to both the best and worst of American attitudes. It is particularly significant that these works come directly from African American culture. These writers share with John Coltrane the legacy of slavery, segregation, and personal experiences. The words of the Negro spiritual, "Sometimes I feel like a motherless child, a long way from home" echo even now. Yet, the pursuit for the true meaning of America in idealism, democratic liberalism, and civil disobedience serves as a harbinger for what is now. The spirituality of hope sustains these writers. That is why they speak. The music reflects their ideals and spiritualism.

[1]Michael S. Harper, "Dear John, Dear Coltrane" from *Songlines in Michaeltree: New and Collected Poems*. Copyright © 2000 by Michael S. Harper. Used with author's permission.

All creative artists are cultural anthropologists, documenters and inter-preters of a culture. Through this prism, the vitality of any age becomes a doorway that can lead to global understanding. In African American life, aesthetics, philosophy, spiritual values, and public protests meld together in enculturation. It is understood that scholars from different backgrounds also contribute to the interpretation of John Coltrane and his musical legacy. But it is a matter of perspective. The contributors whose works appear in this book are immersed in African American lifestyles and come to this moment with a black point of view. This aesthetic is a combination of what is seen, heard, and experienced in both the dominant and segregated society. With an interest in the role of music in a culture, the vision of these contributors is encompassing. Seldom do we hear informed and authoritative voices from within the culture speak in one musical collection. This is an insider's view of the black experience in music and its impact on one musician. The exem-plary musician John Coltrane and his performances serve as catalysts for this compendium.

Preface

The musical and spiritual legacies of John Coltrane are some of the most powerful and significant in the history of American and global music. This work provides important insights into these legacies through an eclectic group of essays, personal reflections, and interviews from leading scholars, media personalities, and musicians of our time. These writings and reflections critically examine Coltrane's mastery of and pioneering efforts in the syntax and semantics of black music vernacular, as well as his incorporation of principles of music making from other world traditions. These writings and reflections also examine how Coltrane was and is perceived and defined by our culture, then and now. Collectively, these works provide insight into how and why Coltrane's musical legacy reflects the spirituality that is linked to the legacy of Black America's continued quest for freedom and liberation. Moreover, the themes of spirituality, music, sound, and freedom unite these works.

This endeavor uses an ethnomusicological approach to examine John Coltrane's musical and spiritual legacies within the context of Black American culture. Ethnomusicology is the study of a people's total involvement in and with music. Within the discipline, there are a variety of conceptual frameworks, approaches, and strategies that may be used to study music within cultural context. This book uses the "insider's approach" because this approach acknowledges and values the study of music in culture as identified and defined in its own terms and viewed in relation to its own society by individuals who can view its field as members of the music culture as musicians and nonmusical specialists. Essential to the purpose of this book is the understanding that John Coltrane's musical and spiritual foundations are rooted in Black American culture.

Portia Maultsby, eminent scholar on black music, has pointed out that those researching Black American culture have a responsibility to first understand how music works in Black American culture and then to use that understanding in conducting and presenting research on Black American music culture.

> Black music is a manifestation of Black culture, and it serves a communication function within this tradition. As such, it expresses the worldviews of Black America. Social and historical environments shape these views, which, in turn, are communicated through music. Black music, consequently, is in a constant stage of evolution and, therefore, encompasses many different genres and styles.
>
> New Black music forms are created when existing ones no longer effectively operate within a given context and when new values alter the cultural significance of old traditions. Changes in cultural values often result from changes in environment; these changes give rise to new contexts for musical expression. Because music exists as a functional entity within Black America, the creation of new styles discloses shifts in values, attitudes, and social needs. These styles do not evolve independently of existing traditions, but rather, they evolve out of them. New forms of Black musical expression are, in essence, new impulses drawn from the environment, blended with old forms and given a new shape, a new style, and a new meaning. The original form persists alongside the new, and remains a vital form of expression within specific contexts.
>
> . . . The lack of systematic efforts to document the Black music tradition as a functional dimension of Black culture has created a void in resource materials that could enhance our understanding of cultural continuity and change.
>
> . . . This void, in part, stems from the use of an inappropriate methodology for research that does not consider music as a manifestation of culture. In addition, conclusions presented by some of these studies are influenced by the biases of primarily white writers, whose cultural orientation limited their capacities to critically assess the social significance of the Black music tradition.[1]

Internationally recognized master musician and educator David Baker spoke of the need to define aspects of Black American culture from the Black American perspective: "Black music must have an articulation and description of its needs from the Black perspective. This is axiomatic. We cannot abdicate from our culture and give it to those who exist outside of it."[2]

Central to the views presented in this volume is the fact that all contributors are insiders. This means all the contributors are Black Americans with extensive knowledge of the roles and functions of Black American music, historical and contemporary. We all grew up in black communities where Black American music culture played and continues to play a central role in how we identify ourselves and how we view the world—past, present, and future. We all have participated in the "doing" of music as a central aspect of our individual personal development, including singing and instrumental performance in church, school, and the community. We all have pursued successful careers and are active as academics/aka "Blackademics" (scholars and researchers), musicians (performers, composers and arrangers), media personalities, writers, and teachers, often functioning in more than one of these capacities. We all are acknowledged authorities in and have made significant contributions to our respective fields, and we all have been "touched," in various ways and to varying degrees, by John Coltrane's sound and his views on music and life.

It is our collective intent that the works in this volume will serve the readers in the following ways:

(1) Acknowledge the continued relevancy and significance of John Coltrane's musical and spiritual legacy in contemporary times.

(2) Provide broad, rich, and possibly new insights and understanding into the roles and functions of music in Black America's continued aspirations for freedom and equality, from then to now.

(3) Contribute to greater knowledge and understanding of how John Coltrane's sound and music are rooted in Black American spirituality.

(4) Increase knowledge and understanding of the majesty of John Coltrane's impact and influence as one of the great master artists and intellectuals.

—Leonard L. Brown

---

[1]Portia Maultsby, "The Role of Scholars in Creating Space and Validity for Ongoing Changes in Black American Culture," in *Black American Culture and Scholarship: Contemporary Issues*, ed. Bernice Johnson Reagon (Washington, D.C.: Smithsonian Institution Press, 1985), 11–14.
[2]David Baker, "A Periodization of Black Music History," in *Reflections on Afro-American Music*, ed. Dominique-Rene de Lerma (Kent, Ohio: Kent State University Press, 1973), 159.

Acknowledgments

To the Creator for all and everything.

To my mother and father, Ione and James B. Brown, for all their love, faith, encouragement and early and consistent exposure to the music.

To my wife, Cheryl, for her love, friendship, patience, and guidance.

To my children, Omrao, Sashi, and Samira, for all the love one could ever need or want.

To John Coltrane for playing the truth and bringing the light.

To my older brother, J.B., for his courage and for leading me deeper into the music.

To my teachers at Mayo-Underwood School and First Baptist Church in Frankfort, Kentucky.

To Clarence Martin, Bill Barron, Ed Blackwell, David McAlester, T. Ranganathan, Eileen Southern and Mary Alexander.

To the estate of Roy Thompson for permission to use the photograph of John Coltrane.

To Michael Harper for inspiration and brotherhood.

To Suzanne Ryan for believing in this endeavor and having the courage to support it.

To each of the contributors for their outstanding work, and a special "shout out" to the elder statesmen of the music: T.J. Anderson, Yusef Lateef, George Russell, Billy Taylor, and Olly Wilson, all of whom have, in various capacities, inspired, encouraged and mentored those of us who walk in their footsteps. We are forever grateful.

Contents

John Coltrane
and Black America's
Quest for Freedom

You Have to Be Invited: Reflections on Music Making and Musician Creation in Black American Culture

LEONARD L. BROWN

In the discipline of ethnomusicology, one of the essential considerations in gaining an understanding of the roles and functions of music in human cultures is learning about the process of transmission, meaning how the music is learned and passed on. Applying this consideration to the legacy of John Coltrane provides significant insight to his spiritual and musical growth and maturation.

One of the oldest human methods of passing the music on is the oral/ aural tradition, in which musical knowledge and performance practice is carried on through a people's memory and history. In North American music cultures, this tradition is shared between certain old indigenous civilizations and the relatively new Black American culture. Given that Coltrane was a black American and grew up in an American community that was black, it is worthwhile to examine how he learned the music of his community.

The Haudenosaunee are longtime inhabitants of North America's eastern regions, with their civilization dating back thousands of years. Transmission of their beliefs and customs, including music knowledge, is a selective process. "Haudenosaunee have an expression that means you have to be invited; it implies that only when you are thought to be ready and able to use certain knowledge responsibly will it be shared. It does not imply that knowledge is secret but rather that those entrusted with knowledge must know how it should be used."[1]

This same belief can also be found in Black American communities before and during Coltrane's time. Historically, the musics commonly labeled "blues" and "jazz" were created by black musicians to meet the needs of their people and community. These musicians were a part of the community and shared common experiences as black Americans. As pioneers, they collectively conceptualized and created the performance and stylistic approaches based on black cultural aesthetics. Much of this music was rooted in practices of the African ancestors, and it often reflected adaptations and innovations resulting from black American life experiences. Acknowledgement of life's difficulties and themes of "perseverance," "resilience," "hope," and "freedom" can be found in much of this music. These were oral and aural traditions passed on through mentoring and apprenticeship. Consequently, the musicians had the responsibility of determining to whom, when, and where this knowledge would be passed. There were no "jazz studies" programs at this time. The musicians were the keepers of musical knowledge and controlled its dissemination.

Early Exposure

In Coltrane's case, his nurturing began in the segregated black community of High Point, North Carolina, where, as a child, he learned principles, practices, and aesthetics of music making in various contexts, including singing in the African Methodist Episcopal Zion churches where his grandfathers were ministers, and hearing music at home, where both his parents engaged in music making—his mother played piano and sang, and his father played violin and ukulele. This exposure and mentoring continued through elementary school and into his early adolescent years, with vocal and instrumental study and performance through high school. He was nurtured by the black American belief that children should be taught to sing; that learning to sing—running sound through one's body—was an essential component in developing to one's full capacity as a human being.

---

[1]Beverley Diamond, *Native American Music in Eastern North America* (New York: Oxford University Press, 2008), 9.

The repertoire Coltrane learned during this time included traditional black sacred music as well as exposure to American popular music of the time performed by black and white musicians and European concert music, primarily through records and the radio. In elementary school, he did a research report on the great black concert singer Marian Anderson. But it was black saxophonists that pulled his ear and by his teenage years, Coltrane had become an admirer of Lester Young, Coleman Hawkins, and Johnny Hodges, illustrating his affinity for the expressive sound of three of the most innovative and expressive musicians in the history of the music.

Philadelphia Apprenticeships

Upon relocating to Philadelphia in 1943 to be with his family, Coltrane moved into one of the richest urban black music scenes in the country at the time. It was here that his musical exposure, training, and education took giant steps. He met up and became friends with both established and upcoming musicians. The former included older swing musicians such as Frankie Fairfax, Jimmie Tisdale, Charles Gaines, Jimmy Golden, and Bill Doggett, all recognized as accomplished musicians on the Philadelphia scene of the 1940s. The latter included Jimmy Oliver, Bill Barron, Jimmy Heath, and Benny Golson, all of whom became master musicians. Oliver was one of the legendary Philadelphia saxophonists of that period who stayed "at home," rarely traveling outside of Philadelphia to perform. Barron went on to become a leading saxophonist, arranger, and composer, spending time in Sweden, where he recorded and broadcasted, and later serving as chairman of the Music Department and head of the Black Music Program at Wesleyan University in Connecticut. As for Golson and Heath, both developed into outstanding artists of international reputation and have been recognized by the National Endowment for the Arts as Jazz Masters because of their superior records of contribution, accomplishment, and achievement.

After attaining a high level of proficiency just three years since his arrival, including studies at both Ornstein's and Granoff's Schools of Music and a one-year stint performing in the U.S. Navy Band, in 1946, Coltrane was recruited by Philadelphia's established black musicians to join their groups. He was invited inside the community, and that invitation signified that the older, established community of black musicians recognized that Coltrane was ready to be exposed to deeper knowledge of the music. They recognized that he had potential to make significant contributions on the bandstand by expressing the aesthetics of the music that was required by the listeners and upheld in the community by the musicians.

The established musicians realized that Coltrane could speak the language in ways that could enhance the tradition. They recognized his attaining a level of musicianship worthy of being invited in. They heard his development to a certain stage of musical proficiency and expressiveness that embraced the established traditions as well as exuding originality. During this period, the cultural traditions of the music were controlled and transmitted by the musicians. The black community had required, even demanded, music of a certain type and feeling—something that expressed their trials and tribulations, hopes and dreams, wants and needs, and that made them want to laugh and cry—on a nightly basis in the 'hood. The musician's role was to understand and express all this through and in the music. This was music that made people want to dance and freed them of the daily hassles of America's segregated practices. It was music that expressed the full range of black life experiences.

The process of transmission of musical knowledge and practices within black American culture in both rural and urban situations had its own belief system that guided and set rules for music making. One of the principal aesthetics of this belief system was to play with a sound and energy that deeply touched the people; to play in ways that connected and communicated. The sincerity and conviction of the sound, the feeling, were two of the most important aesthetics. These performance aesthetics were created by the early black pioneers of the music—women and men, vocalists and instrumentalists. The music had evolved from ancestral legacies of sorrow songs, spirituals, field hollers, shouts, work songs, and sankeys through the blues of deadly Reconstruction into the early- and mid-twentieth-century experiences of black folks migrating north, east, and west seeking, at the very least, a civil living situation not fraught with daily threats of intimidation, dehumanization, humiliation, and death experienced in the American South.

Once he became a member of this inner circle, Coltrane learned the old time ways, the current ways and probably even glimpses into the future. The modern stylistic approaches labeled "bebop" were dominant among the younger musicians with "Bird" and "Diz" having a revered status. In the black neighborhoods, he learned that developing one's own sound was essential and that sound and feeling were paramount over technique. It was there that he learned about maintaining the instrument, selecting and customizing reeds through sanding and shaving, keeping the horn clean, selecting mouthpieces, choosing clothes, and knowing the difference between what to say and what not to say. He learned variations in aesthetic approaches of the different bands for even though they all shared a common root, each group had its own sound in which Coltrane had to fit as well as enhance.

To be invited in, an aspiring musician such as Coltrane had to exhibit these qualities:

–sincere desire to be a musician

–high level of instrumental proficiency

–thorough understanding of melodic, harmonic, and rhythmic performance practices, including a strong understanding of improvisational
  approaches

–potential for continued development and contribution

–the "right" attitude: a thirst for knowledge and a willingness to learn

–respect for previous and existing performance aesthetics and an
  openness to exploring new realms of possibilities

–knowledge and command of the blues and jazz repertoire of the time

–good practice habits

–creativity in solos

–ability to memorize songs

–focused listening ability—an ear for the music

–ability to get along with others in the ensemble

–"saying something" on the horn—the ability to communicate with the
  listeners using the aesthetic vernacular of Black culture

–courage to perform in front of others

Coltrane's Philadelphia apprenticeships happened in the "conservatory
of the community," meaning live performance throughout the black community, not classroom settings. It was on-the-job training within the contexts
of club settings, ballrooms, the black musicians' union, people's living
rooms, and numerous jam sessions, as well as practice sessions with fellow
musicians. These apprenticeships also taught him the art of accompanying
vocalists.

Road Apprenticeships

As a result of his Philadelphia apprenticeships, Coltrane's musicianship and
reputation grew stronger and led to his being invited, in the late 1940s, to
become a member of traveling bands including those led by Joe Webb, King
Kolax, and Eddie Vinson. All these men were accomplished musicians
leading black bands that played across the Midwest and South to predomi-
nantly black audiences in mostly segregated communities. The repertoire of
each featured lots of rhythm and blues with some jazz, including bebop,
thrown in at times. In his travels, Coltrane learned from fellow band members
as well as from black musicians living in the various performance sites.
He was exposed to musical styles, approaches, and sounds that were unique
to specific geographic regions, for during this time there was a black
Chicago sound, a black New York sound, a black New Orleans sound, a

black Baltimore sound, a black Detroit sound, and a black Kansas City sound. He was able to play in jam sessions that exposed him to these regional aesthetics and to even sit in with local masters.

Outside of the musical knowledge and exposure, Coltrane also apprenticed in the daily struggles of black musicians on the road. Segregation was a dominant factor in the majority of performance venues, as well as the surrounding geographical area. This determined where one could eat, use the bathroom, get gasoline, rent a hotel room, or even get a drink of water. And there was always the threat of racist police encounters. These cultural experiences were a part of his mentoring on the road and influenced the evolution of his conscious intent to use music as a force for goodness.

By 1950, Coltrane had developed his musicianship to such a level that he was invited to join the group of one of his heroes, the masterful Dizzy Gillespie. With Gillespie, he came under the tutelage of one of the "creators of bebop" and the father of Latin jazz. Coltrane's time with Gillespie can be considered the equivalent of a PhD in the beliefs, aesthetics, and performance practices of bebop and Afro-Cuban music, both of which were major influences on his later musical creations. After leaving Gillespie, over the next six years he was invited to perform by these leaders: Earl Bostic, who taught Coltrane how to gain greater saxophone command, including extending melodic and harmonic possibilities into the altissimo range; Johnny Hodges, whom he had idolized as an adolescent and who was one of the great saxophone expressionists with a unique sound; and the brilliant Miles Davis, who performed music of the highest level, requiring excellent musicianship consistently, and who garnered national and international visibility.

Along with the musical mentoring and nurturing Coltrane received from these various invitations, in 1948 he picked up the debilitating habit of drug abuse that eventually led to his dismissal by Gillespie, Hodges, and Davis. No doubt his addiction affected his musicianship, but his level of proficiency and expressiveness led to continued employment.

The Epiphany, Monk and Miles Again

Through his own desire to end his addiction and with important encouragement and support from his family and friends, Coltrane quit drug use in the spring of 1957. During this time, he had a spiritual awakening, exhibited remarkable resiliency, and found new energy and purpose in life through music. Coltrane said he wanted to use his music as "a force for good." In this same time period, he was invited by Thelonious Monk to play with him. His time with Monk provided an apprenticeship with one of the greatest musical minds of the twentieth century. While with Monk, Coltrane's conceptual approaches broadened significantly, including melodic invention, rhythmic variations, and mastery of vertical approaches to improvisation and sophisticated harmonic variations. His confidence grew stronger, and through his incredible practice habits (sometimes his practices lasted for eight or more hours), he became a saxophone virtuoso, extending the range of the tenor to four octaves and developing a sound that was uniquely his own.

After his time with Monk, Coltrane was again invited by Davis to become a member of the new Miles Davis Sextet, a group that subsequently made some of the most influential creative music of the twentieth century. In 1960, Coltrane left Davis and formed his own group. Over the next seven years until his death, he was the leader in producing some of the most creative, powerful, and innovative music of all time. The knowledge and experience he gained from the various "invitations" over the years 1946 to 1959 served to give Coltrane a thorough understanding of black American aesthetics for music making and awakened his own brilliance.

In His Own Words: Coltrane's Responses to Critics

LEONARD L. BROWN

Throughout the 1960s until his death in 1967, many critics struggled with Coltrane's music, some even questioning his direction. Despite the fact that he had won praise in a venue very influential with jazz fans—receiving the 1961 *DownBeat* magazine Jazzman of the Year award, a the *DownBeat* International Critics Poll and Reader's Poll award for best tenor saxophonist and miscellaneous instrument (soprano saxophone), and his group being voted the *DownBeat* New Star combo—there was strong controversy about Coltrane, with some of the leading American critics, many affiliated with *DownBeat*, challenging and negatively criticizing his music. Beginning in 1960, *DownBeat* provided a somewhat ongoing forum for criticism of Coltrane's music and for Coltrane's responses. In response to various critics' written opinions that Coltrane's playing was "superficial," "surreal," "neurotic," and "angry," Don DeMicheal, editor of *DownBeat*, featured an article written by Coltrane titled "Coltrane on Coltrane," published in *DownBeat* on September 29, 1960. In this article, Coltrane discussed his musical influences, saxophonists and otherwise. He discussed his Philadelphia experiences and apprenticeships with Gillespie, Bostic, Hodges, Davis (twice), and

Monk and the effects they had on his musicianship and knowledge of jazz history. He also provided insight into the musical concepts and approaches, theoretical and applied, in which he was engaged at the time. In an insert on the first page of the article, DeMicheal wrote that he was impressed with Coltrane's honesty and "lack of pretentiousness or false pride."

In the November 23, 1961, issue of *DownBeat*, however, John Tynan, then associate editor, labeled Coltrane's and Eric Dolphy's music as "anti-jazz." Tynan, who had previously written very negatively about Coltrane's music, said that he felt Coltrane and Dolphy were intent on destroying swing, and he labeled their music "nonsense." "They seem bent on pursuing an anarchistic course in their music that can be termed anti-jazz."[1]

In response to Tynan's and others' attacks on Coltrane's and Dolphy's musical performances, the April 12, 1962, edition of *DownBeat* featured an article by DeMicheal titled "John Coltrane and Eric Dolphy Answer the Jazz Critics." In this article, Coltrane and Dolphy responded to some of the negative criticism, providing clarity on their intents and purposes. Coltrane's answers to the question, "What are they doing?" provides important insight into his consciousness of the role of the musical artist.

> I think the main thing a musician would like to do is give a picture to the listener of the many wonderful things he knows of and senses in the universe. That's what music is to me—it's just another way of saying this is a big, beautiful universe we live in, that's been given to us, and here's an example of just how magnificent it is. That's what I would like to do. I think that's one of the greatest things you can do in life, and we all try to do it in some way. The musician's is through his music.[2]

Coltrane's expressions about the magnificence of the universe and the musician's responsibility to express such illustrate a philosophy that he saw as

> so important to music, and music is so important. Some realize it young and early in their careers. I didn't realize it as early as I should have, as early as I wish I had. Sometimes you have to take a thing when it comes and be glad. I first began to feel this way in '57, when I started to get myself together musically, although at the time I was working academically and technically. It's just recently that I've tried to become even more aware of this other side—the life side of music. I feel I'm just beginning again.[3]

---

[1]Don DeMicheal, "John Coltrane and Eric Dolphy Answer the Jazz Critics," reprint, *DownBeat* (July 12, 1979), 16.
[2]DeMicheal, "John Coltrane and Eric Dolphy," 52.
[3]DeMicheal, "John Coltrane and Eric Dolphy," 54.

This certainly does not sound like someone who was out to destroy swing or create "anti-jazz" or be an anarchist. Coltrane's reference to 1957—the year he kicked the drug habit and experienced an epiphany—and his subsequent awareness of the "life side of music" illustrate a realization that was central to his musical intents and expressions.

On the Outside Looking In

It seems Tynan suffered from a problem similar to a number of white critics at the time—the inability to listen, hear, and appreciate Coltrane's music. Up to this time, jazz criticism had primarily been a white-created and -dominated industry, with many white critics illustrating little to no knowledge of or respect for Black American history and culture. "The role of the Jazz critic (almost always white) is to define, within the structures of the industry, sets of norms concerning aesthetic value and competency based upon reviews of recorded material and to a lesser degree, live performance," wrote the scholar and accomplished bassist Ortiz Walton in his book *Music: Black, White, and Blue*.[4]

More than that, many critics were unable to consider that maybe they were not ready to appreciate what was being offered, that they might need more development and less opinion. In reality, too many of the jazz critics of the time had bought into the false belief that they knew what "real jazz" was, and they relished the power they wielded—a type of cultural imperialism that had been exerted for decades. In Coltrane's time, numerous critics had maintained and expanded this power to define sets of norms based on Euro-American aesthetics that were used to judge what was beautiful and worthy. Most of them were not musicians and were far away from the level of musical understanding, competency, and performance aesthetics of Coltrane. The aesthetics they adhered to were not those of Black American culture, and many showed a lack of respect for the Black American experience and the music that reflected such. They were critiquing a music from a lens entirely outside the cultural context.

As black musicians, Coltrane and Dolphy offered insightful comments in the *DownBeat* interviews that reflected their views on the negative criticism of their music. Dolphy said the critic should consult the musician when there is something the critic doesn't fully understand. "It's kind of alarming to the musician when someone has written something bad about what the musician plays but never asks the musician anything about it. . . . If something

---

[4]Ortiz Walton, *Music: Black, White, and Blue* (New York: William Morrow, 1972), 119.

new has happened, something nobody knows what the musician is doing, he should ask the musician about it."[5] Coltrane added, "Understanding is what is needed. That is all you can do. Get all the understanding for what you're speaking of that you can get. That way you have done your best."[6]

For critics to do this would have required a strong sense of respect for the musicians, as well as sense of humility and a real desire to learn. This obviously escaped the consciousness of Tynan and other critics who chose to put down Coltrane and Dolphy rather than seek to understand through communicating with these great artists. The relationship was further compounded by the fact that, historically, jazz musicians, regardless of skin color, had been seen primarily as entertainers, not artists.

On April 26, 1962, just two weeks after the Coltrane/Dolphy response article, *DownBeat* published two reviews that continued the onslaught on Coltrane's musical approaches. Pete Welding and Ira Gitler were generally negative when discussing Coltrane's "Chasin' the Trane," an extended blues performance recorded live at the Village Vanguard. Welding said Coltrane's performance "lacked the detachment of true art," and Gitler wrote, "This form of yawps, squawks, and countless repetitive runs . . . should be confined to the woodshed."[7]

Once again, these critics illustrated an ignorance of the syntax and semantics of Black American music culture. When listening to "Chasin' the Trane," an informed listener will hear the band move into an extended version of a twelve-bar blues that expands into a fascinating exploration of rhythmic, harmonic, and melodic investigation of blues variations. Moving at a medium tempo, Coltrane, Jones and Workman (Tyner "strolls" on this one) proceed to explore all the nooks and crannies of the blues, using nonvocal instruments to express the various vocal stylings that are the foundation of Black America's blues legacy. Coltrane's uses of harmonics, swoops, overtones, slurs, bends, multiphonics, yawps, and squawks are rooted in the aesthetics of the language of Black American music culture that can be found in performances of spirituals, sankeys, and shouts, as well as gospel, rhythm and blues, fusion, and even today's rap. Archie Shepp's comments on Coltrane's ability to do this on tenor saxophone illustrate Coltrane's incorporation of the sonic traditions of Black American music culture into saxophone performance technique and expression.

From the point of view of the African Diaspora here in the new world, he turned a basically western instrument into a non-western instrument. He

[5]DeMicheal, "John Coltrane and Eric Dolphy," 53.
[6]DeMicheal, "John Coltrane and Eric Dolphy," 53.
[7]Lewis Porter, *John Coltrane: His Life and Music* (Ann Arbor: University of Michigan Press, 2006), 196.

took the saxophone and he did fundamentally non-Western things with it the way the harmonica players used to jackknife keys to get those 12 tones and flat that third, like that. His use of field hollers in his sound really connotes a thorough and passionate understanding of tradition.[8]

Repetition is one of the foundations of Black American music culture that is retained from African traditions. No doubt that for some listeners, the sixteen-minute performance seemed an eternity, but in the tradition of black blues performances, this was relatively short. Many of the great black blues territory bands of the 1930s, '40s, and '50s would often perform blues for an hour or more for all-black audiences who would dance the entire time.

Bringing Some Light

On June 2, 1962, John Coltrane wrote a letter in response to a gift from Don DeMicheal, a book by Aaron Copland titled *Music and Imagination*. This letter provides very important insights into Coltrane's views and consciousness about himself as a black American. It explores his knowledge and understanding of Black American music culture, the roles and functions of music in Black America's continued strivings for equality and freedom, his feelings about critics, and his role as an artist spurred by the creative urge.

This letter can be found in the book *Coltrane: A Biography* by C. O. Simpkins, one of the first biographies published on Coltrane's life and the first by a black author. The inclusion of this letter is significant as Simpkins is a black man who, at the time, was deeply touched by Coltrane's music and the Black Freedom Movement. In fact, his father was one of the black leaders of the Freedom Movement in Shreveport, Louisiana. Because of death threats from racist whites, Simpkins' family moved out of the area to Chicago in 1961. Simpkins' book on Coltrane is clearly from an Afrocentric perspective and provides rich and valuable insight into Coltrane's life and music within the context of the Black American experience. His is the only book to date that includes Coltrane's letter to DeMicheal.

I went about locating Simpkins for purposes of authentication—to find out when, where and how he got the letter. I found him back in Shreveport at the LSU Health Sciences Center Department of Surgery, where he is a professor of surgery and chief of trauma and critical care. On May 6, 2007, I interviewed Simpkins about his book on Coltrane. The following is a portion of the transcribed interview focusing on why he wrote the book and how he accessed Coltrane's letter.

[8]Archie Shepp, "Musicians Talk about John Coltrane," *DownBeat*, July 12, 1979, 20.

LB: Why did you decide to do a biography on Coltrane?

COS: I wanted other people to know of all the beautiful things Coltrane found in the universe. I was curious about who he was, and I wanted to share how deeply I was touched with other people. That's basically it.

LB: Let me ask you about the letter Coltrane sent to Don DeMicheal in '62 that is included in your book. As we talked a little bit earlier today, you said you accessed that letter in 1969 through Naima, Coltrane's first wife. She provided these documents for you.

COS: Yes, she did.

LB: She let you see the letter and hold some of the documents for a while.

COS: She let me keep some of them.

LB: Later, you gave them back to her.

COS: Yes. She gave me a sweater of his and a book on Negro spirituals by James Weldon Johnson and some other documents of his.

LB: As you reflect on this now, what did these documents tell you about John's understanding of music and its roles and functions in Black American culture?

COS: I think that Black American culture was his root. He realized that, and he explored it, and he studied it and wanted to gain greater understanding of it. He studied himself, both individually as well as his cultural roots, and he realized that he had this great heritage. He appreciated and respected it, and he decided to really know about it and dissect it. And that's where I think the source of his power is, other than his extraordinary capability. He knew who he was and what it was that he was made of and what made him, and he valued it. And he drew upon that, and by doing that he struck common veins that exist in everyone.

LB: Why did you put Trane's response letter to DeMicheal in the book? What significance did you see in it?

COS: I think it expressed how Coltrane felt about the ongoing civil rights movement and the struggle for freedom. I think that's what it tells. It was in his own words, so it is an invaluable piece of information.[9]

When reading Coltrane's response letter, one is struck by the sincerity, honesty, passion, clarity, and depth of his knowledge of Black American culture and how the music works within it. Based on his responses, by this time Coltrane had clearly had enough of the negative criticism that *DownBeat* continued to publish under DeMicheal's leadership. Whether or not DeMicheal

[9]Leonard Brown telephone interview with C. O. Simpkins, May 6, 2007.

was of the same opinion as Tynan and others is not the issue. As editor of the magazine, DeMicheal certainly had the authority to determine or at least influence what did and did not get published, and Coltrane would certainly have been aware of that fact.

Why would DeMicheal send such a book to Coltrane? Despite the fact that Coltrane had mentored under Joe Webb, King Kolax, Dizzy Gillespie, Eddie Vinson, Earl Bostic, and Johnny Hodges, had been asked twice by Miles Davis to perform with his groups and sought out by Thelonious Monk, and had recently been honored with multiple awards for his outstanding musicianship by *DownBeat*, it appears that DeMicheal still had to impose his authority as a critic. Whatever the reason(s), it is Coltrane's responses that are so meaningful in the context of this book. As a preface to analysis, Coltrane's letter in its entirety, as presented in Simpkins's *Coltrane: A Biography*, is presented below.

June 2, 1962
Dear Don,

Many thanks for sending Aaron Copland's fine book, "Music And Imagination." I found it historically revealing and on the whole, quite informative. However, I do not feel that all of his tenets are entirely essential or applicable to the "jazz" musician. This book seems to be written more for the American classical or semi-classical composer who has the problem, as Copland sees it, of not finding himself an integral part of the musical community, or having difficulty in finding a positive philosophy or justification for his art. The "jazz" musician (You can have this term along with several other that have been foisted upon us.) does not have this problem at all.

We have absolutely no reason to worry about lack of positive and affirmative philosophy. It's built in us. The phrasing, the sound of the music attest this fact. We are naturally endowed with it. You can believe all of us would have perished long ago if this were not so. As to community, the whole face of the globe is our community. You see, it is really easy for us to create. We are born with this feeling that just comes out no matter what conditions exist. Otherwise, how could our founding fathers have produced this music in the first place when they surely found themselves (as many of us do today) existing in hostile communities where there was everything to fear and damn few to trust. Any music which could grow and propagate itself as our music has, must have a hell of an affirmative belief inherent in it. Any person who claims to doubt this, or claims to believe that the exponents of our music or freedom are not guided by the same entity, is either prejudiced, musically sterile, or just plain stupid or scheming. Believe me, Don, we all know that this word which so many seem to fear today, 'Freedom' has a hell of a lot to do with this music. Anyway, I did find in Copland's book many fine points. For example: "I cannot imagine an art work without implied convictions"—Neither can I. I am sure that you and many others have enjoyed and garnered much of value from this well written book.

If I may, I would like to express a sincere hope that in the near future, a vigorous investigation of the materials presented in this book and others related will help cause an opening up of the ears that are still closed to the progressive music created by the independent thinking artist of today. When this is accomplished, I am certain that the owners of such ears will easily recognize the very vital and highly enjoyable qualities that exist in this music. I also feel that through such honest endeavor, the contributions of future creators will be more easily recognized, appreciated and enjoyed; particularly by the listener who may otherwise miss the point (intellectually, emotionally, sociologically, etc.) because of inhibitions, a lack of understanding, limited means of association or other reasons.

You know, Don, I was reading a book on the life of Van Gogh today, and I had to pause and think of that wonderful and persistent force—the creative urge. The creative urge was in this man who found himself so much at odds with the world he lived in, and in spite of all the adversity, frustrations, rejections and so forth—beautiful and living art came forth abundantly . . . if only he could be here today. Truth is indestructible. It seems history shows (and it's the same way today) that the innovator is more often than not met with some degree of condemnation; usually according to the degree of his departure from the prevailing modes of expression or what have you. Change is always so hard to accept. We also see that these innovators always seek to revitalize, extend and reconstruct the status quo in their given fields, whenever it is needed. Quite often they are the rejects, outcasts, sub-citizens, etc. of the very societies to which they bring so much sustenance. Often they are people who endure great personal tragedy in their lives. Whatever the case, whether accepted or rejected, rich or poor, they are forever guided by that great and eternal constant—the creative urge. Let us cherish it and give all praise to God. Thank you and best wishes to all.

Sincerely,
John Coltrane[10]

From here, I will discuss how Coltrane's response letter illustrated his understanding of the roles and functions of music in Black American culture, the legacy of black aspirations for freedom in the United States, and his intent to follow the "creative urge." His words reveal the depth and breadth of his intellect. His is an "insider's view" of the highest level, a sharing of knowledge and understanding with a confidence and truthfulness that is

[10]C. O. Simpkins, *Coltrane: A Biography* (Perth Amboy, N.J.: Herndon House, 1975), 159–161.

enlightening and informative. In the following analysis of Coltrane's response letter, Coltrane's words are in italic and my comments are in regular type.

Dear Don,

Many thanks for sending Aaron Copland's fine book, "Music And Imagina-tion." I found it historically revealing and on the whole, quite informative. However, I do not feel that all of his tenets are entirely essential or applicable to the "jazz" musician. This book seems to be written more for the American classical or semi-classical composer who has the problem, as Copland sees it, of not finding himself an integral part of the musical community, or having difficulty in finding a positive philosophy or justification for his art.

Coltrane gives thanks and acknowledges the book's value and usefulness but questions its relevance for "jazz" musicians. He sees the book as more appropriate for American classical or semi-classical composers who may be suffering from one or more of three dilemmas. This again leads me to won-der why DeMicheal would send this book to a musician of Coltrane's stature. Could DeMicheal have been engaged, consciously or unconsciously, in a type of cultural arrogance that many white critics had expressed for far too long and that hampered their gaining knowledge, understanding, and appreciation of the rich traditions of music in Black American culture? DeMicheal obviously felt that Coltrane would benefit from Copland's book. Otherwise, why would he send it? It seems DeMicheal believed Coltrane needed to justify his music and/or was having trouble finding a positive philosophy and/or was having difficulty becoming part of the musical community. As the blues lyrics go, "Ain't that a shame."

The "jazz" musician (You can have this term along with several other that have been foisted upon us.) does not have this problem at all.

Here we see that Coltrane clearly feels that the term "jazz" has been imposed, as illustrated by his use of the word "foist," which has nuances of coercion, trickery, deceit, or fraudulence under the guise of being genuine, valuable, or worthy. Coltrane's feelings reflect some black musicians' con-cerns about the use of the term "jazz" to define a style, genre, and/or type of Black America music. An examination of the opinions of some of his peers at the time is insightful and provides a broader perspective.

Max Roach: "Jazz is a word that came from New Orleans. It came from the French. It was spelled j-a-s-s. A jass house was a house of ill repute. In those days they also called them bawdy houses. . . . Our music was first known as the music that came from these bawdy houses, which were referred to colloquially as jazz houses. Therefore when it moved up the Mississippi to Chicago, they made it into jazz . . . It was named jazz, which is why today when you hear people saying: "Don't give me all that jazz," it's synonymous with saying: "Don't give me all that shit." Some of us accept the title, though there are many who don't. Personally I resent the word unequivocally because of our spirituals and our heritage; the work and sweat that went into our music is above shit. . . . The proper name for it, if you want to speak about it historically, is music that has been created and developed by musicians of African descent who are in America."[11]

Dizzy Gillespie: "If we want to call it jazz, we'll make them call it that. It's our music, whatever we want to call it. I don't know who made up the word jazz. The blacks might have named it jazz themselves. . . . It's a misnomer only when it is identified with white musicians. On a television program someone was asked to say who was known as the king of jazz. The answer was supposed to be Paul Whiteman. That's a misnomer, because he couldn't be the king of our music."[12]

Nina Simone: "Jazz is not just music, it's a way of life, it's a way of being, a way of thinking. I think that the Negro in America is jazz. Everything he does—the slang he uses, the way he talks, his jargon, the new inventive phrases we make up to describe things—all that to me is jazz just as much as the music we play. Jazz is not just music. It's the definition of the Afro-American black."[13]

Dissertation research I conducted in the mid 1980s showed that some black musicians saw jazz as a label for African American/Black improvisational music; others saw it as a term whites imposed on African American music; and still others saw it as a performance style that could be applied to any genre of music, from lullabies to symphonies.[14] Coltrane's view in 1962 was to give the term back, reflecting his belief that the label is inappropriate. We also learn that Coltrane saw himself as part of a community of musicians, as illustrated by his use of the term "us." He clearly did not believe the musicians were having difficulty in finding a positive philosophy or justification for their art.

We have absolutely no reason to worry about lack of positive and affirmative philosophy. It's built in us. The phrasing, the sound of the music, attest this

[11]Arthur Taylor, *Notes and Tones* (New York: Perigee Books, 1977), 110.
[12]Taylor, *Notes and Tones*, 126.
[13]Taylor, *Notes and Tones*, 156.
[14]For more information, see Leonard Brown, *Some New England African American Musicians' Views on Jazz: An Ethnomusicological Study*, doctoral dissertation (Middletown, Conn., Wesleyan University, 1989).

fact. We are naturally endowed with it. You can believe all of us would have
perished long ago if this were not so.

Here we can see that what Coltrane means by "us" and "we" are Black Americans, musicians and otherwise. The "we" having a positive and affirmative philosophy is directly related to the attitude that is inherent in Black American culture and was expressed consistently in the musical ancestors of jazz, the spirituals and the blues. The ability to maintain and express strength and hope are essential characteristics of the function of music in Black American culture. These qualities and attitudes were expressed through the phrasing and sound of music, which Coltrane believed was naturally endowed. "All of us would have perished long ago" clearly refers to Coltrane's knowledge of the history of the black American experience. His statement reflects his understanding of the power of the music's sound to sustain his ancestors through three centuries of miserable, often horrific times, to lend strength and resilience to a people, and to serve as an anchor for the Freedom Movement in United States in the mid-twentieth century. This same understanding is why he worked so diligently to develop a sound that was unique and compelling, direct and engaging. "Natural endowment" does not release one from the necessity of having to work hard to cultivate these endowments.

As to community, the whole face of the globe is our community.

By 1962, the music commonly known as jazz had become a global phenomenon, having the ability to appeal and touch listeners of all cultures and races, transcending differences of language, economic status, gender, skin color, economic status, and age. In the same way, Black American spirituals had captivated European audiences when the Fisk Jubilee Singers toured in the 1870s. And musical performances of great black artists since the 1920s—Louis Armstrong, Ella Fitzgerald, Duke Ellington, Alberta Hunter, Dizzy Gillespie, and others—had captured the hearts of listeners worldwide. Coltrane had experienced the international appeal and power of the music while touring Europe as a member of Miles Davis's groups, Norman Granz's "Jazz at the Philharmonic," and his own quartet. Later, in 1966, he would be greeted by overwhelming crowds while touring Japan.

You see, it is really easy for us to create. We are born with this feeling that
just comes out no matter what conditions exist.

Coltrane sounds similar to James Reese Europe, the black musician who, in 1910, organized one of the first black musicians unions in the nation, the Clef Club in New York City. Two years later, Europe led the Clef Club

Orchestra in a concert at Carnegie Hall that astounded white critics and a public that had not yet become acquainted with the sound of syncopated music or "jazz." Later, he organized and led the all-black 369th Infantry Band through a tour of Europe in WWI, exposing the British, French, and other Europeans to the sound of black American music that was labeled "jazz." In a 1919 interview titled "A Negro Explains 'Jazz,'" Europe said, "I have come back from France more firmly convinced than ever that negroes should write negro music. We have our own racial feeling. . . . The music of our race springs from the soul."[15]

Coltrane's reference to "this feeling that comes out no matter what conditions exist" exemplifies his understanding that Black American culture is imbued with the power of music to sustain one through all of life's trials and tribulations, ups and downs, good times and bad. Black Americans and their African ancestors had to be creative to survive in the Americas.

> *Otherwise, how could our founding fathers have produced this music in the first place when they surely found themselves (as many of us do today) existing in hostile communities where there was everything to fear and damn few to trust.*

Here again, Coltrane illustrates his knowledge of black American history and culture and, the roles and functions of music within such. He also indirectly notes the lack of this insight and context on DeMicheal's part. In 1962, the Civil Rights Movement was in full swing and dominated the American landscape. Blacks organized and moved to attain freedom and equality, and in that effort black song and singing served to galvanize, protect, chronicle, and empower. One of the primary genres of black music produced "in the first place" were the spirituals, whose legacy extends back to the earliest days of enslavement. In the history of blacks in America, it is music that has been central to black survival and the continual striving for freedom and equality. Walton argues that the roots of this music are found in West African music cultures.

> It is from Africa that the distinguishing aspects of Afro-American music emerged. The cries, falsettos, slurs and other African expressive modes found their way directly to Afro-American music during the slave era. The tendency for instruments to act as imitations of the human voice is also, I believe, a direct African transmission. . . . African music retained its functional and collective characteristics in America. The mode of improvisation was developed rather than abandoned, and the rhythmic intensity

---

[15]James Reese Europe, "A Negro Explains Jazz, 1919," *Readings in Black American Music*, 2nd ed., ed. Eileen Southern (New York: W.W. Norton, 1983), 238–241.

of the drums was transformed into a heightened rhythmic quality in Afro-American instrumental music.[16]

(Give Me) This Old Time Religion . . . and Some Blues Too

Through the centuries of enslavement when the great majority of Africans and their offspring, Black Americans, were subjected to daily torture, persecution, and torment, music gave the people the strength to keep their spirits up and hope alive. Music is part of Black America's intangible cultural heritage. Song was used to announce one's humanness in a life in which one had been reduced to being nonhuman. Early Black American vocal music genres such as spirituals (aka sorrow songs), work songs, field hollers, sankeys, and shouts served multiple functions, including chronicling events, providing social commentary, celebrating, lamenting, passing messages through codes, maintaining hope for a better day, and expressing the desire for freedom.[17]

Spirituals served as songs of resistance, with many delivering hidden messages of freedom. As Jon Hendricks says on *Evolution of the Blues Song*, " 'Steal Away to Jesus' could be taken a new way when there was three or four of the children run away the very next day and 'Swing Low, Sweet Chariot' made many a sad eye gleam when it meant the Underground Railroad was running full steam."[18]

The lyrics of many spirituals use contexts presented in the Old Testament of the Bible, for enslaved blacks saw themselves in the same situations as the persecuted Jews and the enslaving whites as the Egyptian persecutors. This quote from Bernice Johnson Reagon, founder of "Sweet Honey in the Rock," creator of the Smithsonian Museum's "Programs in Black Culture," and one

---

[16]Walton, *Music: Black, White, and Blue*, 18–19.

[17]For more in-depth knowledge on the history of Black American music, see Eileen Southern, *The Music of Black Americans: A History*; Mellonee Burnim and Portia Maultsby, *African American Music: An Introduction*; LeRoi Jones (later, Amiri Baraka), *Blues People*; Roger Abrams, *Singing the Master*; Sterling Stuckey, *Going through the Storm*; Angela Davis, *Blues Legacies and Black Feminism: Gertrude "Ma" Rainey, Bessie Smith, and Billie Holiday*; Richard Newman, *Go Down, Moses*; W. E. B. DuBois, *The Souls of Black Folk*; Ortiz Walton, *Music: Black, White, and Blue*; Tammy Kernodle, *Soul on Soul: The Life and Music of Mary Lou Williams*; Horace Clarence Boyer and Lloyd Yearwood, *How Sweet the Sound: The Golden Age of Gospel*; Daphne Duval Harrison, *Black Pearls*; Farah Jamine Griffin, *In Search of Billie Holiday*; Dominique-Rene de Lerma, *Black Music in Our Culture* and *Reflections on Afro-American Music*; Samuel Floyd, *The Power of Black Music*; Guthrie Ramsey, *Race Music*; James Cone, *The Spirituals and the Blues*; Amiri Baraka, *Digging, The Afro-American Soul of American Classical Music*.

[18]Transcribed commentary of Jon Hendricks from *Evolution of the Blues* (CD, Sony Music Special Products, WK75069, 1995).

of the leading authorities on Black American music culture, provides insight into the roles and functions of music in the enslaved black community.

> Black culture empowers you to know you are a child of the universe—and produces a strength because so much had to be done. You may not have land or houses and you are enduring dark times, so the culture provides the strength to produce a voice or voices resonating about our special-ness in the universe. We really had to use whatever territory we could create to take care of the business of making a people and often that territory was not land, often that territory was cultural which is why African American culture is one of the most powerful in the world because we had to get so much business done.[19]

Much of that cultural territory to which Reagon refers was sonic and manifested as moans, grunts, screams, hollers—all of which have been incorporated into the sound panorama of black song. Singing was a principal means for enslaved blacks to express their humanity. The rich and powerful vocal traditions of Black American culture have resonated throughout the United States for centuries, even before its founding, and provided the broad aesthetic foundation and sonic palette for black instrumental performance traditions. This sound of freedom, which expressed resistance, hope, faith, determination, resilience, courage, and pride, was carried in the syntax and tones of black voices, male and female, individual and collective. The spirituals became a primary genre of black musical expression and the black community, like the one Coltrane grew up in, was the place where the spirituals were sung—at home, at school, and in church. This is where Coltrane learned about the significance of the music's history, its relevance in current times, and the techniques and use of vocal phrasing to sound the music so that it expressed strength, conviction, courage, and hope. He later transferred this knowledge and understanding to his own unique saxophone performance techniques.

> Black American culture believes it is important to exercise this part of your being—the part of your being that is tampered with when you run this sound through your body is a part of you that our culture believes should be developed and cultured; that you should be familiar with and that you should be able to get to as often as possible. And that if it is not developed, then you are underdeveloped as a human being. If you go through life and you don't meet this part of yourself, somehow the culture has failed you. The songs are free and the meaning is placed in them by the singers.[20]

[19]Transcribed commentary of Bernice Johnson Reagon from *The Songs Are Free, with Bill Moyers* (video, New York: Mystic Fire Video, 1991).
[20]Transcribed commentary of Bernice Johnson Reagon from *The Songs Are Free, with Bill Moyers.*

Many of the titles of spirituals chronicle black views and experiences. An examination of the lyrics to "No More Auction Block for Me," "Go Down Moses," "Didn't My Lord Deliver Daniel," and "Oh Freedom" will provide clear illustrations. The spiritual songs have continued in the black community into the twenty-first century and provided the foundation for the phenomenal development of gospel, blues, and jazz. In the middle of the twentieth century, the spirituals were called on again to provide inspiration, courage, hope, determination, and pride during the civil rights struggle for freedom and equality. Some of Coltrane's compositions reflect his knowledge and understanding of the powerful legacy of the spirituals. Featured on the *Live at the Village Vanguard* Impulse recording is Coltrane's "Spiritual," and he also performed "Song of the Underground Railroad" for his first Impulse recording, later released posthumously on "Africa/Brass, Vol. 2." In 1966, Coltrane recorded "Reverend King," his composition written in honor of the Reverend Dr. Martin Luther King Jr. It appears on *Cosmic Music*, released after Coltrane's death. It is worth noting that one of the books in Coltrane's library that Naima gave Simpkins was *The Book of American Negro Spirituals* by James Weldon Johnson.

Coltrane's reference to "hostile communities where there was everything to fear and damn few to trust" reflects his overall knowledge of the realities of the history of daily existence for blacks, including his own personal experiences growing up in the segregated South, living in Philadelphia, and traveling as a professional musician. It also illustrates his awareness of the continued fear that existed in many black communities all over the United States as the Civil Rights Movement grew and expanded. Black lives were on the line daily, and many were subjected to abuse and even death. Later, Coltrane chronicled one of these tragedies in his composition "Alabama," which was written in the same year, 1963, as the murder of four little black girls in the Sixteenth Street Baptist Church bombing in Birmingham. The late Art Davis, a bassist who performed and recorded with Coltrane, provided these reflections on Coltrane's awareness at the time of the tragedy:

> He was very conscious of what was happening when those girls were murdered in the bombing in Alabama. He was incensed—we talked about that. And for this to happen in a House of God and people were there worshipping God and for people to bomb a church like that, he said, "That's reprehensible. I'm livid with the hate that can happen in this country."[21]

---

[21]Transcribed commentary of Art Davis from *Tell Me How Long Trane's Been Gone*, ed. Steve Rowland and Larry Abrams (ArtistOwned.com, 2000).

Any music which could grow and propagate itself as our music has, must have a hell of an affirmative belief inherent in it.

Just as the spirituals, the blues, too, have an affirmative belief inherent in them. Similar to the spirituals, work songs, field hollers, and shouts in form and feeling, the blues developed as a vocal-dominant music that chronicled Black life experiences, good, bad, happy, and sad, often from an individual perspective that could be understood by and resonated with the many. This has been true of the blues from then to now. Too often, the blues is misunderstood solely as music of sadness, and no doubt much of it is because that is what many blacks experienced from blues' early times. Blues provided a way to "look up at down." But blues is much more than that. The blues, like the spirituals, are about all aspects of life. An examination of blues lyrics will reveal a variety of topics, including economic conditions, antiwar sentiments, social change, lost love, happiness, the election of Barack Obama, and even celestial considerations. The noted black theologian James Cone wrote this about the common origin of the spirituals and the blues:

> Both the spirituals and the blues are the music of black people. They should not be pitted against each other, as if they are alien or radically different. One does not represent good and the other bad, one sacred and the other secular. Both partake of the same black experience in the United States.[22]

Eleanor Taylor asserts that the "blues vision" is the vision of modernity, just as the tragic vision was the vision of antiquity.

> In the tragic tradition, the protagonist ends up mad, blind, castrated, or dead. In the blues tradition, the protagonist descends into his/her pain, claims it and whatever lessons it holds, and then ascends to live again. Stated another way, if Oedipus and his mother/wife had been contemporary blacks, she would not have hanged herself and he certainly would not have blinded himself (Lord knows there are already enough blind blues singers). Instead, he would have composed a foot-thumping (no pun intended), head-shaking refrain. The son/husband and mother/wife would have cried and laughed about life's ironies, bought each other drinks, and gone on about their business, the business of living. . . . The blues tradition demands it. There is no end. Setbacks, yes. Even death. But no end to the imperative to go on living, in spite of . . .[23]

[22]James Cone, *The Spirituals and the Blues* (Maryknoll, N.Y.: Orbis Books, 1991), 129.
[23]"The Blue Vision," *Contributions in Black Studies: A Journal of African and Afro-American Studies* (Five College Black Studies Executive Committee, 1984).

"In spite of" is a key consideration here, illustrating how Black American music culture serves to acknowledge the often tough and trying realities of daily living while maintaining a spiritual essence that provides the strength to "keep on keeping on." Similar to the attitude expressed above, on a National Public Radio "Jazz Profiles" show highlighting his life, the late great saxophonist Johnny Griffin once defined the music commonly known as jazz as "having a good time in spite of."

Coltrane had a deep understanding of the blues and is recognized as one of the great instrumental blues masters. Archie Shepp provides insight.

> I mean you could dance to Trane's music, I don't care how far out he was. He had come through the whole gamut, that training from Billy Eckstine to his stint in the Navy when he was playing alto and after that playing all the blues bands in Philly and Big Maybelle and people like that who loved him. For Big Maybelle, that was her tenor player. Coltrane was one of the most important blues players to ever play the saxophone and I say that about all the players that have achieved some distinction as outstanding soloists and performers. From Duke Ellington through [Art] Tatum through any of them, they were all profound blues players. All of them could play the blues with a certain distinction and identity.[24]

An examination of Coltrane's original compositions reveal over thirty that either use the term "blues" in the title or are harmonically and melodically based on the blues form with some variations. In his renowned and most well-known sacred suite, "A Love Supreme," Coltrane illustrated his understanding of the close relationship between blues and spirituals by incorporating the blues form and feeling as the basis of the third movement, "Pursuance." Coltrane always seemed to personalize his blues performances, which again is in the tradition of the music. In Black American music culture before and during Coltrane's time, each musician, whether vocalist or instrumentalist, was expected to strive to develop his or her unique sound and approach.

The Freedom Sound

Any person who claims to doubt this, or claims to believe that the exponents of our music or freedom are not guided by the same entity, is either prejudiced, musically sterile, or just plain stupid or scheming.

[24]Transcribed commentary of Archie Shepp, from *Tell Me How Long Trane's Been Gone*, ed. Steve Rowland and Larry Abrams (ArtistOwned.com, 2000).

Here we can see Coltrane's understanding that black music and aspirations for freedom are intertwined and that the failure of critics to realize and acknowledge this reveals their shortcomings, whether intentional or not. His use of the term "our" illustrates Black America's ownership of the music. Moreover, he also believes these aspirations are guided by the same entity or being = a Supremeness. He illustrates his understanding of the spirituality that is evident in Black American music culture, and he sees his music as moving within that realm. Additionally, Coltrane's use of the word "exponent" means he saw himself and his fellow musicians who were creating this new and progressive sound as skilled musical artists—not entertainers—who should be regarded as excellent examples of how something should be done.

> *Believe me, Don, we all know that this word which so many seem to fear today, 'Freedom' has a hell of a lot to do with this music.*

How much clearer can it get? Coltrane acknowledges the fear and tension that existed in the mere use of the word "freedom." This fear was not only in the minds of many of the music critics and listeners, but manifested in various ways throughout the United States. This fear was rooted in what was and could happen as blacks moved to obtain the freedom and rights that were guaranteed for all people by the Declaration of Independence, the Constitution, and the Bill of Rights. The freedom that would end white control and domination of black lifestyles and opportunities. The freedom that would move the country toward the attainment of true democracy. The freedom from the inappropriate negativity of critics who were clearly outsiders and used their influence to control, influence, and manipulate. The freedom to create music free of the conventions of the time, which governed chord changes, modal approaches, time signatures, harmony, melody, and rhythm. The freedom to open up and explore new and innovative avenues for creative music. The freedom to create music that challenged the listeners and performers. The freedom that comes with change.

The Believer

> *Anyway, I did find in Copland's book many fine points. For example: "I cannot imagine an art work without implied convictions"—Neither can I. I am sure that you and many others have enjoyed and garnered much of value from this well written book.*

Here we see the compassionate side of Coltrane. He acknowledges his and Copland's common understanding of the artist's responsibility to create work with conviction.

If I may, I would like to express a sincere hope that in the near future, a vigorous investigation of the materials presented in this book and others related will help cause an opening up of the ears that are still closed to the progressive music created by the independent thinking artist of today. When this is accomplished, I am certain that the owners of such ears will easily recognize the very vital and highly enjoyable qualities that exist in this music. I also feel that through such honest endeavor, the contributions of future creators will be more easily recognized, appreciated and enjoyed; particularly by the listener who may otherwise miss the point (intellectually, emotionally, sociologically, etc.) because of inhibitions, a lack of understanding, limited means of association or other reasons.

Coltrane offers a plea for listeners', especially critics', growth and the arrival at an understanding that could result from a strong and active study of Copland's book. From his view as an independent-thinking and progressive artist of the time, Coltrane was deeply involved in imaginative approaches to music making rooted in strong convictions. The problem was that many of the critics did not believe they had a responsibility to also engage in active study, investigation, and examination of the reasons, motivations, and concepts behind the musical explorations of artists such as Coltrane. Coltrane understood that increased knowledge would lead to understanding and possibly a new awareness in listeners, an awakening on the part of those still asleep, those who missed the point because of their own limitations and stagnancy. Coltrane realized that much of problem was attributable to ignorance, a fundamental lack of awareness of how creative musicians work, both within and aside from Black American music culture. He knew that striving to attain such knowledge would very likely lead to a degree of understanding that would benefit all.

You know, Don, I was reading a book on the life of Van Gogh today, and I had to pause and think of that wonderful and persistent force—the creative urge. The creative urge was in this man who found himself so much at odds with the world he lived in, and in spite of all the adversity, frustrations, rejections and so forth—beautiful and living art came forth abundantly . . . if only he could be here today.

Truth is indestructible. It seems history shows (and it's the same way today) that the innovator is more often than not met with some degree of condemnation; usually according to the degree of his departure from the prevailing

modes of expression or what have you. Change is always so hard to accept. We
also see that these innovators always seek to revitalize, extend and reconstruct
the status quo in their given fields, whenever it is needed.

Here we get a glimpse of Coltrane, the creative artist in the true human
sense, the artist who has transcended but not forgotten his cultural ties. One
who can identify with other creative thinkers and doers across the ages—
fellow agents of innovation and change, who are often misunderstood and
persecuted. Coltrane's comments illustrate his intellectual explorations outside of music and his desire to seek out knowledge of the triumphs, trials,
and tribulations of great artists over time. Many people, both inside and
outside of Black American culture, saw Coltrane as the leading creative artist
at the forefront of musical change. These new and innovative approaches to
creative music expression were labeled "avant-garde" and "free jazz." At the
same time, others among his contemporaries, regardless of skin color, did
not understand or embrace his new musical explorations and directions. As
black music authority Portia Maultsby wrote, "Because music exists as a
functional entity within Black America, the creation of new styles discloses
shifts in values, attitudes, and social needs. These styles do not evolve inde-
pendently of existing traditions, but rather, they evolve out of them."[25]
The sociopolitical and cultural dynamics of the times in which Coltrane
was pursuing new and innovative approaches to music expression clearly
exhibited shifts in values, attitudes, and social relations. The Civil Rights
Movement challenged the status quo. It required the entire citizenry to reex-
amine what it meant to have a democracy that guaranteed equal opportunity
for all its citizens. It required the United States to come face-to-face with the
legacy of white supremacy that had handicapped its citizens of color for centuries while reinforcing the ignorance of white racial superiority.

Quite often they are the rejects, outcasts, sub-citizens, etc. of the very
societies to which they bring so much sustenance. Often they are people
who endure great personal tragedy in their lives.

Coltrane understood the ways black folks had been stereotyped, ridi-
culed, and demonized in the United States. He also acknowledged the
incredible rich tradition of Black American music and the contribution
its artists had made to their own country and to the world. Speaking of
Coltrane's artistic impact, Max Roach said,

[25]Portia Maultsby, "The Role of Scholars in Creating Space and Validity for Ongoing Changes in
Black American Culture," in *Black American Culture and Scholarship: Contemporary Issues*, ed. Bernice Johnson Reagon (Washington, D.C.: Smithsonian Institution Press, 1985), 28.

I heard many things in what Trane was doing. I heard the cry and wail of the pain that the society imposes on people and especially black folks and I heard the extraordinary contribution he made to music—rhythmically, melodically and harmonically. And I also heard the innovative use of that instrument. He took it to places that were individual to him and he fed the whole world like that.[26]

Whatever the case, whether accepted or rejected, rich or poor, they are forever guided by that great and eternal constant—the creative urge. Let us cherish it and give all praise to God. Thank you and best wishes to all.

Sincerely,
John Coltrane

In this final statement, Coltrane shows us his belief in a supreme force as the source of the creative urge that guides the innovator. This statement illustrates his steadfastness in the direction in which he moved and his belief that he was being guided by divine providence.

Subsequent to this letter, Coltrane continued to move as the innovative creative artist. He did not wither under the negative criticism. Rather, he stayed focused and continued to follow the creative urge by pursuing a path of exploration, investigation, and innovation. Coltrane's thorough understanding of the roles and functions of music in Black American culture led him to pursue an incredible legacy of practice, rigorous study, self-realization, spiritual awakening, and creative expression that touched listeners worldwide. He expanded the rhythmic, melodic, and harmonic concepts and approaches rooted in Black American creative music expression to realms never before imagined. With Black American culture as his root, Coltrane expanded his study of music to a global level through examining traditions from the Caribbean, South America, Europe, Africa, and Asia. This led to his incorporating relevant elements from these music cultures into his own creations, resulting in the development of a sound that expressed freedom and goodness to all who could hear. In the tradition of his ancestors, Coltrane's conveyance of spirituality through sound endeared him to listeners then and continues to endear him to devoted listeners today.

---

[26]Transcribed commentary of Max Roach, from *Tell Me How Long Trane's Been Gone*, ed. Steve Rowland and Larry Abrams (ArtistOwned.com, 2000).

John Coltrane and the Practice of Freedom

HERMAN GRAY

The main thing a musician would like to do is to give a picture to the listener of the many wonderful things he knows of and senses in the universe. That's what music is to me.

I'll continue to look for truth in music as I see it, and I'll draw on all the sources I can.

John Coltrane

One of the questions that interests me most about the music and life of work of John William Coltrane is how the figure or legend of Trane as distinct from Coltrane came to be constituted.[1] What were social conditions, historical circumstances, discursive practices, signifying systems, and cultural forms by which Trane was constituted and given cultural value by the press, jazz criticism, jazz studies scholarship, and communities of interests? It is this production of Coltrane, not just as a figure from the past but also as a cultural trope in our present, that I explore in this chapter. In other words, I am more interested in the way that we produce and reproduce Trane, continually nominating him as representative of black freedom.

I want to propose that Coltrane's quest for freedom and the basis of our collective nomination of him as representative is not confined to the past or limited to his sound or his way of being in the world, including his ecumenical approach to world sounds and world religions. I want to show

---

[1] I deliberately refer here (and throughout) to Trane and Coltrane to draw a distinction between John Coltrane the man and Trane the mythical and iconic figure.

the specific ways that Coltrane the person and artist used his music, work, spiritual life, identity, and community to express, indeed practice, a conception of freedom that remains useful today. To do this I ask what it was that John Coltrane was seeking freedom from—what was the source of his constraint, his confinement? Though the big answer, the one that satisfies our mythical construction of him, is of course that he was seeking freedom from oppression, domination, racism, and forms of exclusion that plagued most black people of his generation, the fact of the matter is that in interviews with journalists and on the public record Coltrane the person seldom talked about his music and his work in these terms. So following Coltrane's lead I am after a more prosaic account, one more grounded in the everyday world in which he lived and worked: his formation in the segregated South of the 1930s, his early losses—his father's death at an early age; a sojourn that exchanged an insular southern life for an urban northern one; the ceaseless search for a spiritual life that greatly expanded but was ultimately rooted in the southern black Christian tradition of service, education, and religion in which he was formed;[2] his wide and deep experience as a sideman and a journeyman musician; the innovative and joyful work of his classic quartet; his relationship to his community of peers, audiences, and supporters.[3] In other words, Coltrane is profoundly shaped by his generational location and his class position. He was part of the 1930s and 1940s migration of southern black working-class people who moved from agricultural areas of the South to urban cities in the North. For many writers, it is this circumstance that helps to account for Coltrane's freedom quest, his contribution to an "epistemology of black freedom."[4]

Most cultural commentators, critics, and cognoscenti of American music agree on Coltrane's seminal place in the canon of American jazz history. Even such critics as Stanley Crouch and Gerald Early, who are not fans of the late-period Coltrane (Early describes it as being like a cul-de-sac), concede that Coltrane's influence is formidable. While understated, Early speaks clearly on, for example, Coltrane's influence:

---

[2]Coltrane noted that "all musicians are striving for as near certain perfection [sic] they can get, and that's truth there. . . . So in order to play those kind of things, to play truths, you've got to live as much truth as you possibly can . . . and if a guy is religious . . . [he] might call himself religious or he might not." Quoted in Ashley Kahn, *A Love Supreme: The Creation of John Coltrane's Classic Album* (London: Granta Books, 2002), 8.

[3]Lewis Porter, *John Coltrane: His Life and Music* (Ann Arbor: University of Michigan Press, 2001). See also Farah Jasmine Griffin and Salim Washington, *Clawing at the Limits of Cool: Miles Davis, John Coltrane, and the Greatest Collaboration Ever* (New York: St. Martin's Press, 2008), and Ben Ratliff, *Coltrane: The Story of A Sound* (New York: Farrar, Straus and Giroux, 2006).

[4]This phrase is a variation on what Scott Saul calls a "uniquely black epistemology." See Scott Saul, *Freedom Is, Freedom Ain't: Jazz and the Making of the Sixties* (Cambridge, Mass.: Harvard University Press, 2003), 248.

Understandably, several jazz musicians, black and white, have been inspired by Coltrane, who was a very proficient player—arguably the best technician of the tenor and soprano saxophone in the history of jazz, a music that has produced a number of great saxophonists from Sidney Bechet and Lester Young to Coleman Hawkins and Sonny Rollins. Single-handed, he brought to prominence the soprano saxophone, an instrument not played by any noted jazz musicians since Bechet.... Coltrane introduced a particular style of composition utilizing rubato effect, modes, and triads, some of which he learned from stints with Miles Davis and Thelonious Monk, that became widely imitated.[5]

Given (or despite) the range and weight of Coltrane's contributions taken as a whole, his work is primarily arranged into three discernible periods—his early or harmonic period, his middle or modal period, his late or experimental period—to distinguish and weigh the significance of each.[6] To make sense of how Coltrane is represented and constructed in terms of his purported search for freedom, almost any approach to Coltrane's music and practice will of course have to organize and translate Coltrane's genius into legible aesthetic, social, and political claims. In other words, through the image of and stories we tell about Trane and such concepts as freedom, politics, authenticity, or sincerity we attribute to him, we continue to produce "Trane" to make him suit our purposes, and in the process we make him an emblem (and a suitable one, to be sure) of spiritual searching, political radicalism, cultural nationalism, modern (black) collective consciousness, and Third World Internationalism.[7]

The symbolic act (sacrifice really) of turning the man John Coltrane into the mythical Trane ultimately comes at a price. Many in my generation continue to hold the example of Coltrane near, refusing to let him go, to update him, or to release him from our own collective need and search for a normative ideal of what is good and just. Coltrane's freedom quest is ours. His exploration of the outer edges of musical, spiritual, and human experience was possible at least in the universe of the jazz press, music scholarship, and

---

[5]Gerald Early, "Ode to John Coltrane: A Jazz Musician's Influence on African American Culture," *Antioch Review* 57, 3 (1999): 371.

[6]Lewis Porter, *John Coltrane: His Life and Music*; Carl Woideck, ed., *The John Coltrane Companion: Five Decades of Commentary* (New York: Schirmer Books, 1998).

[7]My point is not to suggest that Trane's is merely the symbolic or ritualistic expression of a vacuous black desire; indeed it is quite the opposite, for Coltrane explored links and responded to what Scott Saul calls a "global surge of black consciousness and solidarity [and] movements of liberation that connected Afro-American to black communities of Brazil, South African, the Congo and many other nations" (*Freedom Is*, 210).

cultural politics because he refused the certainty, finality, and fixity that comes with artistic mastery and personal discipline. The clarity of his commitment and the breadth of his interests led him on a quest to imagine, practice, and embody a concept of freedom (in his sound and through his social relations) as a better place, one filled with joy, love, community, and possibility.

For so many of us, Coltrane's music and, especially, the example of his life and everyday practice offers a template through which our own freedom quests, our own aspirations, desires, and needs to confront the constraints, uncertainties, failures, doubts, and cruelties of our times can be weighed and measured. Coltrane and the colleagues, peers, and friends with whom he worked and the audiences and fans with whom he made and shared community realized a kind of freedom in work, sound, community, and personhood. This concrete practice of freedom is what Derrick Bell calls the "nobility of struggle."[8] This practice of freedom, this way of being free in a world of social, political, cultural, and aesthetic constraint and injustice is evident too in the work of Coltrane's contemporaries and influences including Miles Davis, Thelonious Monk, Billie Holiday, Duke Ellington, Muhal Richard Abrams, Cecil Taylor, Abbey Lincoln, Sun Ra, John Gilmore, Sonny Rollins, and James Brown. These artists used music to negotiate and reimagine their time and to make a better, more beautiful life; in doing so they left the means for us to take the measure of their contribution to what Monk's biographer Robin Kelley calls a surreal conception of the good society and a just world.[9]

So I am concerned with Coltrane's professional and personal practice—the literal production and expression of freedom through the formal production of sound (freedom-sound) as much as the social organization and the conditions necessary for those soundings to be generated and produced in the first place. We know that he was a modest man, that he practiced incessantly, that he was generous to younger musicians, and that he loved working in the studio as much as performing on stage. Indeed, for some commentators and observers it is this combination of modesty and personal discipline that is the key to Coltrane's stature among black musicians, intellectuals, and artists. Coltrane's legendary personal discipline took many forms, most notably, his brutal practice regime, which became the basis of his approach to improvisation, composition, and performance. His personal discipline was also expressed through his devotion to an ideal of

[8]Derrick Bell, *And We Are Not Saved: The Elusive Quest for Racial Justice* (Boston: Beacon Press, 1987).
[9]Robin D. G. Kelley, *Freedom Dreams: The Black Radical Imagination* (Boston: Beacon Press, 2002).

purity and spirituality that led him to devote his life and work to the service of God and the human community. And, of course, he did all of this in a community of friends and peers, in the context of work environments and formal contracts involving financial rewards, critical evaluation, travel, family, home, and so on. In this sense, Coltrane's sound of freedom, his infamous quest for perfection and ceaseless search for the "right sound" is, I think, neither mysterious nor otherworldly—but rather it is, I believe, the actual work of making freedom, grounded in the routine and everyday practice of doing and living. In other words, with Coltrane we have the example of a conception of freedom useful for his time (and ours) through making a life and making a living which is as extraordinary as it is routine. It is through this sense of his own practice—social, spiritual, and political as well as musical; his own way of searching, shifting through, combining and reinventing himself and his work—that the example of Coltrane the artist (and not just Trane the mythological figure) is important. Like the innovators who preceded him and the peers with whom he collaborated, Coltrane helped to reinvent the jazz tradition by breaking ground rules, creating challenges in compositional contexts and performance settings, and doggedly pursuing his ideas and ideals. This idea of exposing one's vulnerabilities in pursuit of an ideal, of breaking with the reigning conventions, and of refusing to accept the aesthetic rules of engagement as illustrated in his consistent strivings for the outer reaches of creative expression—all are qualities of Coltrane's professional and personal practice that I have in mind when I refer to his own practice. I think that the jazz scholar Scott Saul gets it just right when he observes that "Coltrane discovered and refined a style whose authority seemed purchased through the publicly performed anguish of his concerts and recordings. He pursued freedom not for the hell of it, but for the heaven of it—and he did so by creating settings of musical purgatory that forced him to confront his own limits."[10] I want to single out Coltrane's example, then, to urge us to continue to see Coltrane in our time not just as "Trane," the memorialized figure from a dead past whom we periodically celebrate and remember, but as a central conduit or means of connecting us to a living tradition and practice. That is, I want to suggest that Coltrane's quest for freedom is not something merely confined to his past or even to his sound, his compositions, or his way of being in the world, including his ecumenical approach to internationalism, to world music, and to religion. I am rather more concerned that we continue to produce and reproduce Coltrane as a cultural figure, creating him anew by mining his music and taking his example as an expression of the fullness and promise of black freedom.

[10]Saul, *Freedom Is*, 212.

So, what are the conditions of possibility both discursive and institutional that make Coltrane meaningful as a cultural figure in his time and ours?[11] This question leads to my concern with the construction in and representation of Coltrane by a range of discourses; of these, jazz criticism and cultural nationalism are the two most significant. Of course Coltrane was not simply a product of discursive production by overzealous black cultural nationalists and committed bebop jazz critics. His own search and practice, understood in relationship to the constant attempts by critics and nationalists to discipline him (e.g., early-, middle- and late-period Coltrane) and fix him as an exemplar of a specific kind of racial, cultural, and masculine identity was as much driven by his own notion of who he was and what mattered to him (spiritually, politically, and intellectually and therefore what constituted his notion of freedom) as by his attempt to realize the sounds in his head, to change the social relations of work in performance spaces from the recording studio to the club and concert stage, to pay musicians a living wage, to be devoted to his family, and to create venues and work for the members of his community. Like so many others of his generation, this life's work—the daily negotiation of these constraints, his specific practice of freedom in the realm of work, identity, community, and spirituality—was in a very real sense transformative.[12] Photographer Roy DeCarava captured the labor and love of Coltrane at work, so to speak, with his peers and in his community. According to Scott Saul, DeCarava appreciated (and captured) Coltrane's routine qualities: "... the way he sweated ... The way he relaxed ... DeCarava preferred to capture how Coltrane gave back to his community in less spectacular ways—through teamwork, offhand joy ... and most of all through perseverance. His Coltrane is the 1930s common man with a modern adjustment."[13] In other words, Coltrane practiced or enacted a concept of tradition, community, and identity (in sound) that sonically expressed and illustrated for black people a range of possibilities for crafting individual and collective selves into a more expansive and complex notion of blackness. Coltrane crafted his notion of personhood and cultural identity in the era that Guy Ramsey richly describes as "Afro Modernism."[14]

[11]Greg Tate, "Coltrane at 80—A Talent Supreme," *San Francisco Chronicle*, September 22, 2006: E1.
[12]Ashley Kahn, *The House That Trane Built: The Story of Impulse Records* (New York: W.W. Norton, 2000); and Kahn, *A Love Supreme*.
[13]Saul, *Freedom Is*, 253; Roy DeCarava, *The Sound I Saw: Improvisation on a Jazz Theme* (New York: Phaidon, 2001).
[14]Guthrie Ramsey, *Race Music: Black Cultures from Bebop to Hip-Hop* (Berkeley: University of California Press, 2003).

Coltrane's freedom quest, then, represents a specific practice; a way of working and living that is expressed individually in terms of Coltrane's own life and work and collectively both in terms of how we remember him and in relationship to his peers, audiences, and communities that he brought together through with his music. I use the term "practice" throughout this chapter in three ways—to denote how Coltrane is produced by various investments, critical communities and the stories they tell; as an expression of Coltrane's own choices and way of working; and as consumptive and interpretive activity, which is to say in the specific ways that Coltrane is taken up and made to matter for various communities beyond his own time.

Fixing Trane, Looking for Coltrane

Columbia University professor and critic Farah Jasmine Griffin has argued that the mid-twentieth-century art discourses and conventions in photography (particularly portraiture and publicity), jazz criticism and scholarship, and culture (especially race, sex, and gender) operated almost imperceptibly to produce quite powerful (and often competing) notions of Billie Holiday as, alternately, an original jazz singer and a tragic mulatto desperately trapped in a life of failed romance, heroin addiction, and the mysterious underworld of jazz.[15] These tropes of mystery and deviance transformed Holiday the master musician and innovator into "Lady Day," the marketing icon through which her sound was heard and through which her body was coded as simultaneously dangerous and desirable. Griffin argues that these depictions and the taken-for-granted rules that organized them and guide practitioners (and audiences) worked to fix different versions of Holiday in the popular imagination. In the way that we remember her, Holiday's musical knowledge, skill, and mastery were anything but musical. Instead by eroticizing her, emphasizing the allure and mystery of her physical beauty and her sound, her musical stature and skill are reduced to innate, even primitive, expressions of the power of addiction and the subsequent mistreatment she endured at the hands of drug dealers, exploitative men, and a racist and sexist society. In other words, the signal and enduring cultural representation of Holiday's genius is not as an accomplished working musician, a respected and contributing member of her chosen profession, but rather as a tragic black jazz singer, whose role was unique—even innovative, to be sure—but saturated with the signs of the exotic and erotic.

[15]Farah Jasmine Griffin, *If You Can't Be Free, Be a Mystery* (New York: Ballantine, 2001).

To illustrate this interpretative overdetermination, Griffin provides a careful and detailed reading of a photograph taken by jazz bassist and photographer Milt Hinton at Holiday's last recording session.[16] Taken in 1958, Hinton's black-and-white photograph is a medium shot of Holiday at the recording session; she holds a partially filled glass and appears completely absorbed in the moment. Her eyes are cast down. She is elegantly dressed with hair pulled tightly back into her signature bun.[17] In several of the frames taken from this session a music stand and microphone are visible in the shot, evidence of the recording session; there is a hard-to-discern look on Holiday's face—it is difficult to tell if it is sadness, concentration, distraction, nodding, or contemplation. Interpretatively, Griffin leaves open the specific question of what's actually going in the session, postponing analytic closure to expose the power of various accounts and the discursive battles that try to fix or foreclose an account of Holiday. Griffin challenges and thereby dislodges the popular interpretation of this photograph of Holiday, that she was in a drug-induced stupor and barely able to stay awake or remain attentive during the session. In an alternative reading, Griffin suggests other accounts of this photograph (and Holiday more generally)—for instance, rather than a portrait of distraction and inattention, this is a photo of an engaged musician caught in a moment of concentration at the session by one of her peers.[18] For Griffin, in the context of a session with fellow musicians and peers, particularly the presence of Hinton—who played a formidable role in creating a documentary archive of the life and work of jazzmen and -women—Holiday's appearance and demeanor suggest that she could well be lost in concentration and preparation rather than drug-induced disengagement and distraction. More important, Griffin argues that alternative interpretations are virtually impossible given the alliance of discursive authority, assumptions, and conventions in popular lore, jazz criticism, and photography about Holiday, all of which work to naturalize or fix Holiday in the dominant national and international imagination.[19]

---

[16]Farah Jasmine Griffin, "Portrait of a Lady: Visual Technology and the Creation of Lady Day," keynote address for the conference "Against the Wire: Interrogating the Relationship among Race, Music, and Technology," popular music research cluster, at the UCSC Center for Cultural Studies, May 2004.

[17]Web site: www.nea.gov/about/40th/milthinton.html, accessed 3/8/07; see also Milton Hinton, *Bass Lines* (Philadelphia: Temple University Press, 1991).

[18]Bassist Milt Hinton clearly brought an insider's intimate knowledge and access (based on friendship and his professional relationship) to the session. It is also the case that this intimate knowledge and working relationship form a basis to challenge the popular and dominant representations of Holiday; Hinton's photographs help to shift our view of Holiday to another register. While Hinton's photos provide an alternative (and one that I prefer) to traditional representations, his photos too are organized by and rooted in a set of discursive conventions and rules.

[19]Hence the book's clever but poignant title, *If You Can't Be Free, Be a Mystery.*

Griffin's analysis shows that this particular account of Holiday is structured in and by criteria that stipulate what can or cannot be said, how it can be said, and through what rules, conventions, and strategies of representation.[20] In other words, the account of Holiday represented in the Hinton photograph (even when viewed by the most sympathetic of insiders), is structured from the outset by terms where the (masculine and racial) subject of the jazz "musician" is already discursively established; these terms make it impossible to see (and hear) Holiday in the fullness and complexity of her life as a musician. By deconstructing and thereby exposing the discursive authority and conventions of representation that govern who can be seen as an accomplished musician, the photo can be read differently. But only after such an analysis has taken place. Griffin offers a critical reading and re-reading of the possibilities of a different interpretation. It is by no means definitive either. There are both the racial and gender logics at work in the production of understandings and representations of jazz musicians. Along with Griffin, such scholars as Eric Porter on Jeanne Lee, Sherrie Tucker on women swing bands, Guy Ramsey on Dinah Washington, and George Lewis on Pamela Z write against similar pressures toward interpretive and discursive closure in the case of black women musicians and singers.[21]

I want to build on Griffin's analysis of the narrative and visual production of Holiday and jazz musicians more generally to suggest that similar operations—in the realm of jazz criticism and cultural politics—also work to transform Coltrane, fixing him as Trane. In the late 1950s and throughout most of the early 1960s, questions of stylistic fidelity and black identity were deeply rooted in social circumstances defined and authorized by certain strands of cultural nationalism in the realm of black cultural politics and jazz criticism (first with bebop, later with hard bop, and later still with the "new thing") could be legible and authorized only through quite limited narrative and representational terms. This is vexed territory, to be sure, since it risks revisionist accounts of the period. Yet the gain is considerable. Rather than just reading onto Coltrane some fixed characterization driven purely by investments in this or that discourse or this or that correct ideological position, I agree with Scott Saul that Coltrane "sustained his connection to the black community and at the same time affirmed the pursuit of

---

[20]See Michel Foucault, *The Archeology of Knowledge*, trans. A. M. Sheridan Smith (London, 1972).
[21]Guthrie Ramsey, *Race Music*; Sherrie Tucker, *Swing Shift: "All-Girl" Bands of the 1940s* (Durham, N.C.: Duke University Press, 2000); Eric Porter, "Jeanne Lee's Voice," *Critical Studies in Improvisation/Etudes critiques en improvisation* 2, 1 (2006); Herman Gray, *Cultural Moves* (Berkeley: University of California Press, 2005).

individuality without supporting an ethic of individualism"[22] and I want to go further to suggest that by doing so Coltrane provides a concrete expression and practice of freedom.

How to get there? Musicologist Ron Radano argues that to avoid both nineteenth-century racialization and twentieth-century essentialism, analysis of the relationship between race and sound is most productively located in cultural and academic discourse—including anthropology, folklore, sociology, musicology, ethnomusicology, nationalism, and raciology.[23] These discourses produce and consolidate the link between race and sound, race and nation, naturalizing this socially constructed link, attributing various characteristics of place, belonging, geography, and disposition to specific bodies. Radano argues that political stakes and cultural claims for the essential and racial nature of this cultural tradition or that racial sound as guarantors of freedom, emblems of resistance, or hedge against domination are already limited. They are limited, since regardless of the critique they exert or radical claims for racial cultures they make, they still depend on racial logics and social relations of power that structure social and cultural systems of production and deployment. However, when claims for the specificity of black musical distinctiveness are made in terms of the specificity of cultural practices, conventions, and traditions produced by communities rooted in historical conditions, social relations, and logics of power, they form the basis not for fixed essentialist claims but for dynamic social and historical ones.

Radano's critical interrogation of racial discourse and its relationship to the production of racial renderings of black music and Griffin's seminal readings of Holiday suggest that we emphasize the role of discourse and practice in Coltrane's life and work as the basis for understanding his quest as a form of negotiating the power of jazz criticism and cultural politics to fix, discipline, and naturalize him. Coltrane's freedom quest was every bit as much his response to critics, his refusal to be fixed either by the musical or cultural conventions of his time. Seeing Coltrane in this way offers a means for understanding exactly how his specific practices of building community, forging working relations with peers, and changing the terms of recordings and performance represents different mobilizations of tradition and struggle and expresses different possibilities for hearing freedom.

[22]Saul, *Freedom Is*, 262.
[23]Ronald Radano, *Lying Up the Nation: Race and Black Music* (Chicago: University of Chicago Press, 2003). See also Jon Cruz, *Cultures on the Margin* (Princeton, N.J.: Princeton University Press, 1999).

Coltrane: An Unlikely Hero

For Gerald Early, Coltrane, when compared with Duke Ellington, Miles Davis, or Charlie Parker, is a most unlikely hero whose adoption by Black Nationalist poets and writers is puzzling.[24] Coltrane, Early claims,

> was not, after all, an especially flamboyant jazz musician as Dizzy Gillespie or Illinois Jacquet or Art Blakey ... ; Coltrane did not embody any sense of masculine cool or Hemingway bravado like Miles Davis; he was not mysterious and enigmatic like Thelonious Monk or Sun Ra; he was not as openly Afrocentric or Pan-Africanist in his religious inclination as Rahsaan Roland Kirk or Yusef Lateef or Sun Ra; nor was he as overtly political with his music as Max Roach or Archie Shepp or Charles Mingus; he was not popular with the masses of working-class blacks as were "Cannonball" Adderley, Jimmy Smith, Les McCann, Horace Silver or Bobby Timmons (although he sold more avant-guard albums than any other jazz musician in that school and his overall sales were in the hundreds of thousands); and he was certainly not as accomplished in the range of what he could do musically or in the way he could exploit the talents of the musicians around him as Duke Ellington. Why were none of these other 'likely' jazz figures adopted as eagerly by black writers, poets particularly, as a muse? Or better put, why, despite his limitations as a symbol or a source of representation, was Coltrane to become what he did?[25]

Despite Early's interesting query, to which I will return momentarily, books continue to testify to Coltrane's importance, and festivals, celebrations, programs, and performances still keep alive his seminal compositions. Critics and academics continue to argue about his most important period and his most lasting contributions. His saxophone mastery and his legendary practice regimen remain a model for new generations of saxophone players. What is it about Coltrane that continues to command attention some forty years after his death? For Gerald Early, it was a combination of factors including the sociology of the time during and immediately after Coltrane's life, the specific qualities of Coltrane's personality and life, and the way that critics and artists deployed Coltrane to perform the critical cultural work of affirming black critical sensibilities, nationalist identity, and transcendent spirituality.

[24]Early, "Ode to John Coltrane," 372.
[25]Early, "Ode to John Coltrane," 372.

Early suggests, for example, that Coltrane's spiritual and political appeal to musicians and the general public rests largely on the fact that he combined "artistic innovation with therapeutic, redemptive spirituality." "It is no accident," says Early,

> that during the time of Coltrane's greatest period as an artist, from 1960 to 1967, Martin Luther King was talking about redemptive love and sacrifice as a solution to the American race problem, many American artists and intellectuals, particularly after 1965 were going "Oriental" and turning to the East for inspiration, particularly to Indian music ..., yoga, and Zen Buddhism. Some jazz of the late 1960s and 1970s took on, at times, the pretentiousness or intentionality of spiritual, blatantly religious themes in its quest for freedom, salvation, and a segment of the young, college-educated, record buying market that was attracted to this sort of thing during the peace and love, anti-Vietnam war years.[26]

Early argues that the influence of the zeitgeist of the time (particularly its emphasis on religion and freedom) on contemporary musicians was in part "a reflection of a broader need for both artists and audiences to make jazz music, which had ceased being a dance music after World War II, something more elastic in its ability to absorb various influences and to express various moods. Part of it reflects the push after World War II, as jazz became more of an art music, to make it more creator-centered rather than audience centered, to make the creator's urges and inclinations of paramount importance—in short to make it a high-culture music."[27]

In addition, the sociological and technological transformations in the circulation and use of music and in the relationship of audiences to music by the 1960s (as distinct from the '20s) helped to make jazz widely available to popular audiences. At the same time, the music shifted from an audience-centered form of popular entertainment to an artist-centered art form. In the context of these shifts and social conditions, Early argues, "Coltrane represented in useful ways for his audience and his marketers the ... growing tendency of jazz to become more nihilistic and more self-consciously technical in its attempt to serve the psychological needs of its marginalized, intellectual audience as well as to become more anti-intellectual as it aspired for transcendence."[28]

For Early, Coltrane became the patron saint of what he calls "a black anti-intellectual movement" in which "the quest for spiritual purity and

[26]Early, "Ode to John Coltrane," 373.
[27]Early, "Ode to John Coltrane," 374.
[28]Early, "Ode to John Coltrane," 379.

racial solidarity became a quest for orthodoxy and the reinvention of alienation, a reaction to ideology of integration or assimilation." Why? Because
Early's Coltrane was a "brilliant but flawed and limited artist with a simplistic and banal approach to religion as revealed in the poem/notes to *A Love
Supreme* and whose modest, even reticent personality became the perfect
template onto which that young black artists could write their nationalist
hopes and dreams; moreover, Coltrane's widely celebrated story of addiction
and redemption was, in so many ways the perfect story onto which to hang
just the sort of authenticating absolutism which cultural nationalism of the
time needed.[29]

Early, like novelist and critic Ralph Ellison, sees Amiri Baraka as the major
intellectual translator and principal artist and critic to deploy Coltrane in
the service of a black liberation project via Baraka's critique (contempt,
really) of the black middle class and his (Baraka's) view of white popular
culture as a lesser expression of true black creative genius. According to
Early, "What the black intellectual liked about jazz was that it was a highly
technical virtuosic art that could be both romanticized and intellectualized
without having to know anything at all about what it was technically because
one's evaluation of the art could be largely based on one's reaction to it....
Jazz evoked purely emotional responses from its audiences, giving the music
the air of transcendence. Coltrane could fulfill these romanticized notions
for black writers and intellectuals better than any other jazz musician."[30]
Writers and intellectuals became interested in the idea of art as weapon, as a
form of revolt, according to Early, and thus Baraka's Coltrane represented
"not merely the emergence of new black expression but the complete
destruction of white ideas, white art."[31]

Coltrane, on the other hand, "felt that his music could explicitly evoke
and render something racial in its sound, just as he felt it could explicitly
render something spiritual in its sound, both of which he felt would be
obvious to a listener."[32] Despite Early's speculation that Coltrane's obsession
with practicing was an indication of an unbalanced personality and that his
grasp of religion was simplistic, I believe that Coltrane, through sheer force
of determination and example, effectively contested (at least in his lifetime)
the terms of musical convention, cultural identity, and racial politics to
which he was subjected. This theme of contestation and reinvention is

[29]This particular story of fall and redemption fits perfectly in the national narrative about jazz as the
quintessential American story of pluralism and jazz's unique expression as the original soundtrack
of the nation. Ken Burns uses this narrative metaphorically in his PBS series *Jazz* by deploying it to
tell individual biographical tales of jazzmen and to tell the grand story of America's racial history.
[30]Early, "Ode to John Coltrane," 380.
[31]Early, "Ode to John Coltrane," 380.
[32]Early, "Ode to John Coltrane," 377.

evident, for example, in most biographical and musical accounts of Coltrane. By approaching his composition and performance as occasions for experimentation and testimony, Coltrane took an opportunity to reinvent the music and himself. Scott Saul writes that "when Coltrane ... reduced 'Tunisa' to its basics, he did so not to claim a higher originality but to reveal an even more direct and powerful drama of energy within the original piece, a charismatic drama that had been hidden by the earlier scaffold of sophistication.... Coltrane dug into 'Tunisa' to rewrite a song of spiritual declaration, the preaching of a particularly bracing sermon."[33]

Coltrane asked his critics to judge his work both by his mastery of the form and the sincerity of his efforts.[34] What might seem naive spiritualism or false modesty might be seen in a different light: as Coltrane's search for and plea for forms that could bear the weight of sincerity and honesty that was too easily masked and burdened by the musical and cultural conventions of the time. "Starting with his famous conversion experience in 1957," Saul writes, "Coltrane sought to purify his life of the corrupting influences of drugs and alcohol; he became the jazz scene's most prominent example of the straight life, its most notable convert to the ethic of sincerity under pressure," and, perhaps more remarkably, "Coltrane achieved this prominence without the usual sort of celebrity self-promotion: he rarely spoke in detail of his personal life, and almost every friend and acquaintance was struck by the degree of his self-effacement."[35] Coltrane simply asked to be understood in terms of the purity of his intention and the sincerity of his work including his quest for mastery, a request that anticipates a theoretical shift for thinking about black identity recently articulated by anthropologist John Jackson. The focus on sincerity and interiority foregrounds the personal qualities that make Early's Coltrane an unlikely figure of Black Nationalist expression.

I want to read Coltrane's personal and professional quest through Jackson's formulation of sincerity and against the discursive operations and assumptions that tried to fix and contain him in his lifetime. As Early and others note, in the 1960s white jazz critics often described Coltrane as an angry young tenor who, it was also said, had contempt for his audience. Yet jazz critics and interviewers were just as often surprised when they met Coltrane, reporting that he was unpretentious, warm, sincere, and open.

[33]Saul, *Freedom Is*, 220.
[34]As evidenced in the following interviews with Coltrane, all in part 2 of *The John Coltrane Companion*, ed. Carl Woideck: August Blume, "An Interview with John Coltrane"; John Coltrane and Don DeMicheal, "Coltrane on Coltrane"; Valerie Wilmer, "Conversation with Coltrane"; Don DeMicheal, "John Coltrane and Eric Dolphy Answer the Jazz Critics"; Benoit Quersin, "La Passe dangereuse"; and Frank Kofsky, "John Coltrane: An Interview."
[35]Saul, *Freedom Is*, 212.

Don DeMicheal, editor *of DownBeat*, for example, reports being surprised at Coltrane's easy and respectful demeanor. "In our initial conversation I was struck by his lack of pretentiousness or false pride. The honesty with which he answered questions ... impressed me deeply."[36] Valerie Wilmer, a British journalist and photographer, formed a similar impression of Coltrane, writing, "the in-person sound of Coltrane was so different from his recorded work that most people wondered whether their auditory processes were in order. It seemed they were, for Coltrane himself confirmed that his music had radically altered over the last twelve months or so. Meeting the man himself, it is hard to believe that such a quiet, calm, and serious individual could be responsible for the frantic 'sheets of sound' which emanate from his tenor saxophone, or that such [a] sensitive person could think of his uglier wailings on soprano as beautiful."[37]

I want to linger a bit on the disparity between these critical evaluations of Trane and the personal impressions that Coltrane made on some writers. I do so to make a point about the discursive production of Trane as a cultural figure and musician. I want to show how the discursive framework of critical appraisal and nationalist claims on the meaning of his work helps to structure some of the social and cultural environment within which Coltrane worked.

As Early suggests, the social creation of Trane in the jazz and cultural nationalist imaginations was organized around two narratives: in the one, bebop was stylistically under assault from an emergent style ("the New Thing"); and in the other, nationalism functions as a radical critique not to be confused with the integrationist solutions to the problem of racial inequality and cultural autonomy. These narratives were represented, on the one hand, by the mainstream jazz press and, on the other, by those who would assimilate jazz to the banalities of white America's cultural, political, and social system. The advocates and defenders of the black jazz avant-garde and the emergent black cultural nationalists had to distance themselves from what they took to be the threat to their project of black freedom—bebop as jazz authenticity, and cultural assimilation as the solution to black cultural subordination. Not surprisingly, both stories depended on an authenticating logic organized by an explicit need for a representation of who and what constituted the subject of their discourse—for both the nationalists and avant-guard, Trane fulfilled this need. But the point is simply that this construction proceeded without Coltrane's complicity. As Saul puts it, "While

---

[36]Valerie Wilmer, "John Coltrane and Eric Dolphy Answer the Jazz Critics," in *John Coltrane Companion*, 198.

[37]Wilmer, "John Coltrane and Eric Dolphy," 104.

Coltrane was loath to attach his music to a specific political ideology, prefer-ring the language of universal spirituality, he became posthumously an icon of a uniquely black epistemology."[38]

Again, according to John Jackson, who has tried to rethink the notion of realness as applied to black cultural politics, an authenticating logic of cul-tural and racial identity is built on subject-object relations (in contrast to subject-subject relations), where the authenticator or the source of authenti-cation resides with the subject who bestows a judgment on the object (in need of authenticating for membership or validity or recognition).[39] Scripts, narratives, and criteria about appropriate or real racial identity or, in Col-trane's case, the real "sound" provide members and aspiring members of a community with clarity and direction about who belongs and who does not, and about which experiences are real and which are imitations—in other words, about what counts as an authentic expression that the validated sub-ject can vouch for. In puzzling through the implications of Jackson's formu-lation as it pertains to the black (and male) jazz musician and largely white (and male) jazz critic (or, as I want to suggest as well, the Black Nationalist guardian of the cultural gates), narratives of authenticity help to organize the terms of legibility (assumptions, concepts, and rules) in which a character-ization such as "angry young tenor" or "ugly sounds" are used to describe (and discipline) musicians who do not conform to the scripted notions of what jazz is purported to be or sound like. Rather than a blank slate onto which the racial and aesthetic battle lines could be read, this persistent posi-tion both by canon protectors and cultural guardians helps to explain in part the social, cultural, even personal impositions that Coltrane (as opposed to Trane) resisted.

Prescribed narratives which declare that black people are this or that, or that jazz is this and not that (bebop is real jazz, and the avant-garde is not) signal to members of the community that which is permitted and that which is forbidden, that which confirms and sustains both the community and the canon as well as that which challenges and unsettles it. In this sense we might suggest that narratives of the sort applied to Coltrane by jazz critics in the 1950s and 1960s (and by nationalists in the 1960s and 1970s) served to locate Coltrane within a worldview that built a normative ideal about what consti-tuted real jazz and designated appropriate representatives.

In contrast to the subject-object formulation of narratives of authenticity are those based in sincerity, where social relations are built on subject-subject relations and none of the parties have a privileged claim on belonging,

[38]Saul, *Freedom Is*, 248.
[39]John L. Jackson Jr., *Real Black: Adventures in Racial Sincerity* (Chicago: University of Chicago Press, 2005).

membership, or the real. These are the terms of encounter that both Wilmer and DeMicheal confronted in their meetings with Coltrane, where his appeal was to openness, dialogue, and exchange. Instead of finding a Coltrane fixed by an authenticating story, ideology, or canon, they discovered an artist who impressed them with his openness and willingness to discuss criticisms of his music as well as his intentions and motivations. Judgments about commitment or fidelity to this or that position are not measured by the distances one travels from some fixed notion of place, but rather by the practice and the capacity of that practice to form the bonds and basis of connection to others. In my view, Coltrane was on a quest to forge such bonds and connections no matter how many of the cultural expectations and canonical rules he violated or how many authenticating narratives about the music, the race, politics, or the imagined nation he transgressed. This quest was not just confined to his relationship with jazz critics and jazz criticism, but extend to matters spiritual, political, and cultural. So in contrast to Early's evaluation of Coltrane's understanding of religion as simplistic and his implicit assumptions about what it takes to sustain a complex view of religion, I want to suggest that the measure of Coltrane's commitment and example resides in his sincerity and practice and not with our judgments.[40]

One of the constants that appear in interviews with Coltrane is his commitment to push the limits of his own mastery regardless of how this mastery is fixed and canonized by the professional jazz critics. As a result, over the course of his career, Coltrane explored a number of different ways of approaching music and absorbed a vast variety of influences. Saul notes that "Coltrane moved from hard bop and modal jazz, to the suite form of 'A Love Supreme' and then the freer combinations that dropped the musical pulse entirely," and he digested "everything from Indian ragas, Buddhist temple music, slave spirituals, Stravinsky, and the harp playing of Harpo Marx."[41] By Coltrane's own account, the period most associated with his first great defining style finds him trying to develop and master complex harmonies and chord structures.[42] His aim, of course, was to expand the limits of the existing styles—swing, R&B, blues, and early bebop—in which he was formed and out of which he played. Coltrane's second great phase finds him engaged in melodic and rhythmic exploration with both Miles and Monk. Both mentors help to free Coltrane from the preoccupations of his prior period of harmonic exploration while building on the important lessons he learned. His body of work produced in this period with the great quartet is

---

[40]I agree with Scott Saul's conclusion that "if Coltrane sounds amateurish [at times] it is because he is willing to try anything . . . that might add to the powers of his testimony" (*Freedom Is*, 222).

[41]Saul, *Freedom Is*, 267.

[42]Woideck, *John Coltrane Companion*.

characterized by greater and greater melodic and rhythmic freedom. This is the period in which Coltrane turns decidedly to Africa and the Third World for influences, producing song titles and arrangements that explicitly gesture to Africa; it is also the period when song titles and subjects are most explicitly political, referencing the racial strife of the time. This move on the part of Coltrane and the force of its appeal among young black intellectuals, writers, and artists was less the expression of a whimsical adventure of happenstance or misdirection than the articulation of a very powerful yearning for black expression and dialogue with powerful emergent forces in the Third World and the African Diaspora.

The final period of his short life finds Coltrane pushing against both of these prior periods while drawing deeply on both. The period from 1965 to 1967 finds Coltrane in search of a new language, a new vocabulary of rhythmic and sonic possibilities. He draws these increasingly from world cultures and his own southern background. This, of course, is the time frame when Coltrane produced work in which the discursive rupture with the established jazz canon is greatest and the criticism is the harshest and most suspicious. For example, Gerald Early claims that the point of the search for freedom was simply the expression of greater freedom. By this time, the force of Coltrane's influence is diminishing; for some he is a threat, for others he is musically illegible and therefore beyond comprehension. For still others, this is the Coltrane of pure sincerity—of pulse, energy, and sound.

I have been suggesting that culturally it is helpful to make sense of Coltrane's career movement through the lens of critical systems of interpretation. At every stage of his career, at every new arrival, Coltrane resisted the temptation by others to fix his musical identity and his work in some definitive sense, confining him to some predetermined generic mold, identity, time, or canon. In terms of the conventional narrative of Coltrane's career (indeed the grandness of this narrative subsumes the biography of almost all of the anointed jazz masters), Coltrane is first intrigued by the masters, then is imprisoned by their influence, and finally seeks release from the hegemony of a given stylistic approach, whether it be swing, bebop, or the New Thing. This is not a story of clear displacement and success but of overlapping and uneven fits and starts. Each of these experiences of influence and the struggle for distinction are formidable, and each prepares Coltrane for the burden of innovation and experimentation.

From the point of view of a canonical project (even narrative of rise and fall), this narrative opens a space and then fixes a specific version of the first two phases of influence in the jazz canon. As with Early's characterization of Coltrane's personality traits as obsessive, this story, as fantastic as it is, centers the inner life of Coltrane as the basis for propelling the story of his career, drive, and innovation forward. It is a powerful story to be sure, but two social dimensions are absent from the conventional narrative that threaten to make it yet another triumphant story of a great man and hence incomplete. The first element is the importance of community, collaboration, colleagues, and the exchange of ideas that made the laboratory of invention and innovation possible. In addition to DeCarava's depiction of Coltrane's membership and relationship to the black working-class community, Lewis Porter recounts Coltrane's legendary support for advocating, sponsoring, and launching the careers of younger musicians, including Pharoah Sanders, Eric Dolphy, Archie Shepp, Freddie Hubbard, Rashied Ali, and many others.[43]

But as I have been suggesting, just as important is the powerful role that critical discourses—jazz in particular—played in setting the terms within which this movement, interpretation, response, and innovation occurs. I am suggesting that Coltrane is shaped as much by his formation and work within a community of practitioners as by the limiting (mis)readings of his work by the jazz press, jazz scholars, and nationalists. By stressing these two social factors, the theme of Coltrane's pursuit of freedom takes on more concrete meanings and can be understood as social and cultural practices involving rules, judgments, conventions, and interpretive communities. In such a context, different discursive communities including musicians, journalists, nationalists, and popular audiences have stakes, make claims, and exercise judgments of all sorts on the practices and expressions within a discernible social and cultural field.[44]

Coltrane's sincere expression of musical restlessness, personal discipline, and sacrifice resulted in the search for personal freedom. In the view of some music critics and popular audiences, Coltrane's constant change and refusal to settle in amounted to abandonment if not a kind of betrayal to the purity of the jazz canon. Politically, Coltrane's perpetual arrival and departure signaled to cultural nationalists, Marxists, and those interested in spirituality, an inspiration, if not soundtrack, for black freedom. These competing and sometimes clashing authenticating narratives were invested, for very different reasons, in claiming Trane, making him and what he represented serve different ends.

---

[43]Lewis Porter, *John Coltrane: His Life and Music*; Woideck, *John Coltrane Companion*; Kahn, *House That Trane Built* and *A Love Supreme*.

[44]Consider, for example, Guy Ramsey's formulation of Afro-modernism as a particular sort of social and cultural field that expressed the sentiment, aspirations, and lifeways of African Americans in mid-twentieth-century America. According to Ramsey, Afro-modernism is a postwar constellation of social forces and relations—urbanization, migration, labor, social relations, and cultural expressions—in which African Americans were constructed as emergent subjects making new lives in large urban centers such as New York and Chicago.

Alternatively, for Guthrie Ramsey, the music(s) generated by blacks expressed the full range—urban/rural, North/South, radical/conservative, work/leisure, art/commercial—of black life in aural form. Particularly important in his formulation is the discursive organization of cultural and aesthetic auralscape in which black music took place in post World War II—art and modern (e.g., bebop), commercial and popular sounds (rhythm and blues), and of course folk or vernacular expressions like (the blues). Ramsey shows that the musics produced by black people in this period were necessarily hybrid and mixed, constitutive of all the available musical elements from the time. This hybridity was present as well in the circuits and spaces where the music was played and experienced—at private house parties, radio broadcasts, jukeboxes, stages, clubs, and so on. Hence Coltrane's negotiation and movement is less abandonment than a reckoning with the sounds available to him, past and present, local and global. In this respect the claim to hybridity is not at all limited to Coltrane but, as Ramsey shows, was also expressed in the music and careers of such people as Dinah Washington, Louis Jordon, and Cootie Williams, each of whom crossed the established genre boundaries—popular, art, and vernacular—thereby expressing what Ramsey regards as the essential quality of Afro-modernism.

Another robust contribution to the idea that Coltrane's search might be understood as both an enactment of hybridity and as a way of pushing against the confinements of musical and ideological identities is suggested in the creative and critical work of poet and critic Nathaniel Mackey. In his writing, Mackey regularly crosses the boundaries of poetry, criticism, music, and the interview. His critical essay "Cante Moro," with its marvelous and extended elucidation of the concept of duende, provides a promising framework through which to understand the importance of hybridity and sincerity to the creative life of Coltrane without resorting to weak speculations about his character or inner life or motivations for abandoning one style for another.[45] For Mackey, duende expresses the often inarticulate but powerful condensation and intensification of experience and tradition in a culture's history and practice. Mackey illustrates this powerful expression and its centrality to the "soul" of creative expression by looking to the work of Spanish poet Federico Garcia Lorca and to the musics of various exemplars of the African Diasporic tradition, Coltrane among them. To conjure the importance of duende in African Diasporic practices, Mackey reads expressive practices of gypsies of Spain, the flamenco musicians of Andalusia, the *son*

---

[45]Nathaniel Mackey, "Conte Moro" and "Paracritical Hinge," in his *Paracritical Hinge: Essays, Talks, Notes, Interviews* (Madison: University of Wisconsin Press, 2005), 181–199 and 207–228.

musicians of Cuba, and the blues musicians of the Mississippi Delta of the United States. In jazz, the equivalent of duende, as Mackey would have it, is expressed in the understanding, for instance, of the blue(s) in Miles Davis's *Kind of Blue*, in which blue signifies across a tonal color palate and the blues form organizes the sonic possibilities that Miles and his colleagues exhaust. In Mackey's account of his own critical and creative writing, he points to what he calls the paracritical form of experimental writing, which stretches across different forms, genres, styles, even media (spoken word and live jazz performance) in search of duende, which is more often revealed through disturbance and unsettling than conformity.

I find this idea especially useful for thinking about those elements of Coltrane's own practice that aroused so much suspicion, scorn, and misunderstanding—for instance, the polyphonic and polyvocal conversations that he carried out in lengthy improvisational performances over the course of his career. This polyphonic sensibility was expressed in different form in the course of the various musical units with which he worked and led; but it was also expressed as a conversation that he sustained with himself, illustrated most explicitly in Mackey's account during Coltrane's time with Miles when Coltrane used the time of Miles's modal period to experiment and exhaust the full range of his ideas on a number of given themes. Stretching across a number of motifs, Coltrane expanded the tenor range to four octaves from its original two-and-one-half-octave range, pioneered new and innovative sounds through his explorations—sheets of sound, running chords— and used many other sonic twists, turns, runs, polyphonics, and harmonics to achieve a kind of self-accompaniment or conversation, call and response if you will.[46] These innovations were central to his quest, his ceaseless and exhaustive expression of a kind of aesthetic, intellectual, spiritual, and personal movement over the course of a tune, a performance, a recording session, a so-called stylistic period, indeed a life.

My contention is that we should read Coltrane's career trajectory and practice through the lens of hybrid disturbance and travel. That is, rather than going through stages of arrival and departure, Coltrane was always invested in a process of producing black hybridity and looking for ways of negotiating the boundaries and territory in which he was formed and in which he lived and worked. Hence it is the rules and conventions of a specific discursive field that constructed Coltrane as this or that, as effective in this phase or that, and hence more or less legitimate in a specific period that propelled him. What makes Coltrane so interesting on these issues is that

---

[46]Thanks to Leonard Brown for the language to describe Coltrane's musical, compositional, and performance innovations.

personally, spiritually, and musically, he exemplifies a kind of hybridization of clashing, seemingly incommensurate forces that can be seen in his some of his signature *performances*—"Africa Brass" and "Dahomey"; "My Favorite Things" and "Out of This World"; "Sun Ship" and "Ascensions," "Ballads" and "My Little Brown Book"; *influences*—southern segregation, cosmopolitanism, global spirituality; and *impact* on harmony, rhythm, and vocabulary. In Ramsey's sense of Afro-modernism, Coltrane represents a kind of blackness (also exemplified by his peers Gillespie, Monk, Davis, Ellington, and Mingus) that understood itself as expansive and cosmopolitan, moored in traditions but yet not captive to them.

John Coltrane as the Personification of Spirituality in Black Music

ANTHONY BROWN

Come on, Bobby,
Blow Robert,
Blow me some Trane, Brother!

—James Brown in "Super Bad," cueing the closing tenor
saxophone solo by Robert McCullough

The title of this essay signifies the prevailing recognition of John Coltrane as a musical and spiritual icon, a man who dedicated the last years of his life to creating an increasingly intense and complex music celebrating spirituality.[1] Coltrane's inclusive nature favored no one religion in his spiritually inspired music, which further distinguishes him in the jazz tradition, if not the entire tradition of African American music. This essay focuses on one of the most radically transitional phases of Coltrane's development, the period marking a dramatic shift in his approach to one of music's most basic organizational concepts: steady time. Following his landmark recording of *A Love Supreme* in December 1964, Coltrane's 1965 studio recordings of his subsequent multimovement extended works document this nearly yearlong transformation wherein Coltrane's primary drummer, Elvin Jones, begins to incorporate extended episodes of unmetered or free-time accompaniment. Paradoxically, Coltrane's incorporation of an inclusive free rhythmic

[1]This article is largely a reworking of two papers I presented at symposiums, first at Northeastern University, Boston, on September 29, 2005, then at the Center for Black Music Research/Society of American Music joint conference in Chicago on March 3, 2006. Also included are quotes from a heretofore-unpublished interview with Elvin Jones that I conducted in New York City on June 10–11, 2003, for the Smithsonian Jazz Oral History Program.

55

foundation would change the sound of his music forever, but it also alienated some of his fan base.

I. Give The Drummer Some!

> *Give the drummer some!*
>
> —James Brown cueing the band to lay out and let the
> drummer solo in "Cold Sweat"

There has been a considerable amount written about John Coltrane's music
over the past fifty years, ever since his first magazine review in the mid-
1950s. But despite a wealth of written words, no study analyzes the evolution
of Coltrane's rhythmic concepts in his music from post-"modern jazz" to
"free jazz." This transformation affecting the entire rhythmic and percussive
undergirding of his music transpired in 1965, while Coltrane was performing at the height of his popularity with the incomparable drummer Elvin
Jones. When queried why he invited other percussionists to perform with
his group, Coltrane claimed, "I feel the need for more time, more rhythm
around me. And with more than one drummer, the rhythm can be more
multi-directional. Someday I may add a conga drummer or even a company
of drummers" (liner notes to *Meditations*). The growth in rhythmic complexity, textural intensity, and further abstraction characterizes the final
stages of Coltrane's musical development and serves as an index of his
realization of a spiritual and musical inclusivity.

Coltrane's rhythmic evolution can be explored through a survey of his
multimovement extended compositions recorded in the studio with his
quartet between his seminal masterwork, *A Love Supreme,* in December
1964, until Elvin Jones's last recording with Coltrane, *Meditations,* in November 1965. Coltrane employed the structural form of a suite in these extended
pieces, which required the compositional acumen to shape music with a
variety of pitch selections, tempos, and moods for his improvisations, while
creating a cohesive, coherent work of spiritual inspiration. The recordings
clearly document the transition of Coltrane's music from its original roots in
post-hard-bop rhythmic approaches, to its increasing incorporation of free
jazz elements characterized by Coltrane's nontonal saxophone wails and an
absence of a basic regulatory pulse or meter maintained by Jones. This innovative approach gives the music a sense of temporal freedom, with the drums
contributing a more textural rather than rhythmic accompaniment. Coltrane and Jones bridged musical time and freedom often intensely, blending

the cadences of speech, prayer, and cries with episodes of driving rhythmic intensity and timelessness.

Coltrane's first two albums for his new label, Impulse Records, signaled his new musical direction in 1961, mirroring the primary influences in his life. Both recordings were major projects, each involving numerous guests artists and new, extended compositions. The inaugural recording's title, *Africa/Brass*, reflects Coltrane's cultural consciousness and origins, as well as an expanded tonal palette. The second project, *Live at the Village Vanguard*, includes the Middle Eastern lute (oud) among the added instruments and features original works titled "India" and "Spiritual." The first work evidences the indelible Indo influences of Ravi Shankar and Hindustani music; Coltrane named one of his sons Ravi. The latter work, *Spiritual*, signifies the lasting influence in Coltrane's musical evolution of that wellspring of African American music, America's original folksong—the spiritual (Johnson 1925: 13).

Coltrane practiced inclusivity in his life's work, particularly in his musical performances. The spirituals tradition served as a primary inspiration, linking Coltrane to his West African musical heritage, which is grounded in the embracing of the collective. In much of sub-Saharan Africa, music making is 24/7, inextricable from daily life, and usually a communal, multimedia, democratic endeavor with everyone participating at some level. It is a vital part of life, a life force. This may be why Coltrane embraced everything. He was dispensing with boundaries in his music and in his spirituality, both of which incorporated multiple cultural and religious influences. When he was exploring ways of freeing up the boundaries in music's tonal and harmonic dimensions, he had not yet fully examined abstracting the temporal dimension, or "freeing up the time." By 1965 Coltrane, in collaboration with Jones, began to explore concepts of abstracting time, pushing "outside" the envelope to free up the fixed, repetitive nature of musical time, to attenuate and ultimately eliminate an underlying, regulating pulse or meter. This led to a point in Coltrane's development, to that juncture in his evolution, when many people listening to these recordings would say, "I can't get into it, or relate to it, it doesn't speak to me." Despite the array of "nonmusical" sounds he produced on his saxophone that people found "objectionable," I believe it was when Coltrane's music ceased to have a fixed pulse undergirding it, when even seasoned listeners could no longer feel the beat or "pat their feet to it," that he lost many of his most ardent followers.

With Jones as his main drummer from late 1960 to early 1966, Coltrane had the most cross-rhythm-oriented percussionist known to play jazz. Coltrane, up until 1965, is documented as always playing with a pulse, or several pulses. He would often begin the introductions to several of his compositions, notably *Spiritual*, *Alabama*, and *A Love Supreme*, with an unmetered beginning (and often ending) before launching into a swinging

accompanied improvisation.[2] On his recordings until 1965, Coltrane impro-
vises over a rhythmically sophisticated, complex, and flowing drum-set
accompaniment improvised by Jones, that still contains at least one identifiable pulse in the music. Even at the most impassioned moments of their live
recordings, the quartet's music is buoyed by Jones's surging syncopated triplet permutations around the drum set generating steady time.

II. Beyond *A Love Supreme*

> *(What) I wanted to do in music ... was to have a band that played like the way we*
> *used to play, and a band that was going in the direction the one I have now is going*
> *in. I could combine these two with these two concepts going. And it could have been*
> *done....*
>
> > *I like to have somebody there in case I can't get that strength, I like to have that*
> > *energy in the band.... There always has to be somebody with a lot of power. In the*
> > *old band, Elvin had this power, I always had to have someone there with it....*
> > *Rashied has it but it hasn't quite unfolded completely. All he needs to do is play.*
>
> —John Coltrane (Kofsky 1970: 232–233)

By the last recordings of Coltrane's "classic" quartet, which had McCoy Tyner
on piano and Jimmy Garrison on bass, Jones was including extended passages of free jazz drumming—using the drum set to create a dynamic, textural wash of unmetered punctuations, phrases, and figures. The May 17,
1965, recording of *Brazilia* is an excellent example of Jones's transition into
free drumming. The thirteen-minute piece opens with an introductory punctuated cymbal crash from Jones and becomes a duet with Coltrane intoning
the melody and improvised elaborations on tenor saxophone. Jones accompanies him with sustained, punctuated snare drum press rolls and accentuates
Coltrane's cadential phrases with crescendos and punctuated cymbal crashes.
The cadence at 1:25 leads to a metered, accompanied improvised saxophone
solo by Coltrane followed by McCoy Tyner's piano solo. Jones is swinging at
a medium tempo, using the full drum set, and bassist Jimmy Garrison primarily walks while Tyner employs his patented 3:2 cross-rhythmic comping.

---

[2]The practice of beginning musical pieces with a seemingly free-form introduction that becomes a
metered ensemble performance is common to India in the alap of a raga in classical Hindustani
music (Wade 1987: 160, 162–164), and in gagaku, the ancient court music of Japan (Malm 1967: 39,
41). This practice can also be seen in sermons delivered by black Baptist ministers, as discussed by
Olly Wilson in my interview with him later in this volume.

At 9:50, during his second solo, Coltrane begins a recapitulation, but Jones does not completely follow the cue and continues to play time. Soon thereafter, there's a temporal shift when Tyner begins to free up his accompaniment, becoming less rhythmically supportive. Garrison becomes less metric in his bass lines as well, while Jones continues to play time. At 10:36 Coltrane again introduces the theme and again Jones continues to swing. At 11:05 Jones joins everyone else in the collective free improvisation by ceasing any ride cymbal patterns carrying the triplet pulsations. He plays unmetered rolls, figures, phrases, and punctuations on the drums, adding crescendi and cymbal crashes for punctuations building to the finale at 12:52.

On June 10, 1965, the John Coltrane Quartet recorded *Suite*, the first multimovement extended work to follow the December 9, 1964, recording of his magnum opus, *A Love Supreme*. The twenty-one-minute *Suite* begins with Coltrane's "Prayer," which serves as the recurring motif between movements. The accompaniment from the rhythm section is much looser in its tracing of the melodic contours with Coltrane's phrasing and timing, creating a temporal elasticity. At 1:09, Coltrane introduces the "Day: Meditation" section, and the band begins a highly dense *agitato* accompaniment with no time referential. Jones's playing uses the entire drum set, maintaining a pan-rhythmic percussive mosaic with a near-constant prestissimo shimmering pulse on the cymbals interjected with drum phrases, figures, punctuations, and cymbal crashes. At 3:15, Coltrane introduces the "Peace" movement, which becomes a loping swing when the rhythm section enters to accompany him. A four-minute unaccompanied bass solo follows before Coltrane reenters with a repeat of the opening "Prayer" movement. Shortly, Jones begins to swing underneath, and Coltrane plays the theme of "Evening: Meditation" with the rhythm section swinging hard in support of Coltrane's saxophone and during Tyner's piano solo. Coltrane reenters with an impassioned solo buoyed by Jones swinging and surging into a drum solo titled "Affirmation" at 17:40. The finale, "4 a.m.: Prayer and Meditation," completes the final three minutes of the work with the ensemble loosely accompanying Coltrane's often straining cries of the melodic phrases. Jones again accompanies primarily with accented drum rolls around the kit and punctuated cymbal crashes, reminiscent of his closing of *Brazilia*.

On June 28, 1965, Coltrane assembled his quartet plus seven guest musicians—tenor saxophonists Pharoah Sanders and Archie Shepp, alto saxophonists Marion Brown and John Tchicai, trumpeters Freddie Hubbard and Dewey Johnson, and Art Davis on bass—to record his most adventurous work to date, *Ascension*. Two takes were recorded of the roughly forty-minute piece, identified as Ascension Editions I & II. Unlike the other multimovement extended works of this period, the structure of *Ascension* is built around alternating ensemble and accompanied solo sections. On both recordings, Jones uses alternating temporal textures (free, metered) to undergird the form of the extended group improvisation. The full ensemble sections are collectively improvised in "real-time generation of musical structure" in an unmetered context (Lewis 1996: 91–92). The solo improvisations modulate from free time to swing with Jones setting up the groove for each soloist before joining in the dissolution of the time at the solo's end to signal the next ensemble section.

Because of the length and character of the *Ascension* recordings, I have graphically represented each edition on a timeline as charts 1 and 2, which provide more detail of the alternating format of both takes. The work's proportional features are clear with each collective improvisation section averaging between one and two and a half minutes, and accompanied improvised solos ranging between one and three and a half minutes. Every musician has an opportunity to solo and to freely join in the collective improvisation sections. Both editions of *Ascension* begin and end with full group improvisations of three to four minutes, with the signature theme played heterophonically in the opening and recapitulated at the end. Both episodes appear to have had someone judiciously keeping time, as several entrances and cues occur conspicuously "by the clock."[3] Jones maintains alternating episodes of free and swing time accompaniment throughout the first edition, and is tacit only during the bass duet in the second. In the metered sections, Jones plays a medium swing beat behind most soloists, ranging in tempo between mm. 96 and 108 per half note. Over the length of the first edition, Jones's accompaniment mixes metered and unmetered elements in his effort to negotiate more variegated temporal shifts. On both editions, his time feel becomes more elastic—if that's possible—as he mixes his trademark swing with episodes of mixed meters, for example, playing waltz time against 4/4 swing and shifting tempos or playing extended fills at nonstructural points. His free playing usually consists of figures and rhythmic phrasings and accents within an undefined metric framework, often supportive of or in counterpoint to the other improvisers.[4]

On September 27, 1965, Coltrane's quartet recorded the first version of his milestone composition *Meditations*, posthumously titled *First Meditations*. The differences in these two suites underscore the evolution of

---

[3]This in no way implies there was a restrictive atmosphere to the recording, but rather that a democratic effort was consciously made to ensure everyone "had their say" within the dictated length equaling both sides of an LP, around forty minutes.

[4]Ornette Coleman's influence on Coltrane is undeniable and documented (*The Avant-Garde*, Atlantic Jazz 7900041-2), and comparisons of Coltrane's *Ascension* to Coleman's 1960 double quartet recording, *Free Jazz*, are warranted. Besides the obvious similarities, they also both employ "clocked" structures with predetermined temporal lengths for ensemble and solo selections. Notably, Coleman's title is actually a misnomer in that both drummers—Ed Blackwell and Billy Higgins—maintain steady pulses throughout the extended recordings; they do not play free time on *Free Jazz*.

Chart 1.   ASCENSION Edition I. Recorded June 28, 1965, NJ. *The Major Works of John Coltrane*, Impulse GRD-2-113

TIMELINE OF EVENTS

Minutes (+/- 3") INSTRUMENTS/SOLOS	5	10	15	20	25	30	35
Theme 0:01-0:30 0:30-4:05							**Theme recap** 35:38 **38:40 End**
Full Ensemble Improv	4:05-6:05 Group Improv	6:10-8:00 Group Improv; 10:10-11:05 Group Improv	11:05-13:35; 13:35-15:00 Group Improv	15:00-; 17:55-19:00 Group Improv	19:05-21:45; 21:45-23:15 Group Improv	25:00-26:25 Group Improv; 28:35-29:35 Group Improv	34:00 Group Improv
TENOR SAX	Coltrane (4:05-6:05)		11:05-13:35 Sanders		19:05-21:45 Shepp		
TRUMPET		8:00-10:10 Johnson	15:00-17:55 Hubbard				
ALTO SAX					23:20-25:00 Tchicai	26:30-28:35 Brown	
PIANO							29:45-31:45 Tyner
BASSES (pizz.)		8:00 arco & walking bass			23:30 arco		33:35 Garrison, Davis
DRUMS 0:01	1:25 Free Loose medium swing, with Free episodes / Free, intermittent time, fills	6:10 8:00 Swing, mixed time	13:50 Free, with fills	15:00 Swing, mixed time; 17:55 Free mixed time	19:05 Swing, Free mixed time; 21:30 Free, with fills; 23:20 Swing, mixed time fills	25:00 Free, with fills; 26:25 Swing, mixed time; 28:50 Free, with time fills; 29:30 Swing, mixed time	31:45 Free time; 29:35-32:05-33:35 Solo; 33:35-34:00 *al fine* Free, with fills

Chart 2.   ASCENSION Edition II. Recorded June 28, 1965, NJ. *The Major Works of John Coltrane*, Impulse GRD-2-113

TIMELINE OF EVENTS

Minutes (+/- 3") INSTRUMENTS/SOLOS	5	10	15	20	25	30	35
Theme 0:01-1:30 1:30-3:15							**Theme recap** 35:55 38:00 **40:30 End**
Full Ensemble Improv	Group Improv 3:15-5:50 5:50-7:50	Group Improv 9:35-11:55 11:55-14:25	Group Improv 14:25-15:40	Group Improv 17:40-18:55 20:00-21:15 21:15-24:15	Group Improv 24:15-25:15 25:15	Group Improv 27:20-30:00	Group Improv 35:55
TENOR SAX	Coltrane	Sanders 7:50-9:35		Shepp 21:15-24:15			
TRUMPET		Johnson	Hubbard 15:40-17:40				
ALTO SAX				Brown 18:55-20:00	Tchicai 25:15-27:20		
PIANO						Tyner 30:00-33:30	
BASSES (pizz.)		arco/pizz. 9:00				33:30-35:55 Garrison, Davis arco/pizz.	
DRUMS 0:01	Free medium swing, mixed time 2:55 Free Cues time 3:10	Free swing with mixed fills time 6:20 7:50 Free, Swing, mixed time with fills 9:25 11:25	Free 3/4, swing, mixed time 14:30 15:40 Free Swing, mixed time with fills 17:35	18:55 Free, Swing, Free mixed with fills time 20:05 21:15 24:15	Swing, mixed time 25:15 Free, with fills 27:15	Swing, mixed time 30:00 Tacit 33:30	Free, with Cues fills group entrance 35:40 35:55 36:30 36:50 Swing Free

Coltrane's music in such a brief but highly transformative period. This version has five movements as does the subsequent sextet recording, but they are not all the same, and they are sequenced differently: "Love," "Compassion," "Joy," "Consequences," and "Serenity" constitute the original version, and "The Father and the Son and the Holy Ghost," "Compassion," "Love," "Consequences," and "Serenity" are on the later version.

The original suite begins with "Love," a simple meditative recitation of a singsong rhythmic theme that builds in intensity. Coltrane's increasingly varied and energized repetitions of the motific phrases ascend with the support of the rhythm section until settling back into a meditative space, ending his solo with an echoed motif reminiscent of his opening theme from *Ascension*. At three minutes into the work, Tyner spins a swirling solo of sublimely balanced delicate force. Coltrane begins a coda at 4:42 that becomes expressively energized before closing with a sense of repose. The rhythm section is completely supportive of the soloists; their accompaniment with Coltrane shadows, punctuates, and buoys his streams of sound. The rhythm section trio is completely in synch as an organic entity, with Tyner soloing in simpatico unison with the bass and drums until the section ends with a decrescendo drum roll at eight minutes.

Jones begins "First Meditations" using timpani mallets, playing punctuated rolls with cymbal crashes around the tom-toms and snare drum with snares off. The rhythmic flow complements and contrasts with the phrasing of the "Love" melody played by Coltrane on tenor saxophone, often synching up with Tyner's piano accompaniment. Jones provides energetic support for Coltrane's impassioned passages with cymbal washes and crashes, dramatic drum rolls and figures, continuing as a sensitive accompaniment for Tyner's open-hearted piano solo. Coltrane reenters at 4:39, reprising the opening melodic ideas and overall contours of the opening's dynamic and textural profile, until coming to a peaceful close.

Coltrane begins the second movement, "Compassion," by intoning the four-measure repetitive triplet figure of the piano accompaniment before being joined by the rhythm section swinging at a medium tempo to support Coltrane's spiritual-like theme. Coltrane's tenor saxophone solo begins with improvisation that becomes more abstract through diminution and rhythmic elasticity in his phrasing of motific cells. The rhythm section is swinging hard with Jones playing his trademark 12/8 swing very forcefully, using what sounds like the stick end of the mallets to propel Coltrane's searing *fortspinnung* of wails and exhortations at 2:00–3:57, and again during his second solo before the recapitulation at 6:30–8:35. Tyner begins his improvised piano solo as Jones switches back to mallets to accompany him. He soon switches one mallet to play a ride pattern on the cymbal but maintains a mallet head on the drums (with snares off since the beginning of the piece), alternating between mixes of mallet heads and wooden ends to build the intensity of Coltrane's solos.

A drum roll again serves as an elision between the movements, the crescendo of Jones's malleted floor tom roll launches Coltrane to begin the uplifting theme of "Joy." The two are joined by Tyner's bright and sparse comping and Garrison's sweeping lines and occasional pedal tones. Jones soon switches to sticks and is driving Coltrane's three-note cell permutations with the rhythm section maintaining a bounce and freshness to sustain the momentum through Tyner's piano solo and usher in Coltrane's plaintive wail at 4:32. Jones foregrounds shifting 3/4 patterns, increasing the dynamism and density to stoke Coltrane's closing solo. A gradual *smorzando* is followed by Jones's eliding tom roll. Coltrane introduces "Consequences," a theme comprising brief bursts of two or three notes, sometimes alternating registers before becoming longer phrases of increasing intensity and complexity. The group is blazing right along with him, Tyner's piano comping is playing out contrasting dramas, while Garrison adds interjected commentary and suggestions. Jones, like a runaway locomotive, is racing at a fast clip, a veritable steamrolling percussive juggernaut. Coltrane bows out at 2:36, and Tyner takes over with fast runs and repeated riffs over a thunderous left hand banging out chords. Coltrane reenters at 5 minutes and resumes the note bursts 20 seconds later, finding the extended ranges on the saxophone before returning to the bursts to end *Consequences*.

Coltrane introduces the repeated three-note motif to "Serenity," with Garrison playing arco phrases, Tyner sustaining shimmering arpeggios, and Jones playing cymbal washes and drum rolls with mallets before all members begin to search along more abstracting and intensifying musical paths. Coltrane ends his solo after two minutes, Tyner continues his contrasting textures of shimmering right hand runs against heavy, often rhythmic chording in the left hand to begin his solo. Coltrane makes a strong reentrance at 3:40 with a tone raspy and urgent. Jones plays a mix of punctuations and an episode of metered accompaniment (4:10–4:40) before they both settle in to a calm finish, capped with a drum roll flourish.

The November 23, 1965, recording of *Meditations* is a closer realization of Coltrane's vision of combining his music's current direction, represented by Sanders and Ali, within his original quartet configuration. This recording is the only extant studio documentation pairing Elvin Jones with his successor, Rashied Ali. The session also features Pharoah Sanders on tenor saxophone and percussion along with the other members of the quartet. It begins with the full ensemble freely improvising in an unmetered structure, the two saxophones maintaining a shimmering texture before Coltrane introduces the sequenced notes that constitute the motific basis for the following improvised explorations of the tenor saxophone's potential. The two drummers are situated in the stereo recording with Ali in the left channel and Jones in the right. Jones begins with mallets in a free-time accompaniment, switching to sticks after three minutes to build intensity. Ali uses sticks on the ride cymbal to maintain rapid, accentuated pulsations, and the rest of the kit to create a continuous unmetered punctuated pointillistic textural wash that builds and ebbs in velocity, intensity and density. Sanders joins in *ad libitum* with tambourine and sleigh bell punctuations behind Coltrane's solo before rejoining on tenor for his solo. At 12:30 minutes into the piece, Jones introduces a medium tempo triplet beat. Ali joins him on drums and percussion, while the rest of the collaborators continue to improvise in their own time zones. By 13:45, the horns and Ali have faded out, and McCoy Tyner takes a swinging piano solo with all players in sync with the drums. Coltrane reenters at 17:20, and the first section, "The Father Son and the Holy Ghost/ Compassion," ends at 19:40 minutes.

The third section, "Love," begins as a bass solo improvisation performed by Jimmy Garrison, an increasingly organic component of the later extended works. Coltrane enters after a bass cadential figure at 2:20, and they continue to explore his new motifs, the drummers joining in shortly with free-time accompaniment. The piano joins in the free play, creating a relaxed, relatively spacious and light texture for Coltrane to spin and weave variations of his motific phrases, edging the intensity with successive iterations and then easing the tension. After eight minutes, "Consequences" begins when Sanders enters, and the rhythm section's accompaniment intensifies in tempo and textural density; even Coltrane is jangling bells and then a tambourine during Pharoah's solo excoriations. Coltrane reenters the fray at 11:40, his horn searing the upper and outer registers in antiphonal dialogue with Sanders before fading out. The accompaniment begins to dissolve in density and momentum at 13:55, with Tyner's piano feature segueing into the final section, "Serenity." The band reenters at 17:25, with Coltrane playing a plaintive theme over an unmetered yet flowing accompaniment provided by the expanded rhythm section, surging and ebbing with Coltrane's phrasing for the closing minutes of the work.

III. A Different Drummer

Elvin was ready, from the first time I heard him, I could hear the genius there—but he had to really play, he had to start playing steadily, steadily every night.... With Miles (Davis) it took me around two and a half years, I think, before it started developing, taking the shape that it was going to take.

—John Coltrane (Kofsky 1970: 233)

The recorded history of jazz drumming documents how the different components of the drum set have shifted in their traditional roles in creating percussive accompaniment (Brown 1997: 102–118). In his work with Ghanaian percussion ensembles, Olly Wilson identified the role of each instrument, whether it played a fixed or a variable rhythm within the composite rhythmic matrix of the whole group (Wilson 1974: 9). Rooted in the march traditions before the turn of the twentieth century that gave birth to ragtime and ultimately jazz, drummers mainly played the snare and bass drums to keep the beat. The pointillistic approaches of modern jazz drummers Kenny Clarke, Max Roach, and others in the 1940s shifted the timekeeping role from the drums to the cymbals, further abstracting their new music now primarily performed for listeners, not dancers.

While with Coltrane, Elvin Jones consummated a stylistic approach to jazz drumming accompaniment that maintained no fixed rhythms on any drum set component; he generated a kaleidoscope of ever-shifting cross-rhythms over at least one underlying pulse, with two or four measures rarely played the same. His accompaniment to "Acknowledgment" from A Love Supreme is exemplary of the full realization of his cross-rhythmic approaches. By 1965, Jones began to incorporate unmetered drumming styles to accompany Coltrane's and later Pharoah Sanders's increasingly intense saxophone improvisations. The symbiotic relationship of Coltrane and Jones is well documented, particularly in their duet recordings, the 1961 live classic, "Chasin' the Trane," and the final one, "Vigil."[5] These improvisational pairings are metered, with rhythmic accompaniment provided by Jones on drums and Coltrane's rhythmic repetitions and phrasings on tenor saxophone. The two did not document any explorations into unmetered dialogue. This concept was to be realized with Rashied Ali in the sui generis recording Interstellar Space, recorded in April 1967, three months before Coltrane's death.

The path of further abstraction would lead drummers to free up the fixed roles of all the drum set's components—cymbals for timekeeping, drums for accents and accompaniment figures—as well as the drummer's role of "playing time," providing a steady beat. Sunny Murray, Andrew Cyrille, Milford Graves, Beaver Harris, Rashied Ali, and others freed cymbals and drums from their traditional timekeeping roles, and transformed the drummer into an orchestrator of musical textures, timbres, and dynamics.

---

[5]"Chasin' the Trane" is actually a trio, since Jimmy Garrison played bass throughout the piece. The driving intensity and near-telepathic simpatico between Coltrane and Jones inspired the misperception of this as a duo performance.

On June 10–11, 2003, I conducted a seven-hour interview with Elvin Jones for the Smithsonian Oral History Program. The prevailing story about Elvin Jones in jazz lore is that he was a self-taught drummer who grew up playing music with his brothers Thad and Hank, that while in the Army he played drums in the band, and that he always wanted to be a jazz drummer. According to his interview, he did not play with his brothers growing up because they were much older than he was and out of the house before Elvin began to play music. In fact, he wanted to be an orchestral drummer, a timpanist, and even studied to become one. He never played in the Army marching band and only performed as a substitute drummer for a variety show program. It became quite clear to me that Elvin Jones had a very different background from what was commonly believed, and a personal quest for what he wanted for his life in music.

In 1960, Dizzy Gillespie offered Elvin Jones the drummer's chair in his new group the night before Coltrane asked Jones to join his group. When I asked Jones why he chose to go with Coltrane instead of Dizzy, he said, "I wanted so desperately to play with him, because he was playing what I thought was a perfect balance for the way that I played at that time. I could always hear myself improving, doing things. I could take chances with Coltrane, and it wouldn't even be noticed. That's one reason (laughs). He was just a nice guy, I didn't know anybody nicer than him."

I also asked when he recognized that the music of the John Coltrane Quartet was something special, and he replied, "I always thought that about the music. I thought that about his music when he was playing with Thelonious Monk, I didn't think anybody could duplicate that. And he just kept getting better. It just expanded from that, a continuation of that development."

When I queried Jones about what types of music he listened to, he mentioned the African Pygmies, Igor Stravinsky, and the London Philharmonic. "It's essential to know a little bit about most of the things that are available in the world, otherwise your education is incomplete. It's helpful to learn as much as one can; just by listening, you learn a lot." I asked Jones to share his views of his relationship with Coltrane in late 1965:

John was studying a lot of the religious philosophies of different parts of the world. He was also interested in Japanese folk songs. He had a shakuhachi (end-blown bamboo flute), and he used to drive on these trips and he'd have it in his mouth, he had one hand on the wheel and one on the shakuhachi. It kept me awake (laughs)! He did not rush into things, he was enthusiastic but not hasty. He wanted to see his ideas become realities in their own way.

By October 1965, Coltrane's continuing explorations with the temporal abstraction of his music extended beyond what Jones was playing by adding another trap set drummer and African percussion to create the denser cross-rhythmic texture he was seeking (*Kulu Se Mama, Selflessness*). Shortly after Coltrane added Rashied Ali as the group's regular second drummer, Jones decided to leave. I asked Jones to talk about the dynamics in Coltrane's group, including his departure while on his last tour with Coltrane in early 1966.

> I did not get along with Rashied that well. I don't know what he was thinking about. We were playing at the Village Gate, and I always went early to get set up. I went out and when I came back when it was almost time to start, he's moved my drums and put his all over. I said, "What you doing here?" We had that going … I said well, if you're going to play, we got to be coordinated when we play together otherwise it sounds like it's just a mess.... At the Jazz Workshop in San Francisco, I went (to John) and said, "I have a headache," so I left, I packed my stuff and I left.... I had told him (earlier) that if I ever feel like I'm not making a contribution to what we're doing, then I am leaving.... I thought it was getting sort of hectic on the stage.... I said, "Well, I'm going, I think they can do that better by themselves." So I just quit. Then I got a phone call from Stevie James, Duke Ellington's nephew. He said, "Duke's looking for you and he wants you to come to Spain—right away!" So, I left there and joined Duke Ellington's band.

The following excerpt from Valerie Wilmer's book, *As Serious as Your Life*, provides a corroborating account of the friction between Ali and Jones. Ali even reveals that he was the main impediment to Coltrane's realizing his goal of combining two complete quintets in one ensemble on the *Ascension* recording date.

> Rashied Ali, later to join the group as its regular drummer, started sitting in with Coltrane at the Half Note in the early 'sixties. His ego was inflated by the realization that whenever he turned up, he was allowed to play. "So, I'm starting to think now, 'Goddamn, I must be a bitch with the drums, because Elvin Jones is the Number One drummer on the scene!' And this is my feeling, my ego shit, and here I am, upsetting this cat every night—in a sense. Actually I wasn't upsetting nobody! It was just gracious of 'Trane to let me play because he heard a different something." One night the saxophonist mentioned to Ali that he was preparing to record and would like him to participate. The drummer agreed, but enquired whether he would be the sole percussionist. "No," was the reply. "Elvin's going to be there. He's in the band, man." Ali: "I said, 'Oh, man, I want to play by *myself*—dig *that*!" (Wilmer 1977: 39)

After Jones's departure from Coltrane's group, Ali became Coltrane's primary percussionist, and Coltrane's improvisational explorations ceased to have a shared metric foundation. Ali's conceptual approach to jazz drumming is identifiably in the style associated with "free jazz" or the "New Thing" developing in the early 1960s. Sunny Murray's sustained free jazz drumming recorded with pianist Cecil Taylor and alto saxophonist Jimmy Lyons at the Club Montmarte in Copenhagen, Denmark, in November 1962 is an early documentation of this innovative approach (*Nefertiti, The Beautiful One Has Come*). In removing the structural barriers of measured time, Coltrane and the members of his last group—Ali, Garrison, Pharoah Sanders, and Coltrane's wife, Alice, on piano—were collectively improvising in a free temporal dimension, exploring music with no one required or expected to provide a steady beat. This concept of nonmetric collective improvisation was wholly unique as practiced by free jazz musicians. It was practiced by Sun Ra's Intergalactic Orchestra, Cecil Taylor's Unit, tenor saxophonist Albert Ayler's groups (with which Rashied Ali played drum set in tandem with Sunny Murray in 1964), and others before Coltrane began to perform regularly in that mode by 1966. Collective free improvisation continues to this day as an international jazz and new music genre.[6]

V. Amen

> *Once you become aware of this force for unity in life, you can never forget it. It becomes a part of everything you do.... My goal in meditating on this through music is ... to uplift people, as much as I can. To inspire them to realize more and more of their capacities for living meaningful lives. Because there certainly is meaning in life.*

> —John Coltrane, liner notes to *Meditations*

During the Civil Rights Movement in the 1960s, John Coltrane's ongoing creation of a music increasingly freed from traditional musical boundaries and conventions was perceived as reflecting this turbulent struggle (Kofsky

---

[6]Other musical cultures have developed varied approaches to measuring musical time. In gagaku, the twelve-hundred-year-old court and religious music of Japan, and shomyo, Buddhist chanting, both make use of a common Japanese principle of elastic or breath rhythm (Malm 1967: 139). Large formal musical structures reflect the basic aesthetic theory of jo-ha-kyu, a tripartite (introduction-exposition-denouement) architecture akin to sonata form, or other traditionally slow-fast-slow temporal templates.

1970: back cover). Seemingly overlooked was that in his last compositions and performances, Coltrane granted each musician an unaccompanied solo feature, thereby expressing an ideal realization of the democratic process in action: artists creatively improvising together and alone to express a spiritual theme. Paradoxically, Coltrane's "free jazz" expressionism—the culmination of his musical evolution to which Elvin Jones contributed—created an antinomy that resulted in Jones and then McCoy Tyner leaving the group. Coltrane's further musical explorations with unmetered collective improvisational modes, inspired by his urgent intellectual, spiritual, and humanistic impulses, exceeded the boundaries of engagement for many of his listeners as well. Nonetheless, Coltrane's quest to express all of the ideas and feelings he had inside produced a music and a sound that continues to captivate new audiences to this day. His musical and cultural influence has been global and intergenerational, and he continues to inspire musicians and nonmusicians alike with a message of unity, dedication and freedom.

Bibliography

Brown, Anthony. 1997. *The Development of Modern Jazz Drumset Performance, 1940–1950*. Ann Arbor, Mich.: UMI.

Hentoff, Nat. 1966. *Meditations* (liner notes). MCA/Impulse, MCAD-39139.

Johnson, James Weldon. 1969 (1925). *American Negro Spirituals*. 2 vols. New York: Da Capo.

Kofsky, Frank. 1970. *Black Nationalism and the Revolution in Music*. New York: Pathfinder Press.

Lewis, George E. 1996. "Improvised Music after 1950: Afrological and Eurological Perspectives." *Black Music Research Journal* 16, 1: 91–122.

Malm, William P. 1967. *Musical Cultures of the Pacific, the Near East, and Asia*. Englewood Cliffs, N.J.: Prentice-Hall.

Wade, Bonnie. 1987 (1979). *Music in India: The Classical Traditions*. Riverdale, Md.: Riverdale Company.

Wilmer, Valerie. 1977. *As Serious as Your Life: The Story of the New Jazz*. London: Quartet Books.

Wilson, Olly. 1974. "The Significance of the Relationship between Afro-American Music and West African Music." *Black Perspective in Music* 2, 1: 3–22.

———. 1983. "Black Music as an Art Form." *Black Music Research Journal* 3, 1: 1–22. New York: Columbia University Press. Reprinted in *The Jazz Cadence of American Culture*, ed. Robert O'Meally (New York: Columbia University Press, 1998).

———. 1992. "The Heterogeneous Sound Ideal in African American Music." In *New Perspectives on Music: Essays in Honor on Eileen Southern*, ed. Josephine Wright and Samuel Floyd. Warren, Mich.: Harmonie Park Press.

Discography (CD, *LP*)

James Brown. *Star Time—The Definitive James Brown Collection* (Polydor 849 108-2).

Ornette Coleman. *Free Jazz A Collective Improvisation by the Ornette Coleman Double Quartet (Atlantic 1364)*.

John Coltrane. *Africa/Brass* (Impulse IMPD-2–168).

———.*Ascension* (Major Works of John Coltrane, Impulse! GRD-2–113).

———.*Brazilia* (Complete Impulse Studio Recordings, Impulse IMPD8–280).

———.*Coltrane: The Classic Quartet—Complete Impulse Studio Recordings* (Impulse IMPD8-280).

———.*The Complete 1961 Village Vanguard Recordings* (Impulse IMPD4-232).

———.*The Complete Africa/Brass Sessions* (Impulse IMPD-2-168)

———.*Major Works of John Coltrane* (Impulse GRD-2-113).

———.*Meditations* (MCA/Impulse, MCAD-39139).

———.*Best of John Coltrane: His Greatest Years, Vol. 2 (Impulse AS-9223-2)*.

———.*Coltrane Plays the Blues (Atlantic 1382)*.

———.*Giant Steps (Atlantic 1311)*.

———.*Interstellar Space (ABC/Impulse ASD 9277)*.

———.*Kulu Se Mama, Selflessness* (Impulse! GRD-2–113).

———.*Live at the Village Vanguard* (Impulse IMPD4–232).

———.*My Favorite Things (Atlantic 1361)*.

———.*Suite (Complete Impulse Studio Recordings*, Impulse! IMPD8–280).

John Coltrane and Don Cherry. *The Avant-Garde* (Atlantic 790041-2)

Cecil Taylor. *Nefertiti, The Beautiful One Has Come (Arista/Freedom AL 1905)*

Freedom Is a Constant Struggle: Alice Coltrane and the Redefining of the Jazz Avant-Garde

TAMMY L. KERNODLE

We were critical of the limits that were being placed on us. And we felt that our musical words could penetrate steel walls, so long as we said them with honesty, and with perseverance and creativity from the deepest of ourselves. So we were political in that way. But things were rather novel, as far as Civil Rights were concerned. There were those who were much more eloquent than we were with words, like the Malcolm Xs and the Martin Luther Kings, the Angela Davises. We let them have that verbally, but we said it in music. And we were able to say it in music. We got across equally as well as they did with what we expressed. So Alice Coltrane, when she arrived, was more subtle in her statements, from a very spiritual point of view. She was very quiet, expressing the various sounds and waves of spirits and essences of the Gods and Earth [pause] where we were trying to come from, with the loudness and bombast of our music. She made these statements in a more delicate, graceful, articulate and uniform way than we did.

—bassist Cecil McBee

Everything I do is an offering to God—that's the truth. The work I am trying to do is a sort of sharing with my sisters and brothers of the world; my all; the results I leave to God. I am really not concerned with results; my only concern is the work—the effort put forth.

—Alice Coltrane

In her lifetime Alice Coltrane bore many names.[1] She was born Alice McLeod, but in 1963 became immortally linked with jazz history when she married John Coltrane. In the years following his death she has recorded

---

[1]I extend a special thanks to Franya Berkman for giving me samples of devotional songs of Alice Coltrane that have not been commercially released. I am also indebted to her for the quotation from Cecil McBee that opens this chapter; it is taken from Berkman's "Divine Songs: The Music of Alice Coltrane," her PhD dissertation, Wesleyan University, 2003, 157. The second quotation is taken from Pauline Rivelli's "Alice Coltrane," in the magazine *Jazz and Pop*.

under her married name, but her pursuit of higher purpose and spiritual guidance garnered her the appellations Swamini Turiyasangitananda and Turiya Aparna. There is distinct and supernatural power in a name, and what we choose to call ourselves and answer to reflects our understanding of who we truly are. In each of these names we discover a musical and spiritual journey that defined or shaped not only a life but a musical genre as well. In the years following the death of John Coltrane the links between jazz and spirituality became so intertwined in the music of Alice Coltrane that it became impossible to separate the two. While the marriage of spirituality and jazz was nothing new in the late 1960s, Alice's musical approaches were unparalleled as she combined the nuanced practices of the traditional Black church with religious and musical traditions of the East. More important she furthered the contextural uses of jazz with the incorporation of her music into the ritual life of the Sai Anantam Ashram, where she served as swami for more than three decades.

Critics, historians, musicians, and jazz enthusiasts debate even today the identity of the heir to the saxophonist's musical throne. Whereas many position Pharoah Sanders, who worked with Coltrane during his last years, as the most obvious choice, others see Ornette Coleman or Albert Ayler as suitable selections. But deeper analysis reveals Alice Coltrane to be not only a musical disciple, but also the one artist who continued in John's experimentations of marrying spirituality and jazz and furthered the exploration of new compositional approaches by introducing African, Indian, and Middle Eastern instruments into the genre. She was the first to develop a jazz harp sound into something more than just a curiosity, and her use of oud, tambouri, and other non-Western instruments predated similar trends in popular music, most notably rock. The albums Alice Coltrane recorded from 1968 until 2005 not only serve as documentation of her development from sideman to innovator, but also offer an alternative reading of the history and evolution of the free jazz or avant-garde movement. The purpose of this discussion is fourfold: it will explore (1) Alice McLeod's early life and musical education as a means of establishing her life and career before her addition to the John Coltrane Quartet in 1966; (2) how cultural revitalization, self-actualization, and spirituality became central themes in Alice Coltrane's music and how these ideals were both extensions of and departures from the spiritual and musical experimentation of John Coltrane's last years; (3) general beliefs regarding free jazz and the avant-garde outside the conventional readings of gender and identity; (4) how the trope of religious conversion or spiritual awakening becomes a theme in the music of various black jazzwomen in the 1960s and '70s; and how subsequent music transitioned jazz into the ritualized religious life of their respective faiths.

Little has been written on Alice Coltrane since John's untimely death in 1967, and over the past forty years she has granted few interviews. Only one large-scale study, a dissertation by Franya Berkman, exists, although Alice is discussed in a number of works on John Coltrane, and numerous reviews of her recordings are available in trade publications such as *DownBeat* and *Billboard*. So it is not surprising at all to hear people at the time of her passing in January 2007 remark, "Alice who?" while others state that they had no knowledge of her death. Even as her name garners curious or blank expressions or is excluded from most major discussions on free jazz, it is one that is perpetually linked with the genre.

Born Alice McLeod on August 27, 1937, the pianist and harpist developed her musical talent within familial circles. Alice had been influenced early by the music making of her mother, which consisted of her playing piano and singing in the church choir. While her half-brother, jazz bassist Ernie Farrow, would prove significant in her transition into the New York jazz scene later, it was this early connection between Alice, her mother, and the church that would have the most direct bearing on her early musical development. Detroit's music scene provided McLeod with a musical training that would extend from the pulpits of local churches to the nightclubs and supper clubs of the city's East Side. It was the extended familial connections of her Detroit neighborhood that helped shaped what would emerge in her early teens as a strong musical identity. At age seven a neighbor began instructing her in piano, harmony, and theory, and by the time she was a teenager she was playing organ for the Mt. Olive Baptist Church her family frequented and accompanying church groups throughout the city. Mt. Olive and the Mac Avenue Church of God in Christ provided Alice with the opportunity not only to navigate the two churches' diverse musical repertoires, but also to gain understanding that the worship of God was not something that had to be dictated by tradition, orthodoxy, or the synthesis of other's ideas. It was in the polarity between Mt. Olive with its hymns, anthems, and spiritual songs and Mac Avenue with its frenetic rhythm and improvised, blues-inflected singing that Alice discovered the freedom to articulate God in her own "language."

> There was another choir that my parents permitted me to be involved in when I was a little older. I must have been around fifteen or sixteen. A chorus called the Lemon Gospel Singers. Now that was the gospel experience, musically, of my life! Because not only were they singing! Some of the time, when we were invited to other churches, I mean, I heard music that was just beyond anything I had heard before. I would hear country gospel. I would hear the down home gospel. I would hear the kind of gospel you almost wouldn't need music with. It was flowing from the heart, from the soul. After a while there was no music. One day we were at this church and I

was with the young people, ages 15 to 19. I happened not to be at the piano at the time because there were two of us, and the other pianist could play anything—she was superb. The choir was singing and there was such a spiritual experience happening in that church. There was such a God feeling. The people in the audience were so overcome with the spirit, they weren't singing anymore; some were just walking around the church. Half of the choir had to be carried out—even young people. The Lord just completely swept through. The pianist started playing at such a rapid pace, and everything just stopped. What could you do? All you could do was go and sit down. There were no closing remarks, there was no more singing, there were nurses attending to those who were highly overcome, and some were carried downstairs and that was it. The service was never dismissed by the minister. Just God. God inspired. An experience filled with the spirit of the Lord.[2]

While her religious beliefs would extend away from the Baptist and sanctified churches later in her life, these early experiences, coupled with the importance of spirituality to the individual being and of diversity in praising God, would permeate her life and music until her death.

The vibrant music scene of Detroit exposed Alice to a steady stream of blues, jazz, and classical music—all of which she consumed voraciously. "I liked all kinds of music—including hymns and anthems, gospel music and music from the sanctified church," she remarked in 1968.[3] In high school she played percussion in the concert band, mastering the timpani, drums, and chimes. But it was bebop, which she heard and mastered during the '50s, that became the basis of her musical style. Through Detroit's jazz scene McLeod also had access to musicians and performance opportunities that other cities and their adjoining jazz circles would have denied her. In addition to nightclubs and bars like the Blue Bird, Klein's or the Crystal, Detroit's scene was also defined by jazz cooperatives that supported young experimental musicians. One was an artist-operated, audience-supported space called the World Stage, which provided musicians with an opportunity to develop their individual musical voices within a space that was totally devoted to the idea of experimentation. The World Stage would birth jazz artists such as Yusef Lateef, Barry Harris, and Kenny Burrell. Another cooperative was the New Music Society, which sponsored jam sessions and concerts throughout the city. This group was the first effort of Detroit jazz musicians to collectively organize and control the conditions of music production aside from their participation in the American Federation of Musicians.[4]

[2]Alice Coltrane, quoted in Berkman, "Divine Songs," 52–53.
[3]Joachim E. Berendt, "Alice Coltrane." *Jazz Forum* (June 1972), 54.
[4]Lars Bjorn and Jim Galbert, *Before Motown: A History of Jazz in Detroit, 1920–60* (Ann Arbor: University of Michigan Press, 2001), 118.

Alice's half-brother would have the most direct bearing on her transition into the Detroit and New York jazz scenes. Although Farrow started with alto sax, he switched to the acoustic bass and earned the distinction of being one of the most influential bassists after World War II. "He was far more advanced than Ron Carter and Paul Chambers because he had a triple finger technique," remarked bassist Cecil McBee years later. "This was rather novel at the time.... He was really a great bass player."[5] Farrow's close relationship with a number of Detroit's jazz musicians turned their home into a musical classroom. Pianists Barry Harris and Terry Pollard as well as Donald Byrd and Paul Chambers were fixtures at the McLeod house. From these encounters Alice learned various techniques and developed into a consummate professional. From 1957 until 1960 she worked with a band called The Premiers that gained a considerable reputation in Detroit. But her musical development was not the only thing that Alice focused on during this period. Alice, who had been described by friends as being so shy that as a teen she had to be coaxed into playing publicly, met and fell in love with singer Kenny "Pancho" Hagood.[6] The two were married, and the union would produce, in 1960, one child—a daughter named Michelle.

Hoping to establish themselves further and find substantial work, the two decided to go to Europe in 1960. They quickly worked their way through the post–World War II Parisian music scene and formed familial bonds with the community of jazz musicians living there, which included Hazel Scott, Kenny Clarke, and Oscar Pettiford. But the one musician who had the most direct influence on Alice was Bud Powell, who became a musical mentor. "I met Bud Powell, his wife Buttercup and son, Johnny in 1960," Alice later recalled. "During the period I learned a great deal from Bud."[7] Although the pianist was not Alice's teacher in a formal sense, he helped her formulate her musical ideas. "He always pointed out something helpful—something you could do right there to bring that out."[8] Europe proved to be just as influential in the pianist's development as it had been to other jazz musicians who had gone there following World War II. But Alice's marriage to Hagood suffered, and in the fall of 1960 they divorced and Alice returned to the United States. She studied classical music for a short time in New York but found it difficult trying to work full time, care for her daughter, and attend school full time. So she returned to Detroit.

She quickly became a fixture on the Detroit jazz scene once again, and subsequent years brought engagements with Johnny Griffin and Kenny

[5]Cecil McBee, quoted in Berkman, "Divine Songs," 68.
[6]Descriptions of Alice Coltrane as a young girl can be found in J. C. Thomas, *Chasin' the Trane: The Music and Mystique of John Coltrane* (New York: Da Capo, 1975), 172.
[7]Berendt, "Alice Coltrane," 54.
[8]Alice quoted in Lewis Porter, *John Coltrane: His Life and Music* (Ann Arbor: University of Michigan Press, 1998), 271.

Burrell. But she mainly played at the Twenty Grand Lounge with a band that included Farrow on bass, Bennie Maupin on reeds, George Bohannon on trombone, and George Goldsmith on drums.[9] At the club she established herself as a leading purveyor of bebop and began playing vibes. McLeod continued to evolve in her musical perspective by listening to the music of other composers and musicians. She was greatly influenced by the modal compositions of John Coltrane and Miles Davis and integrated their ideas into her performances. Even in these early years, her compositions extended beyond the straight-ahead concepts that dominated the Detroit scene. As Bennie Maupin recalls:

> We had these forms that she had created. And so they would be like …
> points of departure, but the improvisation that took place inside them was
> very adventurous. It wasn't like the standard, the AABA kind of tune like
> most bebop forms, or a twelve-bar blues, or something like that. I mean we
> might have some of those too, but some of the forms were sort of extended,
> and the structures, just harmonically, were quite different. So you know,
> there might be things that you couldn't quite put your ear on right away. And
> we were experimenting with the use of … dissonances and … just trying
> different scales and experimenting. And when people hear things that they
> don't, that they aren't familiar with, some people gravitate towards it, some
> people shy away from it because it makes them uncomfortable, you know.…
> Sometimes I would just be standing there on the bandstand listening to how
> she was approaching these pieces.[10]

These early compositions would foreshadow the type of experimentation that McLeod would later incorporate in her work with the John Coltrane Quintet and her subsequent recordings of the late '60s and '70s.

Something about Alice

In 1962, friend and pianist Terry Pollard approached Alice McLeod about taking her place with the Terry Gibbs band. As a vibraphonist Gibbs had established himself as one of the prominent performers of the instrument, and he had worked with Alice's half-brother Ernest and another Detroit bass player named Herman Wright. Although reluctant about leaving Michelle in the care of her elderly parents, Alice consented to an audition and Gibbs offered

[9]Porter, John Coltrane, 271.
[10]Bennie Maupin, quoted in Berkman, "Divine Songs," 75.

her a spot in his band. "Right from the introduction Alice played on the first song," Gibbs remembered, "I knew that she was something else. She sounded just like Bud Powell. She played chorus after chorus and every note was a gem."[11] In 1963 the band was booked opposite John Coltrane's Quartet at Birdland in New York City, which marked the first time that McLeod, who had studied and was inspired by the saxophonist's recordings, would meet John in person. It was Gibbs who introduced Alice to the equally shy John. "I immediately saw a puppy love romance starting," recalled Gibbs in his autobiography. "Alice was very shy and in a way, so was John. You'd never know it from the way John played, because his playing was very extroverted. It seemed like when he played, everything he was hearing in his head came right out of his saxophone."[12] John and Alice were equally infatuated with each other, but both were apprehensive about making the first move. The icebreaker came when John showed up at the club where Gibbs's band was performing. Alice and Gibbs performed a show-stopping routine in which both played vibes, and during intermission John sought out Alice. "I never knew you could play vibes," he remarked. "You never knew a lot of things about me," she replied, which was instantly followed by John's, "Well I'm going to make it my business to find out all I can about you."[13] Later Alice would describe their meeting as being like "two friends that had known each other many, many years, like meeting again."[14] Alice was drawn not only to John the musician, but also to John the introspective man. Nightly she would sit in the back booth at Birdland where the musicians sat when not on stage and stare at John while he played. She was falling in love, and he was too. As Gibbs explained, "You had to know Alice to understand how beautiful she was as a person. John saw that and probably felt her inner beauty, for he fell in love with her too."[15]

In time Alice's playing began to reflect some of the harmonic structures that had recently become a part of the John's music. This influence was first captured on the 1963 recording she made with Gibbs called "Terry Gibbs Plays Jewish Melodies in Jazz Time." The recording focused primarily on Jewish music, and although Gibbs had employed an authentic Jewish band, Alice's solos were the standout performances. Gibbs recounts the recording session as follows:

---

[11]Terry Gibbs and Cary Ginell, *Good Vibes: A Life in Jazz*, (Lanham, Md.: Scarecrow Press, 2003), 228.
[12]Gibbs and Ginell, *Good Vibes*, 228.
[13]Thomas, *Chasin' the Trane*, 173.
[14]Porter, *John Coltrane*, 272.
[15]Gibbs and Ginell, *Good Vibes*, 228.

Alice actually stole that date from me. She started to play runs she got from listening to John and all the musicians flipped out every time she played. She was making those Eastern-style runs on the minor songs and they sounded very authentic. I was the Jew and she was wiping me out.[16]

After several tour dates on the West Coast, the band returned to New York, and John asked Alice to go with him to Sweden. "You are concertizing with this group, but I would like you to get permission from your mother to travel with me wherever I'm going around the world," Alice would recall him as saying. "So I told him that if I got my mother's permission and blessings that I would leave that group and I would travel with him. So I called her and she gave her permission.... I traveled quite a bit with the quartet."[17] Gibbs was initially angry with Alice but realized that there was little he could do. "How do you stop a woman in love from doing anything?" he wrote in his autobiography. So he hired another pianist, and Alice traded in her career for a life of domesticity and security with John.[18] Over the next two years Alice McLeod would transition into a life of relative obscurity.

Although still married to his first wife, Naima, John moved in with Alice, and the two began their family. They would have two sons the first two years of their relationship—John W. Coltrane Jr., born in 1964, and Ravi John Coltrane, born a year later. The life changes that John embarked on with Alice only mildly reflected the musical changes he was experiencing. In 1963, when the two met, John was already integrating new ideas into his compositions. His experimentations drew him closer to the tenets of the free jazz movement, but had not reached their maturity. His solos and compositions were quickly moving away from the hard bop and modal sounds that had endeared his classic quartet to jazz audiences. Now it seemed as if John struggled with the limits of his instrument and its inability to fully articulate all of the musical ideas that were in his mind. His perspectives on spirituality, which had been central in his relationship with his first wife, Naima, and in his ability to overcome his addictions, were slowly emerging as a common theme in his music. The 1964 release of *Crescent* and the very successful, highly influential *A Love Supreme* were emblematic of John Coltrane's marriage of spirituality and jazz. And the next year, his last and most controversial recording with the classic quartet, *Ascension*, would foreshadow the level of experimentation his music was going through. The recording consisted primarily of a forty-minute performance in a free and spontaneous form that featured an enlarged band. To the core group of

[16]Gibbs and Ginell, *Good Vibes*, 229–230.
[17]Porter, *John Coltrane*, 272.
[18]Gibbs and Ginell, *Good Vibes*, 231.

Jimmy Garrison, McCoy Tyner, and Elvin Jones, Coltrane added six horn players and an extra bassist. The album would mark Coltrane's initiation into the New York avant-garde jazz scene and the end of his classic quartet. While the term "the New Thing" was used to describe the music of the avant-garde, the moniker served as the perfect appellation for his life as well. Although he had not lived with her for more than two years, John was still married to Naima. So in 1966 he arranged for a Mexican divorce and married Alice shortly afterward in Juarez. He immediately bought a house in Dix Hills, Huntington, Long Island, and the two settled into their new life—as husband and wife.

A Love Supreme

> We were both traveling in a particular spiritual direction, John and myself.
> So it seemed only natural for us to join forces. It was like God uniting two souls together. I think John could have just as easily married another woman, though. Not myself and not because I was a musician. But any woman who had the particular attributes or qualities to help him fulfill his life mission as God wanted him to.
>
> —Alice Coltrane, quoted in J. C. Thomas, *Chasin' the Trane*

John and Alice's marriage would produce one more child—a son, Oranysan Olabisis Coltrane, in 1967. Alice settled peacefully into her life as mother and wife and did not display any regret about giving up her musical career. Together, she and John explored not only various religious faiths, but also different types of music. In Alice John had seemingly found his soul mate—a loving, spiritual woman who shared his passion for music and had given him the one thing he had wanted most—children. But in the weeks following the recording of *Ascension*, John would need her to move into a role that extended beyond her role as "Mrs. John Coltrane." Coltrane's move closer to the avant-garde, with the addition of drummer Rashied Ali to the quartet and the recording of *Ascension*, would prove to be too experimental for pianist McCoy Tyner and drummer Elvin Jones. At the end of 1965 Tyner left to form his own group, and Jones joined Duke Ellington for a short stint. Undeterred, Coltrane turned to his wife to fill the gap left by Tyner's absence. This decision, along with his addition of Rashied Ali, would for years be the subject of controversy among critics and fans. The criticism leveled against Alice and Rashied varied. Many believed that Ali had been the primary reason for the dissolution of the classic quartet, while others blamed Alice for the changes in John's music. Some even questioned openly Alice's ability to complement Coltrane's robust style. These notions were primarily rooted in the mythology that Coltrane fans and jazz critics had created surrounding the quartet. "I didn't have to inspire John toward the avant-garde," Alice recalled in a 2006 interview with *Essence* magazine. "He led the way on his own. The man was a genius, he didn't need anything from me. That's why it's so interesting that critics decided to dislike me. At some point the members of the quartet felt it was time for a change, and they left on their own. When John said he wanted me to play with him on piano. I told him that there were many others who were qualified. He said, 'I want you there because you can do it.'"[19]

It was thought at the time that Coltrane's musical experiments were just a passing phase, but his new aggregation—Alice on piano, Pharoah Sanders on tenor sax, Jimmy Garrison on bass, and Ali on drums—answered these questions when the band took the stage. American audiences defected in large numbers, but Europeans and Asians, particularly the Japanese, embraced the group's sound.

John seemed undeterred by the criticism his performances and recordings were receiving. He continued with each opportunity to push the boundaries of free expression. For Alice, her role in the quintet led her into stylistic developments that extended past her mastery of bebop. "John showed me how to play fully," she recounted.

> In other words, he'd teach me not to stay in one spot and play in one chord pattern. "Branch out, open up, play your instrument. You have a whole left register—use it. You have an upper register—use it. Play your instrument entirely." These are things he taught. I really think that helped me to understand myself. It was perfect. John not only taught me to explore but to play thoroughly and completely. Not as musicians played years ago. They played on chord changes when they played 32-bar music or 12-bar music: everything was kind of on a limited basis. They couldn't go outside the chord changes and they had to fall in right on the beat, you know. You have got to stress the freedom of music to really branch out and be universal. It was higher than this world's.[20]

The aesthetic approaches described here represented the core ideologies of John Coltrane's music, and in time also those of Alice. These notions are defined in three practices: self-definition, self-assessment, and the

[19]Alice Coltrane, quoted in Susan L. Taylor, "A Love Supreme with Alice Coltrane," *Essence* (September 2006), 200.
[20]Alice Coltrane, quoted in Pauline Rivelli, "Alice Coltrane," *Jazz and Pop*, 29.

act of branching out. Through self-definition, Coltrane advanced notions that music making was defined by the musician and his or her experiences. It was an attempt to reflect the authentic self and have the rest of the world recognize that definition. Self-assessment was based in the praxis that music promoted life, unity, history, and experience through which boundaries and models were dismantled and there was a cessation of the need for approval from the mainstream. This most ardently describes the evolution of Alice Coltrane as a composer and instrumentalist and accounts, in some cases, for the misreading of her musical intentions during the '70s. The final facet of John's musical aesthetic, branching out, reflected his pluralistic spiritual, cultural, and musical beliefs. It was reflected in his interest in the African Diasporic experience and in his adoption of musical practices and instruments from Africa, India, and other Asian cultures. More important, both John's and Alice's use of these cultural identifiers would "free" these cultures to be interpreted beyond the context of colonization and cultural inferiority. Musically, spiritually, and philosophically, both of them made fewer and fewer attempts to identify with the dominant social and cultural paradigm. Their pursuit of what eventually could be defined as a "universal consciousness," was more so an attempt to free oneself from an imposed identity and replace it with more "satisfying, self-realized" identity. John desired to be seen as more than the "sheets of sound"/classic quartet John Coltrane, while Alice fought against being a poor appropriator of his style. But his evolving sense of identity extended beyond the concert stage and recording studio to his life with Alice and their kids.

In a number of ways Coltrane, like Ornette Coleman, as David Ake has pointed out, "remasculated" jazz through his public displays toward Alice.[21] He redefined notions that black male jazz musicians could not have meaningful relationships with black women and that they sought only to display images of hypersexuality, which operated in tandem with their musical genus. "He was an excellent husband, father and obedient son to his mother," remarked Alice in 2006. "We lived on Long Island, New York and he loved to be at home. We always had dinner together and spent a lot of time outdoors taking pictures of our children, watching them play and grow. We were so close; he was so very gentle with us. John never once raised his voice at me or the children. He was at peace with himself and didn't feel he had to use anger to express his feelings. He was fulfilled in his mission in life."[22] When Alice became pianist for his band in 1966, John did not hesitate in extending

---

[21]In the 1998 article "Remasculating Jazz: Ornette Coleman, 'Lonely Woman,' and the New York Jazz Scene of the late 1950s," David Ake explores readings of masculinity and sexuality within the jazz scene of the late 1950s. See the article in *American Music* 16, 1 (Spring 1998): 25–44.

[22]Alice Coltrane, quoted in Taylor, "A Love Supreme," 200.

mutual respect to her. He often escorted Alice to the stage by holding her hand, and he publicly and privately viewed her as his musical and life partner.

John took great care in providing for Alice and his children. By the time of his sudden death in 1967, he had ensured that Alice and the children would be financially secure. She became the sole heir to his estate and gained ownership of Jowcol Music, which also provided the family with a steady income. Even when she decided in the late 1960s to record her own compositions, John's financial planning allowed her to not feel pressured to tour to support the sale of her music. In 1971 she stated:

> I play when I want to ... John worked hard for this. . I am free. John did this.
> I got an offer to go to Japan but I won't go ten thousand miles on someone
> else's terms. I've been taking orders in some form, all my life; being a woman
> I've always been subservient—servant, nurse, cook. The man is number
> one.... My true expression is in my art and my kids."[23]

While Alice's "art" looked, on the surface, to simply be her benefiting from her husband's popularity, in time it would play a significant role in redefining the aesthetic values of the avant-garde movement.

The Female Musician and the Avant-Garde

The emergence of free jazz or the New Thing in the 1960s signaled the further isolation of jazz women from the mainstream jazz scene. As the music moved further and further away from the early traditions of swing and bop, the business of jazz went into decline. Riots at the Newport Jazz Festival in the 1960s had frightened many patrons of the music away, and marketing strategies that had secured the popularity of the genre in the 1950s were, by the mid-1960s, no longer viable. The female jazz musician, much like her male counterpart, searched frantically during the decade to find her own identity within a radically shifting music scene that was being redefined by the British invasion, Motown, and folk and protest music. Increasingly militant attitudes and Black Nationalism loyalties within various musical circles, especially among the jazz avant-garde, further polarized jazz audiences and critics and made it more difficult for jazz-women to secure their place within the paradigm. As Sally Placksin asserts

---

[23]Alice Coltrane, quoted in Angela Dews, "Alice Coltrane," *Essence* (December 1971), 43.

in *American Women in Jazz*, women who had worked diligently throughout the '40s and '50s became "disillusioned enough with the state of the art to quit the business altogether; others were forced to take day jobs and relegate their practicing to evenings and their music jobs to weekend."[24] Vocalist Betty Carter described the time as follows:

> After the Beatles came along the whole business went to pieces. For me, it got scary. On one side there was free jazz, which shook up a lot of black people. Free jazz got a lot of white audiences, but it never played to blacks. On the other side, soul music came in heavy, with free jazz on the white side, and soul on the black side. I was overwhelmed.[25]

The free jazz movement for the most part would subsequently mean the virtual "blackout" of women musicians. As histories of this era continue to be written one finds that historians and scholars have either ignored women musicians altogether or relegated the few active women associated with the avant-garde movement—Abbey Lincoln, Alice Coltrane, Carla Bley—to the role of "minor characters." This practice is emblematic of much of the rhetoric of cultural movements of this period (i.e., the Beat, Black Power, and Black Arts movements) and has shown that the search for creative liberation was centered in the need to liberate oneself and the art from clutches of women—who have been traditionally viewed as the enforcers of the cultural rules of monogamy, the steady job, and the nuclear family.[26] These notions would overtly and covertly shape some of the ideologies of the jazz avant-garde. In other words, the notion of freedom in jazz became an aesthetic value that was defined in a more male-centered construct. Freedom of the black male body, his sexuality and identity from centuries of racial and sexual ideologies, became the standard through which the race would be uplifted.[27] Thus free jazz would serve as the musical embodiment of these notions, and women's musical voices would be collectively folded into this larger racial context. As Scott Saul asserts in *Freedom Is, Freedom Ain't: Jazz and the Making of the Sixties*, "Women within this aesthetic

[24]Sally Placksin, *American Women in Jazz 1900 to the Present: Their Words, Lives, and Music* (New York: Wideview Books, 1982), 250.

[25]John S. Wilson, "Betty Carter Sings Jazz on Broadway," *New York Times*, November 24, 1978. Also quoted in Placksin, *American Women in Music*, 250.

[26]Scott Saul, *Freedom Is, Freedom Ain't: Jazz and the Making of the Sixties* (Cambridge, Mass.: Harvard University Press, 2003), 81.

[27]Such ideals stretch back to the beginning of bebop but are not as visible until the 1960s. Though historians have defined bebop as a concerted effort to reclaim jazz from commercialism and dilution by whites, it was also a reclamation of jazz from female musicians and vocalists, who, like their white counterparts, had found considerable success in the popularity of swing or big band jazz.

[were] given no active vocation, nothing besides their bodies and their affection to offer—in effect no license for heroic improvisation."[28] We can cite, however, two exceptions to these notions: Abbey Lincoln and Alice Coltrane. While the former will not be discussed here, she bears mentioning because of her breakthrough performances and collaborations with Max Roach when they were married. Alice, however, provides us with one of the few perspectives of the female instrumental voice within the 1960s avant-garde. In the 1970s she tangibly found a place in jazz's transition to fusion when she moved beyond the harp and acoustic piano and began playing the Wurlitzer organ and a number of different synthesizers. Yet, these experiments went largely unnoticed as critics and listeners struggled to understand and categorize her music. But at the heart of the exclusion of Alice Coltrane from the literature on free jazz and the avant-garde is that these works are constructed largely in a gendered context that is even reflected in the language used to define the genre and the musicians that represented it. As instruments, the piano and harp have been historically viewed as "feminine" instruments. While the piano has been "masculated" by performers such as Jelly Roll Morton, Duke Ellington, Bud Powell, and Thelonious Monk, it has remained largely the only instrument through which jazzwomen have found an acceptable place as instrumentalist within the jazz aesthetic. But the piano, with the exception of Cecil Taylor, is largely ignored within the free jazz paradigm. The reason for this is threefold: (1) the role of the piano, which has largely been melodically focused or provided harmonic and rhythmic support for other instruments, is greatly diminished in free jazz; (2) few pianists could function outside the structural and harmonic language associated with thirty-two-bar and twelve-bar forms; and (3) the piano is largely dependent upon the Western system of tonality, which free jazz moves away from, and the instrument is not factored in the performative perspective.

The free jazz paradigm is also one that is defined as decidedly masculine, and Alice's role in it moves her from the gendered space of being an appropriator of the music into the realm of composer, something that few female jazz instrumentalists had successfully done. Exceptions to this are Mary Lou Williams, Melba Liston, and Toshiko Aykoshi, but these jazzwomen sought musical expression in other stylistic genres. Alice Coltrane as composer was operating within a masculine-defined context. It was thought that women biologically were deficient in the necessary abilities to master harmony, melody, their emotions, and the complex musical language of free jazz. Alice not only defied these notions, but she, much like Mary Lou Williams in the

---

[28]Saul, *Freedom is, Freedom Ain't*, 81.

1940s with beboppers Thelonious Monk, Bud Powell, and Charlie Parker, served as mentor to a generation of free jazz purveyors. Essentially, free jazz was not just about creating a decidedly "African" art that could not be appropriated by whites, as many musicians, especially those associated with Black Nationalism and the Black Arts Movement, thought. It was about creating a decidedly "African" and "male" art that competing female musicians who had managed to master swing, bebop, cool jazz, and hard bop could not translate or identify with.

But what also shapes Alice's place in jazz history is the common reading of public personality that defines her solely as John Coltrane's widow. Similar to historical readings of other significant widows of the 1960s—Coretta Scott King, Betty Shabazz, and Jacqueline Kennedy—Alice's legacy was defined within the media and the music scene in her role as the widow of a great man who presented significant ideals that ultimately changed the world around him. Within this perspective, what I have deemed the "widow phenomenon," there is no noteworthy public acknowledgment of the woman's contributions to the revolutionary actions that immortalized her husband—so when she attempts to move beyond the image of the mourning widow, her actions are deemed as being inappropriate. But as history has revealed, such labeling is unmerited. Each of the women mentioned here was married to a man who died young and saw her efforts to continue his work met with skepticism. Each labored in subsequent years to secure the legacies of her husband—Kennedy with the invocation of her husband's favorite poem, "Camelot"; King and Shabazz through control over use of Martin's and Malcolm's images, speeches, and writings; and Coltrane through the release of his music and use of his name and image.[29]

Alice's professional aspirations were reshaped by John's death, and in subsequent months she worked to reconcile her music career with motherhood.

---

[29]Coretta Scott King (1927–2006), in the years after Martin's death, worked to preserve his legacy through the King Center of Non-Violence in Atlanta and a successful campaign establishing a national holiday in celebration of his birthday. Coretta and the King family have been highly criticized over the years for declining to allow the image, speeches, and writings of Dr. Martin Luther King Jr. to be public domain. Alice Coltrane (1937–2007) assumed control of Jowcol music, which held rights to his music, in the months following John's death. She became the sole administrator of his image and name, which has resulted in her lawsuit against the Church of John Coltrane in San Francisco in 1981 and the withdrawal of the use of *A Love Supreme* as the title of the Spike Lee movie later called *Mo' Better Blues*. In the years following John F. Kennedy's death, Jacqueline Kennedy (1929–1994) attempted to live a quiet life with her children, but faced widespread public scrutiny when she married Aristole Onassis. Betty Shabazz (1936–1997) also tried to live a quiet life following the assassination of her husband, Malcolm X. After home-schooling her five children, she returned to college and completed a master's and doctoral degrees. In 1992 she served as consultant on Spike Lee's film "Malcolm X," and hired a licensing firm to control the use of her husband's name, speeches, and the symbol X.

Though she did not tour extensively during these initial years, she did record her own original compositions. She had the record studio that John had designed built in the Dix Hills home. It reflected John's attempts to free himself from the restrictions of working in industry-owned studios; he thought that he and Alice could produce the type of music they envisioned, released under their own imprint—the Coltrane label. The Coltrane Recording Corporation had been conceived of through discussions between Alice and John shortly before his death. "He would let me know," she recalled later. "That if there's something you really want done, do it yourself. Not only have a studio, but also make your own recordings. Any of the companies could give you distribution. The whole production would be done by us."[30] Although John was never able to capitalize on the creative freedom he envisioned the studio as offering, it would serve as a musical sanctuary for Alice during the late 1960s and early 1970s.

In addition to recording her own compositions in the home studio, Alice also worked through tapes of unreleased material that John had recorded during the last years of his life. "Cosmic Music," consisting of material recorded in 1966 and two tracks produced by Alice, was the first of many posthumous albums of previously unreleased material. When Impulse executives realized that Alice's Coltrane imprint competed with their releases of new material; they sought a compromise—Impulse would release "Cosmic Music," and Alice would become an Impulse artist. She would, however, continue to have complete control over what material of John's would be released. "I had never really thought much about recording [as a leader] at all," Alice would later assert. "But John would mention it occasionally. And I am sure that he spoke with Bob Thiele, because he said, 'You know, they're very much interested, if you can put out some original music, some new music.' And I said, 'It would be nice to do.'"[31] Alice, who had begun experimenting musically beyond the piano with the harp, set about writing music for her first recordings. Over the next decade, 1968 until 1978, Alice would create, for Impulse Records and Warner Brothers, some of the most highly experimental and spiritual music the labels had ever produced. The aesthetic ideals of freedom in the music and faith, that were associated with the avant-garde, were revealed in the level of experimentation that Alice undertook in her recordings, and her spiritual life and her recordings serve as a record of her self-actualization. The liner notes are a testament of the evolution of her spiritual beliefs and her journey from despair and depression in the

[30]Alice, quoted in Ashley Kahn, *The House That Trane Built: The Story of Impulse Records* (New York: W.W. Norton, 2006), 183.
[31]Alice, quoted in Ashley Kahn, *The House That Trane Built,*185.

years following John's death to the reclamation of her peace and a higher consciousness of God.

A spirit of musical cooperation defined the manner in which Alice approached her music and recording sessions. "She would usually just play something. At that period, especially among the New York players, they thought of themselves as the free guys," remembers producer Ed Michel. "That was where it was headed. You would suggest a harmonic environment, with a bass figure, and open it up from there.... Especially in the beginning she would do that. She shared that desire to take whatever form existed and find a place where it would naturally, organically open up into what was a tremendously empowering space for musicians who had the capacity to deal with it. It was an astonishing experience. A lot of the L.A. studio string players, who were symphony guys, when they first encountered it, thought, 'wow, what's going on here?' and then ate it up. They loved it."[32] Bassist Cecil McBee described the experience as follows:

> She didn't say, "We're going to play spiritual, this is going to be something that is meaningful." No, it was like, "This is the way it feels. This is the way the bass line feels, and I'm going to play this." ... The lights were low and she had incense and there was not much conversation, dictation or verbalization about what was to be. Her desire of your essence was all very, very tangible. The spiritual, emotional, physical statement of the environment, it was just there. You felt it and you just played it. It was very subtle but powerful.[33]

This approach to recording and performing reveals a larger cultural link between the cultural practices of West Africa, jazz, and the African American experience. First is the collective approach to music making, which reflects West African notions that emphasized communal participation. In West African music both musician and audience participate in making music. The audience becomes an extension of the performing, thus forming something that is reflective of both social and communal values. So as Christopher Smalls asserts in *Music of the Common Tongue: Survival and Celebration in African American Music,* value is put not only on technical virtuosity but on "what the performer does with what he or she has."[34] Both Western African music and free jazz encouraged individual expression, but participants knew that they had to submit themselves to the collective to ensure the music-making process was successful.

[32]Ed Michel, quoted in Breckman, "Divine Songs," 151.
[33]Cecil McBee, quoted in Breckman, "Divine Songs," 152.
[34]Christopher Smalls, *Music of the Common Tongue: Survival and Celebration in African American Music* (Hanover, Conn.: Wesleyan University Press, 1987), 464.

Second is the creation of a literal and ephemeral sacred space on the stage, in the studio, and in the music. It is through these spaces that Alice invoked the free and transformative aspects of her experiences in the Holiness churches of her youth which stretched back to the brush harbors and ring shouts of slavery. In Alice's music, like John's, one makes these connections in the collective improvisation of free jazz, and the building rhythmic, melodic tension that begins with a simple motive, these reflecting an ostinato or riff. Both culturally and musically, these approaches illustrate the collective nature of the church moan, the polyrhythmic pulse of stomping feet and clapping hands, the vamp through which embellished texts and melodies intertwine, and the frenetic energy of the dance when the spirit falls. In addition each recorded work reflected musically her articulation of a universal consciousness that drew from African and Indian music, Stravinsky, bebop, the blues, and gospel music. Spiritually, this consciousness (like John's) draws from Hinduism, Islam, Judeo-Christianity, Buddhism, and Egyptology. More important, Alice exercised complete control over the production of her music, with the exception of her first album, "A Monastic Trio," which featured the production work of Bob Thiele. This meant that she controlled every facet of her recordings, thus exercising the type of freedom espoused by her husband and Black Nationalists, over her musical voice. So from the beginning of her recording contract with Impulse, Alice operated in complete autonomy from industry trends that put commodity above art. Few black jazz artists, women or men, could claim the same. As Archie Shepp wrote in a letter to *DownBeat* in 1965:

> Give me leave to state this unequivocal fact: jazz is the product of whites— the ofays—too often my enemy. It is the progeny of the blacks—my kinsmen. By this I mean: you own the music, and we make it. By definition, you own the people who make the music. You own us in whole chunks of flesh. When you dig deep inside our already disemboweled corpses and come up with a solitary diamond—because you don't want to flood the market—how different are you from DeBeers of South Africa or the profligates who fleeced the Gold Coast? All right, there are niggers with a million dollars but ain't no nigger got a *billion* dollars.[35]

While Shepp and many other black jazz musicians focused the struggle of the black artist in the acquisition of artistic freedom, for Alice Coltrane the struggle was rooted in her articulation of her spiritual growth through the one medium in which she could reach others—her music.

[35]Archie Shepp, "An Artist Speaks Bluntly," *DownBeat* (December 16, 1965), 11.

The discography of Alice Coltrane can be divided into four distinct periods that reflect the overall spiritual journey outlined in John's *A Love Supreme*. The first phase reflects the period of acknowledgment in Alice Coltrane. It was during these years that she experienced what she calls a "spiritual awakening," which inspired her to pursue a deeper understanding of the role of God in her life. Listeners were able, through liner notes and exaltations, to chronicle the personal struggles that Alice experienced during the years immediately following John's death through her first three albums, *A Monastic Trio*, *Huntington Ashram Monastery*, and *Ptah the El Daoud*. It is in these recordings as well as subsequent ones that Alice reached back to the roots of her spirituality, back to her early years in the Holiness church, as Franya Berkman asserts, to "testify" about her experiences. For example, the liner notes to *A Monastic Trio* explore her role in furthering the musical and spiritual legacy of John Coltrane and her mind-set during the recording of the music. Written by playwright and activist Amiri Baraka (Leroi Jones), the notes read as follows:

> Alice is one earth bound projection of John's spirit. Spirit of Ohnedaruth. This music is dedicated to the mystic, Ohnedaruth, known as John Coltrane.... I hope to be able to do some of the work thought of by John, with recordings, concerts, and whatever community work, but there is a higher and culminating idea in the mind of John which I hope will become a reality during my lifetime. It is called a monastic trio because John's body has left here. And all the music she has made "more separated" from John than the initial "Ohnedaruth' is monastic (where she has lived, separated from public drain). Monastic and spun solitarily in a string cosmos/universe inhabited by memory, of event and emotional circumstance. But they are all loneliness mentioned, sung about.[36]

Musical representations of Alice's early years in the Holiness and Baptist churches are found in works like "Gospel Trane," and "Lord Help Me to Be" as each invoke a swinging gospel sensibility within a largely free jazz context. One only needs to listen to "Lord Help Me to Be" with the wail of Sanders' horn and the pulsating chords played by Alice under a swinging bass line to understand her musical manifestation of the tormented soul crying out to God from within the chaos of the world and to grasp the emotional, spiritual, and musical connections between her music and that of the Black religious experience.

In the notes to *Ptah the El Daoud*, Alice wrote that her focus was "to express and bring out the feeling of purification." She continued, "Sometimes

---

[36]Alice Coltrane, quoted in the liner notes to *A Monastic Trio*, Impulse IMPD-267.

on earth, we don't have to wait for death to go through a sort of purging, a purification. That march you hear is the march on to purgatory, rather than a series of changes a person might go through."[37] Though these albums sought to establish Alice Coltrane as an individual musical entity independent of her husband, critics and audiences did not readily receive them. The first album, *A Monastic Trio*, received a lukewarm response from critics— who dismissed her abilities and viewed her style as a pale imitation of her husband's. "*A Monastic Trio* showed that as a solo pianist [Alice] relied too much on rococo embellishment and allowed her strong choral patterns to be attenuated by quite trivial decoration," Barry McRae wrote in *Jazz Journal*.[38] *DownBeat* gave the album one and a half stars, declaring that the "piano and harp are unsuitable instruments for transmitting [John's] passionate utterance" and that "Alice [is] an artist in the process of becoming."[39]

But Alice was unyielding in her experimentation and infusion of spiritual ideals. By the next phase of her recorded material, 1970–1972, it was obvious to the listener that Alice had allowed the purging process to proceed and was in pursuit of deeper knowledge of God. Albums such as *Journey in Satchidananda*, *Universal Consciousness*, *World Galaxy*, and *Lord of Lords* mirrored her numerous pilgrimages to the East and her full immersion into Hinduism. *Journey in Satchidananda* was a direct pronunciation of this spiritual journey. The title track, which featured Alice on harp, Pharoah Sanders on soprano sax, Cecil McBee on bass, Tulsi on tamboura, Rashied Ali on drums, and Majid Shabazz on bells and tambourine, was a musical tribute to the Swami Satchidananda, Alice's spiritual advisor. The track "Shiva-Loka," which means God in His myriad forms as the third person in the Hindu Trinity, was, according to her, an attempt to "stretch [her] thoughts over to Shiva-Loka, one of the highest points of the universe."[40] The album *Universal Consciousness* reflected the varied nature of Alice's musical experimentations and her understanding of God. Not only did the recording employ strings, arranged by Ornette Coleman, but mantras such as "Hare Krishna" and "Sita Ram," two traditional Indian hymns she arranged. The liner notes even featured a picture of a meditative Alice with her guru, Satchidananda, beside the Ganges River in the Himalayan Mountains.

Both "Journey in Satchidananda" and "Universal Consciousness" were highly acclaimed by critics, who viewed Alice, by the time of their release, as being "a paragon of the new music."[41] The critic for *Coda* declared that

---

[37]Alice Coltrane, quoted in the liner notes to *Ptah the El Daoud*, Impulse.
[38]Barry McRae, "John Coltrane—The Impulse Years," *Jazz Journal* (July 1971): 5.
[39]"Record Reviews: Alice Coltrane, 'A Monastic Trio,'" *DownBeat* (February 6, 1969), 22.
[40]Alice, quoted in the liner notes to "Journey in Satchidananda," Impulse IMPD-228.
[41]"Record Reviews, 'Universal Consciousness,'" *DownBeat* (February 3, 1972), 18.

Universal Consciousness was "musics of praise ... [that] certainly should be far above pedestrian critical considerations. Regardless of one's own musical standpoints or of the particular cosmology of one's beliefs, this is Devotional music of the highest level, as it must be—majestic, serene, sublime, a richly woven tapestry in sound; music of unsurpassable breadth and beauty to be heard as long as men with souls live."[42] While another critic noted the following in his 1971 review of the album:

> For those within a society whose emotional constitution is considerably developed, we reserve a special place. We look to our artists, our poets, and our musicians for the signs of their feelings and struggles so that we may be able to contrast them with our own. Such an evaluation will, of necessity, be subjective, yet hopefully it will alert us to the unnamed, silent yet persuasive feelings and thought within us, and hence render our view of our lives more accurate and meaningful. Alice Coltrane is such an artist. Her strength supports her ability to face the input from his senses. Her emotional intelligence refines that input and has done so for many years now, thus making her a powerful, yet gentle force in the jazz world. If we recall a few of Alice's previous albums ... we begin to see her unique path toward an understanding of what life and this universe are all about. If we listen to her instrumentation—the harp, the oud, alto flutes, and tamboura—we see that universal orientation expressed through what might be called a Near Eastern or Indian perspective.... With "Universal Consciousness," however, Alice has turned a corner and has discarded entirely, or almost so, any connection with Western music. "Consciousness" is dominated not only by the string and woodwind instrumentation of the East, but it is written in patterns of "chords" and "melodies" which are essentially foreign to the Western ear ... This religious album ... has, then, not the Christian motivation with which we are likely to be familiar, but predominantly Buddhist characteristics.... It is for that reason that this album is unlikely to be easily understood by even the most devoted jazz listener, let alone the occasional listener. This album reflects the highly intricate, highly abstract vision of a highly sensitive and remarkable woman who strives always to understand not only the seen, but the unseen.[43]

World Galaxy was received lukewarmly with its musical spirit thought to have been betrayed by Impulse's insistence to "tone down the weirdness and to give them something that would sell big."[44]

---

[42]"Record Reviews: Alice Coltrane; 'Universal Consciousness,'" *Coda* 8, 10 (1972), 22.

[43]A. D. Saunders, "Alice Coltrane: Universal Consciousness," *Bay State Banner* (October 21, 1971), 11.

[44]"Record Reviews: Alice Coltrane, 'World Galaxy,'" *DownBeat* (May 25, 1972), 21.

The third phase, *Discovery of the Holy Spirit*, is transitional between the end of Alice's commercial recording career and her move to a completely religious life. In 1973 and 1974 she collaborated with Joe Henderson and Carlos Santana on the albums *The Elements* and *Illuminations*, respectively. And in 1976 and 1977 she produced *Radha Krsna Nama Sankirtana* and *Transcendence*, which featured the chanting of members of the Vedantic Center that Alice founded in 1972. Transfiguration, recorded in 1980 for the Warner Brothers label, marked the end of Alice's commercial recording career. For the next twenty years she would focus on noncommercial recordings of her interpretations of *bhajans*, or Indian devotional songs. These songs were recorded on Avatar, an independent label affiliated with the Vedantic Center, and included the following recordings: *Turiya Sings* (1982), *Divine Songs* (1987), *Infinite Chants* (1990), and *Glorious Chants* (1995). These albums mark the fourth and final phase of Alice Coltrane's spiritual journey, which I have deemed "Psalm"—song of praise. These recordings reflect the transition of Alice's music from being driven by commercial appeal to being motivated by its own divinely ordained purpose. More important is the fact that the music from this period moved to a use and purpose that John Coltraine's music, aside from *A Love Supreme*, had yet to achieve.

Alice Coltrane as Spiritual Avatar

The transition of jazz from being the "devil's music" to music of spiritual uplift and gratitude is often defined in John Coltrane's *A Love Supreme* and Duke Ellington's *Sacred Concerts*. But there were a number of black jazz-women during this time who also used the genre to manifest their evolving spiritual identities. The 1960s and 1970s marked an important period in the construction of a conversion narrative of black jazzwomen. Three significant women reflect this idea—Mary Lou Williams, Alice Coltrane, and Hazel Scott—and, in the case of Williams and Coltrane, each not only used their music to reflect their spirituality but also created music that became central to the ritualized life of their respective faiths. All three would look to non-Protestant-based religions as the core of their spiritual identities despite having past relationships with the Baptist and Holiness denominations. Of the three, Mary Lou Williams was the first to integrate her faith into her jazz compositions. Following an emotional breakdown and self-imposed hiatus from the jazz scene, she converted to Catholicism in 1957. She devoted herself to a religious life of prayer and service to others, even turning her Hamilton Terrace apartment into a rehab center for addicted musicians. In the early 1960s she was persuaded by a number of priests to compose some spiritually based jazz compositions. One year before *A Love Supreme* was released, Mary Lou Williams debuted her first religious composition, "A Hymn in Honor of St. Martin de Porres," commemorating the canonization of the first black saint by the Catholic Church. Over the next decade Williams would create an oeuvre of religious jazz compositions that included gospel-inspired hymns and three masses—the last of which was commissioned by the Vatican in 1968. In four short years (1963–1967), Williams managed to play an official role in transforming the music and rituals of the post–Vatican II Catholic Church, introduce jazz education to the Catholic school system in Pittsburgh, Pa., and provide a strong representation of black Catholic identity within the church during this period. While many of the hymns and sections of the masses have been performed in concert settings, it is important to note that Williams' intentions were that they would be performed as liturgy, not concert pieces.

Although not expressed directly in her music, Hazel Scott experienced a strong religious conversion during the late 1950s. According to Adam Clayton Powell Jr., who was then her husband, Scott was drinking heavily as a coping mechanism. But while she was living in Paris, she experienced a "spiritual awakening." He described the event as follows:

> She was living on the Left Bank in Paris, with Skipper's [their son's] godmother and our lifelong friend Mabel Howard. They lived just across the Seine from Notre Dame, whose spires they could see shimmering in the dawn. One morning, accompanied by Mabel, Hazel went to Notre Dame, got down on her knees in front of the altar and vowed she would not move until God gave her strength. She stayed there until her knees actually became bloody. When she finally did rise to her feet, she had the power and strength and the faith never again to touch or desire a drop of alcohol. She became an exceptionally religious person. When I say religious, I use the word in the broadest sense. She became not a Christian, but a religious person. She looked for something of value in every religion of the world. She carried a rosary, which she used. Yet she loved the Baptist church, too. She studied very carefully the best elements of Judaism and Christianity and incorporated them into her philosophy of life.[45]

In subsequent years Scott publicly wore two crosses and claimed to be Baha'i. She herself stated in an interview that her basic belief was in

[45]Adam Clayton Powell Jr. *Adam on Adam: The Autobiography of Adam Clayton Powell, Jr.* (New York: Dial Press, 1971), 228.

"progressive revelation." "We [Baha'i] believe that whenever man has been ready to absorb more knowledge, God has revealed it. Beginning with Abraham right up to now."[46] Despite her strong articulation of faith, Scott never incorporated it into her recorded music; however, she remains important to our understanding of the role spirituality played in the lives of black jazzwomen.

Alice Coltrane's road to religious leader and swami bears similarities to both of these conversion stories. Following John's death, Alice entered a dark period during which she injured herself and was subsequently hospitalized. Mediation and prayer became one of the methods she used to purge herself of her demons, and, in 1969, at the invitation of friend and fellow musician Vishnu Woods, Alice began attending the lectures of Swami Satchidananda (1914–2002), who introduced her to the culture of South Asia.[47] Her interest in the spiritual teaching of the guru deepened, and, following several sojourns to India and other parts of southern Asia, she changed her name to Turiya Aparna and integrated traditional chanting and Asian instruments, such as the shruti box, into her music. In the early 1970s she moved her family to Southern California and, in 1975, founded the Vedantic Center. As she grew spiritually, her music evolved in its expression of her faith. Her albums in the mid-1970s featured her on Wurlitzer organ and a harp, and by the end of her contract with Warner Bros. in 1978, they had come to include tracks of the chanting of religious mantras. When she "retired" from public life in the late 1970s, she donned the orange robes of a swami, renounced secular life, and devoted herself to her religious community. In 1983 she founded the Shanti Anantam Ashram in Agoura Hills, California, which in 1994 became the Sai Anantam Ashram. However, she never stopped composing and playing. Rather, she just turned her attention to creating adaptations of *bhajans* that are still used at the ashram today. These devotional songs are a fusion of Alice's gospel and jazz sensibilities and sacred Hindu text, and these adaptations of sacred texts and melodies, much like the religious compositions of Mary Lou Williams, have created a distinct African American tradition within the larger worship life of the religion.[48] For the most part, the worship music of Alice Coltrane has remained largely unknown by those outside of the religious community, whereas the religious compositions of Mary Lou Williams, especially "Mary Lou's Mass," has been reintroduced to new

---

[46]Hazel Scott, quoted in *Notes and Tone: Musician-to-Musician Interviews*, expanded ed., ed. Arthur Taylor (New York: Da Capo, 1993), 258.

[47]Alice writes extensively about her "spiritual awakening" in her memoir, *Monument Eternal* (Los Angeles: The Vedantic Book Press, 1977).

[48]For more in-depth discussion of the structure and use of these devotional songs, see the chapter "Glorious Chants" in Berkman, "Divine Songs."

generations through multiple live performances and reissues in the last decade.[49] Nevertheless, through the conversion stories of Williams, Coltrane, and Scott, along with the music that emerged from their experiences, one can gather a new perspective on the role of spirituality in jazz during the '60s and '70s.

The music of Alice Coltrane that was commercially recorded from 1969 until 1978 and, much later, in 2005 (*Translinear Light*) creates an unusual paradox for scholars of the free jazz movement as they stretch the context of free jazz or the avant-garde beyond the African Diaspora and Islamic or Judeo-Christian contexts that have been central to understanding it and its relationship with Black Nationalism.

Within the notions of Black Nationalism and the Black Arts Movement, free jazz musicians found an aesthetic that guided articulations of their struggles for identity as Africans in the American context, and as men. Although some Black Nationalists and free jazz musicians divorced themselves from Judeo-Christianity and turned to Islam, Alice Coltrane and other black jazzwomen turned to religions not usually associated with blacks, including Hinduism, and incorporated into them religious teachings associated with other religions. Such syntheses were unique for African Americans, but reflected what Christopher Smalls called the adaptability of the African in constructing his or her identity. He asserts that the African often constructed self-definitions from a variety of sources. That way the African profited "from the potential richness of a number of perspectives simultaneously."

> This can be seen in the way in which Africans seem to be able at one and the same time, and without visible strain, to hold, for example, both polytheistic "pagan" beliefs and practices and those of either Christianity or Islam, to be at the same time "traditional" and "Europeanized" in their daily lives, in ways which often puzzle and even infuriate Europeans; the latter can deal with contradiction only by denying or eliminating one side of it—hence the rejection and even persecution of deviants, both sacred and secular ... while African seem to be able to live happily with both sides. One might say that while the Europeans lives in a world of "either/or," the African's is a world of "both/and."[50]

---

[49]"Mary Lou's Mass" has been performed numerous times across the country the last fifteen years, and recently Folkways re-released Williams's religious compositions on two disks—"Mary Lou's Mass," and "Black Christ of the Andes." Alice Coltrane's music, however, is available only through the Ashram, although many of her recordings with Impulse and Warner Brothers have been reissued on compact disc.

[50]Smalls, *Music of the Common Tongue*, 22–23.

This talent for synthesis is readily reflected in Alice's ability to fuse gospel riffs and nuances with Indian ragas and Hindu devotional texts. The universal consciousness that John and Alice espoused through interviews, liner notes, and their music makes this amalgamation of religious practices plausible. But if one is trying to analyze her music through the lens of Black Nationalism, the going is problematic at best: consider her adaptation of Christianity via harmonies, nuances, and song titles; Hinduism through instruments largely associated with that culture (i.e., oud, harp, alto flute, and tamboura); and chanting and Egyptology through invocation of deities. The cultural revitalization of the free jazz movement was rooted in the creation of a decidedly Black Art movement for many of its practitioners. At the heart of this was also an effort to escape the specter of "white Jesus" and the impenetrable cultural and spiritual oppression that black theology and its cultural practices had constructed. So activists, scholars, and artists turned away from the Baptist, Holiness, and Methodist churches of their youth and found a suitable substitute in the Nation of Islam and orthodox Islam. Nevertheless, Alice Coltrane's fusion of religious practices still speaks to the type of cultural revitalization that Black Nationalists advocated insofar as it allows the realization of new spiritual identities within the black community.

When Bar Walkers Preach: John Coltrane and the Crisis of the Black Intellectual

TOMMY L. LOTT

Many years ago at a convention in Chicago, while in the midst of a conversation with Ghanaian philosopher, Kwasi Wiredu, I noticed that he was swaying to the live music playing in the background. After pointing out that the song we were hearing ("St. Thomas") has a rhythm that is quite popular in West Africa, he added that he had once heard Sonny Rollins play it live. Then, with a frown, he looked at me and said, "How could the intelligence of black people be doubted when you hear music like that?" At that moment I had not yet realized the importance of Wiredu's insight for my consideration of certain philosophical aspects of John Coltrane's music. Of particular significance is the rhetorical nature of his question, for commentators often suggest that music from Coltrane's later avant-garde period would perhaps have been better received had it been less intellectually demanding of the

*Earlier versions of this essay were presented at the annual meeting of the Society for Phenomenology and Existential Philosophy in Boston, November 8, 2003, at the Symposium on John Coltrane, John Coltrane Memorial Concert, Northeastern University, Boston, MA, September 27, 2006, and as part of the Ronald Suter Distinguished Guest Lecture Series, Department of Philosophy, Michigan State University, Fall 2004.

listener. For my purposes it will be needless to dismiss, or deny as illegiti-mate, aesthetic worries that render a certain plausibility to this line of criti-cism. A better way to meet this objection is to accept it.

I present an account of Coltrane's musical development as a search for truth in the sense Plato used this notion to characterize Socrates in the *Apology*. Much like Socrates, who is represented as motivated by an unwavering dedi-cation to his mission, Coltrane's search for truth was driven by a matchless fanaticism for long hours of practice.[1] Perhaps this relentless attitude stemmed from each understanding his mission to be a divinely inspired duty. Critical inquiry is required, even with a spiritual orientation, to seek answers to ques-tions that guide the search, as well as to address new questions generated by it. Coltrane's intellectual pursuit of new ideas, along with the spiritual features of his musical project, dominated his later period. In keeping with cautionary remarks by Andrew White, I highlight the relation between his earlier and later work to draw in question aesthetic concerns, based on an entertainment model, that aim to diminish the significance of his spiritual orientation.[2]

I propose to understand the conceptual unity of his earlier and later per-formances, especially his shift toward the avant-garde, from a philosophical standpoint, as a mature phase of his search for what W. E. B. Du Bois referred to as a "truer self."[3] For both, this meant a newer self that *merges* with, but does not replace entirely, one's earlier self. Recordings of Coltrane's live perfor-mances document his constant critical revision of earlier attempts to express certain musical ideas, a methodology, as it were, that reflects an intellectual dimension of his project. With a conception of his project as a truth-seeking endeavor, he used performance, rather than written composition, as a method of critical inquiry to engage in a systematic investigation of musical ideas.[4]

---

[1]In the case of Coltrane what the term "practice" refers to has a particular significance for the way I propose to understand his methodology as a thinker. Many of his musical ideas were developed from what he practiced. When asked by Frank Kofsky how many hours a day he practiced, he replied, "I find that it's only when something is trying to come through that I really practice. And then I don't even know how many hours—it's all day, on and off. But at this time there's nothing coming out now . . . I need to practice. It's just that I want something to practice, and I'm trying to find out what it is that I want, an area that I want to get into" (1970: 461). As I will indicate in my discussion of Coltrane's avant-garde period, much of the continuity in his different phases is in-debted to his use of Slonimsky's *Thesaurus of Scales and Melodic Patterns*. McCoy Tyner told David Demsey in a 1989 interview, "Coltrane would leave for a road trip with the Quartet carrying nothing but his horn case and the Slonimsky book" (Demsey 1991: 176).

[2]According to Andrew White, Coltrane's music became more abstract in his avant-garde period, starting around 1965, "but the repertoire basically remained the same" (1981: 42).

[3]Du Bois 1903: 11.

[4]The Socratic model of the skeptical, inquiring, and persistent intellectual who subjects every claim to cross-examination applies fully to organic intellectuals operating in an oral tradition. Coltrane once spoke metaphorically of having to keep "cleaning the mirror" to characterize his method of truth-seeking as a progression through different phases, each having a focus on harmony, melody, or rhythm. See *Meditations* CD liner notes, 10.

Triumph of the Oral Tradition: Organic
and Academic Intellectuals

One reason jazz, as an intellectual practice, is less esteemed than classical music is perhaps because of a history of that associates the former with nightclubs and the latter with concert halls.[5] At the turn of the century, when jazz first began, it was against the backdrop of minstrel shows filled with plantation stereotypes. In response, Du Bois and other Harlem Renaissance intellectuals touted the spirituals as authentic black folk music in an effort to ward off the narrow construction of African American music as merely entertainment. They employed an academic account of this folk form to affirm the worth of African American culture and to challenge the proliferation of dehumanizing caricatures in mainstream American culture.[6] As a folk paradigm, the spirituals provided evidence for the idea that, during slavery, various elements of an underlying African heritage influenced the growth and development of African American cultural practices. While certainly not new, this idea was articulated as a full-blown theory by the Oxford-Harvard-trained philosopher Alain Locke. He held that the essence of this distinctively African American folk form would provide a basis for the development of more advanced American music. Although he spoke of the spirituals as a common source for an American national art form, with George Gershwin in mind, he insisted that their *organic* development within a tradition of black music would have a greater potential to yield "a true unison and healthy vigorous fusion of jazz and the classical tradition."[7]

Locke and Zora Neale Hurston were not satisfied with the "sorrow song" conception Du Bois had presented in *Souls of Black Folk*; nonetheless, they were prone to view the spirituals as a primitive folk form that provided

---

[5] I attended every set of Coltrane's engagements at the *It Club* in 1965 and 1966, at which, on any given night, dozens of famous jazz musicians were in the room. (I once sat next to Ray Draper and Gerald Wilson.) During that period, I also worked as an attendant at the Los Angeles County Museum's Monday Night Bing Center Concerts, at which Igor Stravinsky premiered a commissioned work, one of a series of concerts devoted to cutting-edge avant-garde classical music. With regard to posing an intellectual challenge to listeners, I recall Coltrane's tenure at the *It Club* as comparable to many of the Bing Center Concerts. Leonard Brown has addressed this subject of Coltrane's transformation of secular space through his performances in a presentation titled "Sacred Music in Secular Places" Seventh International Conference on Popular Music, University of the Pacific, Stockton, California, July 12, 1993. See Arlen 1966; Kohn, 1965.

[6] Alain Locke's classic essay "The Negro Spirituals" was indebted to writings on the spirituals by W. E. B. Du Bois, as well as to Du Bois's detractor on this subject, Zora Neale Hurston. On Du Bois's view, see Zamir 1994.

[7] Locke 1936: 114.

merely *emotive* evidence of a black soul.[8] While this aspect of the soul grounds an argument for the humanity of black people on their capacity for sentience, it is hardly enough to justify a claim to equality. For Locke, the chief task of the Harlem Renaissance was to create a black tradition in literature and art that would "mine" the raw materials derived from African retentions in black southern folk expression and rediscover a completely lost African tradition of plastic and visual art.[9] He seems to have believed that the development of literature and art, more than advancements in music and dance, would establish that black people have reason and intellect as well as emotions.

While never fully stated in academic studies of the Harlem Renaissance, this suggestion is borne out in their treatment of cases where black music merges with literature, as in the blues poetry of Langston Hughes, the folklore of Zora Neale Hurston, or the modernist storytelling of Jean Toomer. More often than not, these writers are presented as intellectuals influenced by performers such as Bessie Smith, Ma Rainey, and Louis Armstrong (or by the music of composers such as Jelly Roll Morton, Duke Ellington, and Fletcher Henderson), who, in turn, are relegated as entertainers to the social setting.[10] Writers are venerated as the great thinkers, while musicians are viewed as marginal—or are simply excluded from equal consideration. What adjustments to this way of viewing black intellectuals are required when we consider performers such as Coltrane, who, along with being a creative artist, displayed many qualities of a great thinker by transforming an entertainment practice into an intellectual endeavor that conceptually advanced black music?

Cornel West responds to this question in his essay "The Dilemma of the Black Intellectual." He maintains that "black America has yet to produce a great literate intellectual with the exception of Toni Morrison. There indeed have been superb ones—Du Bois, Frazier, Ellison, Baldwin, Hurston—and many good ones. But none can compare to the heights achieved by black preachers and musicians."[11] While West's positioning of musicians and

---

[8]In her anthropological study *The Sanctified Church*, Hurston uses the term "primitive" to refer to the singing of spirituals and to other religious practices in a chapter titled "Characteristics of Negro Expression" (49). In his essay "The Negro Spirituals," Locke proclaims, "They are primitive, but their emotional artistry is perfect" (1925: 201).

[9]Locke 1925: 254.

[10]To cite two examples of this practice: Houston Baker has "Ma" Rainey as cover art for his book *Modernism and the Harlem Renaissance*. And on the cover of her book *Women of the Harlem Renaissance*, Cheryl A. Wall has an Aaron Douglas painting of a black female singer which has a visual insert of the accompanying musical chart. By drawing attention to this issue I do not mean to disparage either of these important books or ignore the abundant research that has been done on music from this period. Rather, my point is that that work has not been marshaled sufficiently to challenge the prevailing notion of the New Negro movement as mainly writers and artists seeking mainstream recognition. Books that treat musicians from that era on an equal footing include Floyd 1990; Stoddard 1982; Vincent 1995; Appel 2002; and Davis 1998.

[11]West 1993: 71.

preachers over writers may be debatable, he rightly grants recognition to black musicians and preachers as organic intellectuals. Unfortunately, he is led by his distinction between intellectuals who are outside academia, or "organic," and those who are academic, or "literate," to conclude that the former's achievement, though inspiring, should not be emulated by the latter. Notice that West is willing to include musicians among the ranks of intellectuals and even to recognize their achievement as greater, yet recommend they *not* be emulated by other intellectuals. The stance West takes here is puzzling because on the one hand he breaks with the practice of excluding musicians, while on the other he reiterates their unequal status as intellectuals.

With regard to Coltrane's intellectual pursuit, I want to consider two issues raised by the position West takes on the question of whether academic intellectuals should emulate organic intellectuals. First, he distinguishes between "literate" and "organic" intellectuals, when he means to distinguish between academic and organic intellectuals. Writers, artists, and musicians may be academics, but when they are not, all may count as *organic* intellectuals. This confusion infects any question regarding the significance of the achievements of various organic intellectuals. It also seems to endorse a positioning of literature over music as intellectual endeavor, for we are left to wonder why the contributions by organic intellectuals who are musicians to a history of ideas are any less significant than those made by writers? As suggested by some of his remarks, West's position may harbor a scholarly worry about a lack of critical scrutiny within black cultural practices.[12] In the case of Coltrane, however, this is a misplaced concern, given his commitment to critical inquiry, as well as his strong resolve to withstand an overwhelmingly negative appraisal of his turn to the avant-garde. Second, West draws a contrast between organic (musicians and preachers) and academic intellectuals (and writers) with respect to the former being less alienated for having found support from strong traditions grounded within black communities. This raises questions regarding criteria used to assess the contribution of organic intellectuals. In the case of music, do we appeal to criteria derived from the Western classical tradition, or criteria derived from African American and other world music traditions? The assessment of Coltrane's contribution as an organic intellectual requires a use of criteria derived from all of these, as well as the *entire* African American corpus—including its sacred music.

[12]West speaks of black preachers and musicians as "historical forerunners" of present-day academic intellectuals. With regard to academic intellectuals, he advocates "the formation of high-quality habits of criticism and international networks of serious intellectual exchange" ("Dilemma," 70 and 84). Scott Saul characterizes Coltrane's *performance* as a critical practice. Emphasizing the collective nature of Coltrane's musical investigations while performing, he states, "They (Coltrane and McCoy Tyner) model an impassioned, self-critical act of discovery, one that allows for digression as much as it welcomes clarity of thought. It is this self-critical aspect of Coltrane that leavens his charismatic power and makes his preacherly saxophone playing seem excruciatingly human" (2003: 239).

Lewis Porter's comparison of Coltrane's musical performance to the delivery of a sermon by a black preacher indicates the literal sense in which Coltrane embodied the overlap of music and religion and the extent to which he combines West's two paradigms of the organic intellectual.[13] Pre-twentieth-century spirituals and contemporary gospel represent a tradition of African American sacred music that is an important part of the oral tradition that has produced black preachers. Although he did not hesitate to declare "I believe in all religions," Coltrane's musical idiom was derived largely from these overlapping traditions. Nevertheless, for several reasons the black preacher construction seems too strong. Coltrane exploited his religious roots with a cosmopolitan outlook that allowed him to incorporate certain ideas pertaining to a religious metaphysics derived from his readings on science, philosophy, and world cultures. He was especially interested in how cultures in Africa and Asia understood the nature of the universe from a spiritual standpoint. Although he studied principles and techniques used in these cultures to present their religious music, in true intellectual fashion, he confessed at one point that his attempt to recover the spiritual nature of African American music only raised more questions—musical and philosophical.[14]

What criteria do we use to assess the achievement of organic intellectuals such as Coltrane and decide the question, posed by West, of whether they should be emulated by other intellectuals? I follow Plato's concept of an intellectual as an inquirer who is systematically engaged in abstract thought with the aim of capturing the essence of the subject being investigated.[15] Coltrane's interrogation of the elements of music accomplished this by employing a method that made possible certain advances in musical performance. His excavation of the system of thought that he inherited from an earlier jazz tradition enabled his further exploration of new ideas that extended that tradition. More important, he began to conceive of music as a sonic language that conveys meanings and allows an exploration of philosophical questions about the nature of reality. What seems to have motivated his refusal to verbalize his philosophical views was his strongly held belief that music can be used to stretch the bounds of language to resist imposition of a conceptual scheme on thought. He tells Kofsky, "You can't ram philosophies down anybody's throat, and the music is enough!"[16] When responding to queries regarding the liner notes for his

---

[13]*Tell Me How Long Trane's Been Gone,* vol. 3; Porter 1998: 245–247.
[14]For Coltrane's remarks regarding his religious beliefs, see Nat Hentoff's liner notes on *Meditations* (1966). With regard to the spiritual nature of his search, he tells Kofsky, "As far as spirituality is concerned—which is very important to me at this time—I've got to grow through certain phases of this to other understanding and more consciousness and awareness of just what it is that I'm supposed to understand about it " (Kofsky 1998: 458).
[15]*Republic* V.
[16]Kofsky 1998: 458.

last studio recording, *Expression*, he told Bob Thiele, "By this point I don't know what else can be said in words about what I'm doing. Let the music speak for itself." Remarks of this sort can also be taken to suggest a reason to resist the positioning of black writers and literature over black musicians and music, along with its underlying implication that a verbal language provides the highest expression of meaning, rationality, and intellect.

Coltrane contributed to a history of ideas in music by employing his craft not only to challenge a fundamental understanding of the basic elements of music as conceived in terms of Western music theories, but also to create new musical ideas, derived from multifarious sources, that he then used to express his thought about metaphysics and the ultimate nature of the universe. Working collectively with a highly select group of musicians in his "classic" quartet, he used live performances as a method of critical inquiry to discover these new ideas, a strategy that enabled the continual change which became a defining characteristic of his music. Moreover, he believed that he would recognize in performance what he had been looking for musically. In this sense he understood music to be a means of expressing the truth he would discover.[17] His transition from a traditional bebop style of playing jazz to a radical avant-garde modernist approach was a necessary step required to accommodate his ongoing reconception of earlier ideas, representing a process of revising his earlier work. The ideas, and saxophone technique, he appropriated from other avant-garde musicians were instrumental in shaping the more abstract direction he began to pursue in 1965. His transition is comparable to transitional periods in the careers of other creative artists and intellectuals who, as they matured, either rejected their earlier views or engaged in a process of critically revising their earlier work to advance new ideas.[18]

---

[17]Several of Coltrane's remarks in different contexts suggest this. Some are geared more toward what happens to the thought process while performing. Eric Dolphy best captured this idea when he responds to a question that Don DeMicheal tells him is of great concern to many critics: "What *are* they doing?" Dolphy responds, "It's like you have no idea what you're going to do next. You have an idea, but there's always that spontaneous thing that happens. This feeling, to me, leads the whole group. When John plays, it might lead into something you had no idea could be done" (Woideck 1998: 113). In keeping with his "cleaning the mirror" metaphor, Coltrane is later quoted by Nat Hentoff making a similar point, "There is never any end. There are always new sounds to imagine, new feelings to get at. And always, there is the need to keep purifying these feelings and sounds so that we can really see what we've discovered in its pure state. So that we can give those who listen to the essence, the best of what we are" (*Meditations* CD liner notes, 10). Other remarks pertain more to what happens when the music is recorded. He tells Valerie Wilmer that sometimes recordings "don't get enough of the real timbre and they miss the whole body of the sound" (Woideck 1998: 104). When asked in his Tokyo interview to recommend some of his recorded works that he likes best, he stated that "some of the best wasn't recorded. Recordings always make you tighten up just a little bit" (*Live in Japan* CD liner notes, 5).

[18]Plato provides us with an example of an ancient philosopher who, in some of his middle and later dialogues, criticized and modified his earlier views. Wittgenstein is a contemporary philosopher who, in his middle and late periods, rejected many of his earlier views.

The spiritual and intellectual dimensions of Coltrane's later work seem to provoke a latent desire, displayed by many commentators, to restrict jazz to its traditional role as a form of musical entertainment. While Coltrane is never condemned wholesale, that is, without praise of his playing on earlier recordings such as *Giant Steps*, the point of such praise seems to be to reposition, and to devalue by doing so, his experimentation with new ideas on later recordings. Scott Saul, for example, presents an analysis of Coltrane's performance of Mongo Santamaria's "Afro Blue" that noticeably ignores the more avant-garde live versions Coltrane performed in Seattle, shortly after Pharoah Sanders had joined the quartet, and again on *Live in Japan* (1966).[19] A preferred tactic seems to be to quote the negative comments of *other* critics and musicians. Many of these negative appraisals of Coltrane's later work are in line with a critique of the avant-garde movement that treats his association with that movement as unfortunate.[20] By focusing on some of the philosophical aspects of Coltrane's experimentation with harmony, melody, and rhythm it is not difficult to show, first of all, that his earlier and later musical ideas did evidence a continuity and, second, that his musical innovations were occurring within a well-established African American music tradition that he and other avant-garde musicians were extending.

C. O. Simpkins and Lewis Porter have located the original spirituals, "The Drinking Gourd" and "Nobody Knows De Trouble I See," that provided a source in folk culture for Coltrane's composition "Song of the Underground Railroad" on *Africa/Brass* (1961) and "Spiritual" on *Live at the Village Vanguard* (1961). With regard to the live recording of "Spiritual," Coltrane pointed out, "I wanted to make sure before we recorded it that we would be able to get the original emotional essence of the spiritual."[21] Unlike James Weldon Johnson, whose collaborative poetic work, *God's Trombones*, sought to achieve this emotional essence using sermons as a basis for orchestral composition, Coltrane placed a greater emphasis on musical performance. He meant by "emotional essence" the feelings expressed by the musicians through their performance of the composition. Several factors may have influenced his decision to go in this direction. *Giant Steps* signaled his dissatisfaction with the limitations of playing chord changes. In an interview in 1962 he spoke of a need to break with playing standards. Eric Dolphy, who was far ahead of Coltrane in his abstract treatment of harmony, and Ornette Coleman, who had given up playing chord changes altogether, were important influences in this regard.[22]

---

[19]Saul 2003: 233–243.
[20]Wilmer 1977; Nisenson 1993; Ratliff 2007; Anderson 2007.
[21]Porter 1998: 206.
[22]Woideck 1998: 107–108, 122–123.

When he decided to form his own band, he needed an answer to the philo-sophical question of "What am I going to play, and why?" and responded to this question by giving his music a spiritual rationale.[23] His desire to express the "emotional essence" of the spirituals is a key to understanding a tandem relation between the intellectual and the spiritual aspects of his project. At this early stage, his performance of "Spiritual" was not based strictly on the principles of music-making that governed the singing of spirituals in black churches—as were some of his later suites, such as *Ascension* (1965) and *Meditations* (1965), that incorpo-rated group improvisation. To show the influence of Ornette Coleman's folk orientation on Coltrane's project I will cite a passage from Hurston's *The Sancti-fied Church*, in which she outlines the defining elements of the spirituals.

> To begin with, Negro spirituals are not solo or quartette material. The jagged harmony is what makes it, and it ceases to be what it was when this is absent. Neither can any group be trained to reproduce it. Its truth dies under training like flowers under hot water. The harmony of the true spiritual is not regular. The dissonances are important and not to be ironed out by the trained musician. The various parts break in at any old time. Falsetto often takes the place of regular voices for short periods. Keys change. Moreover, each singing of the piece is a new creation. The congregation is bound by no rules. No two times singing is alike, so that we must consider the rendition of a song not as a final thing, but as a mood. It won't be the same thing next Sunday.
>
> *Negro songs to be heard truly must be sung by a group, and a group bent on expression of feelings and not on sound effects.*[24]

Hurston's observation of the singing of spirituals in southern black churches led her to conclude that "the real Negro singer cares nothing about pitch. The first notes just burst out and the rest of the church join in—fired by the same inner urge."

With Hurston's rather startling claim in mind, consider the following remarks along the same lines by Ornette Coleman, quoted by Valerie Wilmer, regarding the Moroccan master musicians of Joujouka.

> I saw thirty of them, playing non-tempered instruments in their own intonation, in unison. They would change tempos, intensities and rhythm. They changed together, as if they all had the same idea, yet they hadn't played what they were playing before they played it! . . . Originally, jazz must have been about that: individuals don't have to worry about the written note in order to blend with it.[25]

[23]Woideck 1998: 107.
[24]Hurston 1983: 80.
[25]Quoted in Wilmer 1977: 65.

The principles of music making to which these two examples of folk music allude provide alternatives to those derived from Western music theory. By the end of 1965, when he began to experiment with rhythm and time, Coltrane had embraced many of these alternatives and had incorporated them into his performances.

There are several respects in which Coltrane's music represents a merging of multiple forms of cultural expression. Although he was grounded in Western music theory and African American practice, there were many non-Western sources for the new music he created.[26] The belief that the highest expression of music is in written composition applies mainly to European classical music, in which the performance tradition is closely tied to a specific corpus of written music. In African American musical practices, a largely dance-oriented orchestral tradition has been, in many important ways, dominated by performance.[27] The transformation of jazz bands from marching and rag to dance orchestras, then back to smaller combos represents changing economic and material conditions as well as important ideological and cultural shifts. The music played by the earlier rag musicians and swing orchestras was meant to be entertainment, whereas bebop placed a greater emphasis on solo improvisation that, with each succeeding generation, became increasingly more sophisticated, complex, and abstract. Although Miles Davis, with Sonny Rollins and Coltrane in the group, was

[26]In a *DownBeat* article (1960) with Don DeMicheal, Coltrane states that he likes Eastern music, and he refers to the "exotic-flavored" music of Yusef Lateef and Ornette Coleman. "In these approaches there is something I can draw on and use in the way I like to play," he says (Woideck 1998: 98). Wilmer claims that Coltrane met Ravi Shankar in the 1950s and studied with him for a short period (Wilmer 1977: 36; Nisenson repeats this point in 1993: 185). Ahmed Abdul-Malik, who played bass in Monk's group with Coltrane, may have been an important influence in this regard. With Eastern and African music in mind, he remarked that "most of the things the musicians are searching for are old" (*The Music of Ahmed Abdul-Malik* [New Jazz 8266, reissued on Prestige]); see original liner notes. He plays oud on Coltrane's *Live at the Village Vanguard* (1961).

[27]Duke Ellington once pointed out that the relationship between composition and performance differs in jazz and classical music. "If you are what people usually call a 'serious' composer, what you have done is a theme and variations, and you publish it as part of an opus—or a big piece of work. But if you're a swing musician, you may not publish it at all; just play it, making it a little different each time according to the way you feel, letting it grow as you work on it" (Walser 1999: 10). Coltrane's break with playing standards is important to consider in this regard. In 1960, after expressing a desire to draw upon Eastern music, he refers to the "lines and sketches" he has been writing for the quartet. He then points out a need to "find out what kind of material . . . will carry my musical techniques best" (Woideck 1998: 102). In 1962 he tells Valerie Wilmer, "I think playing and writing go hand in hand. . . . I'm trying to tune myself so I can look to myself and to nature and to other sounds in music and interpret things that I feel there and present them to people" (Woideck 1998: 107). He follows this with the remark that "Duke Ellington is one person who can do this—that's really *heavy* musicianship and I haven't reached that stage yet." He seems to have reached this stage when he began composing suites toward the end of 1964. Anthony Brown brought to my attention important differences between *Ascension* and the other suites, which were written to be *performed* by the classic quartet. In keeping with Coltrane's cosmological view of God, Francis Davis has suggested that the compositions written for *Interstellar Space* also may have been conceived as a spiritual suite. See *Interstellar Space* CD liner notes (1999), 8.

still playing dances at the Audubon in the mid-1950s, by the end of the decade the avant-garde movement was well under way. What makes it difficult to resist a tendency to assess Coltrane's music based on aesthetic criteria derived from an entertainment conception of jazz is that his status as organic intellectual is ascribable to his being a creative artist with a background in the entertainment industry. Nonetheless, against this tendency, I will insist that, rather than ignore, or attempt to downplay the significance of a major influence on his musical development, his body of work must be situated in the context of a developing avant-garde movement in the 1960s if one is to appreciate fully his intellectual orientation.

No Free Jazz: Existential Anxiety and Cultural Autonomy

When considering Coltrane's relationship to the avant-garde movement it is important to keep in mind that his search, much like Socrates', was motivated by a deep-seated anxiety regarding death. Jimmy Cobb observed this aspect of Coltrane's music even earlier, when they were playing together with Miles Davis, and remarked that Coltrane played like he knew he did not have a long time to live.[28] Using colorful visual imagery, Coltrane's mentor from Philadelphia, Jimmy Oliver, claims to have once told Coltrane that he sounded like someone scared, running down the street knocking over trash cans.[29] During his tour of Japan in 1966, Coltrane's response to a question about where he would like be in ten years is revealing. He stated that he would like to be a saint, a remark that can be taken as his acknowledgment of his impending death.[30]

Coltrane's anxiety regarding his early death explains his desire to search continually for a deeper meaning to life. It also explains the agenda he set for himself that included his search for, and attempt to rearticulate, the essence of African American music by returning to its roots in the sacred tradition. While this spiritual turn addressed the question of purpose—"Why play music?"—it also generated a question of how best to execute that purpose. Many of the "free jazz" concepts that were being developed by various avant-garde musicians provided Coltrane with a means of transcending some of

---

[28]Burns 2001, episode 10.

[29]*Tell Me How Long Trane's Been Gone*, vol. 3. In a more negative vein, Nisenson cites an observation of James Collier's that "Coltrane was a certifiably neurotic, if not near-psychotic man, driven by inner demons rather than a search for God." The evidence cited for this claim is Coltrane's compulsive practicing and his candy habit (1993: 194). For a philosophical discussion of existential anxiety, see Slote 1975.

[30]This remark is reported by Nisenson 1993: 212.

the well-established conventions of the post-bop period. His increasing awareness that he had limited time to complete his search was an overriding factor influencing his rapid development and his radical turn toward the avant-garde. Having this awareness also granted him complete autonomy from commercial influences that aimed to discourage this move.

With regard to some of the philosophical implications of Coltrane's music, there are several noteworthy aspects of his project that involve issues pertaining to values, metaphysics, and epistemology. In his dialogue *The Apology*, Plato presents a view of Socrates as totally devoted to a critical examination of basic philosophic questions regarding the meaning of human existence and values. Although Plato's romantic image of Socrates as a truth-seeker has not gone uncontested, we now attribute to him two famous dictums from *The Apology*: "Know thyself" and "The unexamined life is not worth living." Some of Coltrane's remarks, in interviews, about the musical ideas he began to develop after forming the quartet in 1961, indicate that he too had an overriding commitment to these principles.[31] He claimed to have had a spiritual awakening in 1957, and his subsequent musical career became a spiritual search. What is important to note is that from this experience his music acquired a new purpose, and his mission as a bandleader was no longer entertainment. He tells Nat Hentoff, "My goal in meditating on this [force for unity in life] through music . . . is to uplift people, as much as I can. To inspire them to realize more and more of their capacities for living meaningful lives. Because there certainly is meaning to life."[32] Undeniably, his spirituality is rooted in his early childhood religious experience. It is important to add, however, that his musical explorations as a means of seeking knowledge of himself and God can also be understood, as in the case of Socrates, in an existential sense that is concerned with self-knowledge and the ultimate meaning of human existence.

This decidedly philosophical concern with the meaning of existence underlies what Harold Cruse referred to as a "crisis of the black intellectual."[33] In his well-known 1897 address to the Negro Academy, "The Conservation of Races," Du Bois first stated this problem as a dilemma arising from a double consciousness that pervades African American identity. Speaking from a first-person standpoint he asks, "What after all am I? Am I an American or am I a Negro? Can I be both? . . . Is not my only possible practical aim the subduction of all that is Negro in me to the American?" In the first chapter of *Souls of Black Folk*, he gives this idea a positive twist by speaking of the Negro's gift of

---

[31]Coltrane speaks of the need for greater self-knowledge in several places. See his interviews with Wilmer 1977: 107, and Kofsky 1998: 458. On the liner notes for *Kulu Se Mama* (1965), he is quoted as saying he is trying "to reach his better self" (1965).

[32]Hentoff 1966: 3.

[33]Cruse 1984. See also Spillers 2003.

"second-sight in this American world,—a world which yields him no true self-consciousness." He then describes double consciousness as a feeling. More specifically, he refers to it as a "peculiar sensation" of "twoness," "two souls," and "two warring ideals in one dark body." This internal "strife" is characterized by the African American's desire ("longing") "to merge his double self into a better and truer self." It is significant that Du Bois goes on to say, "In this merging he wishes neither of the older selves to be lost." The crisis of the black intellectual is a version of the problem of double consciousness that Du Bois characterized in terms of a divided self. The solution he proposed was black cultural autonomy to avoid "self-obliteration."[34]

Coltrane's search for new musical ideas involved more than simply a movement away from playing chord changes in time. It became a search for a means of expressing a "truer self" by combining traditional jazz with the new music being created by 1960s avant-garde musicians. He is known to have read philosophy books, such as A. J. Ayer's classic analytic tome *Language, Truth, and Logic*, as well as some of Albert Einstein's writings.[35] As his interest in the avant-garde developed, his compositions often incorporated themes that indicate he was thinking about cosmology. His performance of "Spiritual" with Eric Dolphy at the Village Vanguard, and his raising the hymn on *Ascension*, are clear indications of his ever-present religious roots in the southern black church. A much broader spiritual orientation, however, is suggested by the decidedly Eastern and African musical aspects of his performances on original compositions such as "Ole," "India," and "Om"; on standards such as "Summertime," "My Favorite Things," "Afro Blue," and "Clear Out of This World"; on albums such as *Live at the Village Vanguard, Live in Japan*, and *The Olatunji Concert*; and on studio recordings such as *Africa/Brass* and *Kulu Se Mama*.

Some of Coltrane's remarks convey a pantheistic idea of God as nature, or the universe, as a whole. With the exception perhaps of Baruch Spinoza, this notion has been largely associated with Eastern theology.[36] There are, however, many Western philosophers who have espoused similar views. The metaphysical system in Gottfried Leibniz's *Monadology* is committed to a view of God as constituting the universe, such that each individual is a self-contained version of this universe perceived from different perspectives.[37]

---

[34]Gates, Jr. and Oliver 1999: 11.

[35]Coltrane suggested a need to resort to one of the *Philosophy Made Simple* books to understand Ayer (Woideck 1998: 86). Nisenson claims, without references, that Coltrane attempted to apply Einstein's theory of relativity to his music (1993: 193).

[36]According to Spinoza, "Whatsoever is, is in God, and without God nothing can be or be conceived." *Ethics* I, prop. XV, 55.

[37]A monism similar to the view held by Spinoza occurs in Leibniz. He states, "And just as the same town, when looked at from different sides, appears quite different and is, as it were, multiplied *in perspective*, so also it happens that because of the infinite number of simple substances, it is as if

And the Anglo-Irish philosopher George Berkeley argued that the constitution of the external world that we apprehend through sense perception is really immaterial collections of sense data directly imprinted on our senses by God. He believed that sense perception is a divine language God uses to communicate with us on a regular basis.[38] In a fashion very similar to these treatments by major Western philosophers, spirituality was for Coltrane a combination of religion and cosmology.

Along with concepts derived from Eastern philosophy, the much-maligned honks, shrieks, and multiphonic techniques employed by performers such as Eric Dolphy, Ornette Coleman, John Gilmore, Albert Ayler, and Pharoah Sanders provided him the appropriate means of expression needed to represent such a view of spirituality in his music. In his *Critique of Pure Reason*, Immanuel Kant maintained that there is an unknowable reality (noumena) beyond what is apprehended by sense perception that is not organized by space and time, which he understood to be categories that operate like a grid we impose to make intelligible some aspect of that unknowable reality. Hence, the reality we know is constituted by phenomena we can experience.

Some of Coltrane's thinking about cosmology reflects a combination of Eastern and Western metaphysical and epistemological views regarding the ultimate nature of the universe. When Eric Dolphy tells Don DeMicheal, "Music is a reflection of everything," Coltrane adds, "It's a reflection of the universe."[39] Beginning in 1965, especially on recordings of his live performances, whether original compositions such as "Leo" and "Peace on Earth" or standards such as "My Favorite Things" and "Clear Out of This World," a lot of what Coltrane played, sometimes with a distinctly Eastern flavor, can be understood as an attempt to represent, in musical terms, a metaphysical view in conformity with Kant's worldview of superimposed order over a backdrop of chaos.

There is an equally important epistemological dimension of Coltrane's avant-garde phase that ties in with his metaphysical view. Though it is not like a material object, music is nonetheless experienced as something concrete that is occurring in space and time. The transcendental nature of Coltrane's spiritual outlook influenced his belief that music and sounds could be used to communicate at a level of understanding not manifested in sense perception, or at a level that goes beyond what is literally heard by the ear. This is revealed in his remark that he wanted to express the

there were as many different universes, which are however but different perspectives of a single universe in accordance with the different points of view of each monad." *Monadology*, sec. 58, in Parkinson 1973: 187–88.

[38] Berkeley, *Principles of Human Knowledge* and *Alciphron*.

[39] Woideck 1998: 114.

"essence" and captured by his reference to "this force for unity in life."[40] When he tells us, "My conception of that force keeps changing shape," this suggests a need to communicate at a more abstract level in order to express in musical terms a cosmological view imbued with a spiritualism similar to that posited in Eastern thought, as well as by some of the European Enlightenment philosophers I have cited.

I will use a standard line, employed by Rationalists such as Spinoza and Leibniz, to show how this point about epistemology applies to Coltrane's project. His performances were a means of engaging in a form of abstract thinking that allows the intellect, through reason, to grasp an insight by means of sound, but, at once, that insight is unencumbered by the sounds required to apprehend it. The meanings associated with the sounds transform the latter into abstract thought. A blues holler (or moan), for instance, can express the point of a song's lyrics without using words, just as, in a certain context, a grunt or pattern of grunts can function in a more sophisticated manner than ordinary language as an abbreviation of lengthy statements. This phenomenon can be understood in terms of the abstract level at which the meaning of a holler or pattern of grunts is understood when produced in a musical performance. Rashied Ali makes this point with regard to one of Coltrane's last recordings representing his most abstract performance using multidirectional pulse. According to Ali,

> If you listen to *Interstellar Space*, you can hear that something's going on that's holding the whole thing together. I'm not playing regular time, but the feeling of regular time is there. I'm thinking in time. We'd start out in three or four; five-eight or six-eight, whatever. I would anchor it in my mind, but play everything not on it, but against it. I'm hearing the beat and I'm feeling the beat, but I'm not playing it. It's there, but it's not there.[41]

Ali's point about his conceptualization of time while performing with Coltrane on this date had a counterpart in Coltrane's conceptualization of pitch as, at once, "in" and "out" of a harmonic structure. Both represent features of black music that have a structure and dynamic governed by conventions derived from a tradition grounded in religious practice.[42]

---

[40]See *Meditations* CD liner notes. Nisenson sometimes uses the term "essence" with quotes. He refers to Coltrane's "search," but never seems to take the idea seriously. Although, at one place he suggests that Coltrane meant by the term "essence" what Einstein meant—"the ultimate vibration" (1993: 193)—at another, in a rather mocking tone, he defines "essence" as "that sound which would have him directly encounter the mind of God" (178). Statements by Coltrane are important to consider in this regard, for, as I have suggested, his cosmological notion of God as nature in general comes close to views held by Rationalists such as Spinoza and Leibniz.

[41]Davis 1998: 9–10.

[42]See Hurston 1925 and Sterling Brown, "Negro Folk Expression."

Hollers, screams, growls, and other vocal expressions were used by 1960s avant-garde horn players to extend the jazz vocabulary and the boundaries of musical meanings that rely on pitch. The incorporation of these sounds into the jazz lexicon involves a synthesis of thought and feeling such that the *mode* of expression embodies both.

When Coltrane spoke of his desire to express the essence of a song, he was referring to his reliance on his feelings as he plays to know what direction to take.[43] As his interest in the avant-garde developed, earlier conventions governing performance were overridden by his shift toward black sacred music. A frequent criticism was that his solos were too long. For conceptual reasons, however, the critic's demand for editing was misplaced.[44] Black sacred music, as Hurston rightly pointed out, is not based on principles derived from Western music theory.

The Emotional Essence of the Spiritual:
Taking "Giant Steps" to "Mars" and "Venus"

There were several ways in which Coltrane extended his style and technique from a strict adherence to earlier bebop conventions to experimentation with cutting-edge avant-garde principles. The progression of his shift in this direction indicates the extent to which his thinking about various elements of music had become more abstract. His more abstract orientation to harmony, melody, and rhythm—in that order—reached a level that was best expressed, as Coltrane himself once suggested, *could only be expressed*, in live performance.[45] In this regard, his guiding principle of recognizing what

[43]In his conversation with Don DeMicheal and Eric Dolphy some of his statements suggest this. With regard to the general question of what they were trying to do in their performances Coltrane remarked, "It's more than beauty that I feel in music—that I think musicians feel in music. What we know we feel we'd like to convey to the listener" (Woideck 1998: 114).

[44]With regard to the criticism that his performances were too long he replied, "Quite possibly a lot of things about the band need to be done. But everything has to be done in its own time. There are some things that you just grow into. Back to speaking about editing—things like that. I've felt a need for this, and I've felt a need for ensemble work—throughout the songs, a little cement between this block, a pillar here, some more cement there, etc. But as yet I don't know just how I would like to do it. So rather than make a move just because I know it needs to be done, a move that I've not arrived at through work, from what I naturally feel, I won't do it" (Woideck 1998, 115–116). Toward this end he used a suite format on *A Love Supreme, Transition, Ascension, First Meditations*, and *Meditations*, which helped to organize his ideas as his music became more spiritually oriented.

[45]In his conversation with Coltrane and Don DeMicheal, Eric Dolphy makes the point that in live performance "you can feel vibrations from the people." Coltrane adds: "The people can give you something too. If you play in a place where they really like you, like your group, they can make you play like you've *never* felt like playing before" (Woideck 1998: 115).

he was looking for when he heard it included hearing other music that would provide ideas he could incorporate, as well as developing his own ideas and, in an important sense, using both at once.

In the radio documentary *Tell Me How Long Trane's Been Gone*, John Gilmore recalls an event that, as it turns out, marks a milestone in Coltrane's development. As an outsider who finally got a chance to sit in with Willie Bobo's Latin group on a Monday night at Birdland, he reports having been terrified because, fresh from Chicago, he was unfamiliar with the way New York musicians played. Given that his reputation and welfare were at stake, to survive on the bandstand he adopted a strategy that Coltrane, who was present, immediately recognized as something for which he had been searching. According to Gilmore, "I played contrapuntal to what they were doing rather than trying to get into the same groove." With a great deal of excitement, Coltrane told Gilmore afterward, "You got it, you got the concept!"[46]

When asked about his performance on "Chasin' the Trane" at the Village Vanguard in 1961, Coltrane told Kofsky that just prior to making the record he had been listening to Gilmore "kind of closely."[47] In response to Kofsky's inquiry as to whether he ever listens to this classic recording, and whether he was pleased with it, he makes two important points, one regarding the "fairly good amount of intensity" he had managed to get on a record for the first time and a second regarding his realization that he would have "to do that or better." It must be noted here that his reference to the intensity with which he played and a desire to improve upon this achievement indicates criteria he used to gauge his later development. The intensity with which black church-goers sang spirituals, with no overriding concern for pitch or intonation, was a guiding principle identified by Hurston as a more "primitive" form of expression. In keeping with that sacred folk tradition, Coltrane adopted this principle as a means of expressing the "emotional essence" of a song.

Several overlapping conceptual shifts involving his thinking about harmony, melody, and rhythm marked various stages of his development.[48] His earlier harmonic period with Miles Davis dialectically portended the modal period that would follow. While *Giant Steps* is often praised as a masterpiece, for Coltrane it seems to have represented a need to rethink the function of chord progressions. He points out that when Eric Dolphy joined the group they began to play "freer," yet Ornette Coleman's approach to melodic

[46]See Szwed 1998: 189.
[47]Kofsky 1998: 451.
[48]Andrew White identifies four periods: (1) with Miles Davis's group from 1955 to mid-1957; (2) with Thelonious Monk's group from mid-1957 to the end of 1959; (3) with his own band 1960–1964; and (4) 1965 to mid-1967. I use the divisions of harmony, melody, and rhythm suggested by Coltrane to mark the various stages of his musical development—phases which pretty much correspond with White's four periods (1981: 42). It should be noted that, in his latest period, especially his performance on *Stellar Regions,* Coltrane seems to be returning to harmony.

interpretation seems to have exerted a greater influence on the way he im-
provises on the Village Vanguard recordings of "Spiritual" and "Impressions."
In his interview with Benoit Quersin in January 1963, he remarked, "I haven't
forgotten about harmony altogether, but I'm not as interested in it as I was
two years ago." What he had learned from his earlier "experiment" with using
multiple, or stacked, chords, culminating in the recording of *Giant Steps*, was
that the modal concept had become necessary to free the rhythm section.[49]

The notion of "free jazz" is often taken by critics to mean a rejection of
all conventions or rules that apply to music making—and, undoubtedly,
there were some avant-garde musicians who maintained such a view.[50] In
Coltrane's case, though, there is an important difference between the rejection of all music conventions and the inclusion of as many alternatives as
possible. The freedom Coltrane sought was a liberty to explore new dimensions of harmony, melody, and rhythm, but not by *abandoning* his earlier
musical ideas altogether. Rather, he was more interested in *expanding* those
ideas. With reference to the "extended chord structures" of the songs on
Giant Steps, he expressed second thoughts about his use of these "sequences"
to compose an entire piece, when they probably would only be a few bars in
other songs. He then adds a comment that indicates the continuity of *Giant
Steps* with his later performances: "And since then, I've done it, but it hasn't
been so obvious because I've learned to use it as a part of something and not
as a whole."[51] Although this remark was made in 1963, he asserted a similar
view of the place of harmony in his music in 1966. When asked by Kofsky
about the role of the piano in his group, he stated flatly, "I still use the piano,
and I haven't reached the point where I feel I don't need it."[52] What this
suggests is that although his new direction required him to conceptualize
harmonic structure more abstractly—allowing a soloist to elect not to follow
the piano—he never gives it up entirely.

To show this continuity, commentators have compared transcriptions of
Coltrane's recorded performances from his earlier and later periods.[53] David

[49]Woideck 1998: 121.
[50]See Wilmer 1977: chap. 7.
[51]Woideck 1998: 120.
[52]Kofsky 1998: 447.
[53]Porter rightly notes (1998: 81) that Coltrane literally composed music based on the sequential ex-
ercises he studied, which included the Hanon and Czerny piano exercise books. In this regard he
may have been influenced by his association with Eric Dolphy, whose style incorporates a lot of sequences and patterns derived from his classical training. The organist, Jimmy Smith, told an inter-
viewer that he once gave Coltrane a violin exercise book to practice. John Schott has located five
identical patterns using major thirds cycles from Slonimsky's *Thesaurus* in the version of "One
Down, One Up" on *Live at Newport* (1965). "Revealing a Hand That Will Later Reveal Us: Notes on
Form and Harmony," 349. See also Weiskopf 1995: 16. In his dissertation on this topic, Jeff Bair
(2003) traced Coltrane's use of major thirds cycles as chord structure in other compositions, such as
"Countdown," from the *Giant Steps* period through their continuous development as melodic vocabulary in his modal and avant-garde periods.

Demsey's analysis indicates that Coltrane used chromatic third relations in the ii—V—I harmony of "Giant Steps" in a manner that allows the progressions to form a complete cycle, resulting in chords that seem to loop or sequentially perpetuate themselves. Although Coltrane began to play modal improvisation after *Giant Steps*, commentators have shown that he continued to use major thirds cycles as a melodic vocabulary on compositions such as "Impressions." His remark, quoted above, that he has learned to use the ii—V—I harmony in parts of his compositions rather than as a whole song, is a reference to his abstraction of the interval from the chords of "Giant Steps." As Porter and other commentators have pointed out, this allowed him to play "Giant Steps" melodic patterns not only over modal pieces, but in his improvisation on later, more abstract tunes, such as "Mars" and "Venus."[54]

Gilmore's concept of improvising against what the rhythm section plays is key to understanding the shift in Coltrane's thinking about rhythm and time. His interest in cross-rhythms expanded when, around 1965, he began using multiple drummers. This idea broadened even further when Coltrane began to experiment with multidirectional pulse. Though it is important to acknowledge the influence that other avant-garde musicians, such as Albert Ayler, had on his shift in this direction, Coltrane, as a virtuoso saxophonist, brought to the movement a learned sophistication that had been lacking. This virtuosity can be heard on the *Live in Japan* album. His use of a strong Eastern vibrato on soprano and long raga-like melodic passages on "My Favorite Things" and "Afro Blue" added balance to the shout sections involving group improvisation on his own compositions "Peace on Earth" and "Leo." Some of his very last recordings with only a rhythm section, such as *Stellar Regions*, provide evidence of the influence of Ayler and Coleman, as well as that of Coltrane's study of atonal classical composers—the latter, I think, signal his return to harmony. Drawing upon these various sources enabled him to think more broadly about pitch—another important conceptual shift that relinquishes the well-tempered scale in favor of the entire overtone series as a reference point.

When asked in an interview about directions Coltrane gave to members of the group, Elvin Jones explained that Coltrane rarely called any of the tunes they played.[55] The John Gilmore–inspired "Chasin' the Trane" was a tune the group had never played before. This rather telepathic dimension of musical expression was used with a spiritual aim when he raises the hymn on *Ascension* to bring in a multitude of voices that begin to improvise, all at

[54]Porter 1998: 223; Bair 2003.
[55]Jones discusses this in a yet unpublished interview with Anthony Brown. Pharoah Sanders said, "Most of the time he will just start playing something. . . . We're not thinking so much about line or melodies . . . just about music." David Wild, *Live in Seattle*, CD liner notes, 6.

once, on a version of the melody from "A Love Supreme." The group improvisation, which is out of time, is repeated in ensemble sections that are
divided between alternating sections of individual solos played in time. In
several ways, this composition indicates how Coltrane's shift toward the
avant-garde was well grounded in traditional black music. The recording of
Ascension was motivated by his desire to express the "emotional essence" of
the spiritual using horns collectively, instead of voices. Although the melody,
as noted above, is based on "A Love Supreme," from the standpoint of
Coltrane's search, it was also a revision of the earlier Village Vanguard performance, even an attempt to improve upon it with the suite format and the
addition of group improvisation.[56]

Coltrane's decision to use two drummers for the *Ascension* recording session
was based on reasons different from those that motivated Ornette Coleman to
use two drummers on his *Free Jazz* recording. Unlike Coleman, Coltrane had
planned to have Jones playing in time and Ali playing pulse. When asked about
the breakup of the quartet, he tells Kofsky that he wanted both drummers, cor-
recting Sun Ra's accusation that Coltrane intended to drive out members of his
old band.[57] Nonetheless, the tension between the two drummers that led to
their dueling on stage is similar in some ways to the hostility Gilmore faced
that forced him to adopt a strategy of playing against the rhythm section. The
intensity of Coltrane's performance with multiple drummers is legendary. Ben
Ratliff and Eric Nisenson seem obliged to point out, using a lot of authoritative
quotes, that listeners often heard only noise. Coltrane, however, admitted to
having "drum fever" and was more than likely stimulated by the energized
drumming generated by the rivalry between Jones and Ali.[58]

Several elements are combined in *Meditations* (1965) to produce a level of
intensity that has become an earmark of Coltrane's avant-garde period. It is
composed in the suites format he had begun to use for sacred pieces on *A
Love Supreme* (1964) and *Transition* (1965). On *Meditations* he uses both
drummers, with Elvin Jones playing in time and Rashied Ali playing pulse.
The concept of group improvisation used on *Ascension* is transformed when
Pharoah Sanders joined the group. Just as in the case of *Ascension*, however,
Coltrane always included traditional parts in his suites—all of which have
prayer sections played in voice cadence. On some of his recordings with
Sanders, such as *Live in Seattle* (1965) and *Live at the Village Vanguard Again*
(1966), he is noticeably playing in time and within the harmonic structure of

---

[56]Porter 1998: 263.

[57]Kofsky 1998: 449.

[58]This was suggested to me in a conversation with trombonist Bill Lowe. David Wild alludes to this
idea when, with reference to the addition of Sanders and Ali to the original quartet, he remarks that
"the range of not always compatible styles made for a considerably different, quite volatile mix." *First
Meditations* CD liner notes 1992, 5. See also David Wild's comments on the liner notes of *Kulu Se
Mama* CD, 7.

the songs, while Sanders is not. This represents what he meant when he told Benoit Quersin that "the soloist can play any structure he wants to." One of the traditional features of his saxophone style, the blues holler, is expanded as a means of creating the intensity he sought to express using various ideas and techniques he appropriated from other avant-garde musicians. Even the sounds he produces in the shout sections, involving the two horn players engaged in group improvisation, are expansions of his more traditional style of playing. A key ingredient that connects his earlier and later style is the technique he developed using Nicolas Slonimsky's melodic patterns as a musical vocabulary.[59]

In this period it was exclusively through performance, rather than written composition, that he explored musical ideas derived from a more radical line of thought, various strands of which were, at that time, undergoing collective development by a new generation of musicians. As his conception of pitch shifted to the overtone series rather than the more limited well-tempered scales, Coltrane gravitated toward the more abstract style of avant-garde saxophonists such as Pharoah Sanders and Albert Ayler. With the freedom from conventions regarding pitch and time that the avant-garde style permitted, he began to introduce a repertoire of new sounds into his musical vocabulary. Assessments of these later performances often succumb to the lure of an entertainment conception of jazz that tends to reduce musical ideas to what is aesthetically familiar in jazz performed in a conventional style. The expression of sounds that are not aesthetically pleasing, however, has a long history in black sacred music, a context in which the experience of a congregation collectively "moanin'" is far from unfamiliar.

Alienation and Organic Cultural Traditions

Coltrane's lack of recognition as an organic intellectual reflects the uneven status of black literature and black music. Musicians and writers alike draw upon the religious traditions in African American culture. Nonetheless, the historical trajectory of black literature, before and after the Harlem Renaissance, differs from that of African American music in one important respect— and here I want to reiterate the rationale that perhaps motivated West to consider black writers as academic intellectuals rather than as organic intellectuals. The Harlem Renaissance writers aimed to fashion a distinctive black literary voice in an effort to expand the Eurocentric American canon—a voice under pressure to be assimilated into a national literature. With strong roots tied to

[59]Bair 2003; Slonimsky 1947.

an oral tradition that predates slavery, African American music had multifarious functions in the life of black people. Although the primary function of jazz has been to entertain, it has also served as a means to resist assimilation and to preserve a distinctive mode of black musical expression. The domination of African American music practices by mainstream influences has not prevented a protracted challenging of that hegemony. In some musical forms, such as jazz and rap, this has often included resistance to the conventions of Western music. Almost a defining feature of African American music practices—from spirituals, field hollers, blues, rag, bebop, and avant-garde to hip-hop—this resistive element in black music also has been a major source of inspiration for academic intellectuals, and, pace West, an aspect of organic practices that they have sought to emulate.

It was exactly this resistive element, permeating virtually all black music during the Civil Rights Movement of the 1960s, that critics at *DownBeat* and other major outlets attempted to discourage by using their power to censure.[60] Their negative critical reviews reflected the entertainment orientation of the music industry, whose worry about declining record sales and dwindling audiences for live performances certainly was, and still remains, a legitimate economic concern. Economic worry, however, is not a sound basis for the derivation of aesthetic criteria. The criticism that avant-garde jazz became too intellectual often carries the implication that dance music is better. With no intended slight of dance music, I have insisted here that this criticism be reversed for the following reason: if we allow that some black musicians are much like other organic intellectuals, such as writers and artists, who develop their musical ideas the way the latter develop their literary and artistic ideas, then it is a mistake to define black music strictly as entertainment, or, for sheer economic reasons, to place limits on its reach into the intellectual domain.

Coltrane's achievement in music exposes a need, by academics, to reconsider the status accorded to organic intellectuals and African American cultural traditions as a site of intellectual development. By any criteria set by academic intellectuals, his achievement in music excels those standards. West points out that, unlike preachers and musicians, who have strong traditions rooted in black communities, black academics have no such traditions and are marginalized by both the white academic community and the black community.[61] Given that this dual alienation is fostered by the absence of a strong black academic tradition, he proposes, as one means of addressing it, that black academic intellectuals seek to establish that tradition.

There is an important cautionary proviso I would like to add to West's proposal. The African American music tradition that produced Coltrane

[60]See Kofsky 1998: chap. 3; Anderson 2007: chap. 2; and Saul 2003: 224–233.
[61]West 1993: 72.

must be distinguished from the academic tradition of scholars (musicians or otherwise) who teach and publish studies on that tradition. African American music can advance without the latter, but not without the former. Present trends suggest that in the near future, colleges will be a major site of musical training in jazz performance. As we move more in this direction, the tradeoff to be avoided is that often such academic programs are divorced from a black community. We must not lose sight of the fact that the establishment of a post-1960s jazz studies curriculum aimed to create an academic tradition but was never meant to replace the earlier black music tradition. While the present generation of budding jazz musicians has access to both traditions, a major task for future generations will be to innovate musical ideas resulting from their merging. As a major contribution to the intellectual history of the twentieth century, John Coltrane's accomplishment in music provides us with a model of how to draw from all traditions to create something new.

Bibliography

Appel Jr., Alfred. 2002. *Jazz Modernism: From Ellington and Armstrong to Matisse and Joyce*. New York: Knopf, 2002.

Anderson, Iain. 2007. *This Is Our Music: Free Jazz, the Sixties, and American Culture*. Philadelphia: University of Pennsylvania Press.

Arlen, Walter. 1966. "Stravinsky Work Premiered." *Los Angeles Times*, November 2.

Bair, Jeff. 2003. "Cyclic Patterns in John Coltrane's Melodic Vocabulary as Influenced by Nicolas Slominsky's *Thesaurus of Scales and Melodic Patterns*: An Analysis of Selected Improvisations." Ph.D. dissertation, University of North Texas.

Berkeley, George. 1977. In *Principles of Human Knowledge,* ed. Colin Murray Turbayne. Indianapolis: Bobbs-Merrill.

Brown, Sterling. 1953. "Negro Folk Expression: Spirituals, Seculars, Ballads, and Worksongs." *Phylon* 14, 4: 45–61.

Burns, Ken. 2001. *Jazz: A History of America's Music.* 10-DVD set. PBS Online.

Cruse, Harold. *Crisis of the Negro Intellectual: A Historical Analysis of the Failure of Black Leadership*. New York: Quill, 1984.

Davis, Angela Y. 1998. *Blues Legacies and Black Feminism*. New York: Pantheon.

Demsey, David. 1991. "Chromatic Third Relations in the Music of John Coltrane." *Annual Review of Jazz Studies* 5: 145–180.

Du Bois, W. E. B. 1903. *The Souls of Black Folk*. In *"The Souls of Black Folk"*: *Authoritative Text, Contexts, Criticism*, ed. Henry Louis Gates, Jr., and Terri H. Oliver. New York: Norton, 1999.

Floyd, Sam, ed. 1990. *Black Music in the Harlem Renaissance*. New York: Greenwood.

Hurston, Zora Neale. 1983. *The Sanctified Church*. Berkeley, Calif.: Turtle Island.

Kofsky, Frank. 1970. *Black Nationalism and the Revolution in Music*. New York: Pathfinder.

———. 1998. *John Coltrane and the Jazz Revolution*. 2nd ed. New York: Pathfinder.

Kohn, Karl. 1965. "Bing Center Concerts." *Musical Quarterly* 41, 4: 702–708.

Locke, Alain, ed. 1925. *The New Negro: An Interpretation*. New York: A. and C. Boni.

———. 1936. In his *The Negro and His Music* and *Negro Art: Past and Present*. 1991 rpt. Salem, N.H.: Ayer Co.

Nisenson, Eric. 1993. *Ascension: John Coltrane and His Quest*. New York: St. Martin's.

Parkinson, G. H. R., ed. 1973. *Philosophical Writings of Leibniz*. London: Dent.

Porter, Lewis. 1998. *John Coltrane: His Life and Music*. Ann Arbor: University of Michigan Press.

Ratliff, Ben. 2007. *Coltrane: The Story of a Sound*. New York: Farrar, Straus and Giroux.

Saul, Scott. 2003. *Freedom Is, Freedom Ain't: Jazz and the Making of the Sixties*. Cambridge, Mass.: Harvard University Press.

Slonimsky, Nicolas. 1947. *Thesaurus of Scales and Melodic Patterns*. New York: Coleman-Ross.

Slote, Michael A. 1975. "Existentialism and the Fear of Dying." *American Philosophical Quarterly* 12, 1 (January): 17–28.

Spillers, Hortense. 2003. "The Crisis of the Black Intellectual." In *A Companion to African-American Philosophy*, ed. Tommy L. Lott and John P. Pittman. Malden, Mass. Blackwell.

Spinoza, B. 1677. "Ethics." In *The Collected Works of Spinoza*, ed. Edwin Curley. Princeton, N.J.: Princeton University Press, 1985.

Stoddard, Tom. 1982. *Jazz on the Barbary Coast*. Chigwell, U.K. Storyville.

Szwed, John F. 1998. *Space Is the Place: The Lives and Times of Sun Ra*. New York: Da Capo.

Tell Me How Long Trane's Been Gone. Radio documentary. Narrated by Michael S. Harper.

Vincent, Ted. 1995. *Keep Cool: The Black Activists Who Built the Jazz Age*. London: Pluto Press.

Walser, Robert. 1999. *Keeping Time: Readings in Jazz History*. New York: Oxford University Press.

Weiskopf, Walt. 1995. *Intervalic Improvisation*. N.p.: Jamey Aebersold.

West, Cornel. 1993. "The Dilemma of the Black Intellectual." In his *Keeping Faith: Philosophy and Race in America*. New York: Routledge.

White, Andrew. 1981. *Trane 'n Me: A Semi-autobiography*. Washington, D.C.: Andrew's Musical Enterprises.

Wilmer, Valerie. 1977. *As Serious as Your Life: The Story of the New Jazz*. London: Quartet Books.

Woideck, Carl, ed. 1998. *The John Coltrane Companion: Five Decades of Commentary*. New York: Schirmer.

Zamir, Shamoon. 1994. "'The Sorrow Songs'/'Song of Myself': Du Bois, the Crisis of Leadership, and Prophetic Imagination." In *The Black Columbiad: Defining Moments in African American Literature and Culture*, ed. Werner Sollors and Maria Diedrich. Cambridge, Mass.: Harvard University Press.

"Don't Let the Devil (Make You) Lose Your Joy": A Look at Late Coltrane

SALIM WASHINGTON

"As the Spirit moves . . ."

There is a saying in the Holiness church, "Don't let the Devil lose your Joy." It typically signifies as a warning to "saints" who are thought to be in danger of being seduced by "the world." In particular, it is an admonition against adopting secular humanist values that may conflict with faith-based holiness, an ever-growing danger now that the grandchildren of the mostly peasant believers who founded and created the culture of the religion are going to college and enjoying more of the pleasures of the secular world. As each generation within the faith is born and raised further away from the material conditions and cultural values that governed the rural peasants who created the American Pentecostal movement at the turn of the twentieth century, the keepers of the faith are increasingly wary of the effects of higher education, bourgeois living, and the acceptance of more mainstream (lenient) ideas about morality. To the "unsaved," this often seems mere paranoia and ultraconservatism. But to the initiated, to not let the Devil take one's joy is to hold fast to God's unchanging hand in a world that historically marginalized—if not outright despised—poor black people and that lures them away from the straight and narrow path to righteousness. In this formulation, joy is the essence of the religious feeling of being saved, and its ritualized expression is the quintessential religious act of the Pentecostal church—the shout. In its exuberance and in its simultaneous adherence to traditional forms while apparently abandoning the strictures implied by them, the John Coltrane Quartet's rendition of "Joy" resembles the shout, the climactic point of a Holiness worship service.

"Joy" was recorded in September 1965 and released posthumously in a 1977 recording, *First Meditations*.[1] It was from one of the last known recording sessions made with the classic quartet[2] and can be seen as the statement of a spirit-filled man who retained his joy despite the onslaughts of nonbelievers (his naysayers, especially the critics who cried "anti-jazz," and worse, as he developed throughout the 1960s). His sound has the strength and spiritual resolve of a man who survived the seductions of the flesh, whether they be the solaces of heroin and alcohol that ravaged so many jazz musicians of his generation, or the temptation to sacrifice the aesthetics of his jazz practice for the easy acceptance that he would have enjoyed had he contented himself with the usual practice of resting on his laurels. After *A Love Supreme* was recorded almost a year earlier, Coltrane's band was the top combo in jazz, and he had finally been named top tenor and soprano saxophonist by critics and fans alike, and he had even been elected Jazzman of the Year by *DownBeat*. Coltrane risked the comfort and glory of such adulation by continuing to experiment with nonhierarchical, nondiatonic forms of thinking and music making. It was precisely the musical elements outside the strictures of Western musical practice that confounded music critics concerning Coltrane's late work. His use of long vamps over modal passages, and extended soloing; of nontempered tuning including shrieks, honks, and screams; of glissandi like smears; and of melismatic melodic gestures were features that earned Coltrane respect and praise from some quarters and opprobrium from others.[3] In general, as Coltrane continued developing away from the aesthetic comfort zone of most of the critics, who relied principally upon Euro-American-centered values, he began to be associated with the contemporaneous movement of the Black Power strain of the liberation

---

[1]John Coltrane, *First Meditations (for quartet)*.

[2]The "classic quartet" refers to Coltrane's group from 1961 to 1965, and consisted of John Coltrane on tenor and soprano saxophones, Elvin Jones on drums, Jimmy Garrison on bass, and McCoy Tyner on piano. At times others, musicians such as guitarist Wes Montgomery, bassist Reggie Workman, and especially multi-instrumentalist Eric Dolphy joined the group briefly. These additions rarely brought the quartet into the kind of tight arranged sound of the jazz quintet, but sounded more like a quartet + 1.

[3]See, for example, Kofsky, *Black Nationalism*, pp. 133–176; and De Sayles Grey, *Acknowledgment: A John Coltrane Legacy*, pp. 17–45.

movement as its adherents began to move away from some of the goals, and especially the tactics, of integrationists and the politics of respectability that they embodied.[4] Not only was much of Coltrane's late work not considered respectable, he was at times treated as an apostate by the press. It is not surprising, then, that the poets and artists of the Black Arts Movement, with its aesthetic parallels to the non-respectability-seeking Black Power phase of the African American freedom struggle, would choose Coltrane as their patron saint. The saxophonist recoiled from the "angry young tenor" epithet and did not want the descriptions of his music to be reduced to polemical handles; he denied that he felt anger except when he could not make his music work out in a satisfactory manner. Yet his truthfulness within his art allowed him to achieve his goal of representing the zeitgeist, which of course included zealous and spirited utterances.

"Joy" is also a testament to an artist who applied both scientific accuracy and old-fashioned elbow grease to his art. His work ethic helped prepare his mind and body to be a fit vessel for the pouring forth of the Spirit. In other words, Coltrane managed to combine the scientific and the spiritual sides of his muse. At the same time he remained rooted in the African American traditions of music making and spirituality while simultaneously incorporating elements from other traditions. He would ultimately fashion his own musical language and spiritual expressions, all the while carrying the ancestors with him.

Musically, "Joy" realizes almost perfectly the goals toward which the quartet's music had been reaching throughout its four-year existence. It is the quartet's most relaxed and swinging recorded example of how to flow while stretching the formal parameters of music, including melody, harmony, meter, and especially sound. This essay takes a look at what is understood as "late Coltrane" by examining this particular performance. The treatment of these musical factors as I hear them in this recording are remarkable in and of themselves, but also reveal extramusical concerns of Coltrane in particular and African American music in general. The themes dealt with in this regard obviously include spirituality, but also issues of democracy and cultural autonomy in the context of the midcentury social and political struggles of African Americans.

---

[4]Evelyn Brooks Higginbotham, in her *Righteous Discontent: The Women's Movement in the Black Baptist Church, 1880–1920*, pp. 185–229, coins the phrase "politics of respectability" to refer to the assimilationist tendencies and the class and status differentiation practiced by members of the movement in the efforts to present themselves as worthy of the respect for which they fought. Though the Civil Rights Movement and the midcentury jazz musicians who rendered their protests in aesthetic terms were removed in time and actions from the organizers that Higginbotham discusses, there are parallels between the goals and self-imposed restrictions of both movements.

"Way back home . . ."

John Coltrane was born and raised in North Carolina during the Jim Crow era. He was nurtured in a black community with its own sound ideals, institutions, and music. These principles would inform his work throughout his career, no matter how far out his music might sound at times and no matter how widely he searched among other music cultures for information and influences. Coltrane eventually became an iconic figure for enlightened universal consciousness, thanks to his eclectic spiritual views and his pioneering use of musical practices and concepts from various folk traditions, especially those of India and Africa. Yet he never abandoned his roots in the jazz/blues aesthetic. By emphasizing his cultural connection to black people I do not mean to imply that his nurturing community was in any way monolithic, nor that it was uniformly opposed to Euro-American practices in its cultural values. In fact, Coltrane's social and musical upbringing included a mixture of traditions that crossed various lines of class, race, and regional culture.

Both of his grandfathers were ministers in the African Methodist Episcopal (AME) church. His maternal grandfather, the Reverend William Wilson Blair, was a religious and political leader in his community, and he had a reputation for militancy. He commanded respect from all who interacted with him, black and white alike. He would build consensus between the races and marshal resources to get things done, including opening a high school for African American students (which John Coltrane attended). Reverend Blair held a national office in the AME church organization and consequently led parishes in various locales.[5] Despite his peripatetic profession, Blair was clearly the patriarch of his family. Though he moved from town to town every few years, his success was such that his family followed him or, when unable to do so, would remain living in one of his households.

According to Coltrane, his grandfather was "the dominant cat" in his family. Ironically, his ability to become a patriarch and to attain such high social status may have had its roots in slavery. Although he was born into slavery, he was a literate man who became a property owner, a church and community leader, and a patriarch who helped to sustain three generations. Historian David Tegnell suggests that even though Blair and his wife, Alice Virginia Leary, were both born into slavery, they experienced a less harsh version of North Carolina slavery as slaves on a fertile coastline plantation. The slaves on the Skinner plantation lived comparatively stable lives, primarily because their families remained intact, and they did not suffer the

---

[5] For information concerning Coltrane's family history, see David Tegnell, "Hamlet: John Coltrane's Origins."

kind of abuse that was more common with the smaller farms in the central Piedmont counties.[6] Living among the slave quarters of the plantation, the Blairs were raised in a community of African Americans who, though enslaved, enjoyed some hours of autonomy away from the eyes of the master class. The numbers of blacks and the spatial arrangements of their living quarters on the plantation would grant more hours of isolation from the slave owners. It is possible that the socialization in this African American context could better provide coping mechanisms for slavery. Equally important, such a community would also provide normative cultural patterns and resources for living beyond any consideration of the condition of servitude. Perhaps this autonomy and stability translated into greater upward mobility for William and Alice after Emancipation.

The relative cultural advantages of the Blairs' experience of slavery carried over to provide a political advantage after the Civil War. During Reconstruction and the post-Reconstruction period, William Blair's talent and ambition were aided by his circumstances of living in a county with a high percentage of voting African Americans. As a young man he would have a career as a schoolteacher, hold political office, and become a property owner. Later in life he would hold regional office in the A.M.E. Zion denomination and would be awarded an honorary doctorate from Livingstone College.

By contrast, the Coltranes endured a harsher slave experience in the Piedmont region. John William Coltrane's paternal grandparents, Rev. William Henry and Helen Coltrane, were owned by a planter, Abner Coltrane, with a documented history of abusing his slaves. Because there were fewer slaves in the Piedmont, which is the Quaker belt of North Carolina, they lived in greater isolation from other blacks even as their owners were relatively isolated from white society. Slaves in the Piedmont were often subject to harsher treatment, as it was more difficult to enforce normative values (such as they were) about the treatment of slaves. (The apparent irony is explained by the fact that the increased brutality was not due to a lack of toleration on the part of Quakers—who were officially pro-abolition, the only such denomination in the Antebellum period—but rather facilitated by the relative isolation of the slave owners.) This disadvantage would be carried into the political culture after Emancipation since the low percentage of African Americans compromised their ability to build an effective political base.

---

[6]On the North Carolina coast, some former slaves even received their "40 acres and a mule," reparations stemming from Sherman's famous field order. Their descendants held onto their homes until very recently when their property taxes were raised to such levels that they were run off their own land, allowing investors to turn these parcels into resorts. See Elizabeth Leland, *The Vanishing Coast* (Winston-Salem, N.C.: John F. Blair, 1992).

By general standards, the Coltranes were quite successful, though. Helen was a property owner, and William Henry became a preacher (also with A.M.E. Zion) who evidently enjoyed a good reputation. Their son, John Robert Coltrane, would own his own tailor shop. William Henry Coltrane never held high office in the denomination, as did William Blair, and the Coltranes never achieved the level of financial and social status that the Blairs enjoyed. When Alice Blair married John Robert Coltrane, it was clear that the groom was joining the bride's family, and save for a very brief period, the couple lived in Rev. William Blair's household until his death. Coltrane's father was an amateur musician who liked to spend his spare time enjoying a taste and playing for his pleasure at his tailor shop. I do not have direct testimony, but perhaps John Robert's penchant for solitude was partly rooted in the social difference between himself and his adopted family. His wife, after all, attained postsecondary education, played organ for her father's church, and had an interest in performing opera. John William Coltrane, then, had in his immediate family persons of different social classes and was regularly exposed to a wide array of cultural styles and influences. He did not come from a culture of deprivation; his family was relatively well off by the standards of the day, especially for blacks. And he grew up with a model of black manhood that included literacy, dignity, and familial stability, and that did not kowtow to white prejudice or political opinion.[7]

Coltrane listened to the sounds of his community's music and also to the radio, on which he heard Duke Ellington and his star alto saxophonist, Johnny Hodges, who was Coltrane's first musical idol. Though his grandfathers were not involved in the Holiness church, with its rich musical practices, the Pentecostal church with its spirituals and blues-based worship styles were part of his cultural birthright as an African American, and especially as a southerner. The founding of the AME denomination predates the Pente-costal churches by over a century. There are also distinct class and cultural differences between their memberships and worshipping styles. While the AME was founded by and for freedmen during the days of slavery and had its headquarters in Philadelphia, the Church of God in Christ (the first registered Pentecostal church in the United States) was founded at the turn of the twentieth century by and for southern sharecroppers. Of course each denomination has grown to include a more variegated membership, but there remain differences in the worshipping styles and protocols. While the AME church is more staid in its worship, Pentecostals are typically more ecstatic in their singing, preaching, and testifying. I am not claiming that all blacks or southerners invoke the rituals of Holiness, as birthrights can be

[7]See Farah Jasmine Griffin and Salim Washington, *Clawing at the Limits of Cool: Miles Davis, John Coltrane, and the Greatest Jazz Collaboration Ever*, pp. 29–54.

claimed or ignored. But it is fruitful to consider this influence in Coltrane's late music. Much of the apparent spirituality in his music could rightly be understood as sanctified in spirit and form, as well as being in part the result of his studies of sacred music in the Hindu and Sufi traditions. The church in which Coltrane grew up was of a more staid, mainstream denomination, but his mature playing is very reminiscent of the charismata of the Holiness worship styles.

Equally important, Coltrane came from a middle-class family that was able to contribute materially and spiritually to his development and helped to inculcate a sense of love and pride in him for himself and for black people in general.[8] Coltrane would never abandon his musical roots. He would grow to be a great experimenter and is widely regarded as one of the last great innovators in the music, with the blues tradition remaining a constant thread throughout his career.[9] This ability to incorporate disparate influences while maintaining an identifiable connection to his roots was emblematic of the music itself. Jazz has always interacted with other forms and traditions without sacrificing its commitment to its own aesthetic. Even after joining the music's professional ranks, Coltrane would research various folk traditions, including those from disparate parts of Africa, India, and Spain, in search of a universal sound. Similarly, he would study the world's religions, traveling with various sacred scriptures and even mathematical texts as he pursued an ecumenical spiritual enlightenment in service to some notion of a cosmic consciousness. But his foundation never wavered; that is, he remained a jazz musician to the end, and he practiced his art in innovative ways, but always in conversation with the music's established traditions.

Make a joyful noise . . .

Clearly, the suites recorded by John Coltrane's classic quartet (*Transition/ Suite, First Meditations,* and, most famously, *A Love Supreme*) are among the most spiritual documents of all of recorded jazz.[10] With titles that

[8]Interview with Syeeda Andrews (Coltrane's stepdaughter), conducted by the author and Farah Jasmine Griffin, 2006.
[9]I use the term "blues tradition," rather than "jazz tradition," in much the same way that LeRoi Jones (Amiri Baraka) used the term in *Blues People,* to designate the blues as the Ur form of twentieth-century black music in the United States. It is the folk form that has proved to be the most fundamental in the development of other styles of African-American music. It is also the inheritor of many of the meanings and practices of earlier forms of music such as field hollers and spirituals. The term also takes the conversation about the music to consideration of widespread cultural ideals, which can enrich analysis of the musical details of specific texts or performances.
[10]John Coltrane, *Transition/Suite; Meditations; First Meditations (for quartet);* and *A Love Supreme.*

reflected Coltrane's interest in various spiritual and religious traditions, album covers guided readers toward a listening experience that invited a state of transcendence. And often the music that these titles described does evoke such experiences in some listeners and, it would seem, for the musicians themselves. *First Meditations* songs have titles depicting beatific attitudes: "Serenity," "Love," "Compassion," and "Joy."

"Joy" is appropriately named as its sound, tonal and rhythmic arrangements converge to convey a bubbling up of emotions, a state of ecstasy. The sound of Coltrane's saxophone went in excess of a conventional musical tone, much as the term "ecstasy" can carry a connotation of a benign excess of emotion to the point of losing control or even consciousness. The ecstatic voice in African American culture, made popular through rhythm-and-blues singers such as James Brown and Aretha Franklin, is probably most consistently used in Afro-Christianity, a context in which it represents the spirit-filled life. In part the overtone-rich sounds that African Americans have routinely used in singing and instrumental playing throughout their sojourn in America is thought to be derived from what is known as the heterogeneous sound ideal associated with much of West and Central African music. This view holds that in various African music traditions the notion of a beautiful voice (if in fact such a notion is meaningful in the abstract) is quite different from Western ideas about purity and polish of tone. In line with this, different vocal qualities may be used to depict different emotions or scenarios.[11]

The African propensity to use sounds that are not considered beautiful or even musical ("noise") in the Western sense are not limited to vocalizations. Olly Wilson, for example, lists the various traits of African music as including the tendency to play all musical instruments in a percussive manner.[12] (Consider, for example, the piano playing of Little Richard or Cecil Taylor, or the electric bass playing of Paul Jackson or Louis Johnson, the acoustic bass playing of Alex Blake, the saxophone playing of Junior Walker, and so on.) This percussiveness can alter sounds in a way that produces what would be called distortion in other contexts. Recent scholarship, however, seeks to reverse the convention of explaining African music as being qualitatively different from Western music. Kofi Agawu, in particular, interrogates the various myths of African difference, especially when it comes to rhythm.[13] While acknowledging the widespread mistake of denoting an "African" music rather than deal with the multiplicity of traditions in Africa, Agawu speculates that whites posit an African difference for political reasons and that white musicologists emphasize difference for professional reasons. I feel

---

[11]For instance, see Francis Bebey, *African Music: A People's Art*, pp.175–176.
[12]Olly Wilson, "Black Music as an Art Form," in *The Jazz Cadence of American Culture*, p. 84.
[13]See Kofi Agawu, *Representing African Music: Postcolonial Notes, Queries, Positions*.

that Agawu is right in asserting that African cultures are often depicted as "exotic" in the manner of Edward Said's orientalist formulation. Not only is the richness and endless variety of Africa ignored, but even when the continent is not "analyzed" as though it were a country, the putative differences are exaggerated in such a way as to marginalize Africa as being "primitive" and "alien." However, Agawu is no more immune to political sensibility and agency than the rest of us, and perhaps he overstates the "mythic" status of difference here. It *is* possible, after all, to correctly identify music as African in myriad cases. Despite what I consider his stretching to emphasize the sameness of Africans and Europeans, the gist of his argument could even be applicable to black American scholars, who may be particularly susceptible to a romanticization of Africa and especially with respect to music, which is the intellectual and cultural arena in which African Americans are typically valorized.

Whether or not the putative difference in sound ideals is derived from a real or imagined African past, it is certainly a fact that there is a difference in the sound ideals performed and valorized by African Americans and by European Americans. Furthermore, the African-based sound ideal is a mainstay of African American music in a variety of genres and time periods. For examples, one can listen to the "dirtied" tones of early jazz brass players like Tricky Sam Nanton or Bubber Miley and singers like Blind Lemon Jefferson, or the moans and shrieks heard in black religious music by the likes of Shirley Caesar or Aretha Franklin (it is interesting in this regard that Franklin is dubbed the Queen of Soul), the secularized shouts of James Brown (the Godfather of Soul), the blue clusters of Thelonious Monk, the feedback of Jimi Hendrix's guitar, the slapping and popping of Larry Graham's bass playing, the record-scratching of hip-hop DJs, or indeed, the growls and screams of John Coltrane's saxophone.

Church vocalists (and we have to consider "the" black church as the most significant training ground in America for singers) today routinely transform their voices to cover different registers and timbres in the space of one song, and often within the space of one phrase or even one word.[14] The ability to modulate the musical tone is an act of virtuosity, to be sure, but it is also an invitation for the audience to become participants, especially by witnessing or testifying to the spiritual power inherent in such a performance, contributing their own vocalizations and body gestures to the event. In the context of black expressions of religion, the Holy Ghost comes down like an Orisha riding an initiate, and inspires the believer to speak in tongues or to perform

---

[14]Guthrie P. Ramsey, "Jazz and the Church," a lecture presented to the Jazz Study Group at Columbia University, March 3, 2007.

symbolic acts to invoke the personalities of the deities.[15] The overall sound of the John Coltrane quartet in the recorded performance of "Joy", with its power and sense of abandon, gives the impression of a group that is already in the throes of religious ecstasy.

> *What should I hear but Louis Armstrong's "Oh memory" version of "Stardust."*
> *. . . Then there's that scratchiness I've alluded to before, an almost cryptic*
> *hoarseness. Is it the age of the record, the shortcomings of early recording*
> *techniques? Or is it something more primal, something more "ontic" perhaps?*
> *The sense I have is that we're being addressed by a barely audible witness, some*
> *receding medium so heartrendingly remote as to redefine hearing. . . . The*
> *frayed edges of sound are not to be heard as "unheard-of," however much that*
> *handle might appear to apply. The initiatic husk of self-inflicted static or the*
> *residual hum of self-ingesting suns (call it what you will), the raspiness of*
> *Louis's voice against the answering piercingness he gets from the horn*
> *supremely sets up the chorus to be the skinless muse it turns out to be.*
>
> —N.[16]

This flood of sound that Coltrane releases in "Joy" is accentuated by the insistence hinted at in the oft-repeated three-note motif outlining a quartal chord.[17] These repetitions are a trope of soulfulness in black music and are usually used to elicit an audible response from the audience. Black preachers and soul balladeers are the masters of this technique, a fact that underlies its symbolic reference to matters of the spirit. Coltrane's use of a quartal figure,

[15]Orisha are deities from the Yoruba pantheon. These deities are consulted in New World religions such as Santeria, Vodoun, and Candomble. Yoruba-based religions are among the fastest growing in the West, especially in Cuba, Brazil, and the United States, primarily among descendants of African American slaves. During certain rituals the Orisha inhabit the bodies of the initiates in much the same way as the Holy Ghost inhabits the bodies of the saints in the Pentecostal traditions. When the Orisha "rides" the saint in the Yoruba religion the worshipper exhibits the traits and actions of the Orisha according to certain ritualized expectations. This is analogous to the various attitudes that worshippers in the Holiness tradition experience, such as "shouting," speaking in tongues, or being "slain in the spirit."

[16]Nathaniel Mackey, *Bedouin Hornbook*, p. 23. "N" is a Coltrane-inspired character whose letters to the "Angel of Dust" about his traveling band make up Mackey's epistolary romance about the aesthetics of black music. It is one of the most unique and thorough investigations of African American music, as it is rendered in poetic, intellectual, folkloric, and comic wordplay, though it often uses language usually found in a more formal, scholarly context. Mackey's success with reaching deeper interpretations of the music in part relies upon his refusal to be bogged down in the orthodoxies of musicology while maintaining a high level of intellectual sophistication. Accordingly, I have interspersed passages from *Hornbook* as a kind of poetic counterpoint in apposition to portions of my own essay that treat similar themes in relation to Coltrane's music.

[17]Quartal chords comprise stacked intervals of a fourth, whereas the more traditional tertian chords are constructed by stacking thirds. It was one of the innovations of jazz musicians especially during the 1960s and 1970s. The quartal sound is more open and less tied to functional harmony than the tertian harmony.

rather than a more typical blues lick, gives this device a new, more modern spin. The repetition does not necessarily emphasize change or development, but rather places an emphasis on bearing witness as it allows the listener to participate and understand, or rather to feel.

In a discussion of the cultural meaning of repetition, James Snead examines Hegel's dismissal of African culture as being "without history" as a negative to an ever-developing European culture pointing toward progress and future fulfillment.[18] Snead explains that repetition in the natural and physical cycles of many non-Western cultures are celebrated without the burden of the European ritualized expectation of difference and development, as exemplified in the expectations of new records being set at Olympic games, or that the United States' annual presidential State of the Union Address will always announce the imminent health of a bigger, stronger, more prosperous nation. Snead contrasts this with his reading of how repetition signifies in a black context: "Black culture highlights the observance of such repetition, often in homage to an original generative instance or act. Cosmogony, the origins and stability of things, hence prevails because it recurs, not because the world continues to develop from the archetypal moment."[19] Repetition, and most especially trancelike states induced in part by such repetition (such as the interjections used by charismatic preachers and their audiences, or the choruses sung by congregants, or the music and choreography enjoyed in a spirited, dance-oriented party—remember Albert Murray's "Saturday Night Function"[20])—invite the listener (or dancer, or singer) to become a listener/participant, to enter into a sacred space where the paradigmatic acts and words of the gods and ancestors are brought alive in the here and now.[21] In more secular contexts the performer still elicits a spiritual bond of a sort between himself or herself and the audience through the practice of rhythmic repetition making entrée into the thought processes of the musician more accessible.

The effectiveness of the notes in Coltrane's melodic line in "Joy" are part of a swath of sound whose effectiveness is felt not in the individual niches occupied by well-placed tones, but in the overall arc and texture of the entire collection of notes. The notes are not a part of a hierarchy; that is, they are not diatonic. Rather, like much of African American music (and much of the

[18]James A. Snead, "Repetition as a Figure of Black Culture," in *The Jazz Cadence of American Culture*, pp. 62–81.

[19]Snead, "Repetition as a Figure of Black Culture," p. 68.

[20]In his magisterial *Stomping the Blues*, Albert Murray discusses the similarities in function and form between the musical activities in Sunday Morning church worship and what he calls the Saturday Night Function. He explains how the blues-based dancing and frolicking of the Saturday Night Function are not simply frivolous gallivanting but "a ritual of purification and affirmation."

[21]See Lawrence Levine, *Black Culture and Black Consciousness: Afro-American Folk Thought from Slavery to Freedom*, pp. 3–55.

world's folk music), the tonal palette is mostly pentatonic.[22] This lends a communal ethos to the melodic development because of a melodic setting where harmony is a background feature at best, for there are no real or even implied harmonic progressions. Also, any note can sound "good" at any point in the song. Hence, no note is paramount; no note is leading toward any other in any predictable or inevitable way. Here we see another trope of African American music in operation: it's not what you play; it's how you play it that counts. The rapid-fire execution of some of these passages brings to mind Coltrane's "sheets of sounds"[23] phase just because of the sheer velocity of his playing. But in "Joy" there is no attempt to superimpose abstract harmonic relationships throughout the improvisation. Groups of notes, in nonhierarchical fashion, become the sound and focus of the melodic line, and not a series of clever resolutions and modulations that make up much of the value of diatonic music, and some of Coltrane's earlier work. This is one of the clear demarcations of a post-bop aesthetic and praxis.

Coltrane's sound on "Joy" was another indication that he had taken steps beyond the bebop model upon which he cut his teeth on and built his style. That is, his very tone and the way that he produced his sound were different from the established conventions of jazz. The orgiastic richness of overtones found in his tone on the "head" and especially during his solo, were, and still are astonishing, and for some listeners overwhelming. Coltrane's ability to produce these sounds was probably developed during his journeyman days in Philadelphia, when he had to walk the bar on occasion. The midcentury practice of walking the bar was highly controversial among saxophonists. Saxophonists would literally walk atop the bar while playing a wild solo replete with honking and screaming sounds. The more physical gyrations the player made, the more the "house" got into it. Some went so far as to lie on their backs, kicking their legs while screaming through their horns. While many found the connection to audiences worth the effort, some saxophonists detested the practice as an undignified vestige of the minstrel traditions in American music. Lester Young refused to walk the bar,

---

[22]Playing the white notes on a piano from C to C can form a diatonic scale, and it is the do-re-me-fa-sol-la-ti-do scale often taught to children. Playing the black notes on the piano can form a pentatonic scale. The diatonic system is the basis of Western harmony, especially for art music, and implies intricate harmonic possibilities with elaborate rules about how to modulate from one key to another. Pentatonic-based music often does not concern itself with modulation, at least not in the microunits of the tune, as does much of diatonic music. See John Shepherd, *Music as Social Text*, pp. 96–127.

[23]Ira Gitler coined the phrase to describe the rapid passages that Coltrane developed after he played with Thelonious Monk during the summer of 1957. During this phase of his improvisational advancement, Coltrane began experimenting with superimposing as many as three chords over one tonality. By increasing the harmonies, he had to play more rapidly, and at times he had to use unusual rhythmic groupings to fit all the notes in, resulting in a startling new sound.

and even participated in a pro-con debate about it in the famous weekly, the Baltimore *Afro-American*.[24] Coltrane, who during the 1950s sang background vocals and played saxophone in such show bands as Eddie "Cleanhead" Vinson, Daisy Mae and the Hep Cats, and Bullmoose Jackson, was no stranger to the necessity of performing crowd-pleasing antics, but he thought of walking the bar as especially distasteful, even humiliating. He abandoned a gig one night when his friend and fellow saxophonist Benny Golson walked in on his engagement while he was walking the bar. He was also reputed to have refused to walk the bar on at least one occasion.[25]

Many a jazz musician has had to make part of his living playing the vernacular musics that were popular during their time. Even the most adventurous musicians have R&B experience, including not only Coltrane, but also iconoclasts like Ornette Coleman (Silas Greene from New Orleans), Julius Hemphill (Ike and Tina Turner Revue), and Andrew White (the Fifth Dimension). And there are also many musicians—among them, Ramsey Lewis; Nat "King" Cole; Patrice Rushen; George Benson; Earth, Wind, and Fire; Kool and the Gang; and the Crusaders—whose careers started with straight-ahead jazz and eventually shifted to concentrate on more popular styles of music.[26] This should not be altogether surprising, however, as R&B and modern jazz (bebop) began in the same moment, and used the same forms, "blues" and "rhythm changes," as their main vehicles for song format. (Dig Bird and Diz playing with Tiny Grimes, for instance.) The combination of intellectual rigor and drylongso, dance-beat feeling is in fact the magic formula for some of the most compelling jazz statements in history, "Joy" included. While Coltrane might have found walking the bar distasteful, especially during the late 1950s when his stage demeanor was sedate and his playing stance was erect and with little motion save for his fingers, he nevertheless absorbed the lessons to be learned from this extroverted style.

By 1965, when he recorded "Joy," Coltrane's body attitude while performing had changed drastically. Looking at his performance on the 1960 television broadcast while he was with the Miles Davis group, or the many photos extant from that period, we can see the more or less classical performing posture that he preferred in his early career. The DeCarava photographs of the mid-1960s performances, some brief footage from 1966, and the contemporaneous descriptions of his style reveal a different set of practices. Coltrane's shrieks and howls on the horn were then accompanied by body swaying, at times bending and crouching so that his face approached the

[24]Douglass Henry Daniels, *Lester Leaps In: The Life and Times of Lester "Pres" Young*, p. 289.
[25]Lewis Porter, *John Coltrane: His Life and Music*, pp. 91–92.
[26]Aaron Johnson, "The University of Jazz," unpublished paper.

ground as he played. In 1966 he put down his horn in one performance and began beating on his chest while hollering. In the context of 1960s black America, such antics no longer signified minstrelsy, but the serious, fire-branded spirituality that inspired the poets and activists of the day. The furrowed brow and sweat-drenched bodies of Coltrane and Elvin Jones were understood as the products of arduous work and deep concentration of committed artists, not the anti-intellectual gestures of clown-savants.

> But what I saw to be the tactile or coloristic counterpart of hoarseness proposed
> a scratchiness of voice, a self-seeding smudge with overtones of erasure as a
> possible arc along which our music might pass. I tend to pursue resonance
> rather than resolution, so I glimpsed a stubborn, albeit improbable world
> whose arrested glimmer elicited slippages of hieratic drift.
>
> —N[27]

The quartet's performance of "Joy" is communal in that the entire gestalt is important; the improviser is dynamic primarily in relation to the call-and-response rituals of the quartet, and not by the internal logic of his melody, as is the case of styles of jazz more indebted to functional harmony. It is widely acknowledged that the preference for modal systems of tonal organization over the diatonic system in Coltrane's late work in the mid-1960s is as much influenced by his study of African and Indian traditional musics as it was with the modal explorations that he participated in with Miles Davis sextet at the end of the 1950s. Using Indian ragas or rags, Coltrane learned to improvise for long periods of time over static harmonies. The length of time that he would spend in one mode or scale was enough to give the impression that the everyday understanding of time and space was being stretched in some way. The timelessness and otherworldliness of these long improvisations (some going on for forty minutes or more) also helped to underscore the spiritual quest inherent in the music.

Perhaps in no manner is the fullness of the quartet's development represented so dramatically in "Joy" than in its treatment of meter and time. Indeed, the bass is liberated from its traditional timekeeping function. There is a pulse, but the bassist does not consistently reiterate it. Rather, it is implied through the rhythmic background distributed throughout the various parts of the quartet. So although there is a discernible pulse, there is not necessarily a discernible meter. It is difficult to place whether this performance is in duple or treble meter, as at times it seems to coalesce around a common 4/4 meter and at other times seems to be in waltz time. The timelessness that is evoked by the modal character of the melodic/harmonic context is

[27]Mackey, *Bedouin Hornbook*, pp. 26–27.

enhanced by the apparent freedom from meter. Garrison goes throughout the entire piece scarcely playing any quarter notes or any steady rhythms whatsoever in the bass part. On the surface it might seem as though the music has escaped the strictures of meter altogether. If this is so, there is nevertheless a communal sanctioning of the aesthetic through a shared understanding of the pulse. This commitment to dancing with the pulse, that is, to swing no matter how explicitly the pulse is or isn't stated, is what separates the quartet's playing from other players who tried to follow in their wake toward so-called freedom. As in earlier recordings, Jimmy Garrison uses pedal points, asymmetric rhythms, and melodic statements, but here he hardly ever "walks" a traditional bass line and then only briefly. In this group, the bass is freed from the straightjacket of meter and functional harmony. This freedom is not an unrestrained license of the privileged, however. Rather it might be described as the freedom sought by the unfree. There is never even a hint of stepping outside of the groove that is set by the group. Yes, the bassist is no longer tied down to the task of articulating the pulse, as was typical for bassists in 1965, but Garrison is still holding down his responsibilities toward the group in the matter of swing and forward propulsion. There is freedom, but only a freedom as far as consensus can bear it.

Similarly, Elvin Jones provides a catalyst for the sense of metric freedom while simultaneously driving the swinging feeling that traditionally had depended upon, among other things, maintaining an unambiguous metric feeling. In fact, the song begins (and ends) with a tympani-like drum roll with mallets, which is about as far from metric and rhythmic iteration as possible. When the rest of the band comes in, he proceeds to play mostly cymbal crashes and thunderous claps on the various drums. Jones was well known and respected for his fiery eruptions on the drum kit. He was as much a part of the sound of the music referred to as "Trane" as Coltrane himself was. For the entire opening statement, prior to McCoy Tyner's piano solo, Jones delays playing "time" per se. Whereas the bebop drummers revitalized the rhythm sections of the 1940s and 1950s by the way they "dropped bombs" during their timekeeping, Jones found a way to swing the ensemble with a more or less constant sprinkling of bombs and crashes along with his own polyrhythmic way of playing time. (Something that is rarely commented upon is that Jones plays differently in other contexts.) But for the head, though the term hardly seems adequate for what the band plays as its thematic material, Jones does not use bombs to accentuate his time playing; he uses bombs and crashes *as* his time playing.

Tyner, who normally provided a rhythmic anchor in this band of polyrhythmic innovators, joins the spirit with his own rhythmic pedal tones, or, rather pedal chords, as he is playing chords rather than single notes. He does not come down at the beginning of a putative measure, or at any such predictable or consistent place. The result is that the four players make a rhythmic tapestry that is not unlike a choir of West African drummers and dancers in that together as a whole they articulate a gestalt in which each individual voice's relationship to the time and meter may be quite abstract or complicated, direct or simple. But also one in which each voice adds a unique perspective on the rhythm as a whole. Each musician of the quartet is playing in response to the others' circumlocution with respect to meter and time; that is, each responds both to their communal understanding of where the pulse is, how time is swinging in this instance, and also to how each member manages not to articulate it in a straightforward manner. The result is that the whole band swings in a new way, floating over the time and through the meter(s) without destroying either one. Comparing it to the second version of "Joy" recorded twenty days later reveals just how rare an achievement this performance was, even for a band of this caliber and long-standing collaboration. The wonderful metric ambiguity and tonal elisions of the first take are muted in the second version, which seems flat by comparison.

> What you term "the dislocated African's pursuit of a 'metavoice'" bears the weight of a Gnostic, transformative desire to be done with the world. By this I mean the deliberately forced, deliberately "false" voice we get from someone like Al Green creatively hallucinates a "new world," indicts the more insidious falseness of the world as we know it. . . . What is it in the falsetto that thins and threatens to abolish the voice but the wear of so much reaching for heaven? . . . Like the moan or the shout, I'm suggesting, the falsetto explores a redemptive, unworded realm—a meta-word, if you will—where the implied critique or the momentary eclipse of the word curiously rescues, restores and renews it: new word, new world.
>
> —N[28]

The opening statement of "Joy" has the intensity and improvisatory character of a solo but is in reality an opening gambit, setting up the piano solo. During the piano solo Jones begins to play time in a way that places the meter as common time, but still with an unusual amount of counter rhythms and an extremely fluid style, one idea flowing to the next almost as if the entire song were a drum solo. Garrison likewise completely resists the pull to play time or straight walking bass lines. While Jones is giving more hints of where the time and meter might lie, Garrison is dancing with ever more complicated

[28]Mackey, *Bedouin Hornbook*, pp. 62–63.

and free-floating rhythms and pedal points. When Coltrane reenters, he does so by continually reworking and repeating a high A, in the falsetto range of the horn. His playing of the note is so overtone-rich as to sound like chords and clusters. He repeats the note and other figures that also contain an abundance of partial tones, including honks and screams, so insistently that the sympathetic listener is easily carried away into the spirit realm. The sheer emotion of his playing has taken over melodic development per se, making Coltrane sound like a man possessed. The joy of the performance is palpable, as is the beauty of each member's contribution, which without exception is played with irrepressible, effervescent energy, signifying an exalted, transcendent state. But the shouts and screams at the extreme registers of the horn mark Coltrane's conception of joy as otherworldly. It is redolent of power and struggle, even as it is constructed as simple and unadorned. The band is "simply" playing a mode (B-flat major). There is no feeling of "oh, ok. One, two, three, four . . ." No feeling of having to filter what comes out in the service of cleverness or hipness, just unadulterated joy as only the John Coltrane quartet could create it.

In search of the Beloved Community . . .

This performance was recorded in September 1965, a time when the liberal consensus that made the Civil Rights Movement possible had begun to unravel. Just as African Americans were losing faith in the eventuality of King's Beloved Community, jazz musicians were questioning the suitability of European notions of timbre, harmony, and rhythm for their own creative expressions. Already Ornette Coleman had caught the ear and mind—if only to denounce him—of virtually every jazz musician. By 1965 Coleman's music had survived the initial skepticism of the music community, the major dissenters who were part of the old guard, already established aesthetically. However, some musicians who were already established as giants in the field, including Jackie McLean, Charles Mingus, and John Coltrane, were beginning to show their indebtedness to his approaches to music.[29] The radicalism of Ornette's harmolodics was no more unsettling to most established musicians than the increasingly internationalist, anticapitalist leanings of the young leaders in the black liberation struggle were to

[29]Mingus was very critical and even dismissive of Coleman's technique but allowed that he was musically interesting enough to make everyone else's music sound old. Consequently, Mingus made an album using some of the musical approaches that Coleman introduced, *Charles Mingus Presents Charles Mingus*. Coltrane went so far as to take lessons from Coleman, for which he paid $25 per session.

mainstream political organizers. Nineteen sixty-five was the year Malcolm X was assassinated, riots erupted in Watts, and Muhammad Ali knocked out Sonny Liston in less than a minute (his 1964 fight and subsequent announcement of his Nation of Islam affiliation were even more culturally significant). The new face of black leadership and the pace, strategies of political activism, and cultural styles were rapidly developing. The goal of meaningful integration proved to be more complicated than dismantling de jure segregation, and many blacks were listening more sympathetically to the nationalist black leaders. Malcolm X's assassination in February of that year came just as he was launching his political program, free from the political and ideological restrictions of his earlier association with Elijah Muhammad and the Nation of Islam. American political and social traditions were questioned among many young whites as well. The outrage of the Vietnam War informed the anti-imperialist ideologies of student activists and political organizers, a point of consensus between radical blacks and whites. And even though rock music and R&B had replaced jazz as the music of the young, there was a growing politicized audience for the new trends in jazz, which also crossed the color line. Just as in earlier decades when many whites found fuel for their social and cultural transgressions in bebop music, the New Thing (as the au courant jazz came to be called by some) was in part a music for the new-style hipsters of the day. So in addition to the political battles that were central to the times, a countercultural movement attracted many young people who were questioning American values and examining afresh the hypocrisies of our dominant culture. Building upon the Marxist tradition of jazz criticism (Finklestein, Baraka), music critic Frank Kofsky would soon make a famous attempt to link the new music to the Black Nationalist movement, equating the icons John Coltrane and Malcolm X.[30]

But the music made by the classic quartet still modeled an ethos more in line with King's ethic of love and social democracy than it did the separatist ideology of Elijah Muhammad, or the cries of Black Power by Stokely Carmichael or H. Rap Brown. The John Coltrane Quartet perfectly exemplified in music the yearning for egalitarian social arrangements in the body politic. In fact, this quartet forever changed the way that jazz quartets function within the tradition. Thanks to Elvin Jones, gone are the days when drummers are in the background providing time and an occasional bomb. Coltrane's quartet demonstrated how exciting the jazz quartet could be with the drums on an equal level of prominence and strength as the frontline

[30]Sidney Finkelstein, *Jazz: A People's Music*; Amiri Baraka, *Black Music*; LeRoi Jones, *Blues People: The Negro Experience in White America and the Music That Developed from It*; Baraka, "The 'Blues Aesthetic' and the 'Black Aesthetic': Aesthetics as the Continuing Political History of a Culture"; Amiri Baraka and Amina Baraka, *The Music: Reflections on Jazz and Blues*; Kofsky, *Black Nationalism*; and Kofsky, *John Coltrane*.

instrument, in this case the saxophone. The complexity and adventurous-
ness of Coltrane's saxophone lines were matched with the fierce intensity of
Jones's drumming. Without Elvin Jones and his contributions, Coltrane
would have no doubt developed quite differently. In fact, much of what we
think of as "sounding like Coltrane" is actually not even possible without the
type of accompaniment that Jones innovated. And though Jones's contributions are singular, absolutely no less important than those of the bandleader,
we can also truthfully add "and McCoy Tyner, and Jimmy Garrison" when
we are instructing people to "play like Trane." "Joy" is the perfect example of
this; the beauty of this performance lies in the way in which each member
approached the material. The material is being treated in a certain way; that
is, greater degrees of freedom as filtered through timbre, rhythm, melody,
and tonality are very much in evidence.[31]

The John Coltrane Quartet lived up to the ideals of the Civil Rights Movement in that there was a greater inclusion of the ideas, and the potential for
these ideas to shape the direction of the group's music, of all members. Previously, there was a clear hierarchy in jazz in which freer expression was allowed
for some members and others were relegated to supporting roles. The John
Coltrane Quartet eroded some of the prejudices that supported that orthodoxy.
But the overarching goals of mainstream jazz performance such as swinging,
blues articulation, harmonic sophistication, use of Afro-Latin rhythms, all
remained intact.[32] The quartet did perhaps open the door for its own dissolution, however. It extended the freedom within certain musical parameters so far
that the boundaries seemed to stretch to the point of making new formations.
Coltrane thought that he could have had a band that played "both ways."

> There was a thing I wanted to do in music see, and I figured I could do
> two things: I could have a band that played like the way we used to play,
> and a band that was going in the direction that the one I have now is
> going in—I could combine these two, with these two concepts going.
> And it could have been done.[33]

That is, his band could have continued to develop the ideas of the classic
quartet concerning "remaking the blues, the ballad, 4/4, and the Spanish
Tinge," as Stanley Crouch describes it, or it could play in the freer style of
his last band with Alice Coltrane, Jimmy Garrison, Rashied Ali, and
Pharoah Sanders. When Elvin Jones quit at the end of 1965 and McCoy

---

[31]See David G. Such, *Avant-Garde Jazz Musicians Performing "Out There,"* pp. 52–74; and Ekkehard
Jost, *Free Jazz*, pp. 17–34, 84–104.
[32]See Stanley Crouch, "Titan of the Blues: John Coltrane 1987," in his book *Considering Genius:
Writings on Jazz*, pp. 111–115.
[33]John Coltrane, quoted in Kofsky, *Black Nationalism*, p. 232.

Tyner shortly thereafter, that was the end of that particular vision. It did not, however, stop Coltrane from going on; perhaps it was simply true that he was headed in directions for which his new band suited his purposes best. Though it cost him his greatest musical partner and a pianist who was like a son, Coltrane might have chosen to proceed with the newer band in part because the classic quartet was well documented, and it had succeeded in its artistic goals.

Perhaps the perfection of the performance of "Joy" signaled the need to move on from the quartet format. Appropriately, it was one of the last recordings made by the band. There are several accounts of why the group changed personnel, but I am suggesting that the group had achieved in perfect balance so much of what they were after that to continue further would eventually necessitate a change in kind, and not merely a change in degree. When Coltrane recorded the *Meditations* suite again two months later, he added Rashied Ali on drums and Pharoah Sanders on saxophone. He also changed the order of the songs in the suite, deleted "Joy," and added "The Father and the Son and the Holy Ghost." This album, *Meditations*, was released in 1966, whereas the original recording of the Meditations suite was released posthumously more than a decade later. Clearly, Coltrane was not content to stay in any one place. He repeatedly claimed that he wanted to play something that had not been played before. The new version, which was released during his lifetime, was raw with power and vitality, and in it Coltrane furthered his departure from the diatonic system of tonal organization and many of the conventions associated with it. Sanders at the time, at least in the context of this band, was an energy player, who took the techniques of overblowing and the practice of bringing in the shrieks and screams for musical expression to fashion a style of saxophone playing that was apocalyptic and revolutionary.[34] Rashied Ali, for his part, also played with a looser, more rhythmically complex drumming style than even Elvin Jones. Whereas Jones was polyrhythmic and had been Coltrane's musical heartbeat, Ali was pan-rhythmic. Filling the drum chair after Elvin Jones would have been a daunting task for most drummers, but Ali was talented enough and brash enough to not let it bother him. Coltrane was certainly happy; his praise of Ali points not only to his greatness as a musician, but also the aptness of the fit between him and the band:

[34]Forty years later Pharoah Sanders is still capable of the most intense saxophone playing. He has, since his time with Coltrane, found his mature voice and has developed a much wider palette of musical sounds and techniques than were in evidence while with the Coltrane band. One contributing factor to this is the fact that Pharoah's role in that band was to provide Coltrane with energy and a catalyst toward further explorations.

The way he plays . . . allows the soloist maximum freedom. I can really choose just about any direction at just about any time in the confidence that it will be compatible with what he's doing. You see, he's laying down multi-directional rhythms all the time. To me, he's definitely one of the great drummers.[35]

As might be expected, Alice Coltrane also extended the direction of chordal accompaniment into freer realms along the lines already suggested by McCoy Tyner. Tyner fashioned a style that made heavy use of quartal chords, which were placed in such a way as to provide a rhythmic anchor for the group while providing great flexibility in the tonal palette. By building the chords on fourths rather than the usual interval of thirds, the tonality sounded more ambiguous and clashed less with the unorthodox scales and intervals played by Coltrane. Another virtue in this context was that the quartal chords did not carry the weight of centuries of tradition, leading the listener and player alike along well-worn paths to the same tonal resolutions. Tyner also made liberal use of "strolling," that is laying out altogether while the bass and drums (or sometimes just the drums) would accompany the saxophone. Alice Coltrane made her accompaniment even more ambiguous. That is, she abandoned her bebop praxis to a large degree (born Alice McLeod, she grew up in Detroit—then known as "bebop city"—and had studied with none other than Bud Powell) and played rolling tremolos that suggested modes and tonal colors. With her way of realizing harmonies, even the piano was finally freed from traditional timekeeping responsibilities that rhythm sections were accustomed to playing. Rather than play traditional, or even quartal, chords, she made use of the whole piano keyboard to realize her harmonies. Her approach was one that interacted with tonal areas and structural features of the form rather than the measure-by-measure, beat-by-beat articulation favored by the boppers.

Under Coltrane's leadership this band did not revel in the perfection of past achievements; it went full throttle toward the unknown with as much conviction and strength as possible. For many listeners, this music was the contemporaneous soundtrack of a time in which people were questioning the dominant practices and mores. Many were searching for alternatives to rampant materialism and had come to oppose American imperialist wars. At a time when pop music, especially rock, often gave voice to not only adolescent rebelliousness but political and social dissent as well, jazz was eclipsed as the most important art form for youth culture. The John Coltrane Quartet, however, was one of the few jazz bands that played with a visceral power and energy comparable to that of the electrified dissonance and distortion

[35]John Coltrane, quoted in Nat Hentoff, liner notes for *Coltrane "Live" at the Village Vanguard Again.*

that energized the language of rock culture. The dissent from bourgeois aesthetics that resided in the timbral qualities of the new rock was already an
established part of Coltrane's music when he first performed "Chasin' the
Trane" on the classic quartet's first recording, *Live at the Village Vanguard*, in
1961.[36] This aspect of his artistry was even more refined and powerful by the
end of the quartet's tenure. The richness of the soundscape is influenced in
part by the tradition of sound-making in African American music throughout the centuries, but also represents a new emphasis in straight-ahead jazz.
In this arena Coltrane's sound could be understood as new wine seeking new
bottles. That is, the forms and improvisations over them that had provided
sustenance for the jazz community were no longer aesthetically or emotionally wide enough to contain the content of the music that spoke to and for a
growing percentage of the younger players and their audiences.

Coltrane was intensely interested in the struggles of black people. He read
books about black culture and regularly paid attention to the ways in which
the civil rights struggle had captured the imagination of the nation. While
he resisted Frank Kofsky's heavy-handed attempt to depict the raison d'être
of his music as an instrument of social reform according to the principles of
revolutionary Black Nationalism, Coltrane was interested in the political developments of his day.[37] In the words of his stepdaughter, Syeeda (for whom
he wrote the famous "Syeeda's Song Flute"),[38] "he loved his people." On at
least one occasion he made a point of going to hear Malcolm X speak, and
he and his wife at that time, Naima, made sure that their daughter was
knowledgeable about black history. Coltrane's mysticism is often emphasized in such a way as to suggest that he was relatively unconcerned about
worldly matters, and the ecumenical spirit of his religious statements and
views may have also led commentators to deemphasize the degree to which
Coltrane was specifically imbricated in blackness, whether socially, politically, or culturally. But according to Syeeda, their family discussed politics
and social events at the dinner table far more often than they did religion.[39]

Many of the titles that Coltrane chose for his compositions reveal his interest in black culture and history: "Tanganyika Strut," "Dakar," "Reverend
King," "Alabama" (written in memorial for the four girls who died in a racially motivated Birmingham church bombing), "Dahomey Dance," and
"Liberia," for example. It is also true, however, that in his public utterances
Coltrane dedicated his music to the Creator. His expressed interest was in
uplifting people as much as he could through music, and by "people" he

---

[36]Coltrane's first recordings with Impulse were a big band recording, *Africa/Brass*, and *Live at the
Village Vanguard*.
[37]For Coltrane's interview with Kofsky, see Kofsky, *John Coltrane*, pp. 417–460.
[38]This composition was included in Coltrane's signature album, *Giant Steps*.
[39]Interview with Syeeda Andrews conducted by the author and Farah Jasmine Griffin, 2006.

meant all people, whoever could dig the music. In a situation in which one might have expected incendiary public remarks, such as when he and Eric Dolphy used the pages of *DownBeat* to answer the critics who were accusing them of annihilating jazz, we find Coltrane ever gracious and calm. His interests in public statements, at least, were geared toward inculcating greater understanding of what he was trying to do, and the primary focus of his music, at least from 1957 on, was spiritual.[40]

While Coltrane's public statements were more focused upon spiritual matters, many of his musical disciples freely supported the black liberation struggle through the titles of their compositions, musical techniques, civic associations, published writings, public debate, and the like. In addition, there was a cadre of black music critics and theorists of the Black Arts Movement who framed Coltrane's innovations as a call for cultural revolution. It was obvious, even to his detractors, that Coltrane's group had found a new way to present the music. Sympathetic listeners and musicians believed that the music provided a conduit to elevated consciousness, to a new way of being in the world. There were some players like Albert Ayler whose dedication to spirituality through music was as thoroughgoing as Coltrane's and whose political messages were mainly oblique. But many more prominent musicians who were influenced by him, including Archie Shepp, Gary Bartz, and Abbey Lincoln, used their art explicitly toward political ends. Following Coltrane's musical lead, these [mostly] younger musicians used the expanded tonal/rhythmic language that the "classic quartet" explored to help create a new black aesthetic in jazz, an aesthetic that boasted pronounced political and spiritual dimensions.

Through organizations such as the Black Artist Group in St. Louis, the Association for the Advancement of Creative Musicians in Chicago, Collective Black Artists in Brooklyn, the East also in Brooklyn, the Left Bank Society in Baltimore, the Union of God's Musicians and Artists Ascension in Los Angeles, musicians and fans began to promote the new music with a focus on developing black audiences and new artists. Throughout the 1960s and 1970s, legendary events like the October Revolution in Manhattan, the presentation of performances in musician-owned lofts such as Studio Rivbea, The Lady's Fort, and the release of recordings like the Wild Flowers sessions all contributed to the growing commitment to self-determination on the part of young black jazz musicians. They would pick up on the stylistic, spiritual, and political ramifications of Coltrane's life and music and carry it to the stage and beyond.

[40]For Coltrane's response to hostile criticism, see John Coltrane and Don DeMicheal, "Coltrane on Coltrane" and "John Coltrane and Eric Dolphy Answer the Jazz Critics." For Coltrane's dedication of his music, see his liner notes to *A Love Supreme*.

The entire trajectory of Coltrane's music's development pointed toward a relentless pursuit of truth, with the attendant strength and freedom that such a pursuit makes necessary. While "Joy" represented the apotheosis of the classic quartet's democratizing of the jazz quartet, the music continued to pursue new levels of expression. Though Jones and Tyner left the band and continued to have important and brilliant careers, they never explored new musical terrain as consistently and as rigorously as they did in the Coltrane group. With the addition of Sanders, Alice Coltrane, and Ali to the group, the music went further from diatonic melodies, equal temperament, functional harmonies, and simple duple or treble meter. The assault upon the diatonic system inherent in these explorations amounted to an interrogation of Euro-American concepts of beauty, melody, and narrative.

Younger players such as Albert Ayler and Milford Graves would start where he left off, as Coltrane would tell Kofsky. The next generation of free jazz players, those responsible for the aesthetic contours of the New Thing, did not necessarily come up through the bebop ranks the way Coltrane did. Ayler was apparently nicknamed "Little Bird" in his early days in Cleveland, but there is no evidence of Bird in his recording output, nor does he have a significant apprenticeship with any bebopper. Similarly, the struggle for black liberation also began to take on new forms. After King's assassination, the nation erupted in scores of rebellion, marking a clear end to the optimism of the Civil Rights Movement and to widespread faith in the fairness and goodwill of white institutions, including the federal government. Sadly, Coltrane died before 1968, but his music prefigured the political expression of this sentiment. It is especially discernible in his larger groups. Also, 1965 would be the year of Coltrane's most radical and most dissonant recording, *Ascension*.[41] The band that recorded the classic is also one of the largest that Coltrane led. In a way, this recording would also open the door for a new feeling in the music and a new way to organize sound. No longer would Coltrane attack from within, so to speak. That is, he would not make diatonicism his primary approach to melodic/harmonic development, as he did before he convened his classic quartet. In 1957, with original compositions such as "Moment's Notice" and "Lazy Bird," Coltrane worked with conventional harmonies set in unconventional ways. By 1959, in songs like "Giant Steps" and "Countdown," he introduced his unique harmonic formulas, which were based on the diatonic system but divided the octave in three equidistant tonalities, and at times Coltrane superimposed the three derived tonics over one.[42] While there are tonal considerations in the *Ascension*

---

[41]John Coltrane, *Ascension*.
[42] "Moment's Notice" and "Lazy Bird" can be heard on John Coltrane, *Blue Train*. "Giant Steps" and "Countdown" can be heard on *Giant Steps*.

recording made with the quartet augmented by several of the most dynamic young players on the New York scene (which, significantly, some of the soloists chose not to reference in their solos), the music certainly did not adhere to functional harmony in spirit or form. Rather, freedom was sought from the strictures of old forms and ways of thinking. And like the contemporaneous rebellions taking place in America's cities, the music was visceral, and at times violent, in its soundscape.[43] Furthermore, like the mid-twentieth-century black freedom struggle, which started with lobbying for legislation, establishing legal precedents for court battles, and engaging in civil disobedience before adopting the more militant strategies of the Black Power movement, Coltrane's departure from the strictures of functional tonality occurred after exhausting the routes available to him from the hyper diatonic practices of his bebop forebears. Whether one is sympathetic to the Baraka school of jazz criticism (jazz is a repository of the attitudes and history of African Americans) or the Ralph Ellison school (jazz reflects Negro attitude, but is above all a formal art with aesthetic criteria that are universal rather than socially derived) there seems to be a connection between Coltrane's attempts to find a new way to play music in his late phase and what might be seen as the social experiments of the black freedom struggle of the 1960s.

A love supreme . . .

Whatever we may surmise about the relationship between Coltrane's music and the social upheavals of his time (he does, for example, acknowledge that his music was against war in general when Kofsky asked about the Vietnam War), we have his explicit testimony to the centrality of his devotion to the Creator. Perhaps the most famous and most candid instance of this is in his liner notes for his most popular recording, *A Love Supreme*. Coltrane placed special emphasis on this recording. For the first time in his career he took an interest in the packaging of his record. He selected the photograph used for the cover, printed the religious poem that corresponded to "Psalm," the final movement of the suite, and even included a letter to the listener in which he explained how he had dedicated his life and music to the Creator.

According to his friend and fellow saxophonist Yusef Lateef, Coltrane was deeply interested in books on religious and astrological matters. He was

[43]For a discussion that contrasts the relative civility of Ornette Coleman's large band manifesto *Free Jazz* to Coltrane's putatively anarchic *Ascension* recording, see Charles Benjamin Hersch, "Liberating Forms: Politics and the Arts from the New York
Intellectuals to the Counterculture," PhD diss., University of California, Berkeley, 1987.

especially interested in Sufi mysticism. Toward the end of his life Coltrane took to traveling with various sacred texts and math books. One particular Sufi text that he read was *The Music of Life* by Hazrat Inayat Khan.[44] A point of reference that reveals Khan's influence is found in Coltrane's titles for yet another suite recorded in 1965 for the album *Transition*.[45] The movements for the suite are titled: Part 1, Prayer and Meditation: Day; Part 2, Peace and After; Part 3, Prayer and Meditation: Evening; Part 4, Affirmation; and Part 5, Prayer and Meditation: 4 a.m. Khan writes: "Every hour of the day and night, every day, week, month and season has its influence upon man's physical and mental condition. In the same way each raga has power upon the atmosphere as well as upon the health and mind of man."[46] Coltrane's resonance with Khan's ideas goes further than merely adopting specific practices and included the acceptance of certain philosophic ideas about music. For instance when asked to give advice on how to improve as a musician, Coltrane urged musicians to improve themselves as persons to bring them closer to their musical goals. Similarly, Khan advises, "The effect of music depends not only on the proficiency but also upon the evolution of the performer"[47]

Space is the place . . .

It is this second type of lateness as a factor of style that I find deeply interesting. I'd like to explore the experience of late style that involves a nonharmonious, nonserene tension, and above all, a sort of deliberately unproductive productiveness going against.

—Edward Said

Ultimately, our understanding of Coltrane's late art has to rest firmly upon his music and the unfolding of his artistic vision. It is always tempting to see developments in hindsight as inevitable, and Coltrane's music presents no exception. There are turning points accompanied by signposts—leaving Miles Davis's band in 1960, never to be a sideman again, the settling on players for his classic quartet, the dissolution of this quartet—that signal large shifts in Coltrane's music and the kind of recordings that he made.

[44]Hazrat Inayat Khan, *The Music of Life*.
[45]John Coltrane, *Transition*.
[46]Khan, *The Music of Life*, p. 53.
[47]Khan, *The Music of Life*, p. 52.

We are reminded that the material conditions of his life were as important as the cultural and political considerations that have been the subject of this essay. One context that deserves consideration is the brevity of Coltrane's life. Often people speculate about Coltrane's legendary and unique obsession with practicing. One biographer posits that his practicing and his penchant for sweets (which, along with his heroin addiction, led to dental problems) are evidence of an oral fixation. I do not see the need to pathologize Coltrane's legendary practice discipline, especially since his unparalleled virtuosity contributed so mightily to his artistry.

Even so, he practiced as though he knew he didn't have much time. The most significant part of his career was indeed the last ten years of his life, during which his artistic development was steady and accelerated. His death from liver cancer seemed sudden, occurring shortly after he finally checked into the hospital. But there are pictures of him holding his stomach while on tour in Japan shortly before, as though he was in pain. Perhaps Coltrane did in fact know that his time on earth was limited. If so, Edward Said's insights into what he calls "late style" may be instructive.

In *On Late Style: Music and Literature against the Grain*, Said defines two types of lateness in the stylistic development of artists.[48] He contrasts the late works of great artists such as Rembrandt, Matisse, Bach, and Wagner as works that "crown a lifetime of aesthetic endeavor," with those of Ibsen, and we can add Coltrane here, whose late works are understood not as "harmony and resolution but as intransigence, difficulty, and unresolved contradiction"[49] In 1965 John Coltrane was a man at the absolute top of his profession. His group was the most popular in jazz, he was voted Jazzman of the Year by *DownBeat* and inducted into its Jazz Hall of Fame, and his newly released *A Love Supreme* was (as it continues to be) a bestseller. This was surely a vindication of his aesthetic and his principles, as a few years earlier he was a controversial figure within the jazz industry, being accused of incompetence and worse. But with the dissolution of the quartet he neither rested on previous laurels nor tried to re-create his band. If anything, his music became more challenging, more strident and dissonant, and less beholden to the conventions of jazz, even those that he had helped to create. I am not suggesting that Coltrane abandoned jazz. Rather, that he continued to be a pioneer and an innovator, and seemed less concerned than ever about making his music easily understood and marketable. His solos became longer, so much so that his performances for the most part no longer fit the format designed for jazz clubs. His music was a sacred happening that transformed his audiences and performance spaces into a sanctuary, not with congratulatory rituals or other

[48]Edward Said, *On Late Style: Music and Literature against the Grain*.
[49]Said, *On Late Style*, p. 7.

devices of comfort, but with the perpetual unfolding of new dimensions of his musical search.

His music, especially from 1965 until his premature death in 1967, seems a textbook example of Said's notion of late artistry in that it was a music of exile. That is, after firmly establishing himself as the leading jazz musician of his time, Coltrane took a turn away from the comfort zone of most critics and listeners. His was the music that future generations of musicians would follow and emulate. With recordings such as *Interstellar Space*, Coltrane was able to play more freely than ever before, dipping into his unconscious and streaming consciousness to produce works that were at once primal and un-settling as well as intricate and dense. Said makes a metaphor positing that such late art (late either because of the age or failing health of the artist) in-creases the space to compensate for the relative lack of time. This increased "spaciness" seems to declare emphatically that an overriding synthesis of the artist's achievements is not possible. Instead, Coltrane presented an artist whose commitment to seeking (an unattainable) truth was unflagging in sickness or in health, in season or out of season.

Quite simply, as hard as it may be to imagine what more he could have contributed, Coltrane died never feeling that he had attained what he was after. His last recordings would give hints as to what might have happened. Whether because of decreased stamina or more concise thinking, the songs in Coltrane's last studio recording, *Stellar Regions*, are much shorter than usual not only for Trane but for jazz cuts in general. He also seems to be distilling aspects of his music to their basic elemental forms, using trills and chromatic sequences and the like to construct his melodies. The strength and energy in his solos mitigate against interpreting this as a fail-ure of will or as results of the infirmities of the flesh. Likewise, his undis-guised lyricism and the simplicity in his thematic material are not renunciations of his aesthetic, but were integral parts of his music right to the end. What is more beautiful than, say, "Peace On Earth," recorded on his *Live in Japan*? Coltrane's late style was a culminating moment only in the sense that he was creative and courageous enough to continue rein-venting his musical creations to more closely render the beauty of God's natural creation. Sickness and even death did not allow the devil to steal Coltrane's Joy.

Works Cited

Agawu, Kofi. *Representing African Music: Postcolonial Notes, Queries, Positions*. New York: Routledge, 2003.

Andrews, Syeeda. Interview conducted by Farah Jasmine Griffin and Salim Washington, August 13, 2004.

Baraka, Amiri. *Black Music*. New York: Morrow, 1967.

———."The 'Blues Aesthetic' and the 'Black Aesthetic': Aesthetics as the Continuing Political History of a Culture." *Black Music Research Journal* 2, 2 (Fall 1991).

Baraka, Amiri, and Amina Baraka. *The Music: Reflections on Jazz and Blues*. New York: W.W. Morrow, 1987.

Bebey, Francis. *African Music: A People's Art*. New York: Lawrence Hill Books, 1975.

Coltrane, John. *Blue Train*, BN BLP1577, 1957.

———.*Giant Steps*, Atlantic 1311, 1959.

———.*Crescent*, Impulse MCA5889.

———.*A Love Supreme*, Impulse MCD 01648-DMCL1648.

———.*Transition*, Impulse AS9195.

———.*First Meditations* (for quartet), Impulse GRD118.

———.*Meditations*, Impulse MCAD39139.

———.*Ascension*, Imp A95 and AS95 (Ed. II), 1965, released on CD together as complete Ascension, Imp (J) MVCI 23016.

Coltrane, John, and Don DeMicheal, "Coltrane on Coltrane." *DownBeat*, September 29, 1960.

———."John Coltrane and Eric Dolphy Answer the Jazz Critics." *DownBeat*, April 12, 1962.

Crouch, Stanley. "Titan of the Blues: John Coltrane 1987." In Crouch, *Considering Genius: Writings on Jazz*. New York: Basic Civitas Books, 2006.

Daniels, Douglass Henry. *Lester Leaps In: The Life and Times of Lester "Pres" Young*. Boston: Beacon Press, 2002.

Finkelstein, Sidney. *Jazz: A People's Music*. New York: International Publishers, 1988; New York: Citadel Press, 1948.

Grey, De Sayles. *Acknowledgment: A John Coltrane Legacy*. McLean, Va.: IndyPublish, 2001.

Griffin, Farah Jasmine, and Salim Washington. *Clawing at the Limits of Cool: Miles Davis, John Coltrane, and the Greatest Jazz Collaboration Ever*. New York: St.Martin's Press, 2008.

Hentoff, Nat. Liner Notes for Coltrane, *"Live" at the Village Vanguard Again*. Impulse Records, AS-9124, 1966.

Hersch, Charles Benjamin. "Liberating Forms: Politics and the Arts from the New York Intellectuals to the Counterculture," PhD diss., University of California, Berkeley, 1987.

Higginbotham, Evelyn Brooks. *Righteous Discontent: The Women's Movement in the Black Baptist Church, 1880–1920*. Cambridge, Mass.: Harvard University Press, 1993.

Johnson, Aaron. "The University of Jazz." Unpublished paper.

Jones, LeRoi. *Blues People: The Negro Experience in White America and the Music That Developed from It*. New York: Quill, 1963.

Jost, Ekkehard. *Free Jazz*. New York: Da Capo, 1994.

Khan, Hazrat Inayat. *The Music of Life*. Santa Fe: Omega Press, 1983.

Kofsky, Frank. *Black Nationalism and the Revolution in Music*. New York: Pathfinder, 1970.

———. *John Coltrane and the Jazz Revolution of the 1960s*. New York: Pathfinder, 1998.

Leland, Elizabeth. *The Vanishing Coast*. Winston-Salem: John F. Blair, 1992.

Levine, Lawrence. *Black Culture and Black Consciousness: Afro-American Folk Thought from Slavery to Freedom*. New York: Oxford University Press, 1977.

Mackey, Nathaniel. *Bedouin Hornbook*. Los Angeles: Sun and Moon Press, 1997.

Mingus, Charles. *Charles Mingus Presents Charles Mingus*. Candid, 1960.

Murray, Albert. *Stomping the Blues*. New York: Da Capo, 1976.

Porter, Lewis. *John Coltrane: His Life and Music*. Ann Arbor: University of Michigan Press, 1998.

Ramsey, Guthrie P. "Jazz and the Church." Paper presented to the Jazz Study Group at Columbia University, March 3, 2007.

Said, Edward, *On Late Style: Music and Literature against the Grain*. New York: Pantheon, 2006.

Shepherd, John. *Music as Social Text*. Cambridge, Mass. Polity Press, 1991.

Snead, James A. "Repetition as a Figure of Black Culture." In Robert G. O'Meally, *The Jazz Cadence of American Culture*, pp. 62–81. New York: Columbia University Press, 1998.

Such, David G. *Avant-Garde Jazz Musicians Performing "Out There."* Iowa City: Iowa University Press, 1993.

Tegnell, David. "Hamlet: John Coltrane's Origins." *Jazz Perspectives* 2, 2 (2007).

Wilson, Olly. "Black Music as an Art Form." In Robert G. O'Meally, *The Jazz Cadence of American Culture*, pp. 82–101. New York: Columbia University Press, 1998.

The Spiritual Ethos in Black Music and Its Quintessential Exemplar, John Coltrane

EMMETT G. PRICE III

One ever feels his twoness,—an American, a Negro; two souls, two thoughts, two unreconciled strivings; two warring ideals in one dark body, whose dogged strength alone keeps it from being torn asunder.

—W. E. B. Du Bois, *The Souls of Black Folk*

The power of song in the struggle for black survival—that is what the spirituals and blues are about.

—James H. Cone, *The Spirituals and the Blues*

Theorizing about the role of spirituality within black music has never been easy. Many have approached the subject by analyzing the body of songs known as "spirituals"; others have conceptualized the role of religion in African American culture via black music, and still others have focused on the implicit continuum of African cosmology found within the music of the African Diaspora.[1] Part of the difficulty inherent in the topic is that in dealing

---

[1]Numerous works model various approaches to theorizing about the role of spirituality in Black music. A few examples include: James H. Cone, *The Spirituals and the Blues: An Interpretation* (Maryknoll, N.Y.: Orbis Books, 1997 [1972]); Samuel A. Floyd Jr., *The Power of Black Music: Interpreting Its History from Africa to the United States* (New York: Oxford University Press, 1995); Mark Anthony Neal, *What the Music Said: Black Popular Music and Black Popular Culture* (New York: Routledge, 1998); Guthrie P. Ramsey Jr., *Race Music: Black Culture from Bebop to Hip-Hop* (Berkeley: University of California Press, 2003); John Storm Roberts, *Black Music of Two Worlds: African, Caribbean, Latin, and African American Traditions* (New York: Schirmer Books, 1998); Teresa L. Reed, *The Holy Profane: Religion in Black Popular Music* (Lexington: University Press of Kentucky, 2003); and Eileen Southern, *The Music of Black Americans: A History*, 3rd ed. (New York: W. W. Norton, 1997 [1971]).

with spirituality, volatile questions must be exposed and penetrated. Questions such as the following deserve attention: Is the practice of spirituality a religious or nonreligious endeavor? Which higher power among the pantheon of supreme deities offers a baseline through which to approach universal spirituality? What terms, metaphors, and/or system(s) of communication might one use to present universals while retaining the integrity of the search? And how do we speak of the manifestation or presence of spirituality within the confines and limitations of the human experience? These and other self-reflective questions stand as the doorway to a renewed understanding of the role of spirituality within black music, not only within the continental United States but across the entire African Diaspora. Although these questions assist in grounding the context of our inquiry, this writing does not aim to directly approach all (if any) of these questions. This essay will examine the presence and importance of the spiritual ethos in black music, its manifestation in the music of John Coltrane, Thomas A. Dorsey, and Tupac Shakur, and will argue that John Coltrane is the quintessential exemplar of its use in Black America's quest for freedom.[2]

The spiritual ethos is the fundamental character of black music that unifies the various expressions and dimensions of the black experience, connecting the old to the new, the urban to the rural, the traditional to the contemporary, the classical to the popular, all while maintaining the integrity of artistic expression. The spiritual ethos in black music serves as the central fulcrum of the associative black experience by uniting the various social, political, economic, cultural, and religious realities into one essence—the distinctive spirit of the music. To fully appreciate the spiritual ethos we must analyze its impact in a practical manner allowing it to serve as the glue that connects all of the other components of musical expression. The spiritual ethos allows for the cultural context and sociopolitical content of the music to be as important as the performance practice and musicianship of the artist. Music is an expression of the heart and mind; thus our analysis of music should account for the passion and intellect of the artist. The spiritual ethos allows for this integrative mode of analysis.

In 1903, W. E. B. Du Bois published his most noted work, *The Souls of Black Folk*, which prophetically proposed that the greatest problem of the twentieth century would be that of the color line.[3] Du Bois's words not only remain true in the early twenty-first century but ring out with as much force, power and clarity now, as they did then. In this monumental manuscript, Du Bois offers his concept of double consciousness, a mode of survival within the war of identity for the Negro.[4] In his articulation of double

---

[2]For the rest of this essay, all references to Black music will refer to African American music.
[3]W. E. B. Du Bois. *The Souls of Black Folk* (New York, N.Y.: Bantam Books, 1989 [1903]), 3.
[4]Du Bois, *Souls of Black Folk*, 3.

consciousness, it is evident that spirituality and music were (and remain) important tools in Black America's quest for freedom. Not only does Du Bois cleverly title the opening chapter of his book "Of Our Spiritual Strivings," but the title of the book itself, *The Souls of Black Folk,* allows a very poignant glimpse into the level of spiritual inquiry which Du Bois accomplishes in the entire text. Du Bois is clearly interested in the conception and future of black spirituality as manifested through the souls of black folks. The epigraph that opens my essay offers Du Bois's articulation of the rather precarious situation of systematic oppression that black people (at the time of his writing and now) struggle with. It is this double consciousness or internal struggle that forces black musicians to reconcile whether she or he is a musician who is black or a black musician? Similarly, does a musician who is black make music or make black music? Du Bois might suggest these as warring ideas, and perhaps they are, but what is certain is that black music conveys, reveals, and channels the experiences of black people in all of our rich diversity through song. Black music tells multiple stories in a multiplicity of voices through a multitude of perspectives; all connected through what I argue is the spiritual ethos.

In James H. Cone's widely influential book *The Spirituals and the Blues,* the prolific theological scholar and champion of Black Liberation Theology offers a salvific epilogue to Du Bois's statement.[5] Cone proposes that black music contains the tools through which the battle for survival can be fought and won. His clarity in articulating the power of song or the power of music allows for a clearer understanding of the manifestation of the internal struggle of consciousness referenced by Du Bois to occur through music. In this assertion, music becomes not only the potent tool for working through the internal struggles of consciousness, but also the prime battlefield where the struggle occurs. In many ways, it is the presence of spiritual influences or spirituality within the music as expressed through the musicians who create and perform music that should serve as a major focus of exploration for the scholar. Further, one might consider the proposition that it is the spiritual ethos in the music, observed in the spirituals, blues, and other forms of black music, which allows for the possibility of the transition from survival to liberation. Cone, like Du Bois, argues the importance of not only the presence of music, but the ability to understand its role and function in the diachronic experiences of black people. They position spirituality as a key factor in the strength and power of black music.

Both Du Bois and Cone challenge scholars and listeners to delve beyond the sounds of black music into the depths of the experiences that created

---

[5]Cone, *The Spirituals and the Blues,* 1.

the need for the expression or that provided the opportunity for musical exploration. Both clearly understand and acknowledge the social constructs through which the music penetrated. Both offer their individual analyses of the oppressive use of political, social, and economic power against blacks while also proudly amplifying Black America's definitive proclamation that we are survivors, as articulated in the songs, dances, and expressions of thousands of black artists, entertainers, and, especially, musicians over the centuries.

From the early utterances of transplanted Africans, through the evolution of the spirituals and blues onto the development of jazz, gospel, rhythm & blues, soul, funk, and on beyond the late-twentieth-century innovation of hip-hop, spirituality has been an integral and dominant force within the music and the lives of the musicians who create and express it. Previous attempts to articulate the presence of spirituality in black music of the United States have created a superficial polemic between what is sacred (often misunderstood as spiritual) and what is secular (often posed as nonspiritual). This polemic has been widely accepted by scholars, music lovers, and musicians.[6] In the early development of black music, the distinction between the spirituals and blues was often drawn as one of intent. The spirituals were perceived of as examining or professing Christian religious tenets and containing the spiritual ethos of black music, whereas the blues were thought to derive from a more human aesthetic, voicing human frailty, struggle, and hope in a nonreligious and nonspiritual manner. This polemic is far from the reality, as both yearn for the realized possibility of liberation. Both the spirituals and the blues are practical commentaries on life's bittersweet existence for blacks from their first presence within what is now called the United States of America through the present day. Both the spirituals and the blues are simultaneously communal and individual expressions of the persevering strength, fortitudinous courage, and steadfast determination to achieve freedom in some way, shape, or form. Both the spirituals and the blues rely on a culturally based understanding of divine intervention and the probability and power of such intervention. According to Eileen Southern's *The Music of Black Americans,*

---

[6]There are numerous examples of this dynamic. Among them are James Weldon Johnson, "From Preface to the Books of American Negro Spirituals (1925)," as reprinted in *Signifyin(g), Sanctifyin', and Slam Dunking: A Reader in African American Expressive Culture*, ed. Gena Dagel Caponi (Amherst: University of Massachusetts Press, 1999); Portia K. Maultsby, "The Impact of Gospel Music on the Secular Music Industry (1992)," as reprinted in *Signifyin(g), Sanctifyin', and Slam Dunking: A Reader in African American Expressive Culture*, ed. Gena Dagel Caponi (Amherst: University of Massachusetts Press, 1999); Reed, *The Holy Profane*; and Ramsey, *Race Music*.

The dividing line between the blues and some kinds of spirituals cannot always be sharply drawn.... Many spirituals convey to listeners the same feeling of rootlessness and misery as do the blues. The spiritual is religious, however, rather than worldly and tends to be more generalized in its expression than specific, more figurative in its language than direct, and more expressive of group feelings than individual ones. Despite these differences it is nevertheless often difficult to distinguish between the two kinds of songs. Some songs have such vague implications that scholars classify them as "blues-spirituals."[7]

In *The Power of Black Music: Interpreting Its History from Africa to the United States*, Samuel A. Floyd Jr. writes,

Traditionally, the spirituals have been viewed as songs of conventional religious faith, but they are much more than that. In spite of their biblical references, the essence of these songs goes far beyond narrow and conventional religious boundaries. The spirituals are also folk songs of freedom and of faith in the inevitability of freedom. They are quasi-religious songs of longing and aspiration as well as chronicles of the black slave experience in America—documents of impeccable truth and reliability—for they record the transition of the slave from African to African American, from slave to freedman, and the experiences that the African underwent in the transition.[8]

The presupposed sibling rivalry between the spirituals and the blues has been subtly challenged through slight alterations in terminology used by scholars over the years. From Southern's "blues-spirituals" to Michael Harris's "gospel blues" and the "sanctifying blues" in Guthrie Ramsey's *Race Music: Black Cultures from Bebop to Hip-Hop*, new vocabulary has evolved which speaks to the symbiotic connection of the two previously polarized terms.[9] Bracketing the supposed dichotomy allows an analysis in which the spirituals and blues are not opposing forces but different manifestations of the same experience. The blues, which in some cases could outwardly appear vile, profane, and perhaps even carnal, overwhelmingly rely on a spiritual ethos. The spiritual ethos in the blues offers the notion that even within the most nonsacred or nonreligious settings or situations, the presence of God or a greater life source still exists. Furthermore, the blues in many ways

---

[7]Southern, *The Music of Black Americans*, 331.
[8]Floyd, *The Power of Black Music*, 40.
[9]Southern, *The Music of Black Americans*, 331; Michael W. Harris. *The Rise of Gospel Blues: The Music of Thomas Andrew Dorsey in the Urban Church* (New York: Oxford University Press, 1992); and Ramsey, *Race Music*, 202.

exemplifies that the manifestation of spirituality is a unique experiential relationship with God or at least acknowledgment of a greater life source that is often initiated at the lowest or bluest moment in one's life. Spiritually exists, and it matters in all black music.

Twentieth-century mystic Hazrat Inayat Khan, founder of universal Sufism and the Sufi Order International, once wrote, in a document titled "Spiritual Attainment by the Aid of Music,"

> To attain spirituality is to realize that the whole universe is one symphony in which every individual is one note. His happiness lies in becoming perfectly harmonious with the symphony of the universe. It is not following a certain religion that makes one spiritual, or having a certain belief, or being a fanatic in regard to one idea, or by becoming too good to live in this world. Many good people there are, who do not even understand what spirituality means. They are very good, but they do not yet know what ultimate good is. Ultimate good is harmony itself. For instance, all the different principles and beliefs of the religions of this world taught and proclaimed by priests and teachers—but which men are not always able to follow and express—come naturally from the heart of a man who attunes himself to the rhythm of the universe. His every action, every word he speaks, every feeling he has, every sentiment he expresses, is all harmonious; it is all virtue, it is all religion. It is not following a religion, it is living a religion, making one's life a religion, which is necessary.[10]

Khan's notion of harmony offers insight into the presence of spirituality as an underlying notion within religion. This designation is worth distinguishing. Different from religion, spirituality is an individual and unique journey that is not systematic or formulaic but is based on a desire for harmony: harmony with self, harmony with society, and harmony with the cosmic universe. Religion is based on the assumed presence of spirituality, but also offers an institutional framework that grounds beliefs and systematizes worship. Religion articulates the collective process of individual spiritual quests in tangible ways while simultaneously attempting to make sense of the unknown. Religion offers language, liturgy, polity, historical context, an organized system of accountability and a philosophical or theological construct through which people can collectively engage in the individual spiritual quest. In most religious systems, the success of a religion is measured by its success in effecting or aiding spiritual transformation. Yet it is important to note that spiritual transformation is not accomplished only within the

---

[10]The Sufi Message of Hazrat Inayat Khan, "Spiritual Attainment by the Aid of Music," http://www.sufimessage.com/music/spiritual-attainment-by-aid-of-music.html

confines of religious systems. In fact, many argue that spiritual transformation can occur only when one is freed from the strictures of religion. Regardless of context, the ultimate goal of both spirituality and religion is transformation.

A person embarks on a spiritual journey because of a desire to change or enhance a certain aspect of his or her personal life. In Khan's teachings, this journey would be geared toward the pursuit of harmony, with transformation as its goal. Transformation recognizes the move toward more intimate closeness. As the relationship is groomed through whatever rituals or traditions are explored (religion), one realizes hope, love, compassion and a whole host of other emotions that are transferable only once they have been experienced. Thus, the more one experiences (receives), the more one is able to share (transmit), and the more one is transformed. The spiritual ethos allows one to tap into the fundamental character or nature of the believed Supreme Being or deity and embody the manifest connection in personal behavior and attributes. As an example, the closer a Christian is to the Triune God, the more hope, love, and compassion the Christian will experience, and in turn the more hope, love, and compassion, she or he will give—a process of spiritual transformation. In the same vein, the musician uses music as a tool of transformation. The musician creates music that will speak to those willing to listen in such a way that the listener, along with the musician, will be transformed.

Among the pantheon of great innovators and performers of black music praised for their ability to allow their spiritual quest to inform their musical creation (i.e., Robert Johnson, Sister Rosetta Tharpe, Duke Ellington, Mary Lou Williams, Marvin Gaye, Aretha Franklin, Sam Cooke, Nina Simone, Stevie Wonder, Tina Turner, KRS-One, Queen Latifah, and a host of others), John William Coltrane rises among the fold as the most influential of all the generations. His selfless ability to stand as a prophetic voice in black music and his ability to reach folks both within and outside of religious faiths exemplifies the embodiment of the spiritual ethos. Coltrane is the crucial, pivotal innovator who challenged all to hear his music as the urgent, functional expression of heartfelt truth, painful honesty, and vulnerable communication. Simply stated, Coltrane fully acknowledged the spiritual ethos in his music, and he was not limited in its use.

In the realm of black music, John Coltrane stands boldly and authoritatively as a twentieth-century prophet whose expressions gave meaning, whose communication provided direction and whose sound rang forth as an antidote to a prolonged mid-twentieth-century period of chaos and turmoil for blacks in the United States and beyond. Plagued by an amalgam of social, political, economic, cultural, and religious (some might also add spiritual) warfare, blacks and others were in need of a complement to the often polarized political and civic engagement of the times. Coltrane's prophetic sound did more for those who listened to it and heard it than perhaps some of the greatest speeches, sermons, and debates of the day. Even those who were not exposed or did not choose to hear or listen at the time were broadly influenced by Coltrane's quick rise as an iconic figure around the global. It is imperative to approach his music as the culmination of a number of life events and occurrences that dramatically shaped his decisions, desires, and perspectives on life.

Coltrane's spiritual journey has been chronicled and analyzed by many.[11] From his childhood as the grandson of two African Methodist Episcopal Zion preachers through his struggles with self-exploration during the '50 and '60, to his 1964 magnum opus (A Love Supreme) announcing his own conceptual approach to spirituality, Coltrane's journey is well documented. His two spiritual awakenings, occurring in 1957 and 1964, greatly inspired him to realize the importance of the spiritual ethos and led him to define much of his playing as prayer.[12] His determination to be a positive role model for other people (musicians and nonmusicians alike) reveals a strong commitment to be a force for good, a force to help spark transformation.[13] I argue that without attention paid to this spiritual journey and its manifestation as spiritual ethos within his music, the recognition of the power of Coltrane's expression is diminished. Like many other artists who are never fully understood, appreciated, and perhaps never really heard, Coltrane's sound must be heard through the prism of his life experience, and a large part of that experience is his long and contemplative spiritual journey.

Coltrane's sound is girded in the struggle of Black America. His sound was informed by the dark and dim social context faced by black folks during the period. Coltrane witnessed, firsthand, the unjust political contexts where the abuse of governmental power was met with factional approaches to self-determination, Black Nationalism, and the black struggle for equality and justice. Coltrane experienced, firsthand, the dreary economic inequalities that existed for the majority of black folks.

---

[11]See J. C. Thomas's Coltrane: Chasin' the Trane (New York: Da Capo, 1975); John Fraim's Spirit Catcher: The Life and Art of John Coltrane (West Liberty, Ohio: GreatHouse, 1996); Eric Nisenson's Ascension: John Coltrane and His Quest (New York: Da Capo, 1995); Bill Cole's John Coltrane (New York: Da Capo, 1993); Carl Woideck's The John Coltrane Companion: Five Decades of Commentary (New York: Schirmer Books, 1998); Lewis Porter's John Coltrane: His Life and Music (Ann Arbor: University of Michigan Press, 1998); C. O. Simpkins's Coltrane: A Biography (Baltimore: Black Classic Press, 1989); and Emmett G. Price III's "John Coltrane, 'A Love Supreme' and God," available online at http://www.allaboutjazz.com/coltrane/article_003.htm.

[12]Simpkins, Coltrane: A Biography, 57–58, 69; 178–180.

[13]Frank Kofsky, John Coltrane and the Jazz Revolution of the 1960s (New York: Pathfinder Press, 1998). This book is an expanded and revised second edition of Black Nationalism and the Revolution in Music (New York: Pathfinder Press, 1970).

In fact, as an artist he eventually rebelled against the perception that his voice was relevant only if it could sell records. Coltrane was well aware of the cultural wars defined by racism, classism, sexism, and other human expressions of fear, ignorance, and pain. He understood the divisiveness of organized religions. As a revolutionary twentieth-century griot, Coltrane spoke specifically to these situations within a framework that many did not understand, comprehend, or hear. Through his sound, Coltrane depicted an alternative to hatred, pain, evil, and chaos by speaking love, compassion, peace, and healing. His sound was one of unity and reconciliation, a sound that spoke of survival, hope, and liberation.

Unlike many of his predecessors, Coltrane had the unique ability to expand his sound into something that was beyond music. In fact, Coltrane accomplishes three major feats through his sound. First, he used his concept of spirituality to unify social, political, economic, cultural, and religious expression. Coltrane immersed himself in the study of music (including musical systems from India, West Africa, and the indigenous people of the United States) and religions (Christianity, Islam, Hinduism, Judaic mysticism via the Kabbalah as well as the writings and teachings of Jiddu Krishnamurti) as well as such diverse subjects as yoga, math, science, astrology, African history, and philosophy.[14] Coltrane's study was a pursuit with the aim of understanding the unifying nature of the human experience through spirituality. The common denominator of the human experience is spiritual. All humans interact in a social setting under the direct inclination of political and economic influence, within the realm of a cultural context, all under the notion of beliefs, morals, values, and a systematic approach to the acknowledgment of a supreme being (or no being, but still in a systematic manner). To Coltrane, his music was his response to the world. His music was the expression of what he held as most pure, most true, most authentic, most him. In his words, "My music is the spiritual expression of what I am—my faith, my knowledge, my being."[15]

Second, Coltrane used his sound to speak to various constituencies with no discrimination. Through his spirituality, Coltrane was able to reach people of various faiths and beliefs without compromising his mission. Coltrane spoke to the core of humanity; he spoke to the heart of people. Coltrane's concern with humanity was clearly evident in the music that he created. With merciful titles such as "Peace on Earth," "Meditations," "Offering," "Compassion," "Love," "Selflessness," "Joy," and numerous others, Coltrane's desire to reach people with the power of hope, the power of truth, and the gift of love was intentional. Coltrane knew that

[14]Simpkins, *Coltrane: A Biography*, 105–106.
[15]Quoted in *Newsweek*, December 12, 1966, 108.

music could effectively reach people where spoken words and other actions could not. Grounded in a thorough understanding of the depth of black music, Coltrane understood the value of musical expression and the power of sound. As a student of the spiritual, a master of the blues, and an innovator of post-bebop expression, Coltrane used music to reach the hearts and minds of people open to the possibility for a better existence for all. "I think music is an instrument," he said in one interview. "It can create the initial thought patterns that can change the thinking of the people."[16]

Third, Coltrane understood that although music was perceived as entertainment, it was more effective as an agent of empowerment. Coltrane used his music as a tool for liberation; not only his liberation, but the liberation of those who heard and received his message. Coltrane was not afraid to explore the unknown. As a matter of fact, Coltrane's explorations were so futuristic that even present-day listeners are perplexed by the raw, honest, and bold nature of his sound, a noncommercial, nonassimilationist, and uncompromising sound. Coltrane's sound is filled with so much hope that it can empower the serious listener to explore life outside his or her comfort zone. Coltrane challenges the listener to live a life of exploration: living based in the possibilities of equity, justice, unity, peace, and liberation from inner turmoil. Liberation from the inhumane inner self that is self-indulgent on the ills and evils of society.

> Well, I tell you for myself, I make a conscious attempt, I think I can truthfully say that in music I make or I have *tried* to make a conscious attempt to change what I've found, in music. In other words, I've tried to say, "Well, *this* I feel, could be better, in my opinion, so I will try to do this to make it better." This is what I feel that we feel in any situation that we find in our lives, when there's something we think could be better, we must make an effort to try and make it better. So it's the same socially, musically, politically, and in any department of our lives.[17]

It is often easy to isolate Coltrane from the numerous other creative innovators who came before and after him; however, such treatment only serves to minimize Coltrane's dynamic contributions within the Black America's quest for freedom. As a black man born in the Jim Crow South of Hamlet, North Carolina, in the time when black men were perceived as a threat to the stability of society, Coltrane stood on the shoulders of precursors who, although may not have had a direct influence on him, allowed for

[16]Kofsky, *John Coltrane*, 435.
[17]Kofsky, *John Coltrane*, 435.

insightful models of expression. One such precursor was Thomas Andrew Dorsey, the lauded "Father of Black Gospel Music."[18] Similar to Coltrane, Thomas Andrew Dorsey was reared in the south (Villa Rica, Georgia) within a religious family. Although Dorsey's biography has been well constructed by numerous scholars, I wish to illustrate some important points of intersection between Coltrane and Dorsey that will reveal that Coltrane was not the first to understand and utilize the spiritual ethos in black music.[19] Like Coltrane, Dorsey's musical journey was intensified by two "spiritual awakenings." The first occurred in 1921, after he had lived five years in Chicago, where he relocated in hopes of finding work as a full-time musician. Before that, Dorsey was a well-regarded blues and jazz pianist who was musical director for Gertrude "Ma" Rainey, also known as "Mother of the Blues." During a session at the Forty-first Annual Meeting of the National Baptist Convention, in September 1921, Dorsey was struck by the singing of evangelist W. M. Nix as he delivered a rendition of "I Do, Don't You?"[20] Recalling conversations with his mother less than a year earlier as she chided him about straying from his religious roots, Dorsey said that when he heard Nix, "My inner being was thrilled. My soul was a deluge of divine rapture; my emotions were aroused; my heart was inspired to become a great singer and worker in the kingdom of the Lord."[21] Dorsey quickly left blues and jazz in exchange for religious music, but to no avail. Unable to earn reasonable wages and frustrated by the overwhelmingly negative responses of churches to his "secular" sound, Dorsey returned to composing and performing blues and jazz. Upon his return to the Chicago popular music scene, Dorsey again arose as a leading composer, arranger, and performer. However, after a few years of success his personal life was shaken by a deep

[18]Dorsey's title comes from a black tradition in which elders, innovators, and individuals who have made a unique contribution to a local, regional, or community at large are given titles of admiration. Although no one disputes Dorsey's contribution and recognition through the anointing of a title of admiration, the exact nature of the title has been one of confusion. Biographer Michael Harris offers Dorsey's title as the "Father of Gospel Blues"; other scholars have referred to Dorsey as the "Father of Gospel Music"; still others have noted him as the "Father of Black Gospel Music." Regardless of the variations on the title, all recognize his dynamic contribution toward developing a new style of composition and performance that has influenced subsequent composers, musicians, vocalists, and numerous others.

[19]See Horace Clarence Boyer, The Golden Age of Gospel (Urbana: University of Illinois Press, 2000; Robert Darden. People Get Ready! A New History of Black Gospel Music (New York: Continuum, 2004); Harris, Rise of Gospel Blues; Bernice Johnson Reagon, ed., We'll Understand It Better By and By: Pioneering African American Gospel Composers (Washington, D.C.: Smithsonian Institution Press, 1992), and Say Amen, Somebody, video recording (Carmel, Calif.: Pacific Arts Video Records, 1983).

[20]See Michael Harris's chapter, "Conflict and Resolution in the Life of Thomas Andrew Dorsey" in We'll Understand It Better By and By, 173.

[21]Thomas Dorsey, Songs with a Message: With My Ups and Downs (Chicago: Thomas A. Dorsey, 1941), 19–20.

and severe depression. In 1928, after a consultation and spiritual experience with Bishop H. H. Haley, Dorsey once again committed his life to doing the work of the Lord.[22]

This second spiritual awakening served as the catalyst for Dorsey to take the musical expression that chronicled the realities of black southern migrants in the perceived "utopian" and merge them with the music of the Christian faith. Dorsey's "gospel blues" became the sound of the black church during the 1930s and subsequent decades. These "Dorseys" emerged as the main musical manifestation of the sacred message translated to secular folks in plain, everyday language. The songs were accessible, captivating, and aesthetically pleasing. Even though his early days as a gospel music composer and musician were riddled by horrific accounts of being "thrown out of some of the best churches," his perseverance and determination to do what God told him to do eventually resulted in a lasting influence and well-established legacy.[23] Dorsey, like Coltrane, used his own spiritual experiences as a catalyst to establish a musical sound based in the spiritual ethos of black music. With songs such as "You Can't Go through This World by Yourself," "There'll Be Peace in the Valley for Me," "I'm Going to Live the Life I Sing about in My Song," and "How Much More of Life's Burden Can We Bear?" Dorsey's ability to speak to the social, political, economic, and cultural situations of his audience was as clear as his desire to introduce this same audience to Christianity. His spiritual journey was grounded in his personal relationship with God and confirmed by the millions of people whose lives have been touched through his music. Although many scholars have not used the term "spiritual ethos" to describe the essence of Dorsey's sound and music, it is clear that it is not only present, but dominant.

> Try to do my best in service,
> Try to live the best I can,
> When I choose to do the right thing,
> Evil's present on ev'ry hand,
> I look up and wonder why
> That good fortune pass me by,
> Then I say to my soul, be patient,
> The Lord will make a way Somehow.[24]

---

[22]Reagon, *We'll Understand It Better By and By*, 177.
[23]Reagon, *We'll Understand It Better By and By*, 179.
[24]This is an excerpt from "The Lord Will Make a Way Somehow," words and music composed by Thomas Andrew Dorsey in 1943.

Unlike Coltrane, though, Dorsey's use of his sound was not as universal. Dorsey was unapologetically Christian. He did not stray or allow for any misunderstandings concerning the underlying goal of his songs. He aimed to nurture Christians through the gospel and simultaneously use his sound to help introduce others to the Christian religion. Dorsey, in many ways, was not interested in reaching those who had no interest or desire to approach the Christian faith that his songs encouraged unless their experience with his songs might aid in the their transformation. In fact, Dorsey's music allowed for an even greater chasm to be revealed. During his rise to acclaim within the black church, Dorsey's music became the prominent sound within middle-class churches, causing conflict within the ecumenical black church. Further, the unique sound, which clearly departed from earlier black hymnody or the well-established sounds of the spirituals, caused yet another partition among the rural southern transplants (of which Dorsey was one) and the urban northerners (of which Dorsey became). In addition, as Dorsey continued to push the envelope with his unique sound and his ability to manifest that sound through the newly devised gospel choir, tensions arose between the elders of the church and the young adults. The elders in many ways balked at the constant beckoning of the youths to exchange tradition for innovation. Dorsey's "gospel blues" stood at the juncture of these three polarizations (middle class/lower class, southern/northern, and traditional/contemporary) within the black church and thus differs from Coltrane's music in that regard.[25]

Dorsey certainly understood the power of black music as a tool for liberation. To claim that Dorsey was interested only in spiritual liberation would be a misnomer as he was extremely active in the social, political, economic, and cultural struggles of black folk through the church. Although his solution was through acceptance of the Christian faith and spiritual union with God, he was also aware of the external plights of black folks. As a product of the South and as a transplant during the Great Migration, he saw firsthand the unjust, unequal treatment of blacks. He realized, along with many others, that the "better" life that folks fled the South in pursuit of was not what they had imagined. Through his music and certainly through the sound of "gospel blues," Dorsey pierced the hearts of numerous folks who needed a supernatural solution to a superlative problem. Dorsey's sound invoked the presence of a sensitive, nurturing, caring God, a God of mercy, grace, and love. Through Dorsey's sound and his extensive

[25]Even though Coltrane performed blues using the semantics and syntax rooted in southern tradition in a northern context, his goal was inclusion. He had a strong desire to illuminate the awareness and connectedness of the various black experiences and expressions. Coltrane and Dorsey had very different approaches to this idea of polarization versus unification.

catalog of music, he offered insight into a possible solution to the ills of society for countless black Christians and prospective Christians of all colors.

Of all of the post-Coltrane, male prophetic voices of the late twentieth century that reached around the globe and inspired, influenced, and encouraged generations of young people to explore the deeper lessons of life, Tupac Amaru Shakur stands out as one of the most dominant. Like his predecessors Dorsey and Coltrane, Shakur internalized the power of black music and used the inner essence of the expression, the spiritual ethos, to have a lasting influence on millions of lives. Born in the struggle of the 1960s as a son of the Black Panther Movement, Shakur had a strong awareness of the plight of black urban youth in of the United States. He witnessed, firsthand, the unjust system of jurisprudence, and he saw his mother's drug abuse lead to the disassembly of his family. Yet through this bleak situation he clung to the rich heritage of the black experience, learning the nuances of black history and studying with fervor the black artistic expressions of theater, dance, and music. Shakur also clung to spirituality, which permeated his music. Cultural critic and hip-hop intellectual Michael Eric Dyson writes in his book, *Holler If You Hear Me: Searching for Tupac Shakur*, that Shakur "obsessed with God."[26] Shakur's obsession was revealed through his unique sound as expressed through his music and poetry. His sound was not only raw and unconventional but it was bruised by the hardships of life and seasoned with disdain for hypocrisy and injustice.

Like Dorsey and Coltrane, Shakur too was able to pinpoint two visitations or spiritual awakenings. The first, he recounts, occurred when he was shot five times while entering the lobby of a recording studio in New York City on November 20, 1994. In his observation, not only did the presence of God save his life, but God also called Shakur to do even more work through his music.[27] His second spiritual awakening occurred while serving time at the Clinton Correctional Facility in New York State in 1995. While incarcerated, Shakur had another visitation by God. Like Dorsey and Coltrane before him, his spiritual awakenings inspired him to increasingly announce his views on the ills of society through his music. Influenced by his constant questioning of why God would allow so much suffering, his music and sound allowed a very public view of an extremely personal spiritual journey. According to Dyson,

---

[26]Michael Eric Dyson, *Holler If You Hear Me: Searching for Tupac Shakur* (New York: Basic Civitas Books, 2001), 202.

[27]See Tupac Shakur. *Thug Angel: The Life of an Outlaw*, video recording (Chatsworth, Calif.: QD3 Entertainment, 2002); and Tupac Shakur, *Tupac VS*, video recording (Santa Monica, Calif.: Xenon Pictures, 2002).

His relationship with God during his rap career took the form of an ongoing argument about the suffering he saw and the evil he endured and expressed. The compassion he summoned as well as the raps he wrote were meant to expose and relieve the pain he witnessed.[28]

Shakur was immersed in spirituality and effectively used the spiritual ethos in his music. Songs such as "So Many Tears," "Only God Can Judge Me," "I Wonder if Heaven Got a Ghetto," "Picture Me Rolling," and "Bomb First" reveal Shakur's spirituality and exude compassionate cries for divine intervention in a crazy, chaotic, and messed-up world. Shakur's plea for God, the God that is bigger than all religions, offers clear indication that he was dealing with an inner turmoil that only divine intervention could appease.

> High sigh why die wishin', hopin' for possibilities
> I'll mob on, why they copy me sloppily
> Cops patrol projects, hatin' the people livin' in them
> I was born an inmate, waitin' to escape the prison
> Went to church but don't understand it, they underhanded
> God gave me these commandments, the world is scandalous
> Blast 'til they holy high; baptize they evil minds
> Wise, no longer blinded, watch me shine trick
> Which one of y'all wanna feel the degrees?[29]

Different from Dorsey and similar to Coltrane, Shakur's expressions were not focused at one religious community or one community of any sort. Over the years since his death, anecdotal testimony has come from people of various faiths and different generations, economic situations, ethnicities, races, genders, and social standings, that Tupac Shakur was a phenomenal, influential, and dynamic person. In diverse communities across the globe he stands as a martyr, an immortalized saint, which is ironic since he did not openly subscribe to any one religion. He is widely regarded as the most influential voice of America's youth.[30] In fact, his death has remained

---

[28]Dyson, *Holler If You Hear Me*, 229–230.

[29]An excerpt from "Black Jesuz," from the 2Pac + Outlawz album *Still I Rise* (1999, Amaru/Death Row/Interscope). The album was number 6 on the *Billboard* 200 charts.

[30]From acknowledgments on numerous albums, spoken word pieces, poems, and even plays since his death, Tupac's broad and wide influence has been felt. Academic conferences, such as one held at Harvard University on April 17, 2003, reveal that even scholars acknowledge the depth and breadth of Tupac's influence, not only on youth of the United States but across the globe. His dynamic sound and prolific ability to speak truth from his perspective gave voice to many across the world. Numerous journalistic pieces and Web sites have been dedicated to his legacy.

prevalent in contemporary folklore since many still believe he is secretly alive and in hiding.[31] Shakur's music continues to have dynamic effects on the consciousness of America's disenfranchised, ostracized, and "forgotten" individuals as he has had more releases posthumously than when he was alive, which illustrates his profound ability to constantly speak to the urgency of immediate situations through recorded music.[32] He was a voice for everyone who would listen.

Finally, Shakur knew the power of the spoken word and how that power could be further heightened through music. His early poetry offers insight into Shakur's intellectual astuteness and sociopolitical consciousness. A piece written during his brief residence in Baltimore (1984–1988) titled "Liberty Needs Glasses" says in part,

> excuse me but lady liberty needs glasses
> and so does mrs justice by her side
> both the broads r blind as bats
> stumbling thru' the system
> justice bumbed into Mutulu and
> trippen on Geronimo Pratt
> but stepped right over Oliver
> and his crooked partner Ronnie
> justice stubbed her big toe on Mandela
> and liberty was misquoted by the indians
> slavery was a learning phase
> forgotten with out a verdict
> while justice is on a rampage.[33]

Full of social innuendo and clever political references, including mention of the Oliver North/Iran Contra hearings of the 1980s, Shakur was working through his young rage with the gifts of black artistic expression, expression grounded in spirituality and the deeper questions of life. Shakur's willingness to publicly display his private inner turmoil allows for a significant

---

[31]After Shakur's death, numerous print articles and online activity suggested that many thought he was secretly in hiding and would emerge seven or ten years after his assumed death. Sites such as http://alleyeonme.com/alive2pac.html and http://www.cracked.com/article_15659_tupac-shakur-still-alive.html were active as of May 2008.

[32]Of all of Tupac's eleven albums (not including compilations and soundtracks), six were posthumous releases. According to RIAA certification, two went platinum, one went double platinum, another went triple platinum, and yet one another earned quadruple platinum status. According to Billboard's Top 10 Single Chart, of all of Tupac's nineteen singles ranking within the Top 10, eight were from posthumous releases.

[33]Tupac: Resurrection 1971–1996 (New York: Atria Books, 2003), 56.

contribution to the world as we struggle along with him in attempting to figure out the answers to such questions as, Why do bad things happen to good people? Why do people who have never had a chance to thrive not ever get a chance? Or in his own words, "Is there a Heaven for a G?" Through the serious inquiry and ability to work out his painful reality, Shakur found and offered liberation to many. His offering was not just a transcendental liberation that allowed folks to soar above the reality of their own situations and circumstances, but a practical liberation from the societal oppression; liberation guided in hope. His words and his attempts to infuse urban philosophy into the minds of ostracized and disenfranchised people gave an unfamiliar empowerment to a population used to being forgotten. From his completely misunderstood use of the moniker *THUG LIFE* (*The Hate You Gave Little Infants Fucks Everyone*) to the widely controversial redefinition of *NIGGA* (*Never Ignorant Getting Goals Accomplished*), Shakur's ability to inspire a serious cultlike following among people is evidence of his ability to use the spiritual ethos within black music to empower people to change.[34]

Like other innovators of black music, Coltrane, Dorsey, and Shakur all dealt with personal struggle and the need to reconcile the deeper truths of spirituality with the reality of a harsh and cruel world. Unlike Coltrane, Dorsey's approach was to operate solely within the organized religious traditions of the black church. His primary audience and the focus of much of his energy was geared toward Christians and potential converts. From his position within the black community of Chicago as an entrepreneur, minister, and nationally ranked composer and musician, Dorsey's music and lyrics proclaim hope through a personal relationship with God through the Christian doctrine. In many ways, Dorsey's tremendous influence via music was limited by his own religious inclinations. Dorsey's own self-imposed strictures limited the wide-range influence his music might have had on non-Protestant populations. Dorsey rarely mentioned his pre-gospel days as a highly regarded jazz and blues musician.[35] His practice of disassociating himself from secular living in many ways disconnected him from folks looking for a sacred message without being converted. Dorsey privileged religion with a subtext of social, political, economic, and cultural commentary within his music.

Similarly, Shakur disconnected himself from the religious communities by focusing on reaching young, ostracized, and disenfranchised youth who were not strictly devout to any sect, denomination, or established faith. With

[34]Shakur's acronyms are addressed in Dyson *Holler If You Hear Me*, 112–115; 144–147.
[35]See the *Say Amen, Somebody*, 1983, for a visual depiction of this hesitancy to reconcile the pre-gospel Dorsey (aka Georgia Tom and other nicknames) with the "Father of Black Gospel Music," Thomas A. Dorsey (later, Rev. Thomas A. Dorsey).

the aim of connecting to the struggle of urban youth and identifying as a lay leader, he attacked the crises of generational divide, injustice, and inequity. Shakur approached an audience very different from Dorsey's. Shakur's audience was influenced by his sheer brilliance, his impressive skill at rhyme play, wordsmithing, and his technical mastery of flow and rhythmical dexterity. Yet Shakur, like Dorsey, was isolated to a population that had been compartmentalized as hip-hop. Although Shakur had phenomenal success in influencing many outside the hip-hop generation, he still had a segmented audience.[36] Whereas Dorsey privileged religion to formulate his strategic reach, Shakur privileged the social, political, economic, and cultural aspects of life as they pertain to ostracized and disenfranchised youth and young adults.

Coltrane provides the greatest example of one who used the spiritual ethos within black music to bridge and unify the youth and the elders, the poor and the wealthy, the religious and the spiritual, the southern and the northern, and numerous other groups that are supposedly disparate. Coltrane's influence expanded far beyond the music known as "jazz" and even further beyond music itself. When chastised by the critics for playing "anti-jazz" or playing angry music, Coltrane always responded that his music was an attempt to fix what he found wrong within society. Musicians from the concert world, the rock world, the folk world, and beyond were enamored by his unique, intense, honest, and sincere sound. Coltrane accomplished what most have not been bold enough to endeavor—to allow spirituality to be present, front and center in his music, as its own entity separate from any system of religion. Coltrane knew and proved that spiritually mattered in black music.

The spiritual ethos in black music is the urgent cry for a liberating prognosis to the complexities of human existence that only a nonhuman force can provide. It is the transformative moan that simultaneously gives credence to the past and present suffering of black folks while also presenting the possibility of hope for a brighter today and tomorrow. The spiritual ethos in black music is the alarming holler of pain, hurt, destitution, and devastation harmonized with the healing growl of potential, salvation, deliverance, and delight. The spiritual ethos in black music is the ecstatic wail of oppression waiting to be transformed into liberation; hatred waiting to be mutated into love; and evil waiting to be morphed into good. The spiritual ethos in black music is the reviving force that flows from generation through generation exposing traditions, exploiting legacies, and constantly

---

[36]Bakari Kitwani introduces the notion of hip-hop generation in his book *The Hip Hop Generation: Young Blacks and the Crisis in African-American Culture* (New York: Basic Civitas Books, 2002). He defines the "hip-hop generation" as those born between 1965 and 1984.

illuminating heritage to make known the repetitive cycle of life that comes from beyond. The spiritual ethos in black music is the constant in all black music that relates, reveals, and reflects the chronicle of the black experience. It is the reality that allows black music to be a means of communication and expression.

John William Coltrane, Thomas Andrew Dorsey, and Tupac Amaru Shakur each experienced and used the power of the spiritual ethos in their music. Each served their communities in uniquely visionary, intellectually affirming, and innovative ways. They offered not only a voluminous amount of published and recorded music but, more important, a legacy of prophetic voice. Through their music, their respective prophetic voices provided practical resolutions to everyday challenges in an extremely intimate manner. Their prophetic voices embraced communities of people in need of the intimacy that would not only nourish their souls as they embarked on spiritual journeys but would also unify disenfranchised, ostracized, and oppressed people. The spiritual ethos in black music is the key that unlocks the true power of black music; without it, we have not fully appreciated the expansive, divine power of the music.

In the concluding chapter of *Souls of Black Folk*, titled "Of the Sorrow Songs," Du Bois writes:

> And so by fateful chance the Negro folk-song—the rhythmic cry of the slave—stands to-day not simply as the sole American music, but as the most beautiful expression of human experience born this side the seas. It has been neglected, it has been, and is, half despised, and above all it has been persistently mistaken and misunderstood; but notwithstanding, it still remains as the singular spiritual heritage of the nation and the greatest gift of the Negro people.[37]

Black America's quest for freedom has taken many shapes and forms over the years, yet the one consistent and fluid realm has been through music. Coltrane, Dorsey, and Shakur most effectively voiced Black America's quest for freedom through the sounds of their prophetic expressions. Dorsey's expression catered to a religious community raised on spirituals and grounded in the communal congregational singing of hymns. Shakur's expression catered to a youth-oriented, nontraditional community of believers who placed more stock in the urban-based hip-hop culture than in any one religious system. Both were effective in speaking truth to their constituencies; both were powerful prophets to their people. But neither was ever as

---

[37]Du Bois, *Souls of Black Folk*, 178.

effective as Coltrane, whose self-defined community bridged the traditional black ecumenical Christian believers and the nontraditional, unorthodox believers in a greater good. Coltrane was able to nurture and empower youth while also comforting and recognizing the wisdom of elders. His prophetic voice was not restricted by the limitations of religion but open to the possibilities of spirituality. Perhaps Cone says it best in these powerful words:

> Whatever form black music takes, it is always an expression of black life in America and what the people must do to survive with a measure of dignity in a society which seems bent on destroying their right to be human beings. The fact that black people keep making music means that we as a people refuse to be destroyed. We refuse to allow the people who oppress us to have the last word about our humanity. The last word belongs to us and music is our way of saying it. Contrary to popular opinion, therefore, the spirituals and the blues are not songs of despair or of a defeated people. On the contrary, they are songs which represent one of the great triumphs of the human spirit.[38]

Through Coltrane's prophetic voice and demonstrative use of the spiritual ethos in black music, we experience a unique sense of hope, love, and compassion not grounded on any institutional system of faith or belief, but based on the fact that we as humans have more in common than we do in difference, and that music can be the bridge toward a love supreme.

"To me, you know, I feel I want to be a force for good."[39]
—John Coltrane

---

[38]Cone, *Spirituals and the Blues*, 130.
[39]Kofsky, *John Coltrane*, 450–451.

Somebody Please Say, "Amen!"

ERIC D. JACKSON

Editor's Note: I asked Eric Jackson to write from a personal viewpoint about his relationship with John Coltrane's music because of his legacy as one of the nation's leading jazz radio personalities for more than three decades. His is an honest testimony to the power of Coltrane's music to influence and change people's lives, including his own.

I am a witness to the power of music to change a life. I admit it! I heard Miles Davis and John Coltrane, and I was hooked. I mean I forgot about going to med school and I forgot about my plans to study psychiatry. Amazed by the music of Trane and Miles, I decided I had a mission. I wanted to tell everybody about the great music some call "jazz." I wanted to tell everybody about all the wonderful music and the exciting music makers who had come out of the African American community. Not just the well-known folks, but I wanted people to know, to hear the great music that came out of the African American community in spite of the life that many members of that community were forced to live. I was already doing a radio show, and I knew that was a perfect place to turn others on to the treasures to which I was listening.

I grew up in the '50s and '60s listening to a lot of the same music that most African American young folks were listening to at that time. I remember dancing the Twist, the Monkey, and lots of other dances. Even earlier, I remember visiting neighbors' homes and hearing a kind of music different from what I usually heard at home. It was a bluesier sound. What I was hearing was the blues or early rhythm and blues, and some was the music of the church.

I've often said that the music of the church was just "in the air" in the African American community. Maybe they didn't sing those old songs in your church, or maybe you didn't even go to church, but you knew many of those songs because they were in the air. Grandmom or Mom or some neighbor sang them around the house. People often quoted them, extracting some gem that they thought was appropriate for the moment. The Reverend Martin Luther King, Jr., often quoted them in his speeches, and W. E. B. Du Bois used their wisdom to open the chapters in his book, *The Souls of Black Folk*.

At home, I grew up with the sounds of Duke Ellington's music frequently being played on records. My father was an avid Ellington fan. Often he played the latest release from Duke while he enthusiastically told his friends to "listen to Paul, (Gonsalves)," or he exclaimed "Johnny (Hodges)" or one of the other names of the many masters in that great band! We lived in Camden, New Jersey, near Philadelphia so we had several good jazz stations on the radio to listen to.

That's the kind of musical environment I grew up in. I think I was comfortable listening to all the styles I mentioned. To me, even as a youngster, mood dictated what I wanted to hear. At times I turned on the radio to either of the two Philly R&B stations but at other times I chose to listen to one of the two commercial jazz stations. But hearing Coltrane was like a revelation. It was a whole new world of hearing.

I fell in love with Trane's work with his great quartet. I think that real love affair started with *A Love Supreme* although I had listened to Trane's *Live at Birdland* and what seemed to me to be a very exotic, "Afro-Blue." To hear someone play soprano saxophone was still unusual. Trane had already recorded "My Favorite Things", and his use of the instrument helped spark a revival of the soprano sax's use, but I didn't know any of that at the time. Coltrane played the soprano on three tunes on *Live at Birdland* but it was "Afro-Blue" that caught my ear.

I think I was also fascinated by the title. Just the word "Afro-Blue" brought images to mind. Oscar Brown Jr. later wrote lyrics to the tune, and the first line captures some of what I felt listening to Trane's wordless version. Brown wrote, "Dream of a land my soul is from . . ." This was the late '60s, and many African Americans were looking at Africa with new eyes. They began to look at the continent with a sense of pride. I also couldn't overlook the word "blue." It reminded me with sadness of the condition that African people and the people of the African Diaspora were struggling through. But the mood of the song was joyful. It was an uplifting, optimistic, hopeful sound. Amira Baraka (LeRoi Jones) wrote in his liner notes for the recording that drummer Elvin Jones's "thrashing" was "unbelievable." He found himself up and dancing to the sound of "Afro-Blue" while writing the notes. Even earlier, I had heard that classic album Coltrane did with vocalist Johnny Hartman. I did really like the album, so I played it frequently, giving myself a dose of Trane's playing each time.

But listening to A Love Supreme was another experience for me as a college freshman. Its beginning sounds served to open my ears, just as the rest of Trane's music would open my vision and tap feelings and emotions that seemed to be deep inside. I found myself wanting to listen to it over and over. I began to carry the album with me. When visiting almost anyone, after sitting for just a few moments, I often asked my host to put on A Love Supreme! Usually most folks were agreeable, and so, happily, at least for me, they played Trane's epic work. Let's hope it also won some converts to Trane's music. That A Love Supreme album was such a constant traveling companion of mine that at least one friend called me "Coltrane."

A Love Supreme spoke to a hunger I had inside. I had grown up in the church, but as the '60s closed I became disillusioned, specifically with my local church but also with the church in general. I just could not understand how racial injustice and its many ugly faces was not the constant topic of Sunday sermons. In my local church I found that many shunned me because I was involved in some nonviolent protests in my hometown. I was confused. Hadn't Jesus, according to the Bible, challenged injustice? Hadn't he even got so upset that he overturned the tables of the money changers? So I began drifting away from the church. A Love Supreme served to help keep alive a love of God. I knew that even if I was disillusioned with the actions of the members of the church, Trane helped me to remember that there is a God of the universe. It was a revival in the truest sense. Eventually his music and the music and titles of other Impulse Records artists, like Pharoah Sanders, led me to look at other religions, other paths to God and enlightenment, but A Love Supreme kept the spark alive.

I had an interesting conversation with a longtime friend, author Mary Ann French, some years ago. I was talking to her about the power of the African American spirituals. She said to me, "John Coltrane's music is my spirituals." Somebody please say, "Amen!"

I am reminded of these words, spoken about jazz in Berlin in 1964:

> God has wrought many things out of oppression. He has endowed his
> creatures with the capacity to create—and from this capacity has flowed the
> sweet songs of sorrow and joy that have allowed man to cope with his
> environment and many different situations.

Jazz speaks for life. The Blues tell the story of life's difficulties, and if you think for a moment, you will realize that they take the hardest realities of life and put them into music, only to come out with some new hope or sense of triumph.

This is triumphant music.

Modern jazz has continued in this tradition, singing the songs of a more complicated urban existence. When life itself offers no order and meaning, the musician creates an order and meaning from the sounds of the earth which flow through his instrument.

It is no wonder that so much of the search for identity among American Negroes was championed by Jazz musicians. Long before the modern essayists and scholars wrote of racial identity as a problem for a multiracial world, musicians were returning to their roots to affirm that which was stirring within their souls.

Much of the power of our Freedom Movement in the United States has come from this music. It has strengthened us with its sweet rhythms when courage began to fail. It has calmed us with its rich harmonies when spirits were down.

And now, Jazz is exported to the world. For in the particular struggle of the Negro in America there is something akin to the universal struggle of modern man. Everybody has the Blues. Everybody longs for meaning. Everybody needs to love and be loved. Everybody needs to clap hands and be happy. Everybody longs for faith.

In music, especially this broad category called Jazz, there is a stepping stone towards all of these.

—Dr. Martin Luther King Jr., opening address to the 1964
Berlin Jazz Festival

It got to a point that my friends and I only wanted to listen to Trane in a kind of ritualistic way. I mean, this wasn't music to be played as background to conversation. This was music that was meant to be listened to. So there were times when it was right to hear Trane, when you knew that you could sit and listen without interruption. This was serious music, and I enjoyed it best when I could give it my full attention. We approached his music like a religious encounter.

I recall listening to *A Love Supreme* and other recordings by Coltrane's quartet and being amazed that four musicians could make that much music. How could all of that sound come from just four musicians? No I don't mean volume, although they certainly used dynamics in their music, ranging from quiet and peaceful to highly energetic and passionate moments, but the word that came to mind as I listened to that music was "majestic."

That struck me even then as odd. At that age, I'm not sure how many times I would have used the term to describe anything, but to me it was an accurate description of the way I saw and heard the music.

I purposefully used the term "saw." When I listened to John's music, it produced a mental image in me. A picture that seemed clear in my mind. Later I would find out that Trane was trying to produce mental images. On a Web site called Tubegator (tubegator.com), I found this quote from Coltrane, "I think the main thing a musician would like to do is to give a picture to the listener of the many wonderful things that he knows of and senses in the universe. . . . That's what I would like to do. I think that's one of the greatest things in life and we all try to do it in some way. The musician's is through his music."

In the 1996 movie *Mr. Holland's Opus*, Richard Dreyfus's character, a music professor, talked about listening to Coltrane's music. He said that for him, it was a building process. The more he listened, the more he wanted to listen, even if he didn't understand what was going on. I think that's the way I was as I started to listen to more and more of his music. I just wanted to hear everything I could of Coltrane's 1960s bands. No, I can't say that the first time I heard some of the music that I got it right away. I can say that there was always something there that made me want to hear it again. It got to the point that I even became a kind of snob! All I wanted to hear was the music called by some as jazz. No Temptations or Four Tops. No Miracles. I didn't want to hear anything but so-called jazz, and Coltrane's music was usually my first choice.

It's ironic that I use the term "so-called jazz" in conjunction with Coltrane. Often someone who disapproved of Coltrane's music from that period would say his music wasn't jazz. Early on, my defense for that argument was that perhaps that person needed to expand his definition of what jazz is. Later my reply to that statement would be different. "That's not jazz!" "Maybe you are right," I might have replied. But at some point I don't think Coltrane was as concerned about what is jazz or what is not as he was concerned about making music. If Trane changed the rhythmic, harmonic, and melodic concept away from someone's predefined concept of jazz, maybe he wasn't playing jazz to that person's ears. In fact, many musicians during the late '60s and early '70s showed some reluctance to use the term "jazz." Herbie Hancock and Yusef Lateef are two that come to mind. Some musicians simply were more interested as to whether you liked their music, not how you defined it. So maybe you are right. Maybe it's not jazz. But I sure love it, no matter what you call it.

Kulu Se Mama, with its accompanying poem by New Orleans–born composer and percussionist Juno Lewis, spoke of a need to preserve African and African American culture. (It is significant that one of Coltrane's last public appearances was at Olatunji's Center of African Culture in New York, a center that had similar goals.) It was a theme that was heard frequently from many different voices in the African American community during the mid- to late '60s. Many Afro-centric centers emerged in cities with those goals in mind. In Boston, one of the largest and most well known was run by Elma Lewis. It ran for many years as a place for people to come and study different forms of artistic expression. Miss Lewis received encouragement from many significant people, including Bostonian minister Louis Farrakhan, who played violin and sang in Boston nightspots during the 1950s. He often returned home to appear at her events. Another big supporter of Miss Lewis's work was the pianist Randy Weston. He recorded a tune dedicated to her called "Blues For Elma Lewis." To my mind, there is still a need for these kinds of centers today. Maybe the need is even greater than it was in the past.

When I listened to *Kulu Se Mama* I saw scenes of an Africa that I had yet to visit. In 1973, I did get to visit Africa as I spent about two weeks in Morocco. I had taken some Coltrane recordings with me, including some of the music from the European tours that would later be released by Norman Granz on Pablo. At that time, that music was not easy to find. I remember listening to Trane playing soprano on one of the tapes one evening as I got ready to go out to dinner. The restaurant we chose to eat in that night featured live Moroccan music. There was what I think was an oud, a violin that was played upright, like a cello, some small clay hand drums, and finger cymbals. Hearing the music, I could barely sit still! I remember saying excitedly, "This sounds like Trane! This sounds like the music we were just listening to."

I had always thought that I had a special connection to music. And I guess it was obvious to others because I heard my father say to Leonard Brown that I always liked music. Coltrane's music touched me in an entirely different way. Often as I listen to Coltrane's music, tears run down my face. Are they tears of sadness? No, I don't think so. I certainly don't feel sad when listening to his music. Are they tears of joy? To tell you the truth, I don't know. What I do know is that Trane's music touched me inside, reached into places where no music had gone before, and when the music hit that spot, tears flowed. Perhaps that's why I knew that I couldn't listen to this music as some kind of background music while entertaining company. It's not the face that I want to present publicly. And after a musical experience like that, somehow a conversation about the Red Sox, the White Sox, or even the Black Sox just wouldn't fit the moment. At times, my friend Boo, with whom I often listened to Trane in those early days, and I were just stunned, and we only manage to get out something monosyllabic, like "damn!"

I have been told that when some people heard John's music live, they screamed while listening. Perhaps this was a kind of release because Trane's music had touched them. They couldn't find the right words to say at that moment, so they let out a yell. Maybe it was like those folks in the church. The minister's sermon gets hot. The music gets hotter, and the intensity grows. The spirit is moving in the church, and all of a sudden the sister in the corner starts speaking in tongues. It's not a language the people around her understand in any rational way, but it's an expression or reaction caused by the intensity of the moment. Mike Canterino, one of the former owners of New York's Half Note Club, mentioned seeing and hearing a different reaction. Canterino said listeners often yelled "Freedom Now" as Trane soloed.

Trane was no holy man or preacher. Both his grandfathers were ministers, and John grew up in the home of his maternal grandfather, Reverend Blair. But the ministry was not John's calling. Even as a youngster, he seemed attracted by the sound of music. It's no secret that Trane had problems with substance abuse, both alcohol and drugs. Starting in the late '40s, heroin use seems to have become popular with a number of jazz musicians. There is much too long a list of jazz musicians, including many well-known performers, who found themselves captured by the addictive powers of heroin. John fell into that hole.

The bassist Reggie Workman told of seeing Coltrane once when Trane had been using. Horrified at seeing John in that condition, Reggie just kept repeating, "You're John Coltrane!" It certainly wasn't this human weakness that I admired about Trane. What really impressed me was Coltrane's human strength. Anyone can fall, stumble, or have problems dealing with life. John had the strength to see that he had fallen and the strength to stand himself back up again. It's been said that to kick his habit, he locked himself in his room and asked to not be disturbed. He kicked his habit cold-turkey. To me, this is a sign of human strength. I'm sure being isolated and locked in a room with only himself and his demons, the temptation would have been to give in, to decide to have "just one more bag."

Coltrane talked about his struggles in the notes to *A Love Supreme*. In fact, as Lewis Porter pointed out in his book *John Coltrane: His Life and Music*, the four sections of that work suggest a path to be traveled in life, from "Acknowledgment" to "Resolution" to "Pursuance" and "Psalm." That is, the acknowledgment of the Higher Force and His plan, the Resolution to serve and follow that Force and His plan. Pursuance is the struggle to live that life, and that pursuit should lead to a level of satisfaction as shown in "Psalm." Trane doesn't say that this is the exclusive path of a member of the AMEZ Church he grew up in or any other church. He doesn't say this is the path of a Muslim. No. It's a record of his path. But it is a universal path, not exclusive to this faith or that.

I think it's Coltrane's character that is so important to many musicians. In addition to the strength he showed in conquering his addiction in an effort to become both a better musician and a better person, there are many stories that tell of his desire to practice constantly. Stories have circulated about visitors coming by the saxophonist's house early in the day and finding John practicing. Repeatedly, visitors tell of returning to his house hours later to find Trane still practicing. It's even been said that sometimes while resting on the couch, he would be practicing his flute work. So in addition to the human strength he exhibited, he also showed an intense dedication to his craft. That dedication led him to produce the music that he made, music that some forty plus years after his death we, fans and musicians alike, still want to hear and enjoy and scholars and musicians still want to study and analyze.

As a Boston jazz radio show host for over three decades, I might say that Coltrane's music must be played simply because it's beautiful music that must be heard. But that's too easy. There is also a timelessness to much of Coltrane's music that just about requires me to play it. Though decades have gone by since his passing, his music still sounds fresh and inspiring. Many of the ideas that the quartet were dealing with are still a part of the music scene. The influence of McCoy Tyner and Elvin Jones certainly continued even with the dissolution of the quartet. The list of musicians who would count Coltrane and the members of his quartet as major influences would be too long to print.

There has always been a feeling among European classical music enthusiasts that certain works by certain composers must remain a part of the classical repertoire. Many radio programmers feel that those works must be included in their programming or else they aren't properly supporting the music. The popular music world works differently. There is little value placed on older music, even when "older" means just a few years old. For radio, a record would be considered new for just a few months. It would get a certain amount of airplay during that initial release period, and after that only the most popular selections ever get aired again. Unlike the classical music stations, perhaps because of marketing techniques, most popular music stations don't feel that it's necessary to play the music of "masters" or founding fathers or to play some older songs as essential to the sound of the station or the format. In many ways, jazz radio has followed this model with some variations. Many give lip service to jazz classics but rarely, and in some cases never, play them.

For me, I prefer the attitude of classical music stations. Certain jazz masters must be heard. The music of the masters must be played so that younger audiences will become familiar with the history of this music. Also there are still jazz fans alive who've heard even the earliest jazz recordings when they were first released. There are certainly many Coltrane fans today who saw him live. His music must be played to satisfy the taste of those jazz veterans.

Even after saying that, I think the real reason I play his music is not something he did technically. I think I play his music because it's simply beautiful and as I said, I got into radio because I wanted others to know about the beautiful things I was hearing.

Although I've said how I often could listen to John's music only in certain situations, really Trane left us with a rich legacy and a wide variety of music. I certainly remember watching the *Cosby Show* and hearing Trane's music while the Huxtables were in a romantic embrace, dancing across the floor.

In these troubling times, many can probably use the uplifting effect of Trane's music, perhaps sharing in that vision of a better life that John wanted to communicate though his music.

Recently I found this poem by Franz Von Schober that Franz Schubert put to music in his 1817 work "An die Musik."

> O gracious Art, in how many gray hours
> When life's fierce orbit encompassed me,
> Hast thou kindled my heart to warm love,
> Hast charmed me into a better world.
> Oft has a sigh, issuing from thy harp,
> A sweet, blest chord of thine,
> Thrown open the heaven of better times;
> O gracious Art, for that I thank thee!

"Somebody please say, Amen!"

Masters on a Master Introduction

The following three sections are edited conversations beginning with Anthony Brown's interview of Olly Wilson, followed by my dialogues with Yusef Lateef and Billy Taylor. The purpose of these discussions is to provide a unique opportunity for readers to gain insightful knowledge about John Coltrane's musical and spiritual legacy from masters of the music. The opportunity was created by reaching out to the trio of Professor Lateef, Professor Taylor, and Professor Wilson, each recognized throughout the world as a musician and educator of great accomplishment, integrity, and humility. Each is a master African American musician with deep and insightful knowledgeable of John Coltrane's accomplishments, contributions, and achievements. Along with the contributors' outstanding work, these transcribed conversations capture the spirit, knowledge, and understanding of the search for truth that defines this endeavor to share new and important light on the legacies of John Coltrane within the context of Black American culture.

Olly Wilson's comments reflect on Coltrane's artistry and innovations, the development and incorporation of spirituality in his music, his extraordinary contributions and his iconic stature in music. Yusef Lateef's comments include reflections on his relationship with Coltrane as a fellow musician and friend. They spent significant time together, on and off the bandstand. They had many discussions about music, and Lateef's remarks provide rich insight into Coltrane's musical concepts and approaches, spiritual evolution, and global influences. Billy Taylor's comments reflect on Coltrane as a contemporary of his time, his significance in the community of his peers, and his lasting influence on our times. Collectively, the comments of this "masters trio" provide a richness and truthfulness that can come only from the inside view of the Black American musician.

—Leonard L. Brown

Conversation with Olly Wilson

Given my orientation as an ethnomusicologist, I believe an examination of Coltrane's musical origins, in particular his West African roots, contributes to a deeper understanding of his music. In preparing a contextual framework for my contribution to this collection of scholarly writings about Coltrane, I conducted an interview with preeminent composer and professor emeritus Olly Wilson at his home in Berkeley, Calif., on December 7, 2006. The Spring 1974 issue of *The Black Perspective in Music* includes Wilson's seminal article *The Significance of the Relationship between Afro-American Music and West African Music*, which introduced a theoretical framework that examines a core of conceptual approaches to processes of music making that are shared throughout the African Diaspora. This work has informed most scholarly research in African American musical culture since, even broadening the range of descriptive musical transcriptions by inclusion of an excerpt from James Brown's recording *Super Bad* (*Star Time—The Definitive James Brown Collection*), a first in scholarly music journals. Wilson's 1983 article, *Black Music as an Art Form,* further examines this relationship in the music of Miles Davis, and a 1992 article, *The Heterogeneous Sound Ideal in African American Music,* explores musical commonalities found in the seemingly disparate music of the Central African Ba-Benzele Pygmies and that of Duke Ellington. Because Wilson is an internationally honored composer and scholar, I felt that his insights into Coltrane's compositional craft would provide a fresh understanding of Coltrane's music, sound, and stature as an artist. [*Editor's note*: Prior to publication, Professor Wilson reviewed his comments and corrected as he deemed appropriate. Therefore the interview as presented is an edited version.]

—Anthony Brown

AB: Dr. Wilson, would you please share your views on John Coltrane's contributions to African American culture?

OW: John Coltrane made a major contribution by helping to define the nature and reflect the character of American urban culture in the latter half of the century, a time of significant cultural, social, and political turbulence—including the Civil Rights Movement, the Black Power Movement, and the anti–Vietnam War Movement.

His emergence as a major artist in this time period also coincides with the development of the Black Art cultural movement in the United States. For many African Americans who were his contemporaries, John Coltrane is seen not only as a major cultural icon of the period, but his career also embodies the intersection of the social, cultural, and political dynamics that dominated this era. In many respects, his life and music epitomized the ideals of the Black Arts cultural movement in the 1960s.

As an artist, Coltrane, as had others before him, developed a distinct approach to improvisation that reflected his unique vision of the art, and that vision enabled him to explore aspects of the performance experience that few had focused on to the same degree. Among his most unique qualities as an improvising artist is the palpable intensity of his performances, and the resultant gravitas that this quality imbues in the entire performance experience. Coltrane consistently managed to convey a sense of urgency, power, and insistent communicability in his performances that required the listener to sit up and pay attention. His music was the antithesis of the subtle understatement that characterizes some genres of jazz that possess a sensibility of quiet contemplation and cool detachment. His music, rather, exudes fire and direct, unequivocal statements; perhaps the musical equivalents of political exhortations of his time such as "Freedom Now!" This distinct quality was an intrinsic part of his basic approach to creating music and is also evident in varying degrees in his early recordings, although the various means that he employed in achieving this goal evolved over his entire career. He was a man whose apprenticeship as a young musician included exposure to religious music in rural African American churches, performing brass and woodwind instruments in bands, and, ultimately, performing and recording hard-driving rhythm and blues as a saxophonist. All of these experiences enabled him to develop an understanding and appreciation of music as an intense, affective force—music that had a direct appeal to one's inner soul and required one's personal emotional involvement.

Another salient aspect of Coltrane's artistry was his conscious effort to invoke his personal spirituality as a fundamental component of his artistry. Many observers have noted this quality early in his career, and it became a central part of his life in the early '60s as he began consciously to explore Hinduism, Buddhism, and African culture in search of his personal spiritual enlightenment. Coltrane's quest for spiritual enlightenment has a lot to do with his background as well as the nature of his personal life. His grandfathers were ministers, and he, as a child, was exposed to the notion of spiritual power. Moreover, the trajectory of his personal life also mirrors the Christian "Prodigal Son" narrative. He reached a crisis when, at a high point of his professional career, his drug and alcohol addiction endangered his life. Fortunately, he had a personal epiphany that enabled him to overcome his addictions. He then resumes his musical career with a commitment to embrace his spirituality as an essential part of his artistry. The seminal 1964 recording of *A Love Supreme* by his classic quartet, consisting of [Coltrane and] McCoy Tyner, piano, Elvin Jones, drummer, and Jimmy Garrison, bass, is the landmark work in this development. After this recording, most of his work reflected his spiritual quest explicitly.

I believe this experience gave him a heightened sensibility, an acute understanding of the multiple levels of communication that are possible within the context of musical experiences that also embody dimensions of spirituality. He brings that sensitivity to bear on his approach to performance for the remainder of his life. In a broad sense, perhaps because of this personal epiphany, this new understanding of the multiple dimensions of the music experience, he perceived the nature of music to have been expanded exponentially. This experience gave him a clearer understanding about the importance of communicating more profoundly with each individual listener, and, simultaneously, communicating more effectively with larger groups of people in an interactive manner.

One of the most notable things about Coltrane is that he built upon all of his experiences. If he learned something new musically, he became vitally interested in that phenomenon, and it became part of his musical personality. He never threw anything away, but continually developed, in imaginative ways, new means of transforming that which had previously existed. His brilliant transformation of the Richard Rodgers show tune "My Favorite Things" from a interesting diatonic melody supported by a harmonic underpinning based on the circle of fifths to a piece that explores and expands the pedal point and the modal implications of the original first four measures of the original piece is a case in point. Here he creates a fresh harmonically static structure for the entire song that both supports the original melody, and contrasts with the improvised, soaring, modal, soprano-saxophone melodic excursions that swirl in an arabesque manner above a constant rhythmic pattern in the ensemble and pedal point in the bass.

In a broad sense, the idea of transforming previous existing techniques, musical ideas, and concepts is central to the modern jazz ethos. Charlie Parker, Dizzy Gillespie, Thelonious Monk, Max Roach, and Kenny Clarke all made great contributions to redefining the nature and substance of the jazz tradition that they found as young musicians. Coltrane is a central figure in the history of jazz because he also was an agent of significant artistic change. He was the creator of a new paradigm of improvisation. I also think Coltrane's high status among the jazz giants was achieved as a result of his intensity and spirituality as well as his exceptional dedication to his art. This combination of personal qualities coupled with his fertile musical imagination and superb technical skill as a performer enabled him to attain the highest levels of musical artistry.

From a musical point of view, Coltrane's contributions to music are extraordinary. He was, in my opinion, more of a consolidator, than an innovator. Of course, he was also an innovator, and he consistently worked in innovative ways, but, most important, he consolidated what he and others had done earlier and produced viable new ways of making powerful musical statements that reflect influences from a number of sources. *A Love Supreme* is a case in point. In this work we have an extended improvised work whose musical structure is influenced by the modal improvisation that was established in the late '50s in seminal recordings such as "Kind Of Blue," but whose rhythmic background freely employs nonregular pulse techniques, whose overall harmonic structure is not dependent upon Western functional harmony, and whose overall extended structure is preconceived although most of the music is improvised. Moreover, the basic reason for this work's existence is firmly rooted in his personal spiritual quest.

In his latest recordings Coltrane moved beyond modal improvisation to embrace atonality in his work as well as an approach to utilizing musical timbre and textures as shaping forces in his improvisations, although spiritual intensity continues to be fundamental to his ideal. This step also reflects Coltrane's role as a consolidator in that he incorporated techniques associated with several of his contemporaries, such as Ornette Coleman, Cecil Taylor, and Sun Ra, but maintained his personal musical identity.

To summarize, John Coltrane is significant because his music is an exemplar of superb musicality and aesthetic integrity, particularly as it relates to intensity and spirituality. Second, his work often consolidates a number of innovative concepts that other imaginative musicians were exploring and synthesizes them in a very powerful artistic package that reflected the ethos of many people in the major urban centers of the United States in the 1960s. It was this accomplishment that large numbers of people recognized immediately. Sometimes artists who attain enormous critical acclaim and popularity during their lifetime are recognized because their work cogently reflects the ideas and the values of that generation. I think that John Coltrane was such an artist. Moreover, because the role of spirituality was so vital to Coltrane as an artist, he redefined the role of the so-called jazz performer in ways that were fundamentally different.

AB Commentary: At this point I played an excerpt from James Brown's "Super Bad" containing a Coltrane-inspired tenor saxophone solo to underscore that Coltrane has become an important figure outside of the jazz world. In fact, in the 2005 movie *Beauty Shop* starring Queen Latifah, the film's musician character plays only Stevie Wonder tunes and John Coltrane's "Giant Steps." I then asked Professor Wilson to comment on Coltrane's impact on the wider musical world.

OW: The usage of extended "free" modal or atonal improvisation as an expression of a concept, general idea, or emotion became an iconic sound. It signified the embodiment of something that was intense, powerful, emotional, and implied spirituality. It also signified a musical experience that was desirable and therapeutic. At this point, it began to imply that the musical experience had become a spiritual experience—intense, powerful, and emotional.

In the 1960s, when John Coltrane becomes "Trane," he becomes an icon. As a consolidator he pulls many things together (different musical styles, cultures, and genres, his intensity, his political consciousness, his spirituality), and all of this becomes identified with the musical period, and becomes the kind of music that many people listened to, beginning with "My Favorite Things." And his name, "Trane," is suggestive of the period because it's a powerful symbol that is also associated with African American spirituals, and conveys the image of a train ... the moving, the running away, the getting away, the going to a better place, is all part of that metaphor.

Coltrane's compositional craft is rooted in improvisation. A couple of techniques he commonly employs are characteristic of his work. One is his usage of motivic figures. He will often take a short motivic idea, 2, 3, or 4 notes, and use that short fragment repeatedly. And he'll use it in a number of different ways ... sometimes placed in different places in the rhythmic continuum. Or he'll perform a simple motivic idea [*sings "Giant Steps"*], and then take that same musical contour and harmonic structure associated with the idea and create a series of sequences on that musical idea. This is a common technique of developing the musical material in many cultures. Beethoven did that a lot, especially with the usage of fragmentation at the end of a sequence of statements.

I believe when Coltrane thought of a piece, he thought about the music's motivic structure, and that motivic structure identifies the piece. The repetition of short motivic ideas becomes a very common characteristic of his work [*sings "Acknowledgment" of "A Love Supreme"*]. Listen to "Blues for Bechet" [*sings excerpt*]. It's the same kind of structure—the usage of short motives to construct larger phrases that are also based on the development of the original motives. It's relentless, trancelike in a way, but ingeniously done—his judicious choice of the notes, the choice of the ranges, the timbres, and where and when he moves or doesn't move harmonically. Nevertheless, all of this creates a sense of direction and builds a discernible musical structure. So ultimately, Coltrane creates a logical musical structure that has a purposeful direction. There is clearly a teleological basis underlying Coltrane's improvisations. If you listen to several extended sections you will notice there is always a sense of direction, that he is moving toward specific goals or climactic points.

In "Giant Steps," Coltrane uses cyclical melodic and harmonic progressions [the iii-V-I and ii-V-I chord progressions] that shift to unexpected places. It's an ingenious way of using standard harmonic themes or ideas, but always presenting them in novel and musically compelling ways. The circle of fifths is again used here as a harmonic anchor, but the intervallic relationships between the melodic line and bass line, and the surprising harmonic sequences at the end of every two measures at the beginning of the piece are artistically inspired. Another aspect of Coltrane's music is his tendency to fill up all of the musical space. That intensity, that relentlessness is engendered by the fact that he seems to have so much to say and not enough time to say it.

With Coltrane [*Wilson's speech increases in volume and its cadence accelerates*], it's "I got to get it all out. And I want to tell you something very quickly, because I may not get it all out. I want you to know. Do you hear me? I want you to know, explicitly ..." Often, there are no pauses, or cadences in his improvisations, even when he comes to a formal structural point, he'll go right through it! Other hallmarks of his improvisational technique include focusing on the melodic, especially against a pedal point; the use of simple motives and their ingenious repetition and development; his usage of scales, runs, and swoops, sometimes referred to as "sheets of sound," or textures; that is, a series of notes that are going so fast that they can be recognized only as rapid melodic flourishes filling up the space. These flourishes of notes move from one point to another in rapid succession, sometimes stating the same scale a half step or whole step away in a manner that creates momentum. The primary shaping force of the music is in the hands of the improviser, so that the performer can create, in the moment of performance, the content and nature of his specific musical statement.

Coltrane shapes the melodic dimension of his improvisations in a myriad of ways. He does this by employing a wide range of techniques, including influences from non-Western cultures. In his last recordings, he appears to expand the emotional content of his music, particularly when playing soprano saxophone in a modal context, which may superficially resemble Middle Eastern music. But his way of expressing it is his personal way of doing it; that is, he brought everything into his own compositional sphere. By playing phrases fast enough using his personal phrasing on his saxophone, he approaches the instrument like a voice, and the voice like an instrument, projecting a wide range of vocal nuances like screams and shrieks. It seems to come naturally to him. He appears to view his instrument as an inexhaustible vehicle for expression, just like the voice. He uses a wide range of intensifiers ... timbral variations that intensify the repetitions of musical gestures, such as shrieks and howls to add to the intensity. Most of his pieces start out slowly and gradually evolve into climactic high points where the tension generated by the experience is ultimately released.

The combination of Coltrane's personal musical proclivities, coupled with his rich, fertile artistic imagination and magnificent technical skill as a performer enable him to create extended improvised works that work on many levels. He understands how to shape music of longer time dimensions. You often know what he's going to do before he starts doing it. Just as you often know what's going to happen in terms of the dynamic progress of many African American ministers' sermons in a traditional Baptist or Pentecostal church. You know the preacher is going to gradually build the emotional tension up slowly. And you know he's going to have some interesting, humorous, and philosophical comments to state along the way. But when he gets ready to say, "Open the doors of the church," the tension in the room is going to be high, and a lot of people in the congregation are going to be moving in their seats in an agitated manner. By that time, in some churches, the organist has eased over to the piano, the music is sliding around harmonically, or repeating a rhythmic vamp on a dominant pedal point, and thereby creating expectations for a tremendous climax, and everybody is excited, and the minister reiterates shorter and shorter phrases, and the people respond by saying, "Yes! Yes! Yes!" and then, you reach the highest point of a collective emotional climax, and everybody's feeling the heat. And finally, things slow down, and a cathartic release of emotional energy is achieved.

Coltrane often uses that kind of overall structure, but what makes it interesting is, like every Sunday morning, you know the minister's going to do it, but you don't know exactly how he's going to do it that day. What interesting side stories is he going to tell; is he going to get there rapidly or slowly … ? There are many ways to creatively shape that climax. So, in some respects, perhaps, this is what Coltrane is about artistically, I think, as I listen to and, more important, experience his music.

Conversation with Yusef Lateef

The following conversation with Yusef Lateef took place on July 28, 2006, via telephone as he was at home in western Massachusetts. I have known Yusef Lateef for a number of years and have been listening to his music since I was a young teenager. He is one of the great human beings and artists of our time. As his Web site (www.yuseflateef.com) states, "Yusef Lateef is a Grammy Award–winning composer, performer, recording artist, author, educator, and philosopher who has been a major force on the international musical scene for more than six decades. He is universally acknowledged as one of the great living masters and innovators in the African American tradition of autophysiopsychic music—that which comes from one's spiritual, physical, and emotional self." Beginning in the mid-1950s, Professor Lateef pioneered the investigation and incorporation of the use of global music traditions, including instruments and music forms, in his own compositions and influenced Coltrane's later explorations into similar sonic territories and considerations. I asked Professor Lateef to talk with me about John Coltrane because I knew they had significant personal and professional relationships.

—Leonard L. Brown

LB: How did you come to know John Coltrane?

YL: Well, see, I met John Coltrane when I was with Dizzy Gillespie's big band, 1949. We were rehearsing in Philadelphia, and we had an engagement at the same time. And Jimmy Heath came to the rehearsal, and that's when I first met John.

LB: What type of individual was he? What were your initial impressions of him as a person and as a musician?

YL: He was a very quiet person, and what impressed me was that he was serious about developing himself as a musician and as a performer.

LB: You knew him for pretty much the rest of his life until he passed in 1967?

YL: Yes, I knew him up until two weeks . . . in fact, I saw him about two weeks before he died.

LB: How would you describe your relationship with him over those years?

YL: It was an amiable relationship. Every time that we would meet, musically, the same thing. And it seemed to be a continuous camaraderie between the two of us, and we both were imbued with a feeling of development of our music.

LB: Were there some particular things that you both were interested in musically during these periods of time—of exploring or learning more about?

YL: When he was with Miles Davis, he came to Detroit, and I was in Detroit then, where I grew up, and I would listen to him play all night, you know. He took most of the solos, you know. And after he got off at 2 A.M., we went to breakfast, and he asked me, "What two keys give you twelve different tones, and what two keys will give you eleven tones?" and subsequently, on down the ladder. And we stayed up maybe two or three hours figuring that out. And that was the kind of eclectic attitude—he was searching.

LB: What would you say about his personality and his character qualities? What type of human being was he?

YL: Well, he was a very kind, humble, humble person. The impression was very humble ... that's the impression I always got from him.

LB: What would you say about his evolution and development as a man and also as a musician?

YL: Well, he was a person who was mainly eclectic by nature, or he developed that attitude. And if he was on the road, there would always be several books in his room. He'd be studying something, whether it would be mathematics or esoteric astrology. I remember that once he and Naima recommended a book called *Esoteric Astrology*, which dealt with the hidden planets and things of that nature, and Naima would see that the various books and things were in his study. She was very essential to his growth.

I remember when the critics were saying John was playing what sounded like "sheets of sound." Well, they didn't know that Naima had seen to it that a harp was in his study, and of course you could just set the pedals and pull your fingers over it and you would get the idea of "sheets of sound." Among other books that she made available for him included violin books that he used to practice out of, things of that nature. And of course, when he discovered the secondary dominants that were used by European composers decades ago, he brought in, he introduced it into autophysiopsychic music. Heart music, I call it. And he took the secondary dominants and applied them to standard songs, like "Body and Soul" and several other songs. "Giant Steps" was the first introduction. And he told me that, "I know that pattern backwards," and it was obvious in his playing.

LB: What about his musical and spiritual influences?

YL: Well, you know it was evident in the poem he wrote in *A Love Supreme*, I think it is ... I could hear, semantically, the songs of Islam, if you will, and he was married to a Muslim lady.

LB: This was Naima.

YL: Naima Coltrane. And of course, as you know, Muslims pray five times a day, and the first chapter of the holy Qur'an, which is the religious book of

Muslims, it's called "Al Fatihah." And when John would say in this poem—
I'm paraphrasing—"God is the greatest, no matter what" ... and you heard
that suffix and this keeps repeating. It reminds me of the second sentence
of the Holy Qur'an which says, "All praises to God, the Lord of all the
worlds." And so it seems as though he was imbued with this love of God in
this poem. Islam teaches that he who is grateful to God is grateful to
mankind. And in this poem, he thanked all those people who recorded and
played with him, if you remember that. He picked them out one by one and
said how gracious he was. And this is an Islamic attitude. Now, when you
talk about spirituality, this is a very personal thing. Spiritual experiences, as
I see it, are between the individual and the Creator. It was obvious that he
had a love for God in his writings. Another thing that the Holy Qur'an
teaches is that God creates things in pairs, so in interpreting this phrase, I
like to say that, for example, when a man hears a beautiful voice or a
beautiful sound, in being drawn towards it, it's not the person who the
sound is coming to. It's the Creator who has invested, impregnated this
sound with this particular quality that only he can give. And I think that's
what John was talking about when he spoke about spirituality. It is the
spirit of God, which can be seen in the universe. If we look out into the
galaxy, galaxies, we see all this beauty, and we know that no man created it.
Things happen because they are created, and John knew that. You see one
cannot induce spirituality because he has so many degrees, or intellect, or if
he has billions of dollars. It has to be the will of Providence that one
becomes anointed with that. That's what I think John was striving for, and
one could feel certain moments of this Providential experience in listening
to some of his music.

LB: Do you think he manifested some of that through the actual sound he was
able to create through his instruments?

YL: What I'm saying is it's likely that he was anointed with that in periods of
time during his life.

LB: One of the things that John says about his life is that he had an experience
in 1957. Sometimes I call it an epiphany. Clearly, he had a kind of
awakening in '57 that caused him to really reflect on what his life was
about, why he was here on earth, and in what directions he should be
moving. He began to get his life in order and consider those types of
things. What's your take on that?

YL: Well, I guess I have some fragments. You know like impressions, the word
impressions? ... He named a song that, right? Now, I think, there are
moments when one gets the impression of the awareness of God, you see.
And I think him being a creation of God and loving God, and so I believe
that he had some impressions of the Creator as a godly force, and that's
why his poem was so much about praising the Creator, it was like a prayer.

LB: During this period of time in the late '50s, early '60s, it seems there was a move by a lot of African American musicians to see themselves more as artists and identifying oneself with what the purpose of life was on Earth, and also in terms of being aware of issues linked with fair treatment for African Americans in this country. Do you think that some of that touched John or came out in John's music some way?

YL: Oh, yeah, I do. I think the grief that human beings experienced during the '60s touched John like it touched many others. Now, what is the piece he wrote ... ?

LB: "Alabama" was one he wrote.

YL: You see? ... It touched me. I wrote a piece called "Down in Atlanta." Same thing. Love for people, preparedness for love and compassion. John wished that for humanity, and so did I. And so it was reflected in what he did. I think Naima, the song "Naima" ... it's a love poem, what you call a love song. He told me ... me and my wife would meet him and Naima when they'd come to Detroit. We'd have dinner. And once, later on, after John got his own group, I met him in Chicago. I was in Chicago playing also, and he told me that he and Naima had split up. He said it was one of those things. You know, people part for some reasons. I don't know the reasons, but he said, "Yusef, I still love her." And shortly after that, he recorded that song "Naima." It was the most lovely love song I've ever heard. You can hear it. You can hear it in the music that he certainly cared.

LB: Did you know Alice, his second wife?

YL: I knew Alice. Her brother used to play bass with me, Ernie Farrow.

LB: Do you think they had just as strong a connection? She was also in the music with him as a performer, and it seems like they had a deep, loving relationship also.

YL: I agree, yeah. Well, that's the kind of person John was. I mean he was a serious person, and I'm sure he loved Alice dearly.

LB: Do you feel she made a significant musical contribution to the band?

YL: I don't know. I don't listen to much music. Maybe I haven't heard the things you're talking about. I think a lot about music, but I don't play a lot of music on records. But I know that when we played this concert at Olatunji's, John was just as strong as ever after he married Alice.

LB: Was this a part of that concert in 1967, or did you do more than one concert at Tunji's Center?

YL: Well, we did one concert, but we had planned another at Lincoln Center. In fact, we got the hall, and it was going to be a kind of an anthology, if you will, an anthology of our music, starting in Africa, the Americas, its development. In fact, at that time John wanted to buy a location in New York, without whiskey, without alcohol—sandwiches and teas so children could come and hear the music. And he asked to see my realtor. I lived in Teaneck [New Jersey]. So he came over to my house that day—this is about two weeks before he passed—and he went out and found a place that he liked. He was going to move, 'cause he lived way out on Long Island, you know. So he found a place in Teaneck, and I had to leave for England the next day, but the day before I left, he found this place, and he came by the house, and I fixed some chocolate for him. It's called "Pretty Quick," and you mix milk with it. Now he didn't tell me he was sick or nothing. He just looked at the jar and he said "pretty quick" out loud, as though he was thinking of something. I never knew what he was thinking. And so I gave him my greetings and peace, and I was looking forward to him opening the place in New York. And I got to London, and about five days after I was in London, I picked up the morning paper, and he had died.

LB: What would you say about his innovations and contributions to music?

YL: Well, see, that's a big question. There are many. Number one, he had a sound like no one else on his instrument which is what the masters, like Lester Young and Coleman Hawkins and Ben Webster, showed us—that you can have your own sound. So John produced that. And like Charlie Parker, he introduced different harmonic structures to improvise, if you will . . . to perform over. John introduced that, of course, with the secondary dominants, which is a very fast harmonic structure, but he made it sound so beautiful and so easy. That shows you how much ability he had. He took the saxophone to a level that no one else had in terms of melody, if you will. Melody became something else. He presented never before heard "melodicals," if you will. . . . And, of course, he brought sounds out of the instrument that no one had ever heard before. The same as Lester Young was an innovator of new timbres to the saxophone. Oh, yeah, he's the first person I heard to develop at least two themes. During the length of the solo, he would develop one theme in one register, and almost simultaneously he would develop another one in another register, and he would leave some rests in one theme, and go to the other and develop it, and come back. It's as though he had two kinds of consciousness, if you will, for one soul. And he explored tonality and like the song, *A Love Supreme*? [Yusef sings the melody as he says these words.]

LB: Acknowledgment. That's the first movement, Acknowledgment.

YL: Right, right, which made me think of the night we sat up to find out which two keys give you twelve tones . . . [*chuckles*] . . . and give you eleven too. So I have one analogy. I had a student from Russia, and I asked him just about the same question you just asked me about John, and he said, "Oh, I know what John did." He said what John did was collect many things and put them in a bottle, and then when he poured them out, they would come out connected.

LB: That's a heck of an analogy.

YL: Yeah, I think that's a terrific analogy, and it hit home, you know … in collecting things, you know? Which reminds me, you heard that last interview John had in Sweden?

LB: Yes.

YL: Before he left Miles?

LB: Yes, sir.

YL: And remember when the deejay told him, "People think you're angry the way you play those twenty-five-minute solos." And John said, "No, I'm not angry." You remember that?

LB: I remember him specifically saying that he wasn't angry at all.

YL: Right! John said: "Maybe the people think that because I've found so many things, I'm trying to see which works the best."

LB: Yeah, he was working things out.

YL: He was working it out.

LB: I think maybe the Swedish people picked up on what some of the American critics were saying, but I always find it interesting as to why somebody would make that assumption because he was playing that way. What kind of mentality would lead somebody to label it like that, because there were a lot of other ways you could look at it at the time.

YL: Absolutely. I don't think that's fair to label it like that. You know, John wasn't what you would call "a mouthy person." He didn't talk a lot. He was very terse, you know? But that didn't mean he wasn't thinking, you know what I'm saying? You see, that's an attitude that I observed back in the '40s when Billy Eckstine had his band, and there was Dizzy Gillespie's band after that with Gene Ammons, Dexter Gordon … What I would like to point out is that the musicians didn't talk a lot. It was as though if you talked a lot, you weren't thinking about how to develop what you wanted to play. That's the kind of an attitude that … Sonny Stitt was on the scene too. Musicians didn't talk much. They would think a great deal, and John came out of that school.

LB: It seems like at that period of time, the musicians were seeing themselves more as serious artists, rather than entertainers.

YL: Oh, it was very serious. Absolutely. It certainly did. That music that Dizzy and them was playing, they hadn't written any music like that before. And Ernie Henry and Fats Navarro were very serious in taking an uphill lunge.

LB: Wardell Gray and other people were in that.

YL: Wardell, Tad Dameron, yeah.

LB: What would you say about John's influence on showing musicians that one didn't need any drugs or anything else to play the music? What you needed was faith and conviction and some serious discipline and to believe in the music.

YL: Absolutely. He did make that type of impression. John would be eating pumpkin seeds and nuts.

LB: Do you think he had any spiritual contributions or spiritual impact on other musicians during his time or since then?

YL: Yeah, well, you know, I guess time will tell, you know? I hear that some preacher has a church called the Church of John Coltrane in California, so obviously he has made some spiritual impressions on people. And I don't doubt that John didn't know that [Lateef meant that Coltrane did not know he had this impact], as the Holy Qur'an says, God says, "I will create what you do not know." And Naima knew about this because she read the book. And John wouldn't have moved into the realm of the things that no one had heard before, if God hadn't let it be revealed.

LB: Did he ever talk his intentions as a musician to you, or did you ever hear him say anything about what he wanted to express to people? Is there anything different than what you may have shared with me already?

YL: Well, only thing I remember of that nature was he was concerned about composition that sounded like glass.

LB: Help me get some insight into that.

YL: Well, I don't know. That's some type of timbre that he was looking for in the crafting of music, of composition.

LB: That would sound like glass?

YL: Yeah, that would sound like glass.

LB: One of the things I noticed as I was reading Olatunji's autobiography is him writing that you, John, and he had similar visions about where the music should be performed. And what you've done in your life with the music; defining it as autophysiopsychic music, moving it out of the whole aspect of jazz and defining it from your perspective in terms of what it's about. I think venues have something to do with that—getting it out of the places where there is liquor and alcohol, to places where anybody can come, little kids can come, grandmothers can come, everybody. Did you and John talk about that at all because it seems like some of these efforts, like Tunji's center, seem to reflect a consciousness on the part of him (Coltrane) and you to move the music into an environment that was more conducive for the music and not for making money.

YL: Yeah, it was clear that he thought the music deserved a different venue, therefore he wanted to move closer to New York and find a place to have the music played where children could come and there wouldn't be no alcohol and things of that nature. That was what he wanted to achieve in his lifetime. I personally think the music deserves better venues. There's too much blood, sweat, and tears has gone into the development of the music for it not to be in a better, have a better venue. That's what I think, and I'm pretty sure that John felt the same way about that.

LB: Then you clearly believe musicians should play an active role in putting it into those venues. Not just waiting for club owners or promoters.

YL: You have to do it for yourself, you know. You can't wait to do it. That's why I stopped playing nightclubs in 1980. I mean those venues where they have alcohol. You just can't ... you have to do it for yourself, you know. That's the way I see it.

LB: How was he looked at in the music community and then, how was he looked at in the black community?

YL: He was given the utmost respect in the musical community. On the other hand, there were people during the '60s ... I mean there were schoolteachers who didn't know who John Coltrane was [*laughing*]. It's not their fault. People who play autophysiopsychic music don't get as much PR as some others might, so subsequently they're not known by certain people who you'd think would be aware of them. That's why books of this nature will help, particularly for people who read, you know.

LB: Did he have any particular stature in the black community?

YL: Well, he did as far as I was concerned [*laughing*]. He was evolutionary, an evolutionist. That's what I would say. You know music can have various affects on the listener, and it has some type of, you know, I can't prove this, maybe Noam Chomsky could [*laughing*]. But I think it has something to do with the syntactical relationships that one forms, and what one listens to. It's the same way ideas are transmitted through language—reading language or hearing spoken ideas. Ideas come from listening to music also ... that influence the thinking patterns. And so this music is not heard. People, they don't have the benefits that can come from such, if you will. Do you believe that?

LB: I definitely believe that. I believe music has that power. You know, I've had people talk to me about how hearing John's music touched them in ways that really changed their life, made them think about things differently, made them consider things that they were just kind of overlooking in their life. Hearing somebody's sound, or hearing somebody sing something in a certain way, touched them in a way that made them re-reflect and really look at what they should be about, and where they were going with their lives, and what should they be doing and those types of things. So, I've had that experience myself.

YL: You know it.

LB: All the way back when I was little, growing up in the black Baptist church in Frankfort, Kentucky, some of that old-time music touched me that way.

YL: I hear you.

LB: If the music hadn't manifest, I'm not so sure there would be any African Americans alive today. I don't know if we, if our ancestors, would have survived those terrible times … with some degree of sanity and aspirations and hope. We didn't dwell on all the negative, even though there was plenty of negative to dwell on. But we took a very, very bad situation and made the best we could make out of it and one of the things that came out is this music that's touched everybody around the world. Transcends skin color, sex, how much money you make, who your mother and father were, what language you speak. This music appeals and touches people and it becomes meaningful in their lives. That's the reason it survived.

YL: Right. The same way it caused the joy, it gave people hope and feelings of compassion toward their families, to humanity. John heralded an evolution of that thought. That was the "NOW" version of that beauty that African Americans were blessed with.

LB: A lot of times people write about John, and they want to talk about his knowledge and the incorporation of musical and spiritual principles and maybe some religious concepts that come from Asia, it could be India, and they also talk about West Africa. But for a lot of those folks, I never see them want to acknowledge the root of that spirituality being in the segregated Black American culture he grew up in North Carolina, where both his grandfathers were ministers.

YL: Right, right.

LB: So there's a tendency to want to forget that, or leave that out. There is a tendency to want to jump international with John, and my belief is that where his real roots are is in the spirituality that comes through our collective experiences as black people in this part of the world. It is that spirituality that led him, along with his curiosity and his musicianship. The Creator led him to see these connections, these other ways of conceiving music and spirituality, religious beliefs in other parts of the world, as he matured and grew and developed and evolved. And I believe the root of that is in Black American culture right here in this country.

YL: Yeah, I agree with you. If we examine the syntax of some of his solos, you see glimpses of our forefathers, the southern preachers. You hear the glimpses of their prototype that came out of the church. They're imbedded in the syntactical relationships that form some of the solos. And also the semantics that come from the church. You know those old southern preachers … you hear that in "Naima," in that beauty. It's a different sound, you see, it's the saxophone. He made the saxophone sound semantically and syntactically … he makes you think of those prototypes that you mentioned.

LB: John got the benefit of all that. He comes through all that, you know, growing up in North Carolina in a segregated black community. One of his grandfathers, Reverend Blair, was very much an activist for black rights during that time. Reverend Blair had to leave North Carolina two or three times—he came back—because of threats on his life and things like that, and I think all of that impacted on John. When I look at the sound that he manifested, the titles of some of his songs and things like that, I believe that was in his heart and the sound quality he manifested carried a lot of those aesthetics, and that intent.

YL: Absolutely. Yeah, he was imbedded. I remember ... who is that alto saxophone player that used to wear kilts?

LB: Earl Bostic?

YL: Earl Bostic! I was in New York and Bostic offered me a job, and I had an offer from Ernie Fields.

LB: [Fields was] from Oklahoma.

YL: Yeah, Oklahoma, Tulsa. Right. And John went with Bostic, and I think he learned a lot from Bostic too.

LB: He said that. John said he was greatest saxophone player, in terms of technique, that he ever saw.

YL: Yeah, you see what I mean? Oh yeah, the music definitely was learned outside of school. The university of life! Yeah. He never lost sight of development. I remember I came to New York, it was in the '50s, to make a record, and he was playing with Miles at the club in the Village. Oscar Pettiford used to play there.

LB: Birdland.

YL: Yeah. Anyway, we played "Woody n You." I sat in with them, you know, and I played a solo, and when John finished his solo, Miles said to John, "You ain't playin' nothing," and John didn't say anything, and then right after that is when he started that practicing. And I've never seen anyone practice as much as he did, and he just got moving up the steps of evolution, you know. I remember once I went to visit him on 103rd Street, after I moved to New York. And I heard him practicing on my way up the steps, and I knocked on the door, and he let me in, and he welcomed me, and I sat down, and he went back to practicing. And I listened about twenty minutes ... and then I got up and I left ... [*laughter*], and went home and started practicing!

LB: [*Laughter*]. Yourself ... yes sir, I understand. Yeah, it's contagious! It's not a bad contagion to have.

YL: Yeah, you know, I said, "He's really got it." And it becomes a practice habit, you know?

LB: That practicing also led to a command of the instrument that I don't think had ever been seen before, which opened up all of these other possibilities of, like you said before, manifestation of sound the people hadn't heard before out of the saxophone. You know, the tenor, all of a sudden, is four octaves!

YL: That's right!

LB: In tune!

YL: Right!

LB: I mean those are just some of the things; the "sheets of sound" and all those other things, and then when you get to the compositional things and those aspects of it, all come through that diligence.

YL: Right, right.

LB: Let me ask you this, Brother Yusef. One of things John said was that he wanted to be "a force for good." Clearly this is one of his quotes that show he realized the Creator had put him here for a purpose, and he asked the Creator to give him strength to get himself back in order, after he had a few bouts and struggles, as we all have had with various things. He wanted to be a force for good, to use his music as a force for good. What do you think about that statement, and what do you think about how he moved on that?

YL: Well, you know, what comes to my mind is him being married to Naima. There's a statement in the Qur'an that God says, "I have created the man and the jinn so that they should worship me." And I think John realized that his life should be spent worshipping the Creator, the one who created him, gave him the life that he had. I think he realized that more and more as time passed. That's what comes to my mind—that he wanted to manifest that love for God, and there's a saying, "He who loves God, loves God's creation." So therefore John loved God's creation. He wanted to show them that love that he felt inside. That's why he wanted children, to play for children to come and hear the music—where he could let them experience what God had given him. That's what comes to my mind. I think he found out that's the purpose of life. That's one of the great purposes, to be compassionate.

LB: He wrote a song called "Compassion."

YL: Oh, I didn't know that.

LB: Yeah, he wrote a song called "Compassion," and I think of the name that Alice and some of her people sometimes used to refer to him after he passed—Ohnedaruth. When you take that back to the Sanskrit, it means compassion. It's a Sanskrit term that means compassion.

YL: Aha! That it's in your heart. Yeah, I see, yeah, he became aware of that.

LB: From my view on it, the messages through John's music are as relevant today as they were forty years ago, maybe more. I think his music sounds as fresh as anything I'm hearing out there today. It's as if John was playing twenty-fifth-century music, you know.

YL: That's it.

LB: I think the messages in his music about compassion and loving one another and humbleness to the Creator are messages that we need to hear in today's time.

YL: Well, I certainly agree with you. I would say all of the same things you just said.

LB: His music doesn't sound dated to me. Sometimes you can put something on, and it sounds like it was recorded in 1960. His music sounds just like it was recorded today.

YL: Absolutely. And that's because it was so … it's his prototype, you know? He really developed his own voice. It was so unique, and that's why it's so lasting. His music is an example of the providential beauty being made available in sound through his soul. It's like in the visual world we can become elated over a sunset in the sky, the colors of the sky. You know, like the Qur'an says, "I've given you eyes, and I've given you ears." God has given those faculties to show us things, show us His beauty. And John was a vehicle to produce the beauty that's possible for a soul to bring forth. Beauty is something that fills one, and that's why it's so lasting.

LB: Did John ever get close to becoming Muslim?

YL: Well, I never talked to him about Islam.

LB: I also hear that he was reading a series of books on the Sufis, or Sufism.

YL: Sufism, yeah. Inayat Khan, yeah, *The Mysticism of Sound*.

LB: George Russell told me about this. The George Russell up here in Boston, the musician.

YL: Yeah, I know him.

LB: George Russell was saying that John began to read some of these books by Inayat Khan, about the Sufi message and the meaning of life and the meaning of music within that. Do you have any knowledge of that, or do you have any personal knowledge yourself of this message that came out of Sufism, and particularly with Brother Khan?

YL: Yeah, I read Inayat Khan's *The Mysticism of Sound* in the '50s, and I still retain some of the things. He said, and I paraphrase, "You should be able to hear the love in your mother's voice when she speaks to you. You should be able to hear your own love that you have for a person when you speak to them." He used to be a vina player, you know. He was a musician before he became a philosopher.

LB: I know. I've read some of those books.

YL: You read them, OK.

LB: He stopped playing the instrument because he realized he was the instrument.

YL: [*Laughter*]. Uhh Hunh. That makes sense.

LB: What a state of awareness.

YL: Yes, that's a real state of awareness.

LB: I'm kind of familiar with it. It opened me up to thinking about things that I'd never really thought about.

YL: Right! Well see, now what you just said, that's what music can do, certain music, John's music. It can make you think of things that you haven't thought of before. Like you've read some things that you'd never thought of before. Do you see that?

LB: I see that.

YL: It can happen with music. It could be why some people don't want to hear that. [*Laughter*]

LB: I hear that one. That's the reason I believe music has the power that reading doesn't. Music can touch you, and you don't have to be literate in any written language.

YL: That's right, you're right!

LB: And so music, to me, has a more powerful role in terms of that aspect of it because it can touch us and stay with us in ways we might not realize. It can touch us, and it's almost like you can plant a seed and then a little later on, it begins to grow and sprout. And I feel John's music definitely did that for me, and many of my musician friends. The reason we started the John Coltrane Memorial Concert, Yusef, is because of our love for John and his music and our belief in some of the things he believed in. We didn't start it for anything else but that.

YL: That's beautiful.

LB: We've put our own energies into it, and we've maintained it all these years! Again, we've learned a lot and moving it on into the twenty-first century, you know, into places where kids can come, and everybody can come, grandma, grandkids, and everybody.

Editor's note: For more information about the John Coltrane Memorial Concert, go to www.jcmc.neu.edu.

Conversation with Billy Taylor

This conversation between Professor Billy Taylor and me took place on August 21, 2006, via telephone as he was at his home in New York City. I have known Professor Taylor for a number of years and have worked with him in various educational endeavors including the creation of the American Jazz Museum in Kansas City, Missouri. Considered to be one of the giants in the music, he fills that capacity in multiple roles: as a great pianist, composer, and arranger; as an outstanding educator; as a pioneer in broadcasting, including being the first black artist to host a daily show on a major New York City radio station, WNEW, as well as hosting NPR's *Jazz Alive* and *Taylor Made Piano*. He appeared on CBS *Sunday Morning* for years and has been artistic director for the Kennedy Center since 1994. A visit to his Web site (www.billytaylorjazz.net) will provide a wealth of knowledge about his legacy. I asked Professor Taylor to talk with me about John Coltrane because I knew that as a peer of Coltrane, he would provide unique and important insight, knowledge, and understanding of Coltrane's legacy.

—Leonard L. Brown

LB: This is for the book that we're doing on John called *John Coltrane and Black America's Quest for Freedom: Spirituality and the Music*. I appreciate your giving me your time and insight to contribute to it.

BT: OK.

LB: The first question is how did you know John Coltrane?

BT: I knew him from Philly. I mean he had been playing around in different places with Jimmy Heath and other people, so I knew him by reputation actually before I knew who he was because he was a saxophone player, and I knew Jimmy and I knew the Heath brothers and several other guys down there that he had worked with, and then I didn't remember him much from that particular period, from that experience. But I did remember him when he came to start to play with all different kinds of people in New York and recording for Blue Note and [Art] Blakey and all those kinds of things that he was kind of getting into on the New York scene. And that was very interesting to me because I was on the air [radio], and I could hear a lot of the things that he was doing. But even before then, when we played at [*pause*] I was the house pianist at Birdland. He was with the all-star groups on many occasions. He would be one of the guys that would come in whenever they had some good players; they'd put them all together and call them "all-stars." And they were. I mean because these guys were really carrying the load. They were taking all of the chances and doing all of the things that most of the other people weren't doing. So Marty K would put these guys together and it would be Blakey playing drums and he'd have Oscar Pettiford sometimes on bass and other guys like that.

LB: So these were like all-star bands.

BT: Well, I mean really, literally "all-stars" even though they didn't have the reputation that individually they should have had at that point.

LB: When was it in Philadelphia that you first heard John play?

BT: Well that would be in about 19 [*pause*] I think about '48, '49.

LB: OK, and then you heard him more when he moved to New York.

BT: Yeah, when he came to New York. At that time I was freelancing and doing a lot of other things and trying to put together groups and everything, so I would get to meet a lot of the guys because I was getting around to see what was going on and trying to play a few gigs here and there.

LB: How would you describe your relationship with him over the years, Billy?

BT: Very good. He was a very interesting man. One of the things that I remembered about him was that most guys who play saxophone, if you go see them or something like that or if you see them in a personal area, where they were practicing or something like that, the guy would have the chord from his saxophone around his neck ... many guys. He [Coltrane] would have his whole saxophone and walk around with his saxophone all the time. And I always got the feeling that he just wanted to have the horn that close in case he thought of something, and he usually did. He'd be talking to someone, and he'd play something, and it would not have a relation to anything. Like we're talking, and I'd say something that doesn't make sense over here, and it's not like what we're talking about.

LB: What could you say about his personality and character qualities?

BT: He was a relatively quiet guy. The thing I liked about him was when we got to talk [*pause*] he was interested in some of the things that I was studying and stuff, and I got the feeling [*pause*]. He didn't do academically many things that I remembered, but he seemed to have a kind of feeling for academic things in terms of getting information and putting it in some kind of form that was useful.

LB: What would you say about his evolution and development? And I kind of look at it in two categories: one as a man and then as a musician.

BT: Well, I liked him as a man because he was straight-ahead. There was nothing false in our relationship, and he was all straight-ahead. He was never dubious and beating around the bush. He'd just say what he had to say. He didn't talk a lot, but what he had to say was cool. And he was interesting, and, in general, things interested him. He had some interesting things to say about what was going on when Bud got beat up.

LB: Got beat up in Philadelphia?

BT: Yeah [*pause*] and, you know, he [Coltrane] really took that kind of seriously. He said, "Why would anyone do that?" He [Bud Powell] was beaten up by the cops.

LB: A lot of people said that changed Bud forever.

BT: It did! It did! No question about it. It was a terrible beating, and he was really a changed person. People don't realize how bad you can bang a guy around on his head and everything else, and you know it may very well have a very serious after-effect. I know with Bud it did. I know we [Coltrane and I] got in a conversation one time about Lester Young, who lived right across the street from Birdland in the hotel. And he [Coltrane] was talking about what a sound … the kind of things he [Young] did and how he did certain things as opposed to Coleman Hawkins. He [Coltrane] loved the way Hawk went over the keys. Hawk knew every change you could think about, man. And he [Coltrane] was aware of that. He was aware of that aspect of what Hawk did. And he wondered what would have had happened if Prez [Lester Young] had chosen to do what Hawk did with that sound.

LB: What about him as a musician, his evolution and development? What would you say about that?

BT: Well, he really got serious. I don't know, maybe he was always serious. I don't know, but he got really serious when he got to playing with a wide variety of guys in New York. I mean the guys who were really on the cutting edge and the guys that were doing everything and playing the changes and trying to develop something. One of the things that he asked me about—he knew that I was Art Tatum's protégé at the time and so he said, "How did he do some of those things, it sounded like a glissando?" I said, "Well, man, his fingering was so expert that what he did, even though it was sounding like he was just running his hand down the key, he was actually playing specific notes that he wanted to hear." And he [Coltrane] found that fascinating. He said, "Oh yeah? I've got to check him out some more." Obviously Tatum had played Philly, and so he [Coltrane] had heard him play, and that was why he had asked me. He said, "Well, you know, you were influenced by Tatum, so tell me about him." I told him what I knew about him. I said Art was a wonderful musician and a wonderful cat, and for me it was like going to school, and I learned so much from just being around him. So at that point, that was when I became aware of some of the harmonic things that he was beginning to focus on. I had a book called *Mastering the Scales and Arpeggios* that I had worked on for many years. Already I had been using it for about ten years or something like that, and that had helped me develop a lot of the technical things that I had heard Tatum and other people do and I told him about that, about what I learned from piano students studying about tonal quality and stuff like that, and he found that interesting. We had interesting conversations because not many guys who didn't play piano would ask those kinds of questions.

LB: Did you hear him when he was with Monk?

BT: Oh, yeah.

LB: What are your recollections, and what would you say about what was happening? What they were doing, and what impact may that have had on John?

BT: He was like a student to Monk. He was really one of the first guys that realized that Monk's approach was very personal, but there was something that he could get from the way Monk handled the music that he played. What he [Coltrane] did with those different rhythms and his approach to rhythm and his approach to really getting over the horn, and I think that was probably when he really put the Tatum thing that we had talked about in a different context and really began to use that, not just the kind of scales that were diatonic or something like that. These were all kinds of scales and things like that, and he could hear other kinds of not just harmonies but spaces in the work that Monk was doing, and he wanted to put that to use, and he did.

LB: What would you say about any links that John has to Black American musical aesthetics and principles of music making?

BT: Well, I think that being from the South, he had a sense of wanting to contribute something to African American music, and when he got to Philadelphia, it was a place where people articulated that. Jimmy Heath was a good example around his age and my age, but there were a lot of other folks that wanted to say something in the music, in the tradition of the music. We knew about our predecessors, and a lot of the musicians came down from Philadelphia to Washington and went further south on tours and everything, so we got to hear a lot of guys. Jimmy Oliver and a lot of the other guys that were playing locally in the bands around there. Even though it wasn't acknowledged as such, there was a kind of feeling that guys from Philadelphia had. That's why Dizzy Gillespie and some of those guys went down there because they were approaching jazz in ways that you couldn't put a name on it or anything, but their approach was a Philadelphia approach, if you will. It's like somebody has an accent, speaking or something like that, and there are certain things that all the guys there were party to that, and they could kind of feel their way. It's like Detroit led at a later period when those guys came through. The same thing happen. I mean, different people, different problems, but the same result in that you got something that really spoke to and for the black community as they felt it and saw it. Because all of these guys played R&B and there was no separation in those days. You could play R&B, and you played jazz, and it was a part of it. R&B was really just a way of playing jazz, in some respects, for dances and for parties and stuff like that.

LB: What would you say about John's influences—musical or spiritual or religious?

BT: Well, his influences are really phenomenal when you look back. I was too close to him to see some of those things until after the fact, but when I saw some of the things that he began to do with his quartet, man, I could see the effect that he had on people. I remember one time Mary Lou Williams put on a festival out in Pittsburgh, and Catholic people backed it, and finally they couldn't handle it business-wise, so George Wein jumped in and helped 'em out and made that particular festival a real special one. And man, it was a great weekend or week, whatever it was. The thing that I remember—I was one of the MCs—and I did a thing where we had a piano section because of Mary Lou, and we invited a lot of people, man. We invited Duke Ellington to play on it, to play on the festival. We had Ellington, Earl Hines—who is from Pittsburgh—and a whole bunch of other people. It was really nice, but the thing that I remember from the festival itself was the John Coltrane Quartet played the first half, ended the first half of one of the concerts that we gave, and, man, I mean I have never heard such a loud and constant outpouring from people. I mean that was one of the best things that I personally heard him do with the audience. The audience could not get enough of him. We literally had to stop the show right there, and it took us a while to get the next act on, and by the time we got the next act on, which was Stan Getz, the only thing that Getz could do was to bring his vibraphone player up and do a vibraphone solo to get everyone's attention, and then the group started playing.

LB: What about any other things that you think may have influenced John? You talked a little bit about Monk's influence and his period of time with Monk, you talked a little bit about his awareness of Lester, and that he talked to you about Art Tatum. Is there anything else that may stand out that you think is significant?

BT: Well, he was curious and I think that there were a lot of things that he wanted to do. This thing about scales and arpeggios that I was talking about, and he wanted to play on the horn something that sounded like a glissando, like what he was hearing Tatum [do], and to me, that's what the "sheets of sound" were. I mean because that's exactly what he heard and what he reproduced on the saxophone. No separation between the notes.

LB: What would you say about his innovations and contributions to the music?

BT: Well, he really showed his spirituality when he realized that there were certain things that he wanted to say and he wanted to say them in a way that was not only interesting but available to everybody. He really wanted to make something, as far as he could, universal. He wanted it to be something that people say, "Well, yeah, this brotherhood thing" and this thing's appealing for other people. If you can get that into music, that's worth anything else that it requires to be able to do. And he worked really hard on that. It wasn't just one or two pieces or something like that. He said, (paraphrasing) "I want to get this feeling, spiritual feeling that I feel into the melodies and into all of the aspects of the music that I create. To me, that's why I'm doing it. That's music for me." He was very clear on that, I thought, at a time when people had a different approach to brotherhood and took it in other directions; his was the one that I thought was more all inclusive in terms of saying, (paraphrasing) "Well here is an opportunity for me to say something personally, which is a lesson, I hope, for other people, and so they'll take stock of that and do something with it."

LB: Do you feel there are any roots of that vision, that aspiration that he expressed through his musical performance, in Black American traditions?

BT: Absolutely, sure. You know, he's from the South, man. You can't grow up in the South, and be a young person [*pause*] Dizzy was from the South, Monk was from the South, I was from the South.

LB: You and John are both from North Carolina.

BT: As a matter of fact, we were born just a few miles away from each other. I was born in Greenville, North Carolina, which is a hop, skip, and a jump from where he was actually born. You couldn't have any . . . I have to back up a little. If you were growing up at the time that I was making a reputation on trying to put together groups and do something in music, I had always in my mind, I couldn't go South. I could not take my son and daughter to the South because I couldn't protect them. I mean that's a terrible thing to live with. Greenville was a nice little country town when I grew up, when I was born. It became a university place later, but it was a very nice place, but it was not a place that I could take my family and not run into a real terrible type of prejudice in that whole area. Not in the specific area where I was but anywhere around that area, I could get it. So it wasn't that I was threatened or anything like that, but I knew that I could not protect my family, and I guess John and Monk and everybody else who [felt that way], because we were all about the same age, and we experienced some of the same things. We knew about people being lynched down the street or down the corner or not far from where we lived and all that kind of stuff. That's not something that you can explain to somebody today and say, "Well, this is how I felt about that." It's a very serious and frightening kind of thing where you felt helpless, There is nothing that I can do individually, I thought. And so most of us had to deal with that and say, "Well, OK, how can I deal with that, and what can I do about that? What can I say that will have an effect on somebody that has another opinion of my race and who I am and what my family is capable of doing?"

LB: I understand. I grew up in Kentucky during segregation, so I understand. I'm a little bit behind you, but I know what you're talking about.

BT: Well, you know what I'm talking about.

LB: I know exactly what you're talking about.

BT: And really people do not today, young people do not realize the weight that puts on people. Many people became drug addicts like John. Part of that was frustration and not, at some point, just saying, "Nah, man, let me walk away from that for a minute and let me get that out of my mind, get everything out of my mind." A lot of the guys in that period were drunkards, and they drank enormous amounts and there were all kinds of drugs. You know, when I was a kid, guys were "smoking tea" and all that kind of stuff. But that's an escape that some people find that that's the only way that they can live with it, with what's going on. It's unfortunate. Like with Bird, it's the thing that made him so much less than he could have been, simply because he couldn't handle it. John was fortunate in that he got to a place where he could handle it and could then turn around and do something that was really more in keeping with the spirituality and not just spirituality, but the feeling of oneness that he tried to express in a lot of his music and the community, to speak to his community and for his community. He did that musically in his own way.

LB: Considering John being able to come through these trials and tribulations, experience them and then pull out of them, what impact do you think that had on how he was viewed as a musician among the other musicians and the listeners?

BT: A lot of that, people didn't understand anything. It reminds me of something that Tatum said to me one time. We were—I took him to an after-hours club and a guy came in and told him, "I've been admiring you for so many years and I'd just love to play 'Tiger Rag' for you. I made a transcription of your record of that, and I'd love to play it for you." So Art said, "OK," and so the guy sat down and played it, and my mouth fell down, and I said, "Man, this guy has really got an ear on Tatum." And Art Tatum couldn't have cared less. He said, "Well, he knows what I do, but he doesn't know why I do it." And so that was the same kind of thing that I felt with John. Here's a guy that a lot of people heard the notes that he played, but they didn't get the spirit behind it.

LB: Do you think he had influence on musicians in terms of helping them being able to look at what their lifestyles could be about?

BT: To some extent, yeah. Because by the time he was really doing what he did at the top of his game, a lot of guys were beginning to get a much broader idea of what he was doing. It wasn't just, "This guy could play a lot of notes." I mean, Don Byas could play a lot of notes but it was from a different perspective, you know. And speaking of Don Byas, I often wondered what would have happened if Don had come back from Europe and been playing on Fifty-second Street or somewhere that was available to Coltrane, what the effect would have been on both of them?

LB: What makes you wonder that, Billy?

BT: Well, because Don was one of the first non-beboppers to be able to play bebop. I mean he played with Dizzy Gillespie's first bebop group on Fifty-second Street. They couldn't get Bird, so he came in and played all those parts. He could play good bebop because he did that when he went over to Europe with Don Redman. He didn't choose to do, stylistically, the things that made bebop, bebop. He was still of the school, that "Well, these are things that I want to do, that are me, and I can do that, and I'm not going to change that because it's important for me to say it that way." ... And so he could play bebop and he did, in a lot of different kinds of groups, but he played 'em his way, you know. That's why I wondered if he had come back, whether he would have had—because he was a strong player—if he had been on the bandstand with John, it would have had some effect, I don't know what, because he was—if you listened to what he was doing with that duet he did with Slam Stewart, I mean with just the two of them ... I mean this guy was doing "sheets of sound" then, you know ... because he was influenced by Tatum.

LB: Fascinating. Jon Hendricks believes that Bird was very much influenced by Art Tatum.

BT: Unquestionably.

LB: You know that because you worked with Charles [Parker]. Tatum's influence seems to be immense.

BT: The thing that Bird loved was—two things: not only the facility, but his harmonies. He heard some of those upper voicings in those chords from Tatum.

LB: What would you say about the particular sound that John manifested? I mean, along with all the technique, he had a sound that touched people. Is there anything about John's sound that you remember; any unique qualities or things that you can speak to?

BT: Oh yeah, sure. Especially, you know I knew early on before he made the ballad album, that he had a certain thing about playing ballads, and I really related to that because that was a period that I was really focusing on playing ballads in a way that could express certain things that I wanted to do. And I could hear that, and he really was making the saxophone sound or sing in a way that Hodges and Benny Carter and a lot of other guys had done before them. Not in their way, but I could hear that polarity in approach, and that was one of the areas that he had concentrated on, and he really got that together a lot quicker than most people realize.

LB: How would you say he was regarded in the music community?

BT: It was mixed. He was fortunate in that he got to record for a large company when he did because as long as he was playing for Blue Note and all that, and even though he was playing with other people, he really didn't have an opportunity to do his own thing as he did when he got with ABC/Paramount [the parent company of Impulse Records]. He actually changed the label. He changed the quality and the character of the label. They weren't doing anything near what he was doing. He had done some things for Atlantic and stuff like that, but when he really hit his stride, he had a big influence on listeners because they put out many more records on him than a lot of guys. Outside of Miles, I don't know of many other guys that made as many recordings in that period of time.

LB: How would you say he was regarded in the black community?

BT: Well, he was too far out for many people. And people didn't take the time to listen to what he was doing. I think if it had been a different time, a few years before where there were still places for him to play dances and things like that, if musicians were doing that to the extent they had been doing earlier when the black community was into dancing—John would have played some more rhythmic things and some of the things that he actually did in his other playing because the feeling is there, but the purpose isn't there. If he had been playing dances, he would have communicated with a lot more people in the black community.

LB: What would you say about his awareness of issues of his time, say in the mid-'60s, of the conditions in Black America in specific, and the world in general?

BT: Hey, you couldn't avoid it in the '60s. By that time, being from where he came and what he was capable of doing and the way he felt, he could express that musically, he could express that verbally. He was very clear on the fact that he really hoped that people would use the roots of the music and all of the experiences that we had in the community and learn from it. He was very clear on that.

LB: Do you feel that his clarity on that has something to do with the way he was embraced and appreciated on a global scope?

BT: Because he had to be asking the question to himself, "Well, if people all around the world are this enthused about what I'm doing, why is it that Harlem and the black community ain't jumping up and down and saying the same thing?" That bothers almost all of the adventurers—

Miles, Diz, Bird, everybody that I can think of. Cannonball Adderley. Any number of them used to look at the people of that period, and I'm talking of people that were influencing one another during that period.

LB: You know, one of the things was his involvement with Olatunji, with the center he had up in Harlem. Do you have any knowledge of what Tunji's center was about?

BT: Yes, Olatunji was an African, and he really started something. He was one of the few people that really started something in Harlem that he wanted to be a link between who we were as Africans, people from African origins, and who we were at that particular period of time. So he's right in the center of Harlem. He's got a school. He had public things that were taking place there. He tried to do many of the things that would have happened had he been able to do them at home and bring them, in total, to the black community. Inasmuch as he could, he did that. He arranged for people to come in a variety of ways and say and do things which he hoped would have a positive impact on the black community. And in many cases it really did. It's not documented as such, but he was well thought of. He didn't have the money. He didn't have the backing of certain organizations that were doing things. His studio was literally right around the corner from WLIB, and so that was why he asked me to do it, and I had to do it in between—I was in radio so I couldn't get off. [Taylor is referring to his involvement with Olatunji's center] I tried to get somebody to take my time, my place, but I couldn't get it for the whole length of time, so I spent as much time as I could, but then I had to go back and finish the show. He was aware of the impact that black radio was having on the community, and he was delighted with the fact that some of the things that he was famous for—he had recorded with a lot of people and he had played with his own groups in other places, and he took that money and those opportunities to spread that. And he had a feeling about John because he said [paraphrasing], "Well, man, here's a guy who's doing something very special, and so when I do this concert then I want people to come out and check him out there, as opposed to Town Hall or something like that."

LB: I don't know if you've heard the Impulse recording they call Trane's Last Live Concert.

BT: I haven't. I know it's out there, but I haven't.

LB: You introduce it. You're the host. Your words were, "One of the most remarkable forces in the jazz today. And the only person who can really discuss what he does to the music, which is so important to us, is John Coltrane." I wondered whether you have any recollection on that or memories worthy of sharing?

BT: Yea, sure. One of the reasons that I said it that way is because already at that time everybody was speaking for John. There were people talking, "Oh yeah, I knew him." By that time, there were a couple of books out. At any rate, there were people that were saying, "I know him very well and so on, so on, so on and he had been trying to do this." Everybody was an expert because he [Coltrane] had been off the scene. So once he was off the scene, other people spoke up and said, well, "I knew him." A lot of the stuff that they were talking about was bull, man. Somebody just trying to get over using his name.

LB: When you say "off the scene," what do you mean?

BT: He was not as active as he had been prior to that. So he had been off the scene working, writing, and composing and really thinking about some of the things that he wanted to do in this concert at the center. Olatunju's Center was a good focus, a place for him to focus on the things that he was trying to say from an African American point of view. And who better to do it with than a guy who was African and who also had the same kinds of desire to do something like that for the community.

LB: When I interviewed Yusef about a month ago, I asked him some of these questions. We got to this one, and Yusef said that John had actually come to him and talked about wanting to get his own place for a venue to present the music. He said John felt like the club scene, with the alcohol and the background and all that, was just not appropriate for the music anymore. Yusef had plugged John into a real estate agent and John was looking to buy a place where he could present the music where families could come and children could come and people like that. There wouldn't be any alcohol. He wanted to move the music into other venues. Do you have any knowledge of that?

BT: Ahmad Jamal had done the same thing, and several other musicians who had serious intent for their music and for the community had tried to do the same thing. There were several musicians—especially in the '50s and '60s—these were musicians who, at some point, had said, "Man, I would like to do something where the cash register is not making all this noise, and the people are not using alcohol and other things. It should be cleaner, it should be better, it should be something that is more representative of the things that I'm trying to present."

LB: What would you say about John saying he wanted "to be a force for good," to use his music as a force for good?

BT: I thought it, oddly enough, may have been a reaction to some of the things that Miles was doing. I think that he thought that Miles, given his popularity and his position, could have done more. He was around when Miles was getting all these opportunities to be on television, to do other things like that. I think he just thought, "Well if I did that, then I think I would do it a little differently."

LB: What would you say about the relevance of Trane's music, and any messages in it, today—in current times?

BT: Well, I think that anyone who listens to Trane has to listen to not just something that they may feel is the epitome of what he does. You need to listen to as much of it as you can, simply because it's so vast in terms of what he actually was able to do. There are so many lessons and so many things that could be extracted from that. The problem is that most people will get "Giant Steps" and specific things and say, "Well, that's it," and it's not it. I mean that's one of the things that I took great delight in explaining to a lot of my students was the fact that "Giant Steps" is based on the middle part of a tune by Rodgers and Hart, and harmonically a lot of things like that would happen. Benny Carter dared some things like that, that were going on. But he [Coltrane] took that harmonic structure and just made something that changed the way people approach harmony. Many other people, Ellington and others, have done similar things, but didn't get the credit for it because they didn't do it as succinctly as he did.

LB: Do you feel like the message that he has put out there—which consciously took a much more clear spiritual intent—is still relevant today for us as a people and also for the world in general?

BT: Not as relevant as he would have liked for it to be. Most people who are getting his music now, unless they are really turned on and want to focus on the music as music, don't hear deep enough in the music to get the kind of message that he was trying to convey. It's a different time. People want to hear something that's instantly satisfying. A lot of people don't come to places to hear music in the way that they did when I was talking about that festival that we did in Pittsburgh and some of the clubs that everybody played. We had developed people that actually heard the music; who said that this is what melodically, harmonically, and rhythmically is going on. Not musicians, but they could hear the difference in that culture and country and western and pop music. Indeed, many of the things that he came up with had elements of all those things. What was "movie music" or "music for movies" or whether it was something that just came from a favorite phrase that he just turned around or heard in his playing exercise or something like that. He said, "Yeah, I think I'll make something out of this." He just took all kinds of things as tools to help him say, "Well, I want to say this. Here's something I want to say rhythmically. Here's something I want to say about Cousin Mary. Here's something I want to say about the blues." He would take little things and say, "Well, you know, I want to say that." He may not go back and do it again, but he said it there.

LB: Any last comments you want to say about what we're trying to do here, the intent, and any advice you want to give us as we move down this road?

BT: He's still one of the most remarkable forces in the music. I have to stick with what I said. The only person who could really discuss what he did to the music was John Coltrane, and he did. He said it in his words, and he said it in his music, and we need to look carefully at both aspects of that and go back to where he was and how he presented it. I'm glad you're doing it man. I mean, somebody like you has to step up and do the right thing.

Coda: George Russell on John Coltrane

As closure to this work, here is the wisdom of the late George Russell, recognized worldwide as one of the most brilliant minds in theoretical and applied aspects of twentieth-century creative music. In an interview I conducted in his home during August 1997, I asked the Maestro what did he consider as some of Coltrane's significant achievements. His answer is below.

—Leonard L. Brown

There's no "some of it." Everything he did was not only significant; it was monumentally significant. The scope of what he has left is on a monumental level as an inheritance to us, and at the key of that inheritance is this very essence of the music and that essence is originality and innovation on a high level that carries within it the imprint of the originator and the innovator and carries with it the essence of that innovator. Coltrane had enormous essence, you know, and an essence that was always pushing him on to re-create himself. That's part of it—you don't keep on repeating. I don't know of anybody on his level of improvisation. I don't know anybody at that level of intensity and that sound. But the beautiful thing was that that's what Trane was, he was so full of the true spirit of the music and of creating and re-creating.

Index

221